SEA

CREATURES

Praise for

SEA CREATURES

"A tangled, tenderly believable love story. . . . A gorgeous story that spans the full experiential spectrum of romantic and parental love, artistic impulse, betrayal, sacrifice, and redemption, *Sea Creatures* satisfies on every level."

—Amazon.com

"There's a charmer at the heart of *Sea Creatures*. . . . Almost like an action-filled, emotional memoir. . . . Gripping."

—Associated Press

"While Miami has inspired its satirical works of genius, chilling mystery novels, and excellent accounts of Cuban exile, we've mostly run short on first-rate literature that takes the city seriously enough to capture its eccentricities without flinching. A writer can't just roll into town for a few months and hope to understand the soul of this place. But Daniel, with *Sea Creatures*, gets it absolutely pitch-perfect."

—*Miami Herald*

"An undercurrent of disaster pervades the novel. . . . Yet Daniel's celebration of life is so quietly joyous . . . that we cast our fears aside much as Georgia does. 'Traffic, heights, waters,' Graham says. 'There's always something.' He's right, of course. But the real risks Daniel asks us to consider are the inevitable ones that accompany love, including the hard and sometimes dangerous bargains we make to hold onto it."

—*Atlanta Journal-Constitution*

"Daniel returns to Stiltsville's South Florida in a second novel filled with domestic upheaval, difficult choices, and far-reaching consequences. . . . Daniel's verdant descriptions of salt and sea continue to shine, as does her portrayal of a mother struggling to protect her son."

—*Publishers Weekly*

"An intelligent page-turner (that is, the dream combination) about, among other things, South Florida, art, insomnia, and marriage."

—Curtis Sittenfeld, author of *Prep* and *Sisterland*

"Utterly enthralling. . . . [*Sea Creatures* is] about love, loss, and longing in their most familiar forms. Brace yourself: you'll fall hard for the characters, and your heart will break preemptively—even before the hurricane blows through."

—More.com

"A captivating, haunting novel about the complexities of the human heart and its attachments, terrain as slippery and beautiful and disaster-prone as Daniel's South Florida."

—Abraham Verghese, author of *Cutting for Stone*

"A sophisticated story that holds the reader rapt. . . . [Daniel] sets up each scene in *Sea Creatures* with masterful strokes. . . . She builds momentum from the opening chapter, leading up to the crescendo. . . . Daniel drives into tumultuous waters and emerges with a mesmerizing, beautiful novel."

—*Wisconsin State Journal*

"Susanna Daniel's powers of creation are so vast, and the South Floridian landscape she describes so vivid, that this lifelong Manhattanite briefly thought of hurricane-proofing her own windows. But what I found most stirring in *Sea Creatures* is how deftly Daniel exposes one of the most agonizing realities of parenthood: that no matter how hard we try, or how endless our love for our children may be, we are hampered by our own limitations, sometimes even tragically."

—Helen Schulman, author of *This Beautiful Life*

"Don't confuse the waterfront setting with light beach reading; this is substantive domestic drama. . . . Readers interested in families coping with disabilities will find Frankie particularly compelling as he navigates changing relationships and obstacles."

—*Library Journal*

SEA

CREATURES

SUSANNA

DANIEL

HARPER PERENNIAL

NEW YORK • LONDON • TORONTO • SYDNEY • NEW DELHI • AUCKLAND

HARPER ● PERENNIAL

A hardcover edition of this book was published in 2013 by HarperCollins Publishers.

P.S.™ is a trademark of HarperCollins Publishers.

HarperCollins books may be purchased for educational, business, or sales promotional use. For information please e-mail the Special Markets Department at SPsales@harpercollins.com.

FIRST HARPER PERENNIAL EDITION PUBLISHED 2014.

Designed by Michael Correy

The Library of Congress has catalogued the hardcover edition as follows:

Daniel, Susanna.
    Sea creatures / Susanna Daniel.—First edition.
        p.   cm
    ISBN 978-0-06-221960-2
        1. Families—Fiction. 2. Life change events—Fiction. 3. Mutism—Fiction.
4. Houseboats—Fiction. I. Title.
PS3604.A5258S43   2013
813'.6—dc23

                                                              201203180913

ISBN 978-0-06-221961-9 (pbk.)

14 15 16 17 18   OV/RRD   10 9 8 7 6 5 4 3 2 1

for John
who has given us his heart

one

IT WAS MY HUSBAND GRAHAM'S idea to buy the houseboat. The notion took shape on the first leg of our move from Illinois to Miami, between pulling away from the cottage in Round Lake and stopping at the county fair outside of Peoria, where we urged our three-year-old, Frankie, into a gargantuan bouncy castle. For a few minutes Frankie seemed to take some pleasure in jumping haphazardly among strangers, until he remembered that he didn't like strangers, and staggered lock-kneed toward the exit. I mention this interlude in the long drive for one reason: a few minutes after we walked away from the enormous cartoonish castle, a gust of wind upended it, bouncing children and all. Ambulances arrived quickly. As we stood among the anxious crowd, I thought—not for the first time and not for the last—that to be a parent is terrifying. Graham once told me how the Stoics practiced imagining their own worst fears had come to pass, to make peace. But it seems to me that what worries us most—pedophiles, kidnappers, dog attacks—is least likely to happen, while what is most likely is some unimagined event. And how do we prepare for that?

We debated the pros and cons of the houseboat through Tennessee and Georgia. An adventure, Graham said, and relatively inexpensive. Naive, I thought, considering neither of us knew much about boats. Making the most of the locale, he argued. Soggy and mildewed, I said. We'd intended to rent a house on Key Biscayne, near the Rosenstiel School of Marine and Atmospheric Science, where Graham would occupy a two-year research fellowship. But once my husband latched on to an idea, it was difficult to shake him loose. And the truth was that I wondered if living on a houseboat might be every bit the adventure he hoped. Sometimes you have to remind yourself after adventure comes that there was a time when you went looking for it.

We stopped for fuel outside of Gainesville, and Graham picked up a boat trader magazine, then made a few calls when we stopped again in St. Cloud. By the time we reached Miami, he'd found three candidates, all in the Pompano area. After we unloaded the trailer into the spare room of my father's wife's house, Graham got back on the road with my father at the wheel.

Graham didn't drive, not since he was a teenager. I'd done all of the driving from Illinois while he fidgeted in the passenger seat and Frankie slept openmouthed in his car seat, a coloring book open across his thighs and a crayon in his fleshy fist, waking every so often to give the sign for milk and dig into a sleeve of crackers. We stopped every few hours at a rest area, and while I plotted our route and fetched cold drinks, Graham led Frankie in a vigorous game of freeze tag, and they returned to the car red-faced and panting. For much of the ride, I eyed our hulking trailer in the side-view mirror, my gut lurching each time it swerved with the contours of the road. When I started off from a stop, the heavy pull of the trailer reminded me of the lifeguard tests I'd taken in junior high, when I'd swum the length of a pool wearing two pair of blue jeans and three sweaters. It was exactly the same feeling: I knew where I was going, and I was damned if I wouldn't break away from something powerful to get there.

To the extent that Graham would have admitted that his aversion to driving was a phobia, it was incongruent with his bold and blustery personality, his assertiveness, even his maturity. When we'd gotten serious, I'd thought I might ingratiate him to the act of driving with subtle, loving encouragement. He'd been in the backseat, sixteen years old, when his mother's car had jumped the median on the way home from a birthday party. It was February; the roads were icy. His sister, Lauren, fourteen at the time and in the passenger seat, was thrown clear and never regained consciousness. Graham insisted that the event had been so sterilized by retelling and scrubbed by time that the two things—witnessing his sister's death and not driving—were unrelated. This was a testament not to Graham's lack of self-awareness, I believe, but to the confused nature of each of our personal histories, the mess of contradicting passions and aversions developed over a lifetime. To love one's sister for indulging their mother by singing along on road trips, and to hate one's sister for refusing to wear a seat belt. To love the car trips of one's childhood, the ambling farm roads and lush hillsides, and to hate the heavy inertial machinery of a car, particularly when measured against glass, body, and brain.

GRAHAM CALLED FROM POMPANO. I was drinking a beer in the kitchen while Frankie played with blocks at the table. My father's wife, Lidia, who was Puerto Rican by birth and spoke perfect English with a heavy accent, stood at the counter, wiping crumbs. Her home was on the Coral Gables waterway, and she'd prepared the spare room by piling towels and toys on the bed and clearing dresser drawers. On the nightstand she'd set out framed photos of me and my family, including one from Frankie's bald and blotchy first weeks. There was one of me and Graham standing on a volcano in Pico, Portugal, and one of my high school portraits, which I hadn't known still existed. The latter called to mind a memory of my mother, who'd ordered it mistakenly after I'd marked the few that I'd *not* liked. We'd ended up with a stack of glossy photos of me with my eyes in slits, chin pimple glowing, upper lip stuck to my teeth. I'd berated my mother soundly. It's disconcerting how often, after a deeply loved person dies, the memories that return are not reverent or nostalgic, but disquieting. My mother was prone to making flighty mistakes, yes, but not until I became a mother did I understand what the flightiness meant: she was overwhelmed at the basic level. More times than I care to admit, I've come home with the incorrect item from the grocery store. The nonfat instead of low-fat, the vanilla instead of plain. And every time I do, I think of how I ridiculed my mother for doing the same thing, how I rolled my sullen-teenager eyes at her, and how it seems, in retrospect, that she adopted my interpretation of these nonevents—that she was flighty—instead of regarding them the way I've come to: a parent's brain is rarely in one place at a time, and the grocery store does not command one's precious minutes of focus.

I stuffed the portrait into a drawer. Not because the photo was unflattering, but because the memory was.

Lidia handed me the phone. The overspiraled cord pulled annoyingly against my hand. This was exactly the way in which other people's homes are unlivable, I thought, which led me to the opposite thought: I was grateful to Lidia. I was touched by her efforts. She was generous of time and spirit, eager to be a grandmother to Frankie, and she was not some shiny young thing—she was only a few years younger than my father.

Still, I was relieved when Graham told me on the phone that he'd found us a home of our own. It was a 1974 Sumerset, fifty feet in length and fourteen in width, with a propane stove and refrigerator, and a new 30-amp inlet. My father would run shore power and water from the main house, and we could drive the boat to a local marina every few weeks to empty the sewage tanks. The engines and bilge were in good shape, he said. I calculated the square footage in my head: the size of a tiny city apartment.

"She's not pretty," he said, "but there's a berth for us and a bunk for Frankie."

I pictured him scraping the stubble of his chin and squinting in the sunlight. I could hear the cries of the gulls in the background, could almost smell the marina, that stew of seaweed and engine oil and fuel. My father had owned boats when I was a child, first a cabin cruiser with a tuna tower that he'd shared with two other musicians, then a heavy trawler that took several seconds to respond. I was comfortable riding in boats but had only driven one a handful of times. I'd never known my husband, the midwesterner, to use the words *bilge* and *berth*.

"Buy it," I said.

"Why not?" said Graham.

After I hung up, Lidia presented me with an old coffeemaker. "I knew I had one somewhere," she said, pushing it into my hands. Lidia and my father drank only tea, which was one of a dozen little things that had made me wonder, in the time since they'd married four years before, if she was a better match for him than my mother had been.

"Normalcy," she said.

"Normalcy," I said, nodding.

Lidia had a way of getting to the heart of it. A year before, I'd been running a business that if not thriving, exactly, then still had potential. A year before, Graham had still had a shot at tenure, and his sleep troubles were more or less under control. Frankie had been a well-adjusted two-and-a-half-year-old, a little slow to talk but not yet entirely mute.

Time is tricky. Time is surprising. Time and age play important roles in my story, so I will say right away that at the time of these events, during the summer of 1992, I was thirty-six years old. Graham was forty-four and Frankie was three and a half. My marriage was ten. The hermit, Charlie Hicks, was sixty-one, the same age as my father and three years older than my father's new wife. My mother, had she been alive, would have been sixty-two.

The boat cost roughly two thousand dollars less than we had in the bank. Our reserves had been sapped—first by the collapse of my business, into which we'd sunk three years of time and savings, and then by moving and renting our home in Round Lake, which had needed work to be ready to show to prospective renters, then more work once a lease had been signed. The cottage was on the lake, which was a big part of its appeal and its decline, both. We'd replaced every other plank in the pier. We'd replaced the soffits and roof and water heater, and installed a sump pump. We were landlords now, which was not something either of us had ever wanted to be.

We'd brought our clothes, some books, both of Graham's bicycles, and Frankie's favorite toys. Each decision, to leave behind or bring along, had been more grueling than the last. It wasn't that we believed we'd be back—in fact, I hoped we never would be, even as I hoped I'd change my mind—but more that we felt selling the house, which had been in Graham's family for three generations, was not an option. Our renters were a visiting professor in Graham's former department at Northwestern, and the professor's young wife. No matter how ready I'd been to flee, when I thought of them using our bed, clipping herbs from Graham's garden, crossing the lake in our kayaks, I had to turn away from the thoughts as if from something bright and hot.

Behind Lidia's home was a kidney-shaped swimming pool and a rectangle of green lawn that sloped down to a canal. A narrow cement pier ran parallel to the house, and a slip was carved from the limestone bank at one corner, shaded by a tangle of mangroves between her yard and her neighbor's. Lidia owned a little two-seater Zodiac—the red inflated collar reminded me of a child's pool—that she moved to the pier so the houseboat could dock in the slip. She'd assured us that we could dock behind her house as long as we wanted, but had given no thought, it seemed, as to whether the manicured and bucolic city of Coral Gables (a cut above the modest South Miami neighborhood where I'd grown up) would allow a houseboat to reside in its canals. I'd decided to give this no thought, either. It wasn't the kind of thing that would occur to my father, and Graham had only visited Miami three times in a decade, and had no sense of the laws of the land. For the time being, I put the whole question out of my mind.

That evening, Lidia and Frankie and I romped around in the backyard, throwing an old Frisbee. I amused Frankie by lunging into the grass to catch his misfired throws, streaking my knees with green stains. He made the sign for *Swim* over and over, and I signed *Tomorrow* and *I promise*. Lidia and I let him spray us with a garden hose. After a bath, I put him down in the guest room. My father arrived home in my car, then left for a gig, and Lidia poured a glass of wine for herself and said good night. After midnight, as I sat out back watching the slow crawl of the dark water, I heard the houseboat choking its way up the canal. When it came into view, I could make out Graham inside at the helm, waving through a window. Why he was willing to captain this hulking vessel and not our sedan, I wasn't certain. One was a burden, I guessed, and the other a lark. The houseboat was plodding and boxy and took up more than its share of the waterway's width. If ever its paint had gleamed, that time was long gone. Over the back deck, a white scalloped awning flapped in the wind. Graham throttled down and nosed toward the pier, and when he cut the engine and the noise died, I tied off the lines and stepped aboard. On the brief rectangle of faded Formica in the houseboat's galley, I set down Lidia's coffeemaker.

GRAHAM AND MY FATHER COOKED up a plan to christen the houseboat while they were out late together after one of my father's gigs. It had to happen quickly, Graham explained—the ocean gods are finicky about these things. So just two days after we moved aboard, I found him digging through the bunk under our berth to locate a guayabera Lidia had sent the Christmas before. I retrieved the matching one she'd sent for Frankie. Once we were dressed, we stepped onto the pier to find my father and Lidia waiting for us in the steeped-tea sunlight of early evening. Graham carried a bag of painting supplies, and on the limestone parapet that hemmed Lidia's backyard was an ice bucket of champagne and bottled water.

Graham clapped gamely. "Master of ceremonies?" he said to my father.

"Aye, Captain," said my father.

They were a mismatched pair, Graham and my father. Graham was tall—six feet and four inches—and my father was my height, almost a foot shorter. Graham had storklike, sinewy limbs and broad palms and a slight belly that never went away, no matter how many miles he rode in a week. The word most often used to describe him was *gaunt*, and though I don't think that's inaccurate, the word that came readily to my mind was *angular*. Once, sitting behind him at a wedding where we'd arrived to find no two seats together, I'd studied the jutting walkways of his shoulders before realizing that they belonged to him. He had a habit of gesturing wildly to emphasize a point, flexing his fingers in a way that reminded me of a bear showing its claws. He was handsome, my husband, though too striking to be conventionally so, with his heavy helmet of silver hair and bluish circles beneath his eyes. Still, women stared. I think they assumed from the way he looked that he was a little wild at heart, which was not entirely off the mark. He had a deep, powerful speaking voice that some found overbearing, and though he grew bored in casual conversation, when he was in the mood to chat he could be so chummy and attentive that mere acquaintances found themselves confiding in him. He wasn't easily amused, though he did possess an infectious, seldom-used giggle, and there was one thing that reliably brought it out: baby animals. A chick attempting to walk, bear cubs stumbling in play, a piglet cradled in a person's arms— this kind of thing never failed to make Graham laugh. If we had not had a child, which introduced into our lives a stream of animal-themed books and videos, I might never have known this about him.

Beside Graham, my father was short and fleshy. Every few years he took up a new form of exercise—aqua jogging, most recently—and lost ten pounds, then slowly gained them back. For the christening, he wore a linen shirt unbuttoned to midchest and a gold chain around his meaty neck. He wore his graying hair a little shaggy, so that it hung over his collar and into his eyes, and he had an inch-long scar beside his lip that over the years had folded into the lines of his face—it had happened in a bar in Key West when I was a kid, during his drinking days. Carcinomas had been removed at both corners of his mouth, leaving two small white craters. For a performance, he'd always worn white slacks and sandals, but at home he preferred deck shoes and blue jeans. A clunky gold bracelet glinted on his wrist—a gift from Lidia, I assumed, along with a thinner chain around his neck. The jewelry suited him.

My father and Graham were in cahoots—we were all meant to take this christening thing seriously. On the houseboat's flank, between the windows and gunwale, was a bright green stripe; it was here that Graham would paint the new name. He stepped onto the boat and pulled items from a bag: gold metallic paint, brush, stencils, tape. He shuffled through the stencils and found the one he wanted, then held it up against the green.

"Here?" he said.

My father motioned for him to adjust, then gave a thumbs-up.

The first letter was *L*. Graham had promised I'd love the name—he'd come up with it himself—but wouldn't reveal what it was. I saw now that he planned to unveil it letter by letter, like a host on a game show. This was exactly the kind of thing Graham relished.

My father studied a piece of lined paper, then cleared his throat to get our attention. Lidia, who had been playing the game with Frankie where he had to guess which of her hands held a prize—a sticker—pulled Frankie to her side. I was a little nervous about having him on the narrow pier, which sloped slightly toward the water, so that when you walked its length there was the sensation that one leg was shorter than the other.

We must have appeared suitably solemn. My father trotted out his performance voice. "They say every vessel is known personally by Poseidon, god of the ocean, and that every vessel's name is recorded in a Ledger of the Deep. An unnamed boat, like this one here, tempts the gods."

My mother had raised me to have a good deal of reverence for my father, but Lidia had no such upbringing. She elbowed me and whispered, "Mercy!"

My father gave her a hard look. Graham finished the first letter and moved on to the second: *U.*

"For thousands of years," my father boomed, "we have gone to sea. We have crafted vessels to usher us and we have called them by name. Our ships nurture and guide us through rough waters and stormy weather, through all peril, and so we refer to them, with great affection, as *she.*"

It was hot. My father's thick neck glistened, Frankie's dark hair stuck to his temples, and sweat trickled between my breasts. I looked to the canal, hoping for a breeze from the bay. Directly across was a stucco manse that spanned a lot twice the size of Lidia's. Its layers of balustrade-lined balconies and exterior staircases confused the question of its height—was it two stories, or three?

My father caught my eye. "Do we wish to tempt the gods, Georgia?"

"We do not," I said.

He went on to tell a story about a man down in Islamorada who'd believed he'd purged every mention of his boat's old name, then found a key chain with the old name on it, and decided to chuck the key chain instead of starting over with a new christening. That year, his boat was hit by lightning, and sank. "The gods had their revenge," my father said.

Of all of us, only Lidia was a believer—a Catholic, to boot. My mother had been a member of the First Unitarian Church, though my father had refused to go. So she and I had gone together, and after each service—comprised, more or less, of lessons we already knew—we joined the congregation for coffee from silver urns and cookies on doilies, and I sat in the corner and watched the boys. My mother hadn't liked to drive, so she'd taught me early, and even before I had my license would nudge me toward the driver's side. After services, which seemed to wear her out, she would settle into the passenger seat of the hot car, roll down the window, pull her straight hair from her face, and say something like, "Another week behind us, just like that." She'd given the impression, from time to time, of surviving her own life.

There was a glint in my father's eyes. He savored having an audience when he wanted one, and the invented ceremony and shadowy superstition held a certain appeal. He reached into a bag and pulled out a stack of papers. "The boat's captain has assembled all items bearing the boat's former name," he said. "You'll notice that each instance of the former name has been expunged."

He passed the papers to Lidia, who passed them to me. This was the boat's title and registration, and in each square where the boat's name had once appeared—it wasn't painted on the boat itself—there was a smear of white liquid eraser. I passed the papers back to my father, who said, "No mention of the boat's name remains aboard. Is that right, Captain?"

"Not a one," said Graham over his shoulder. He had moved on to the fourth letter: another *L*, the third so far. He'd selected a romantic, lilting script—not what I would have chosen, but it was coming along nicely. He had a way with straight lines and spacing, which had come in handy when hanging shelves or framed pictures at the cottage. When I glanced at the letters, each gleaming wetly, I couldn't help but take a guess. Graham was right. The name was perfect.

My father saw me smiling. He raised his eyebrows. "The new name will not be spoken until this ceremony is complete. You hear me, Georgia?"

I nodded.

"Harvey," said Lidia, "dinner is in the oven. You have ten minutes."

"You can't rush the gods, darling," he said, but he started speaking more quickly anyway. "Oh, mighty ruler of the seas, to whom all sailors pay homage, we implore you to expunge for all time the former name of this vessel from your watery kingdom."

He pulled a slip of paper from his pocket—this was the last written mention of the boat's old name, *Carpe Diem*—and tossed it into the canal.

"Litterbug," said Lidia.

He ignored her. "To convey our gratitude, we offer this drink with the hope that it will move you to do as we request." He took a bottle of champagne, popped the cork, and poured half into the canal. He divvied the rest into two cups and handed one to me and one to Lidia. For Graham and himself, he poured water. "Oh, great ruler of the seas! To whom all sailors pay homage! We implore you to include in your records and memory this worthy vessel, from now and for all time to be known as"—here he paused, grinning widely—"the *Lullaby*!"

"Hear, hear!" I said.

"Amen," said Lidia.

My father's voice softened. "Guard her, please, with your powerful arm and trident, and ensure her safe and rapid passage through all her journeys on your realm."

I drank. Frankie looked up at us, hoping whatever we'd been doing was over. Graham finished the last letter and came down from the boat to admire his work. This boat, our new home, was a relic from the days of pinkie rings and white patent leather shoes, and the gold paint he'd chosen, emblazoned across the green stripe, was if not tasteful then at least fitting.

My father snapped his fingers to get Frankie's attention. "Son," he said, "what you've witnessed here today is very important. It means your home is safe now."

Frankie nodded, his dark eyes wide. *Safe*, he signed: arms crossed against the chest, then spread, hands in fists.

"Time to dine," said my father, heading toward the house. At the cracked limestone steps, he extended one meaty hand toward Frankie, and Frankie took it. The way they looked in that moment, holding hands up the steps, brought my mother achingly to mind, and I had to look away.

Coppery sunlight sliced across the surface of the canal and played in the mangroves. At the pier across the water, a gleaming white yacht rested on bright, clean lines, its windshield black as ink. If there had been a photo of that segment of the canal, it would belong on the wall of a travel agency: *Come to Coral Gables!* But the air was thick with no-see-ums and humidity, which made it a little difficult to breathe.

My father's words to Frankie lingered. What if there was something to the purging and renaming, the appeasing of gods? What if I'd missed my chance to take it seriously, and had put all I had in the world—husband, son, squalid little home—in grave danger? A house-boat was a peculiar choice for any family, but particularly for us. When I'd mentioned this, Graham had brushed me off. "Traffic, heights, water," he said. "There's always something." He had the cuff now, he added, and we could put alarms on the doors and windows, if it would make me feel better. Still, since we'd arrived in Miami, I'd had the woozy, uncertain, sea-legless feeling of time moving too rapidly, of not being able to catch up with the changes in our lives. I looked to my husband, who seemed never to doubt his own decisions once they were made. If he believed everything would be fine, I could almost believe it, myself.

Graham saw my unease. He put his arm around me and gestured to the boat. "Onward," he said.

"Maybe here, we'll sleep," I said.

"It's a nice thought," he said.

MY FATHER, HARVEY WALKER HYDE Quillian—I give his full name because that's how he was billed in every performance of his career—played guitar, banjo, piano, ukulele, and a little flute, which he didn't pick up until he was in his fifties. To this day, he is one of the only people I've ever known to make a life as a musician, and for the most part that life has been good to him. People tend to think that if you don't make it big as an artist—musician, painter, writer, what have you—you've failed, though if you never make a ton of money as a lawyer or contractor or teacher, no one thinks the same thing. We never had surplus cash, but the bills were always paid and I never thought of myself as one of the poor kids, though certainly we were closer to poor than to rich.

For most of my childhood, my father worked five or six nights a week, regular gigs, and traveled two or three times a year for a month at a time. My mother worked, too, as the office manager for a tightly wound young pediatrician named Dr. Albee Fuller. We didn't travel much as a family, but when my father was on the road, my mother was given to spreading her wings in questionable ways. At least once a year, for example, she picked me up from school with packed luggage, and we drove straight to Government Cut and boarded a cruise ship bound for the Bahamas. My mother loved cruises, which later I came to realize was uncharacteristic of her. Normally, she had low tolerance for tackiness and strangers. She'd been raised in a swampy, unripe Miami; her father had helped build Freedom Tower, the first building in the city's skyline. She remembered Tequestas riding on horseback down Tamiami Trail, panthers chasing bicyclists along the waterfront. She spoke of her childhood in post-pioneer Florida with a heavy dose of nostalgia, but I think cruises were exempt from her sense of hometown ruin because they did what no one else could. They took care of all the details of daily life, from cooking and cleaning to entertaining her curious, energetic, and—I realize the burden of this now—highly attentive child. On a cruise, she encouraged me to wander for hours as long as I checked in. She didn't drink regularly at home, but on a cruise she had champagne with breakfast and a margarita with lunch, and more often than not we went straight from dinner to bed, sunburned and sapped. My father never knew about our gallivanting until he'd returned home, and I understood even at a young age that this was a way for my mother to rebel against my father's schedule and the tight limits of his ambitions, against their shared burdens and regrets. But she wasn't angry on cruises: she was relaxed, even flirtatious. She made friends and played cards in the sea of loungers while I lazed in the pool and ordered ice cream sandwiches from the cabana boys. Cruises are not a particularly expensive way to travel, all told, and though I know my father did a lot of teeth-gritting when he got home, and usually my mother picked up more hours at the office, I think she could have done a lot worse. I don't plan a vacation, still, without feeling a little rebellious myself.

I was named for my mother, though she was known as *Gigi* her entire life, even as an adult. When I married Graham, I kept my own last name, mostly because I couldn't imagine no longer sharing this one basic thing with her.

The other thing she did when my father was on the road was host house parties that lasted two or three days, attended by close friends: two gay neighbors, Bernie and Tom; her childhood friend Vivian; and a few coworkers. Often, even Dr. Fuller stopped by, looking stern and tucking his chin to his chest as he handed over an expensive-looking bottle of wine. The parties started in our backyard after work on Fridays. My mother hauled out Hula-Hoops and mixed sloe gin fizzes by the pitcher. Someone always had a radio or guitar, and they all stayed outside until after midnight, snacking on fruit and playing parlor games. Bernie and Tom were older than my mother, and I knew—how I knew it, I'm not sure—that Tom (or was it Bernie?) had been sick with some sort of cancer, and now he used a cane and coughed a great deal, as if punctuating the ends of his sentences. Vivian had a husband who worked a lot—again I'm not sure how I knew this, except that my mother wasn't the type to send me to my room or cup my ears with her palms—and when she came for the parties, she lied to her husband about where she was going. Dr. Fuller had a wife and young children. He sipped at his drink, kept his shirt tucked into his madras shorts, stared absently at my mother when she wasn't watching, and frowned when she caught him. I understood at the time that the adults were all being dishonest to some degree, to their spouses and children and themselves. They drank Bloody Marys in the morning and in the afternoon they dozed in our living room, then someone lit a joint and it started up again. To this day, I think of those marathon parties whenever I hear the term *second wind*. My father knew about the parties, and they ranked lower in sin level than the cruises did, but he didn't ask questions beyond the minimal: "Did you enjoy yourself while I was gone? Did you finish hemming my new pants? I'll be home for dinner—make the bayou casserole?"

By the time Graham and I moved to Miami, my mother had been dead five years, and my father had sold our small home in South Miami to a developer who razed it to build a Spanish-style duplex. My father had long since scaled back on the traveling—hardly ever, anymore—and worked only three standing weekly gigs: one at a bar downtown, one at a hotel on South Beach, and one at a piano bar in Coconut Grove. He'd developed a reputation as a good man at the back of the band, probably because he'd given up alcohol ages back and was always on time and had a working telephone. Whenever one gig disintegrated, another rose to fill the void.

Graham enjoyed going out and my father always had somewhere to go. My father liked to unwind from his own gigs at later shows, which often led to jam sessions at another musician's apartment. Neither man drank, so I didn't worry if they came in past dawn, as they often did. Graham liked live music—he'd taught himself to play a little guitar—and because of his sleep disorder, bed held no appeal. This had been true since long before we met, so I didn't take it personally. In fact, Graham's sleep problems and my lesser ones had brought us together in the first place: we'd met on the first day of my brief stint at the Illinois Regional Center for the Study of Sleep, which we'd dubbed Detention. I was two years out of Northwestern at the time, living with a roommate and her cat in Bucktown, working on campus as an admissions officer. I'd become disillusioned with the opaque and arbitrary nature of the admissions process, and was considering starting a college counseling business of my own. My doctor had admitted me to Detention after weeks without more than three consecutive hours of sleep, and I was there just long enough to get a diagnosis—unexplained insomnia, what they called a *brown-bag* diagnosis—and a prescription for sleeping pills. I left with the understanding that without pharmaceutical assistance, I might never sleep well again. I was still young enough to feel a certain tragedy in this, a black mark on the unspooling story of my life.

Graham had checked himself into Detention—his second time—after sleepwalking across Chicago's Cortland Street drawbridge in the middle of the night. He'd caused a fender bender. A piece ran in the *Tribune*, along with a grainy photograph taken by a passerby. In the photo, Graham was midstride over the yellow line, eyes open but vacant, like Bigfoot marching through woods. To the best of his knowledge, he'd been on his way to the ice cream shop on Webster Avenue for a bowl of mint chocolate chip. The doctors had asked if this was the first time something like this had happened, and he told them it was the first time he'd made it so far from home: a quarter mile, give or take. Following pressure from the dean, he'd taken a leave of absence. It hadn't yet dawned on him that his disorder might cost him anything as important as tenure.

While I still felt no small amount of anxiety about sleep, Graham was terrified of it. Sleep was the yardstick by which all other fears were measured, and everything else dwarfed. It's the stuff of horror films, sleep terror, but the sleep goblins of films are imaginary. Graham's goblins were real, and all the more alarming for their unpredictability. A month or so after being photographed on the drawbridge, shortly after we met, he was evicted from his apartment. He'd been waking his neighbors in the night, playing guitar and shouting nonsense and stomping across the floor at all hours. They'd assumed he was horribly inconsiderate or mentally ill or on drugs, or some combination. When he explained his disorder, the building manager didn't believe him. Graham put his things in storage and stayed with an old teammate from the two seasons he'd spent playing first base for the Evansville Triplets. The friend's name was Jackson. A week into Graham's stay, Jackson's wife woke to find Graham standing naked on her side of the bed. She screamed. Graham woke and fell to the floor and seized for a full minute while Jackson and his wife scrambled to hold him down. Graham came out of it with a migraine that lasted forty-eight hours. The seizures had happened twice before, he admitted. His doctor increased his medication and added a muscle relaxant.

The night terrors lessened, and it was around this point that he stopped trying to sleep most nights, which helped things as well.

We moved in together, and he developed the habit parasomniacs—people with disorders like his—call *nesting*, where he napped outside of the bedroom, as if trying to trick himself into getting some sleep. He spent only the occasional night in bed with me. I knew some spouses of parasomniacs locked their bedroom doors at night, to thwart the occasional violent attack, which happened even with parasomniacs who were unfailingly gentle when awake. But Graham had never shown any violence toward me or anyone else, awake or asleep. After we moved from our apartment in Chicago to the cottage, he hung a hammock on the back porch and stowed a sleeping bag in the basement, and these were his nests, though he used them rarely. We installed a house alarm at my insistence, because of our proximity to the water, but he liked to go walking at night and kept forgetting the code, and eventually we let it lapse into disuse. Over the years, there was the occasional incident. There was the time he woke partially undressed on the dock, preparing to take a swim. And one morning I found an ashtray of still-burning cigarettes on the dining room table. Graham had no idea how they'd gotten there; he didn't smoke. He slept less and less. As for me, I came to rely on my nightly pill not only to get much-needed sleep, but also to shut out the fear of what might happen to Graham in the dark hours. Otherwise, being the wife of a parasomniac could come to resemble a sleep disorder in itself.

After a night out, my father came home to draw the blinds in his bedroom and sleep heavily until early afternoon. Graham came home to shower, dress, and get on with the day. Sleeplessness was a lifestyle for Graham, a handicap with which he coped rather well. He did not doze off in meetings, did not stumble or stutter or even seem particularly bleary, aside from the dampness in his large eyes. I think the most obvious physical manifestation of Graham's long-term lack of sleep was probably his silvery white hair, though I can't prove the two are related. He also had the rough, lined face of an older man and bluish bruises beneath his eyes. Then again, his mother had slighter versions of those bruises and no sleep problems at all.

A WEEK AFTER WE ARRIVED, just after dawn, Graham took off for work on his bicycle, a band of reflective tape around one pant leg and panniers packed with a change of clothes. I got up to see him off, then through the little window in the houseboat's galley watched Lidia's twice-weekly prayer group assemble on the lawn. She brought out tea and muffins and they talked and held hands. Like Lidia, these women wore chunky gold jewelry and sheer scarves and brightly colored, draping blouses, wide-legged pants or layered skirts. They were the kind of women who looked like their lives, inner and outer, were *composed* in a way that mine had never been. As I stood barefoot on the galley's patch of faded linoleum, wearing a tank top and Bermuda shorts, I both admired and resented them. I was a person who was usually able to ignore the inherent competition of life, the how-far-have-you-come and how-much-have-you-got. But I'd lost my business and my husband had lost his job, and I'd moved back to my hometown after almost two decades away, which has a way of bringing to bear the passage of time.

The Rosenstiel job had rescued us. I don't mean to be dramatic, but this is how it felt at the time. The position, or one like it, had been out there for years, a vague possibility brought up every so often by Graham's old friend Larry Birnbaum, who was tenured at Rosenstiel. Not until Graham faced extinction at Northwestern and we'd been shunned in Round Lake had the idea grown legs. Graham had a Ph.D. from McGill in marine physics and a master's degree in computer science, and it was because of the latter degree that he'd been rushed through Rosenstiel's hiring process and dropped onto this team, which had lost a key member to Scripps in San Diego. I knew of Rosenstiel, though I'd never been enrolled at the University of Miami. In high school, I'd had a boyfriend who took classes there, and on Thursdays and Fridays, if you parked on the sandy street outside Rosenstiel and walked down a corridor lined with stuffed sharks baring their menacing teeth, you'd find yourself in a tiny bar that served beer on tap and had one of the best sunset views in South Florida.

But the truth was—and we'd stopped acknowledging this after the decision was made—Graham had never much liked my hometown. This had wounded my pride at the start of our marriage, especially since I'd adopted his hometown—moreover, his entire region of the country—as my own. Miami was too hot, too crowded, too bicycle-unfriendly. There were no gentle green hills, no farmsteads, no mid-westerners (there were tons of them up the coast, especially on the Gulf, but in Miami the midwesterner remained a breed apart). He felt like the city had a lot going on but nothing to *do*. During a visit, my father's shows might be the only things to lure him out of the air-conditioning. He liked the idea of a multicultural city but was intimidated by the chore of learning a new language. On this point, he made a complete reversal the day after we arrived. He bought language tapes and started spending his night hours listening to them on bulbous headphones. He even subscribed—ambitious, I thought, but that was his way—to *El Nuevo Herald*, using Lidia's address.

I no longer had a job beyond taking care of Frankie, and I found that with Lidia around, this was less than all-consuming. It's a testament to the pull of family that although we'd never before lived in the same city, Frankie treated Lidia and my father—we all called them *Mimi* and *Papi*—like he treated me and Graham, with no suspicion or shyness and with a powerful sense of entitlement to their adoration. He assumed that, inasmuch as he was a prince, they were among his minions.

So I found myself partly absorbed by nesting—organizing, sprucing, and, frustratingly, getting rid of things we'd transported from Illinois but now had no room for—and partly adrift. My business had disinte-grated a year earlier, but still I had the feeling during idle hours that I'd forgotten some vital phone call or meeting. I found myself spending a lot of time in Lidia's backyard, setting up obstacle courses for Frankie with the sprinklers and the patio furniture, using a stopwatch to time him as he ran laps. Lidia's next-door neighbor, Mr. Genovese, dotted his lawn with meticulously pruned fruit trees and topiary shrubs, each a different shape or animal—cylinder, rectangle, oval, rabbit, squirrel, manatee—and though I had little landscaping experience, this inspired me to do a little upkeep in Lidia's overgrown bushes. I took to rooting through her unwieldy begonias and ferns with a pair of old clippers while my father and Frankie tossed a beach ball and paddled around on floats in the pool.

It was after Lidia found me in her hedges the third time—I'd been overzealous, and things were looking bare and asymmetrical—that she mentioned her plan. "There's a job for you, if you want it," she said.

I wiped my hands on my shorts. She stood between me and the sun, her rusted brown hair glowing a little around the edges, as if on fire. "What kind of job?"

"You need something to do. Take Frankie along."

Lidia, who kept busy every moment, paying work or no, was retired after having been a flight attendant for Pan Am for twenty-five years and working at a bank for another fifteen.

I vacillated. I could tell Lidia I could run my own life, thank you very much, or I could take the outstretched hand and whatever it offered. Lidia had never been anything but kind to me.

"All right," I said.

"It's maybe a little odd."

"Just tell me."

"It's a personal assistant thing," she said. "You have a problem carrying water?"

"Whose personal assistant?"

She pursed her lips. It seemed that she'd concocted a whole plan without any notion of how to convey it. "You'll take my boat," she said.

"Your boat? Where am I going?" I said.

"Stiltsville," she said. Then my father called from the backyard, using the voice that meant he needed all of her attention immediately, and she backed away. Before she was out of sight, she said, "If you're up for it, you can start Monday."

WINE LOOSENED LIDIA'S TONGUE. LATER that night, in the creaky chaise lounges we'd pulled from her garage onto the *Lullaby*'s roof deck, with Frankie asleep in his little bunk and Graham and my father out at a gig, she described the situation.

"Errand girl?" I said, after she started to explain.

"You're too proud? At the most, it's a few hours a day, three days a week."

What she told me was this: her old friend Vivian Hicks, who had Alzheimer's and lived in a rest home in Kissimmee, had asked her during a lucid spell more than a year earlier to find someone reliable to take care of her husband. There was already a young man doing her husband's shopping and running supplies out to the stilt house, but Vivian didn't trust him.

Vivian didn't have lucid spells anymore. "She was always forgetting that he wasn't her husband anymore, really," said Lidia, waving a hand to acknowledge a longer story that she wasn't going to tell. "She would think he was still living in their house, but he's been at Stiltsville for— *dios mio*—ten years or so."

"The hermit," I said. I thought of my mother's second-wind parties all those years before, where Vivian had always shown up alone. Once, my mother had mentioned that Vivian's husband had left her to live full-time at their stilt house. People, including my mother, started referring to him as *the hermit*. This was as much of the story as I recalled. "Vivian was a friend of my mother's."

"Of course," she said. "They all know each other."

I knew what she meant. There were circles of women in South Florida, and my mother, having grown up in the area herself, was at least distantly attached to several of these circles. If you didn't know someone well, you at least knew her by name. My mother's reputation in these circles was good—this was my understanding, formed over decades—but my father's was considerably less so. There's a segment of society that easily forgives a working mother her modest income—how much could my mother have made as the keeper of Dr. Fuller's calendar and inventory?—but does not do the same for a working father. To many, my father, with his traveling and late-sleeping and unclassifiable income sources, was a decidedly unenviable husband. I'm sure there were times, especially in the later years, when my mother agreed.

"I did find someone right after she asked me to," said Lidia. "The son of a friend of a friend. But he quit a few months ago." I gave her a look, and she added, "Not for any awful reason, I promise."

Lidia's blue eyes were a little glassy, her cheeks high in color. She was one of these women who had never had a manicure or needed one. Her nails were white-tipped and grew naturally in a squarish shape. Her thick dark hair winged out in a wide, feathery bob—a style, I gleaned from old photos, she'd been wearing for decades. She wore chunky cork platform sandals every day of the week, even with her swimsuit while lying beside her pool, a wide-brimmed hat over her hair and a muslin cloth over her legs. She was attractive, if slightly outmoded. More attractive than my mother in some ways, less so in others. Where my mother had been slim-shouldered and large-breasted, widebottomed and thin-ankled—floral in shape, like a tulip—Lidia was a little plump but vigorous and strong. She had curvy calves beneath her culottes, round hips and high breasts, shoulders and biceps that resembled plump fruit. Her skin was sun-darkened and freckled at the collar of her blouse. My mother's skin had been ivory, unblemished, her thin hair ash-blond, her nose narrow and long in a way that on a man is considered potent, but on a woman is perhaps sexy but not very pretty. My mother had hated her nose. Lidia's nose bloomed at the tip, like a new bud. She wore very red lipstick almost all the time.

"I think my mother said he went crazy," I said to Lidia. "Is that right?"

She raised her eyebrows. "I doubt your mom used the word *crazy*."

Lidia had known my mother, too, but barely. I'd gone to school with Lidia's son, Roberto, who was now a real estate agent in California. He had five young kids—their names were, I promise, particularly impossible to recall—and didn't visit often. He wanted Lidia to move to Fresno. She'd told me this in a way that communicated that the prospect was not only unfeasible but appalling. When she spoke of Roberto and his family, she didn't try to hide her sadness, which was something I liked about her.

"I can't remember what word she used," I said, thinking that it was true that it would have been unlike her. My mother had been something of an armchair psychologist. She'd told me she thought a neighbor who talked a lot and left trash on our lawn was a narcissist, that her estranged brother, who lived in Key Largo, was a depressive. Where she got this information—surely not from the pediatric office—I don't know. She had antennae for that kind of thing, as people do. But her self-training on the subject would have kept her from using the word *crazy*. Not only was it unkind, but it was also unspecific.

"What's wrong with him, exactly?" I said to Lidia.

"If you don't count living alone in the middle of the bay," she said, "nothing."

"Is it safe to take Frankie?"

"Would I recommend it if it wasn't?"

"You're sure?"

She didn't have much patience for reassurance. "Look, run a few errands and take him some supplies. Put it on your credit card and keep the receipts. His lawyer handles the money. Give it a week. You don't want the job, I'll find someone else."

I was too old to take on a second mother, but the way she treated me, in this instance and in others, smacked of maternal doublespeak, as if circling around what she really wanted to tell me, which was to buck up. My own mother had danced around the truth enough for me to recognize the behavior. One afternoon at the start of my mother's long illness, I'd visited for the weekend, and she'd needled me into helping her sort something—photographs? silver? I don't recall. I'd recently spent my time in Detention and was dizzy with thoughts of Graham. I took a break from the sorting to show her a photograph of him. "He looks like a silent-film star," she said, staring closely. "You said he doesn't drive?" In the photo, Graham leaned against the passenger door of a shiny black sedan, a cornfield in the background. His hair was a slightly muddier white. He had given me the photo for just this purpose, to show my mother, but I remember thinking that it took a certain kind of man to give a girl a photo that was so obviously taken by another woman. Instead of saying this outright, my mother added that he seemed mighty self-assured, which in her book was a mixed bag.

Spoons. We'd been sorting my mother's collection of antique spoons.

LIDIA TAUGHT ME TO DRIVE the Zodiac that same night, after another several inches of wine for us both. I was nervous leaving Frankie alone, even while he slept. I locked the *Lullaby*'s sliding doors and goaded Lidia into leaning over the hedges and asking her neighbor, Zola Genovese, who was sitting on her own back deck, to keep an eye on the *Lullaby* until we returned. Zola said it was her pleasure, then made a point to reassure me that she, too, had driven herself mad with worry when her kids were young.

The moonshine off the water had the soft blue glow of a night-light in a dark room. I reminded Lidia that we needed to hurry, but she just shushed me and gestured for me to follow her to the far end of the pier, where the Zodiac rested. She stepped aboard. "There's nothing to it," she said, handing me a key attached to a bright yellow float.

She showed me how to check the fuel level and lower the engine and prime the choke. The engine roared into the night and Lidia shushed

again, then laughed. She's *fun*, I thought. She told me to throw the
stern and bow lines into the well, and I dropped down onto the boat's
gunwale as we pulled away. We swapped places and she barked instructions over the engine noise: how to ease forward on the throttle, how to
shift into neutral and reverse. We headed toward the bay. I reminded
her again that I didn't want to go too far, but she just kept issuing instructions. We practiced turning around and slowing and reversing,
and then suddenly we were at the start of the canal, where it opens to
spit out the bay, and while Lidia explained the channel markers—the
Zodiac had very little draw, she said, so I would have to really load it
down to run aground—I marveled at the canopy of star-salted night,
the dark open water spotted by whitecaps, the indistinct indigo horizon. Then Lidia leaned against the boat's two-seater bench and refused
to answer any more questions. It was up to me to navigate back up
the canal, leaving the bay at our backs. I eased up to the pier and cut
the engine, and the still, silent darkness pooled around us. Over the
hedges, Zola Genovese waved good night and went into her house.

Inside the *Lullaby*, Frankie slept with one arm flung over the side
of the bunk, his face open to the room, lips as bright as bougainvillea
blossoms. The bedsheet was twisted around his legs as if he'd tossed
and turned. I had the thought—it skipped through my mind and
dissolved—that I couldn't believe I had left Miami in the first place.

GRAHAM'S ILLNESS ANNOUNCED ITSELF THE summer he was eleven years old. One night after his family arrived home to the cottage after a long day at the state fair, Graham and his sister, who was nine, bathed and got into bed, and their mother looked in on them and encouraged each child to share a favorite moment from the trip. His sister's—he could hear her voice through the wall between their rooms—was the crayon-colored Ferris wheel, which had stalled when they'd reached the top and swayed a little in the high winds, giving them all a thrill. Graham told his mother that his favorite had been the rifle range, where he'd won a giant lollipop.

In actuality, though, his favorite had been the haunted house. His father had taken him against his mother's wishes, while she and Lauren were taking another turn on the Ferris wheel. Just inside, Graham and his father had been ushered with a large group into an airless black room, and the lights had dimmed. He'd thought for a moment that there had been some kind of mistake, but then a deep, echoey voice came from overhead, narrating a history of the house and the robber baron who'd owned it, telling how the baron and his wife had been slaughtered by Indians and now haunted the rooms, headless. The door they'd come through was a seamless wall. There was no discernible way out. Graham felt ghost-fingers on the back of his neck.

He went to sleep that night thinking of the crowded room, the old-fashioned portraits on the wall, and the handsome striped wallpaper. He was worn out from the trip and fell quickly into a heavy sleep. In his experience, even at that young age, there were half a dozen types of sleep, and this was a seductive, serpentine sleep, bent on smothering. He startled breathlessly awake after an hour or so, and something pushed him to rise to his feet. There he stood in his pajamas in the dark. He was middream, still, though he didn't realize it. In his dream, he stood alone in that suffocating haunted house. The lights had gone off. This had been done deliberately, he understood, to scare him. They knew he was afraid of the dark. He took a few tentative steps, hands out, and touched the wall. He felt his way along the wall, and within a few steps his fingers met the square edge of a frame: a portrait. He continued to edge around the room, bumping into a second frame.

On Graham's birthday the year before, his father had handed down to him two of his own cherished possessions: framed prints, one from the 1933 Chicago Fair, and one from the 1948 summer Olympics in London, where his father had watched from the stands as right-handed Hungarian pistol-shooter Károly Takács, whose hand had been destroyed by a grenade, won the gold medal using his left hand. Because Graham's birthday was in the summer, the prints came to hang in Graham's bedroom at the cottage, instead of in the apartment in Chicago.

Graham's eyes were open in the dark, but he could see nothing, not even shadows. On a night with a moon, the surface of the lake outside his window doubled the light, but on this night there was no moon, no starlight. His heart beat fast. He told himself to stay calm. Distantly, he heard the call of a loon. Some summers were thick with them. When he was fifteen they would disappear entirely for years, but by the time we lived there they'd returned, though he would swear the numbers had thinned.

It was the loon that pulled him out of it. He felt again for the wall, and this time the glass beneath his fingers, the edge of the picture frame, revealed itself for what it was: one of the prized posters.

Graham blinked a few times and stood still. The understanding—that he was in his own bedroom, that he'd been asleep and then had woken, or half-woken—came gradually. He didn't trust it. He clung to the idea of being trapped, as if it were the reality and the physical world the dream. When finally he was fully awake, he made his way to the bed and climbed in. He didn't sleep. As the sun rose, the weeping willow outside his window made lacy patterns on his walls, and the light glinted off the glass frames.

After this, he understood that the human brain has the ability to lose its way, like a boy without light.

When Graham was fifteen—long after the episode in his bedroom on Round Lake—he spent a summer in Cadiz, Spain, as an exchange student. He lived in an apartment with a family who had three boys, and he shared a room with the youngest. They ate chocolate and bread for breakfast and spent all day at the beach. Graham had always had a lot of dreams during his scarce sleep, and he'd always remembered them vividly, and one night he woke sweating in the early morning, the light outside a shade short of black, parrots cawing across the building's courtyard. He woke not peacefully but with the sound of his own screams competing with the cries of the parrots. In the dream that receded too slowly, he was being chased by something terrifying and deadly. The mother of the family, a stout woman with a mustache, held him and shushed him brusquely, and the youngest brother stared in annoyance. This was the summer Graham grew his first white hair. By the time he was twenty, there would be no brown left at all.

Because we met through sleep, people assumed that our troubles were similar, or at least neighbors on the same spectrum. But my sleep troubles and Graham's were never related, not in symptom or treatment or prognosis. Nothing that helped me could have helped him. The furthest reach of my troubles—the long hours, the heavy pharmaceutical coating that remained after pill-induced sleep, and the terrible humming alertness that followed the shattering of such sleep, like the vibration of a gong after being struck—were insignificant compared to the terrifying unpredictability of extreme parasomnia.

Although it might have seemed as if we were in the same place, working toward the same goal—healthy sleep—we were not at all. By the time we met, Graham knew that no real cure existed for him. I was still hopeful on leaving Detention that the long hours might end. I'd fooled myself into thinking that my insomnia was a sleep disorder, or I'd been fooled by doctors. I don't sleep well—it's a problem, yes, but it's a problem on a par with losing your grocery list before getting to the store. I don't talk about it, but when it does come up, people are sympathetic. Most people have a passing association with insomnia, and they know it's an experience they don't care to repeat. I want to tell them how much worse it can be. Perhaps the closest relative to Graham's experience is chronic pain—recurrent migraines or crippling arthritis, for example. Living under the thumb not only of the pain itself, but also of the threat of full-on outbreak. People with these conditions know a bit about what it's like to live as Graham did, in perpetual discomfort and perpetual fear.

THERE WAS A BRASS BELL suspended from the wide trim alongside the *Lullaby*'s sliding doors, and this was how Lidia announced her presence the first morning I was expected at Stiltsville. She didn't wait for an answer. The screen's metal track was chalky and warped, and the door stuck in phases—*stut stut stut*—as she strong-armed it open.

"*Madre de dios*," she said. "You must fix that."

"It's on the list," I said.

I wore a towel around my torso and another around my hair. Frankie was on a colorful patterned rug in the corner of the salon, practicing his monkey jumps. He signed to Lidia, two fingers pointing at his own eyes: *Watch! Watch!*

"He wants you to watch him," I said to Lidia.

"Certainly!"

He placed his hands on the rug, fingers splayed and head tucked, then bucked and twisted in one motion. Then he thrust both hands into the air, smiling largely, showing his boxy little teeth. There were times when I could almost hear the sounds he would make if he spoke: *Ta-da!* he might have said. A few times, in reality, he'd laughed faintly; there had been days when getting him to laugh was my singular objective. There were sounds of pain sometimes, if he skinned a knee or whacked his head, a cry muffled by closed lips. Otherwise, I hadn't heard him form a word—an intentional, coherent word—in eighteen months, almost half his lifetime, and back then the only words he'd spoken had been *mama*, *dada*, *flower*, *doggie*, and *ball*. Just as he'd started to speak words, he'd stopped. We'd dragged him to the doctor, had speech therapists out to the cottage. They'd confirmed there was nothing wrong with his hearing. They said he was making a choice, shutting his mouth when another child would open it. They said there was likely a reason, and they quizzed me about my marriage and about Graham and his parasomnia, which led me to understand that children in difficult homes sometimes go mute—but they settled on no clear explanation.

When I thought of what life would be like for Frankie in school and as an adult if he never started to talk, I felt a fist tighten around my heart.

I asked Lidia to watch him while I dressed. As I retreated to the main berth—this was the first time since we'd moved aboard that I would close the room's flimsy accordion door—she said, "Move it. You're running late."

I pulled on shorts and ran a brush through my hair. I dug through the storage trundle for a crushable straw hat that had belonged to my mother, which I'd adopted as my own long before she died. I dropped a towel and sunscreen into a tote.

Through the thin door, I heard Lidia saying, "Sweet boy, can you say *Mimi*? *Meee-Meee* . . ."

I opened the door. "Lidia," I said, "please don't." I'd made the request three or four times since we'd arrived.

"Mama's right," she said to Frankie. "No pressure. This isn't the military, it's Mimi's house. *Meeee-meee*'s house—"

I shut the door.

When we were ready to leave, Lidia handed me a photocopy of a handwritten list. It wasn't in her handwriting, which was loopy and illegible. This handwriting was tiny and precise, all the letters capitalized, as if shouting in a small voice. There were four stores listed and about thirty items total. From a bait and tackle shop in the Grove, several items. CREAM KROMKA CRAB BONEFISH FLY (4), for example; 1 LB SPOOL CLEAR MONO FILAMENT LINE (ANY BRAND). From a place called the Knitting Garden: 1/2 DOZ 11 MM ENGLISH RIM WOODEN BUTTONS (ASH) and 1/2 DOZ 11 MM COCONUT BUTTONS (UNCARVED), as well as three types and colors of yarn. Beneath the name of the print shop, FAX COPY PRINT, there was only one line: SEE MR. HENRY GALE. The list alone begged the question of what I was getting myself into.

By June in South Florida, it's more or less as hot as it will remain through the middle of October, when finally the heat relents for a few months. Some women—my childhood friend Sally was one example—were either so accustomed to the heat or so immune to it that they coiffed the way they might if they lived in permanent winter, where the crisp and dry air was more skin- and hair-compliant. Maybe there were products I'd never heard of that could have helped, but for me, being in Miami meant dispensing of makeup, dry-cleaned clothing, and smartly styled hair. I'd inherited my grandmother's coarse dark curls, and my round face meant a shorter cut would be unflattering, so there was little to be done. In Miami, I secured my hair in a messy bun or ponytail at the nape of my neck, curls fat and frizzy in the humidity. I wore sleeveless shirts and Bermudas or cotton skirts every day. In South Florida, it's not the intensity of heat or humidity that wears you down—it's the perseverance of it.

Lidia, who'd mentioned she was running late to meet her power-walkers club, escorted us to the driveway. She hovered in the driver's-side window as I started the car. I tended to drive with the windows down and the air-conditioning fully throttled, and always had. It blasted my face as we idled. Up close, Lidia's skin showed age—deep lines around her mouth, creases down her thin lips, faint speckled scars along her jawbone—though generally she gave the impression of a much younger woman. She squinted at me and adjusted her visor. "You're all right?" she said, then answered herself. "You're all right."

"We'll be fine."

"Maybe this isn't a great idea."

"Maybe not. We'll give it a shot."

"I haven't seen him since they were married," she said. "Really married, you know—dinner parties and that sort of thing. He was polite enough but didn't smile. I talked with him once about a bridge he'd designed or engineered or I don't know what, somewhere up the turnpike." She smacked the car roof lightly. "Off you go, anyway."

At the bait and tackle shop, I handed the list to the man behind the counter, who looked surprised not at its existence, but at mine. He ignored Frankie, who stood close at my side. He said, "I was wondering when he'd run out of lures." The man—his name tag said BILL—had skin that looked carved from rough, wet stone. He didn't smile, but when he loaded the contents of the list into a bag, he said, "Tell Charlie we miss him out on the flats." He delivered this line without meeting my eyes, in a way that conveyed he'd said it many times before, without much hope of ever seeing Charlie on the flats again.

At the knitting store, several women sat in a huddle of armchairs, their hands working mechanically and their heads tipped, like a colony of birds. Frankie went to inspect a wall of cubbies filled with brightly dyed yarns heaped in soft figure-eights.

Don't touch, I signed. I didn't have to sign, but in public I found myself doing it without thinking, for no other reason than to keep him company.

He stuffed his hands in the pockets of his shorts emphatically, to make a point.

One of the knitting women met me at the counter. When I handed her the list, she appraised me over cat-eye glasses. "Where's the other guy?" she said.

"I wouldn't know," I said.

She looked back at the list, frowning. "More pea soup angora already? How's that possible?"

I didn't answer.

"I'm out of the medium-weight cactus flower. I'll have it next time." She started to hand back the list, then stopped and looked at me again. She had pink, gently sagging cheeks and a silver stripe in her black hair. "I find it interesting, this list." Her tone was confidential. "Sometimes more of one thing, less of another."

"I saw it for the first time this morning," I said.

After I paid, Frankie and I walked to the print shop, one block away in a different strip mall. We passed a small, crowded diner, outside of which men and women in suits smoked cigarettes and chatted, waiting for a table. Inside, people sat shoulder to shoulder on benches at stainless steel tables. A few doors down, the print shop was bookended by empty storefronts with FOR LEASE signs in the windows. I was struck by Miami's easy relationship with contradiction, economic upswing and downturn jumbled together. In other cities, there seemed to be ways to predict which homes would sell, which restaurants would close. Maybe there were Miamians who could predict these things, but whenever I hazarded a guess, I was wrong.

Even after walking only a block, the air-conditioning was a relief. Frankie's hair was too long for this weather. Dark, leafy chunks were pasted to his forehead, and his cheeks were bright pink. He peered over the counter at the maze of industrial printers being manned by gum-smacking teenagers, their faces glowing with each pass of the developer under the glass.

Mr. Henry Gale was in the back. I asked for him, and the man who emerged was broad-shouldered and barrel-chested, with a vo-luminous dark beard that covered most of his face—an *un-Floridian* beard, was my thought. He wore a short-sleeved plaid button-down and long shorts with a surfeit of many-size pockets, an oatmeal-colored waist apron, and leather sandals. This man, with his ruddy cheeks and easy stroll, was clearly not a person one would address as *Mister*, which furthered my notion that the hermit was formal and old-fashioned.

The man whistled as he navigated the bunker of copiers. "You must be Georgia," he said in a deep, softly articulated voice. We shook hands. To Frankie, he said, "Little man! How's it going?"

"I'm sorry," I said. "But may I ask who told you I was coming?"

"Riggs said a new runner would be stopping by. You've got to ex-plain something to Charlie for me—on the nautilus, I subbed vermill-lion red for the carmine red he requested." He searched behind the counter, then pulled up an oversize brown bag. "It's a little brighter, a little *orangey*, but I think it works better with the dark water. Make sure to let me know if he doesn't like it, and I'll do it again."

"Who is Riggs?"

"Charlie's lawyer. He called yesterday."

"And what is vermillion red?"

He smiled. His teeth were very bright and straight, the teeth of a more sophisticated man. It wasn't that he wasn't attractive—he was—

but it was the offhand kind of attractive that's composed mostly of confidence and cool, with physical attributes an afterthought.

He said, "Look here," and pulled from the paper bag a stack of prints. He sorted through them gingerly, touching only the corners. The topmost piece, which Henry tipped toward me as he searched, was two things at once: a page from some kind of reference book, covered margin to margin in very small type; and also, superimposed over the type, a precisely drawn portrait of a multicolored jellyfish—or was it a man-of-war? Each tentacle was a different shade of yellow or green, its tendrils rendered painstakingly, some entwined and some jagged, some thin as noodles, some stubby and muscular. The dome of the creature was a soft emerald in color, its crown delicate as a snowflake. It appeared midswim, pushing itself across the page. Henry slipped another picture from the stack: a candy-striped nautilus (I didn't know what the creature was called at the time), its one visible eye cold but frantic, the rectangular pupil stamped and goatlike. This creature, too, was superimposed over a reference book page.

Beside the stack of prints, Henry placed a paper bag. "The originals," he said, pushing them toward me.

I opened the bag and leafed through. These portraits were black and white, drawn on oversize book pages in what looked like charcoal pencil. My understanding was that it was Henry's job to add color to the drawings by hand, then print them on heavier stock using his equipment. Without color, the jellyfish was ruthless and astringent, masterfully depicted and beautiful in its way, but also cold, without the colored version's hint of playfulness.

"This is the vermillion," Henry said, pointing to the nautilus's striped shell. "You see? Orangey."

I closed the bag of originals and carefully picked up the jellyfish print. Frankie rose on his toes to peer over the edge of the counter. I signed to him, *What's that?*

Fish, he signed, one hand swimming in the air in front of his face.

"Jellyfish," I said. "We'll look it up."

We kept a big book of American Sign Language and consulted it daily, sometimes three or four times in an afternoon. We were constantly running up against the limits of a vocabulary acquired on an as-needed basis.

Henry looked back and forth between us. "You like fish, little man?" he said to Frankie, who gave an exaggerated nod. "Check this out." He thumbed through the prints, then pulled out a drawing of a giant octopus attacking a clipper ship. The ship's bow was consumed by the water and its stern hovered tenuously above it. Each of its three masts was wrapped in a ropey lavender tentacle lined with fleshy pink suckers. I caught the typed heading of the page beneath the drawing, which read ABSTRACT OF STATE LAWS REGARDING WILLS. I marveled at the technical ability, the artistry, of rendering an animal so vividly on the page. "What do you think of *that*?" Henry said.

Frankie had ways of making up for his lack of speech. His eyes devoured the drawing. They spoke for him. He looked up at Henry, cocked his head, pushed out his lower lip, and blinked once—a gesture of pleasure.

Henry came around the counter and handed me two small boxes. "This one goes to Charlie," he said, indicating the bottom box. "And this one," he said, pointing to the top box, "goes to the RZ Gallery on LeJeune. Drop it off with the curator—I think her name is Helen? Elena? Something like that."

"Today?" I said.

"She's waiting. I can't leave the shop, and a messenger will take too long." He put the prints back in the bag and handed it over, along with the bag of originals. He shook my hand again, but this time he cupped mine in both of his for a moment, as if we were old friends. To Frankie, he gave a salute. "Until next time, little man," he said, and Frankie waved.

FRANKIE PLAYED IN LIDIA'S BACKYARD while I unpacked the car. Since leaving the printer, we'd unloaded the drawings at RZ

Gallery—the curator was reading a gossip magazine and wearing a wool turtleneck in the gallery's biting chill—and spent over an hour at the grocery store. It was one o'clock; Lidia had implored me to get to Stiltsville before noon. I rushed back and forth from the boat to the car, checking on Frankie each time I rounded the corner of the house. He was a passable swimmer for his age, but I didn't like having him unsupervised around the pool, even for a minute. After several trips, the Zodiac's aft deck was crowded with bags and boxes, including three twenty-pound bags of ice that each required its own trip. These, I crowded under the captain's bench to keep out of the sunlight. I fastened down the boxes and bags with bungee cords I'd found in the garage.

At the tackle shop, I'd picked up the only life jacket on the shelf that came close to fitting Frankie. It was purple and had a pink butterfly across the back, and even on the smallest setting rose up around his shoulders. He kept pulling it down, patting his front and shaking his head, as if the foamy presence were a mosquito he could shoo. I stepped onto the boat and pushed off, and in that moment felt the clutch of anxiety.

The Zodiac had a two-seater captain's bench where I leaned and Frankie sat with his legs dangling. I pushed forward on the throttle as a Jet Ski raced by—too fast for the canal, I thought—and the Zodiac rocked on its waves. I signed to Frankie: *Hold on.*

The Coral Gables waterway was dredged in 1925. Back then, gondoliers ferried residents out to the bay down the eight miles of snaking green canal. Now the homes that lined the banks were Mediterranean in style, the nearby streets named for places in Spain—*Seville, Andalusia, Granada*—and lined with banyans that fractured the sunlight into spires. Some canal-front homes, like Lidia's, were modest, outdated ranches with large backyards and terra-cotta tiles and sunken great rooms, called Florida rooms, their stucco exteriors painted hibiscus colors. But many of the old homes had been razed and replaced or swallowed by additions. The newer homes were similar in style but strangers in soul, some pretty and some grotesque. Along the canal, each lot was belted by a pier and a boathouse or a slip. Many bulwarks, Lidia's included, were crumbling, and they were all marbled in green algae and pocked with butterscotch snails as big as Ping-Pong balls. Between many of the homes, swampy mangroves or sea grape trees rose like haphazard fences, sending dark roots into the water to claw for space. There were boats at most of the piers, and several of these were gleaming yachts with broad white hulls and no obvious signs of use. They blocked the sky as we passed beneath them. I drove slowly. We were passed twice, once by a lone man in a cabin cruiser and once by a little Mako so crowded with teenagers that it rode frighteningly low in the water.

The course of a life will shift—really shift—many times over the years. But rarely will there be a shift that you can feel gathering in the distance like a storm, rarely will you notice the pressure drop before the skies open. That morning, as Frankie and I had plodded from errand to errand, led around by the hermit's list like animals on leashes, I'd known on some level that this was one of those times. I would like to believe that I wouldn't again make the mistake of walking in blindly. Then again, blindly is the only way I would have walked in.

In the clear light of afternoon, the canal was transformed. The bay opened not like an unfurling serpent but like a feat of engineering, cleanly and without fuss. I followed the channel markers and kept our speed low, but the water was a little rough and without some momentum we rose too high and fell too hard. I sped up, and the bow bucked and planed and the ride smoothed out. The jostling waves were mild compared to those of the open ocean, beyond the continental shelf, and after several minutes, Frankie loosened his grip on the bench and I started to enjoy the sunshine and breeze and blue expanse of the water. The bay was sparsely dotted by boats in every direction. Behind us, my hometown gathered itself neatly on the shoreline, as if seeing us off. To the south wound the muddy green shoreline, and to the north rose the silver spires of downtown. A milky span of bridge linked the mainland to Key Biscayne.

The success of piloting midway across the bay buoyed me. I no longer felt unwise. I felt brave, as if I were the kind of mother who does not think, when her child has a nosebleed, of the potentially fatal ailments the nosebleed might augur. I felt like the mother who hands her child a tissue and tells him to wash his hands. At some point, I looked over my shoulder, and what I saw tripped my heartbeat: the yawing mouth of the canal had been sealed by distance.

It was ten minutes before Stiltsville—fourteen homes built on pilings in the middle of the bay—took shape along the horizon. From that distance, the houses resembled toy blocks on pins. Two channels ran through Stiltsville, and shallower grooves laced the northeastern quadrant of Biscayne Bay. From above, in aerial photos I've seen, these grooves look exactly as if a giant raked its fingers across the seabed. I knew from Lidia that the hermit's house was in the far channel, shingled in weathered gray cedar, with an exterior staircase that jutted out over the water before angling back to the dock, like a crooked elbow.

It was Monday, and most of Stiltsville's weekend residents were back on dry land. The place was empty of boats. From a distance, it had seemed as if the houses bundled together, but in actuality each stood alone on its own piece of narrow shoal, shouting distance from the closest neighbor. When you build a house beyond the edge of a continent, you're not looking to make friends. We passed a light blue house with an L-shaped dock, all the windows shuttered and a gate across the staircase. Next was a lemon-colored house with a wraparound porch, and, on the opposite shoal, a light pink house with plastic owls rooted to every dock piling.

The hermit's house was next. Lidia had mentioned that it would be the only one with the windows and gate open but no boat at the dock—still, the sight was jarring. Each house was a kind of island, yes, but especially the one inhabited by a person with no means of getting off. The Mansard roof was flat and thickly shingled, giving the house a top-heavy, vaguely French appearance. I approached slowly, the Zodiac's engine stuttering, intending to give the hermit some warning. Like the others, his house was raised above the water by cement pilings, so I could see underneath it to the open water beyond.

We reached the dock, which snaked back and forth toward the house like a line at an amusement park. There was a brief, alarming moment when I forgot how to cut the engine, but then I turned the key and that was that. I signed to Frankie to stay put, then stepped onto the dock with the spring line and secured it to a cleat. He watched me, then slipped off the captain's bench and stepped over to the gunwale. His arms came up and I lifted him onto the dock. When I turned—I suppose I knew this would be the case—there was a man standing on the upstairs porch wearing a faded gray T-shirt and jeans with the cuffs rolled up. He stood with both palms on the porch railing, one bare foot perched on top of the other, as if there was all the time in the world for greeting, and for the moment he was content to stare down at us, these two strangers trespassing on his island.

THE FIRST THING I SAID to the hermit was: "You're very precise."
I handed over his list, items crossed out, exceptions noted.

He was slim with broad shoulders and a narrow waist, only two or
three inches taller than I was. His large gray eyes folded at the corners
and he was due for a shave. He didn't meet my eyes.

"I used to try to be easygoing," he said, rubbing his chin with his
thumb. "It didn't work out."

I told him my name and introduced Frankie, laying a hand on
Frankie's head, which Frankie shook off. The man told us his name—
Charlie Hicks—then stepped into the Zodiac and started hefting boxes
onto the dock. The muscles in his forearms tightened as he lifted. I
signed to Frankie—*Stay there*—and stepped down to help, and within
a few minutes the Zodiac's deck was bare.

Charlie pulled a small plastic bag of lures from the pile and held
it out to Frankie. "Can you carry this for me, please?" he said quietly.

Frankie nodded solemnly and clutched the lures to his chest, then
followed Charlie toward the staircase. I grabbed a couple of bags

and hurried to catch up. Frankie took the stairs deliberately, and
Charlie glanced back every few steps to check on him. We emerged
onto a broad wraparound porch rimmed by a white wooden railing.
Each segment of the railing was comprised of four horizontal two-
by-fours that angled slightly toward the water, like oversize blinds.
The bottommost rung was about three feet from the porch floor,
which left plenty of room, I thought, for a toddler to fall through.
In one corner was a metal toolbox, a hammer and jar of nails beside
it. I kept careful watch over Frankie, wondering again if this was
such a great idea.

We dropped the bags on the linoleum floor of the kitchen and
went back downstairs. Again, Charlie handed Frankie something of
his own to carry. Frankie took great care. I fretted that we were seconds away from some drama that would end the whole enterprise.
Frankie might drop something into the water or tumble down the
stairs or off the dock. It looked to me like the water beneath the
house and surrounding the dock was only four or five feet deep, which
was somewhat reassuring. We made several trips, Charlie leading
and Frankie close behind, eager to be handed his next assignment.
Each trip, I took in a little of the house's interior: sagging sectional
sofa in faded gray corduroy, plywood coffee table covered in books
and magazines, Formica breakfast bar rimmed by four cracked red
vinyl stools, faded oval braided rug in the living room, wood-paneled
walls painted a chalky off-white. Above the kitchen window hung a
wooden clock in the shape of a knobby ship's wheel, the hands frozen
in place. On the walls of the living room were half a dozen framed
paintings, all Florida landscapes of a similar, realistic style. In one,
the long neck of a wind-blown palm tree curved over a pale beach.
In another, a stately bright poinciana shaded a dirt road. In a third,
an anhinga took flight through dense wetlands beneath dark clouds
ringed by silvery sunlight. Off the main room of the house was a brief
hallway and three closed doors.

When we were done, Frankie scrambled onto the sofa and looked through a large window at the open ocean. I noticed a canvas bag on the seat beside him, overstuffed with mounds of yarn pierced by a pair of knitting needles.

"Frankie, come back," I said.

"He's fine there," said Charlie.

There were two large coolers stacked beneath a window in the kitchen. Charlie started filling them with the ice I'd brought.

"Did you build this house?" I said.

"No."

"Who did?"

"My uncle." He washed his hands at the sink. "Did you have time for lunch?" he said without looking up. For a moment I thought he might not have been talking to me. "Is the boy hungry?"

Frankie spun around and waved both arms—this was how he signaled me—and signed: *Banana.*

We hadn't eaten. "I brought snacks," I said to Frankie, signing as I spoke.

"It's late," said Charlie. "We'll have a meal." He looked up quickly, then away again. He was so wary of making eye contact that I watched him unheeded. He had the compact, stocky-legged body of a wrestler or swimmer, and his face was square in shape and sun-worn, deeply lined across the forehead and around the mouth and eyes. His straight hair was brown with a lot of white at the temples, parted messily. His lips were thin and pale, his mouth set in concentration. I would have guessed he was older than he was, older than my father.

"We don't want to put you out," I said. "Tell me what I can do."

"Sit down." He pointed at a low wooden armchair with leather cushions. "That's the comfortable one."

I brought a bottle of water, now warm, to Frankie. *Boat,* Frankie signed, pointing through the window at a distant ship, smokestacks branching into the sky.

"Cruise ship," I said. I didn't know the sign.

Charlie opened and closed the refrigerator, putting away groceries, but no light went on inside.

"Is there electricity?" I said.

"Generators," he said, motioning downstairs, where I'd noticed a small room in one corner beneath the house, across from the stairway.

"Water?" I said.

"There's a rainwater tank," he said. "The commode flushes, the sink works. But drink only bottled water, please."

He filled a glass from a gallon jug of water and placed it on the coffee table in front of me. Then he brought down a tray from a cabinet and started pulling items from the coolers, chopping and arranging them in white bowls: strawberries, squares of pineapple, green olives, hunks of French bread, two kinds of cheese, carrots.

When he was done, he moved a stool from the breakfast bar to the sink, then said Frankie's name to get his attention. "Come wash your hands," he said.

Frankie complied, cupping the wedge of soap Charlie handed him, then taking a long time to dry his hands on a faded green dish towel. He raised both arms toward Charlie before climbing down from the stool, and before I could step forward to help, Charlie had lifted Frankie under the arms and set him on his feet. Frankie made his way back to the sofa. Charlie turned on a radio that sat on the ledge above the sink, and from it came a scratchy thread of classical music. The tray he'd prepared reminded me of a kaleidoscope, all the colors distinct but nestled tightly. He sat on the sofa and handed me a plate.

"Eat," he said, offering the bread. His eyes landed briefly on mine. To Frankie, he said, "You, too."

"This is lovely," I said. "Thank you."

Frankie bounced down onto his rump and ambled to the table, eyes wide. Charlie chewed slowly, glancing at Frankie, who ignored his plate and went from bowl to bowl, choosing each bite. After eating his first chunk of pineapple—it wasn't a fruit I tended to buy—he emitted the softest sigh of pleasure. This gave me a little thrill, but I kept my cool. He pointed to the bowl of pineapple and signed, *What name?*

"Pineapple," I said. "We'll look it up when we get home."

And the fish, he signed.

"And the jellyfish," I said.

Charlie watched us but didn't say anything.

I said to Charlie, "Henry wanted to make sure you're okay with one of the reds he used."

"I'm sure it's fine," he said.

Maybe it was the heat, but I felt no urge to stoke conversation. The air was still. In the distance came the buzz of a boat engine, but then it passed. Gulls squawked. After a while, all that was left on the tray were the stubby green heads of the strawberries and a small mound of wrinkled olive pits. I offered to clean up. Charlie shrugged by way of agreement. As I worked, Frankie dropped to the linoleum and army-crawled to the open doorway, where sunlight spread across the floor. He placed his hands in the patch of light, keeping his fingers inside its boundaries, then rearranged them and did it again. This was the kind of thing that could occupy him for long stretches. Charlie watched him.

I said, "I was told it was no problem if he came along."

"It's fine," said Charlie, wiping his face. To Frankie, he said, "You're what—four?"

Frankie held up two fingers, then corrected himself by adding one more.

"I see," said Charlie. He brought his hands—they were thick-fingered, nails neatly trimmed—to his knees and rubbed the worn denim. "I gather you don't like a lot of talky talk."

Frankie nodded, then shook his head.

"I don't much care for it, either," said Charlie.

I dried the last of the bowls and put them away, then returned to the living room, where Frankie now crouched over a laminated fishing map of Biscayne Bay. I wasn't sure what was supposed to happen next. In awkward situations, I called on my manners; this was my mother in me. "You were nice to feed us," I said.

Charlie stood and crossed his arms against his chest. "I hate this beginning part," he said. "Every time, all uphill."

"You've had a lot of assistants?"

"A handful. The last fellow was with me almost a year. You won't last that long."

I couldn't read his tone. "Probably not."

He went to the corner and brought back an empty white cooler. "Keep this. Every time, bring me ice. As much as you can handle."

"No problem," I said.

"And take away the trash. I try to keep it to a minimum, but there's always some."

I went to the kitchen and pulled the bag from the trash can. He took it from me, saying, "You'll need a library card if you don't have one already. And you'll need to get my mail from the post office once a week, I don't care what day. There's a Friday list—you have it already? Did you talk to Riggs?"

"Not yet."

He went through a hallway door and came out again, closing the door behind him. He handed me a piece of paper, another photocopied list. "I have a project. We'll start Friday, if you can spare a few hours. If you want to get paid, I'd call Riggs right away."

I scanned the list. "You eat a lot of fruit."

"I was in the navy," he said. "There's a history of scurvy."

I assumed this was a joke, but he gave no indication. I had questions—I would have liked to know how often I'd be coming, what exactly I'd be doing, and how much I'd be paid—but the way he avoided my eyes discouraged me from asking. I signed to Frankie: *Let's go.*

Charlie followed us downstairs and lifted Frankie into the boat, then dropped the garbage bag into the well. I stuck out my hand and Charlie shook it. "Friday?" I said.

"Before noon, please."

I turned to get into the boat, but he put a hand on my elbow. He spoke in a low, rough voice. "One more thing. The boy's vest—it's too big. He'll need one that fits. Don't bring him back otherwise." He put up his hands to indicate the obvious: we were in the middle of open water. The current carried on beneath our feet. The porch and the stairs were nominally railed, the dock not at all. One could step off and be swallowed. In addition to a new vest, he would need more swim lessons.

"Got it," I said.

Charlie handled the boat lines, then stood on the dock with his hands in his pockets while I started the engine. At the mouth of the channel, I looked back, and he was out of sight. The water was smooth and the sun high. In the distance, the Miami skyline was a low cluster of sun-washed buildings, insubstantial as watercolors. As we neared, the shoreline parted, revealing our path. I throttled down and peered into the dark hollows of the mangrove roots, searching for an ibis or heron or turtle to show Frankie. A footprint-shaped swirl rose in the water off the port side.

Look, I signed to Frankie, pointing with my index and middle fingers from my eyes toward the water.

He jumped down from the bench and I put the boat into neutral. Together we watched the manatee's dome break the surface. Its molded-clay face appeared for a long moment, then it sloughed past, tail waving in slow motion.

BEFORE GRAHAM GOT HOME THAT night, Frankie and I sat at the kitchen table with the *American Sign Language Dictionary*. I'd gotten pretty good at understanding the ASL's descriptions of signs, and the *jellyfish* one was a breeze. Frankie and I did it together: one palm out flat, the other open above it, then all fingertips brought together, then open again, in imitation of the creature's movement in the

water. For *pineapple*, we made a *P* at the corners of our mouths and
jiggled a little, which Frankie found hilarious. His mouth opened wide
and out came quick gusts of breath, a silent guffaw.

Graham struggled through the sliding glass door and dropped his
panniers. He frowned at the dictionary on the table; he'd lost patience
with the speech problem. He opened his arms to Frankie, who scrambled up the trunk of his father like a monkey, then sat complacently in
his arms without holding on, as if perched on a throne.

Over dinner on the *Lullaby*'s back deck, we exchanged details of the
day. Graham had been assigned to a team that was developing a new
kind of weather buoy, and he was in charge of improving the software
that collected and transmitted the buoy's data. I described our trip to
Stiltsville. When I mentioned lunch, Graham cocked his head at me,
his fork paused in the air above his plate.

"What kind of job is this?"

"I really don't know."

"So what's he like, this hermit?"

I thought about how to answer. "He's intense, quiet. Kind of formal."

"Is he strange?"

"Not particularly. Not that I could tell."

"Seems as if he'd be strange, living like that."

When he was done eating—Frankie relished snacks but at meal-
times became suddenly disinterested in food—he emptied the contents
of his pockets onto the table, item by item. This was a habit he'd developed: he stashed things in his pockets during the day, and at night he
presented them to us like treasures: stickers backed with lint, a tiny elephant from the toy box, a sugar packet from Lidia's kitchen. Tonight,
the last item was a plastic yellow sea horse the size of my pinkie finger.
I touched the sharp ridges along its spine.

"Where did you get this?" I said.

His hands came up. *Man give it to me.*

I signed: *When?*

"Speak?" said Graham to me.

"When?" I said to Frankie.

Frankie looked back and forth between us, his mouth turned down at the edges and his shoulders slumped. *You in kitchen*, he signed. *Washing dishes*.

I've been asked time and again—by doctors and speech therapists, who had failed to find anything physically wrong; by Lidia and my father; even by friends back in Illinois, whose calls I'd stopped returning as their children's vocabularies multiplied—why sometimes I chose to sign instead of speaking. When I'd first started with the signing, not realizing how instrumental it would become, I'd pressed Graham to learn some basics. He'd said, "The boy can hear, right? Why are we doing this?" I'd said, "He can hear, but he can't talk. I don't want him to feel alone." I hadn't known why I was doing it until the words left my mouth. I knew people believed I should have been doing something quantifiable to help Frankie, and I didn't disagree. But so far, no diagnosis or treatment had been chosen for him. And I believed strongly that until we knew why he refused to speak, we would not entice him to start.

I cleared the table. Frankie's eyelids were heavy, his stare unfocused. He made the sign for *Sleep*: one hand cupping his soft, full cheek. Graham lifted him and playfully slung him over one shoulder, then stooped to let me say good night before taking him inside. I poured myself a glass of wine. When Graham came back out, he stumbled over the doorway and dropped into a patio chair. He stretched his long legs and sighed. The *Lullaby* docked bow-in, so the wide stern patio—fully a third of the boat's living space—faced the canal. Breeze trembled in the mangroves and across the surface of the water.

"I like what you did with the—what do you call them—area rugs," said Graham, his voice a little shaky.

"We needed a little sprucing," I said, but I could tell he barely heard me.

Every few weeks it hit him, the need for sleep. I knew tonight he would take his pills, would lie down in our bed, and would fasten the soft black cuff that we'd leashed to the wall. He hated the pills, hated the cuff, but every couple of weeks he was forced to spend a few nights more or less the way regular people did. The cuff had come home with him after his third and final visit to Detention, after the incident on our anniversary. The doctor who gave it to him had said that he'd treated patients with such extreme parasomnia only a few times in his career. One patient had sex with strangers in her sleep; another stabbed her husband. He told Graham—and I hated that doctor for it, though I never met him or even knew his name—that the worst was likely still to come.

I sipped my wine. I'd steam-cleaned the houseboat's carpet after we'd moved aboard, but the industrial gray stuff remained faded and stained. Frankie and I had gone from store to store, digging through sale piles, until I'd found a jute rug for the deck, a small braided mat in sherbet colors for the kitchen, and a large, colorful wool one in Moroccan patterns for the salon. On the deck I'd hung hurricane lamps, and on the sofa I'd arranged bright pillows in orange, grassy green, magenta. The *Lullaby* was not pretty, no, but she was showing a little personality.

Graham rubbed his eyes and tried to focus. He gave me an effortful smile.

"Why don't you lie down?" I said.

"We should get a new mattress." He'd lain on our mattress two or three times, total, since we'd moved aboard, and never for more than an hour or two. "That old one gives me the creeps."

"Good idea."

"And a new pediatrician, for heaven's sake."

I said something about taking the time to interview a few doctors, to find someone who was a good fit.

"Just ask Sally," he said.

My old friend and I had swapped messages but had yet to see each other. She had three boys under the age of eight; surely, she knew a good pediatrician. "It's just the talking thing—I don't want anyone too strict."

"Maybe strict would be good, babe."

It was a conversation we'd had a dozen times. Neither of us wanted to get into it. The plastic table where we sat—it had been included, along with all of the furniture, in the price of the boat—rocked a little. Graham pushed against it, then slogged inside and came out with a few paper towels. He kneeled beneath the table, stuffing them under one leg and then another. He had a restless, struggling energy about him. It might have been a cousin of unhappiness or anxiety—he'd been sent to a shrink by every sleep doctor he'd ever seen, with no clear diagnosis— but I didn't think so. It seemed to me that when other people's brains started to turn off at night, after the day's work was finished, Graham's struggled to stay on, as if sleep were a kind of death and only by remaining awake could he survive. Sometimes I wondered about the prohibition against alcohol. Graham seemed like a person who could use a drink.

"Sit down," I said.

He continued to try to fix the table, one leg at a time. Finally, he gave up. "Your stepmother is driving me a little crazy," he said.

I shushed him. There was only the lawn between the *Lullaby* and Lidia's house. "Don't call her that," I said.

He reached over and pinched me lightly on the arm, pleased to have gotten my goat. He tried to whisper, but it was hard for him, his gruff voice. "All the jibber-jabber, every time I come up the driveway. It's like she's waiting to pounce."

Lidia was a talker, it was true, but I had found I didn't mind it. Those early days on the *Lullaby* would have been awfully quiet otherwise. "I miss privacy," I said, and Graham sighed heavily.

But our privacy had been compromised before we'd even left Round Lake. It had only been a matter of time before the neighborhood had known our business. Late one spring night, Graham had rung the bell of our closest neighbor. It was after midnight. When she answered, he asked if she wanted him to build a bat house for her backyard, to keep the mosquitoes under control in the summer. (This was something we'd discussed doing in our own yard, but never got around to.) She'd said no, thank you, and closed the door, and once he was gone she debated calling the police. She didn't call. I didn't know this had happened until much later, when I read about it in the newspaper.

Across the canal, inside the grand multilevel home, a family was seated at an enormous glass dining table, spotlighted under a pinecone-shaped chandelier. The parents, grandmother, and four children all had lacquered dark hair and caramel skin. Now the children wore pajamas, but I'd seen them in their matching church clothes, white shirts and navy knee-skirts for the girls, navy trousers for the boys. The word *family*—in my mind, both hands made the letter *F*, forming a semicircle away from the torso—encompassed so many possible configurations. What did we have in common with this neatly dressed brood in their enormous home?

When I was a kid, roaming the decks of a cruise ship, I'd studied the families from behind my sunglasses. To me, they'd been unknowable as wild animals. They'd sulked and shouted and laughed and nagged. The fathers came from the blackjack table to dinner, suited and smelling of aftershave. I'd assumed that when I grew up and had a family of my own, we would resemble the families I'd observed, as they'd—at least from a distance—resembled one another.

And there were moments when I thought we *did* resemble them. The weekend before, in fact, we'd driven down to Shark Valley and biked the trails, gawking at alligators and stopping every hour to reapply sunscreen. Graham had secured Frankie in a child seat mounted just behind his own, and spent a long time fitting Frankie's helmet before starting out. Though Graham tended to bike fast, Frankie had only to tap his shoulder two times to convey that he wanted to see something—a gator or iguana or turtle—up close, and Graham would brake, prop the kickstand, and pull Frankie from his seat. I'd pedaled behind, studying them as they studied the wildlife.

Graham's head hit the back of his chair. I brought two pills from the stash above the sink and forced a cup of water between his lips. I coaxed him to stand and supported his weight through the salon, then eased him onto our mattress. His head thumped the wall and he moaned, then settled again. His eyes were almost closed but not quite. They never closed fully, even when he made it through the night. I pulled off his shoes and unbuttoned his shirt and pants. The cuff dangled from a bolt he'd drilled into the wall, the leash about two feet long, enough to allow some movement but not to get tangled around his neck or mine. The first one he'd brought home had secured with a nylon strap that was easy enough, we soon learned, for a sleeping Graham to unfasten himself. Now he wore a heavy leather version with an embedded lock. At the cottage, the key had gone in my nightstand. On the *Lullaby*, I put it on a high shelf in the kitchen, inside a Tupperware container. Graham could get himself into the cuff without help, but I'd gotten into the habit of doing it for him, of kissing the inside of his wrist before tightening the strap. I doubted I'd ever be entirely comfortable forcing him into captivity, but I didn't like him doing it alone.

The thing about pharmaceutical sleep, at my dosage but much more so at Graham's, was that waking up was no minor matter. Before Frankie was born, I'd woken to the loud clanging of a twin-bell alarm clock Graham had ordered from a catalog. After Frankie, my insomnia disappeared and didn't return for ten months. When it marched back arm in arm with my menstrual cycle just after Frankie weaned, it devastated me all over again. Frankie was big for his age and walked early, and by that time he was already climbing out of his crib, landing on his feet, and coming into my room to pull on my arm until I woke. He was running and jumping before his first birthday. After we moved him to a twin bed at the cottage, he figured out that the plastic pyramid-shaped object on his nightstand carried sounds from his room into mine, and stopped getting up to wake me. Instead, he would rap his knuckles against the monitor, which transmitted a series of jarring gongs to the speaker beside my head, and launched me from sleep with the force of a cannon. The first several times this happened, I shot up before my eyes opened, then asked myself where I was. My brain had to work to reorder itself, as if after a fainting episode or a stroke.

Graham always claimed to know hours before bedtime whether the pills might work and he would be able to sleep. He'd fought the feeling for years, but it was never wrong. He said the foreknowledge felt like the taut vibration of a tuning fork inside him; there was no use trying to still it. Early in our relationship, I gave up even asking whether he planned to come to bed. It was an act of love, my letting go. Not only of trying to share a bed more than once in a while, but of the whole notion of the marriage bed. I knew he was grateful to me.

Now, in the *Lullaby*'s cramped main berth, where Graham hovered in fragile presleep, one wrist leashed to the wall, eyes slatted, I realized that against all logic, some small part of me *had* hoped that uprooting our lives might have precipitated a change. Or even that the christening ceremony, the aptly named boat, might have sprinkled some magic over us.

Graham licked his lips and made a sound. I leaned over him. "What's that?" I whispered.

He summoned the energy to speak. "My love," he said.

I kissed him. There was a hint of cologne long since applied. His lips were chapped from biking in the wind. I counted the days since he'd last come to bed, taken his pills, fastened his cuff. It had been more than three weeks, since before we'd left Round Lake.

SALLY DROVE OVER ONE NIGHT after her kids were in bed. I waited on the upper deck of the *Lullaby*. Though it was unlikely that

Frankie would get up in the night, and I doubted he could pull open the screen door even if he wanted to, I'd suspended a bouquet of bells from the door, to sound an alarm if it opened. After sleeping through the night three times that week, Graham was out with my father; the stint was finished. To the east, the coppery sunset bled through the banyans and royal palms. The water in the canal wore a sheer, golden cloak.

Sally climbed the ladder to the roof deck with a bottle of wine under one arm and a bar of chocolate between her teeth, kicking off her heels. They landed on the pier.

"I met your stepmother," she said in a stage whisper. "My, she's friendly. I think her perfume rubbed off on my neck."

After I recovered from the sight of her—we talked occasionally on the phone, but hadn't seen each other in more than two years—we embraced. I spread my arms. "My new digs."

"You made it sound worse than it is."

"Don't lie."

"I expected rats and an unidentifiable smell."

Sally was tall and wore her brassy red hair straight. Her skin was creamy—expensively moisturized, was my thought—and smooth. She wore a salmon-colored dress with a yellow belt, and diamond stud earrings. She was, as usual, unfussy and immaculate, just short of conventionally pretty, with her up-slanted nose and widely spaced eyes. She had what I thought of as a swimmer's body, broad across the back and padded in the muscles of her arms and legs, strong and slender and flat-stomached, but far from slight. Her face, unmade, had a lunar quality, translucent and freckled and only subtly contoured. It was a face—I realized this in that moment—I'd been missing for years.

I said, "I'll give you the tour some other time."

She collapsed into one of the loungers and dropped a bare foot to the deck. "I feel as if I've escaped my life. Offer me shelter."

"Busy day?"

"Little men, everywhere I look. They have their probes primed for me every morning."

"How are they?"

"Let's not talk about them. I want to hear all about Frankie, of course, but not tonight. Let's pretend we're unencumbered."

Before kids, Sally had worked long hours as a financial planner—her husband, Stanley, still did—but in the past years she'd cut back so severely that I had the idea she let months go between clients. She'd helped me get my own business started; we'd spent so many hours on the phone, faxing loan documents and my business plan back and forth, that I'd insisted on paying her. She'd never cashed my check. When my profits started to decline—a former colleague, Ross Stern, adopted my business model and improved on it, marketing not to teenagers but to fretful parents, offering a *guarantee* of college acceptance, emphasizing his experience as an *insider* and promising "tricks and tips no one else can provide"—I'd asked again for advice. It was her response as much as anything that forced me to face facts, though at the time I'd resented it. "There comes a point," she'd said, "when it's not investment anymore, it's going down with the ship. You passed that point a while back."

I descended the ladder and went to the galley for glasses and a corkscrew. When I returned, Sally was lying on a chaise with her arms stretched above her head. "I feel like I'm in a tree house," she said, smiling.

"It's not so awful," I said. "But sometimes I find myself looking for the bilge pump." I mimed pulling a plug.

"I can't imagine why."

The breeze through the hammocks gave off faint applause. Lying beside Sally on our twinned loungers reminded me of my childhood, of the physicality of friendship in youth. There was a time when not a week had passed when Sally didn't hold one of my hands in her own and painstakingly paint each of my nails, then softly blow on them until they were dry. When we'd walked together, our shoulders had touched and neither of us shifted away. Did that ever happen with friends I'd made as an adult? Now it seemed we all treated our bodies like armored cars, unlocking for brief hugs and battening back up.

"How do you like having a stepmother?" said Sally.

"I don't think of her that way," I said. "How do you like it?"

"They divorced last year. We weren't close."

Sally's mother died of melanoma two weeks before we graduated from high school. I'd barely known her mother; she'd worked as an attorney and wore fine, dark suits. Her father was well meaning but lost, after, and Sally spent that summer with me and my mother, sleeping over every night. I assumed there was some arrangement with Sally's father that I never knew about. We spent much of the summer at the neighborhood pool, reading magazines and drinking virgin piña coladas. Afternoons, Sally and I would take my mother's car to the beach or the movies and pick up my mother from Dr. Fuller's on the way home. My mother would take us to the mall to get our makeup done, then give Sally the free samples from her purchases. She even gave Sally one of her own push-up bras, a blue satin one, and Sally wore it every day for weeks. When Sally cried, my mother held her and sang to her. She drew Sally a bath and poured in lilac salts, then sat on the toilet seat and gently probed Sally with questions about her mother. I lingered in the doorway, thinking that my mother was being rude, that surely Sally would have preferred not to talk about her mom, since every time she did it ended in tears. But then my mother brought her a towel warmed from the dryer and Sally's tears dried and she returned to herself. I'd been proud of my mother, of the way she'd known what Sally needed.

The summer before, I'd worked at a bookstore, but that year my mother let me off the hook and even cut back on her own work hours. Somehow, Sally's mother's death had granted us all a suspended vacation. At the end of the summer, just before we left for college—Sally to the dorms at the University of Miami, where her father taught economics, and me to Northwestern—my mother took us on a cruise to

St. Johns and let us drink real daiquiris and spend all night in the dance club with boys. It might have been, all told, the best summer of my life.

We watched as across the canal the mother of the dark-haired family went from room to room, turning off lights. I refilled Sally's glass. "How is your dad?" I said.

"Looking for number three. Healthy. Plays a lot—and I mean a lot—of racquetball. How's Harvey?"

"In love."

"What do we think of her?"

"She's very nice."

"Vague."

"She treats Frankie like her own grandson."

"That's saying a lot," she said. Her voice changed. "You know, I really miss your mother. I miss her almost as much as my own."

I couldn't speak for a moment. "Sometimes it feels like I'm the only one still thinking about her."

"I think about her all the time."

I'd often thought that if I were to be lost to Frankie while he was still young enough, I would want his new parent—another wife for Graham—to step so fully into the role of his mother that I would be digested by the gullet of history, leaving the merest residue of maternal love.

At other times, I worried that I should have been recording every thought I wanted to convey, so that if I were lost to him in the physical world, he would still own me in the words I'd chosen for him, as he had owned me in the flesh.

5

FRANKIE AND I PRACTICED THE signs for *canal, bay, ocean.* (The one I remember best is *ocean*: both hands in front of the chest, pushing down and rising again, miming the surf as it surges.) It looked, when Frankie copied my hands, like he was doing a little dance, a kind of hip-hop move, and I laughed out loud. He smiled proudly. We agreed to use the capital *C* to refer to Charlie. Before leaving for Stiltsville the second time, I loaded five bags of ice into the cooler on the Zodiac, and Frankie propped open the top and sat inside, then signed, *Cold butt!*

The sky was full of viscous white clouds. The air in the bay gusted against the brim of my hat and the hem of my skirt. Frankie wore a new, bright orange life vest cinched across his belly. The Zodiac's engine gunned in the troughs of larger waves, and each time this happened we slid sideways for a breath, then found our way forward again. We arrived at the stilt house panting a little from the choppy crossing, relieved to tie up and step onto solid dock.

Charlie met us downstairs wearing blue jeans and a linen shirt unbuttoned to midchest, the sleeves rolled to his elbows. "You're here," he said. He sounded as if he'd been waiting for us and was surprised to see us, simultaneously.

"Hello!" I said, signing reflexively.

He hefted a bag of ice onto one shoulder and I did the same. Frankie carried my tote. It was made of heavy cream-colored canvas, with straps as wide as his palms. When he realized he couldn't hold it the way I did, over the shoulder, he resorted to dragging it behind him. We struggled up the stairs, then down again and back up. By the time all the ice was in the kitchen coolers, I was sweating. That morning, I'd trimmed a few branches from the bougainvillea in Lidia's side yard and put them in a milk-glass vase I'd bought at a garage sale. Now I pulled the whole mess from my tote. I filled the vase at the sink and placed it on the kitchen counter.

Frankie waved with both hands above his head to get Charlie's attention, then signed: *Flowers for you.*

"For me?" said Charlie. His eyes passed over my face. "Why?"

"A token of appreciation," I said. "For the job."

He came forward and studied the vase. Here in the middle of the bay, the bright blooms were misplaced and gaudy. I reached to arrange the branches a little—whether the flowers would last the day, I wasn't sure—and an alarm went off in my brain. I turned. Frankie wasn't there.

It had happened a dozen times: that hysterical instant when I didn't know my son's exact location. It had happened in malls, grocery stores, the backyard. It had happened when he was standing immediately behind me, out of my peripheral vision. Each time, I'd been reminded that I'm no good in a crisis. My vision narrows and the recent minutes flee from memory, leaving me disoriented. Sometimes in my alarm, I don't see Frankie even when he's in my line of sight.

I said his name loudly. Of course he didn't answer. But as I started toward the open doorway to the front porch, he stepped from the hallway.

"No," I said, my voice shaking.

I pulled him to the sofa and sat him down. I was reminded again that it was a dubious proposition, bringing a toddler to a place like this, so remote and lacking in physical barriers. What could be gained, when compared with what might be lost? I would have given anything, in that moment, to be in a place where there was no porch or dock to fall from, no ocean stretching in every direction. But there was nothing I could do to make the stilt house truly safe, so I had two choices: I could take us back to land and stay there, or I could teach Frankie what to fear, and trust that he would heed my warning.

I signed: *Look at me.* He reluctantly met my eyes. "It's not like on land," I said. "You can't walk away from me. I have to be able to see you *all the time.*" He looked down and I raised his chin. "Do you understand?"

He nodded.

"I need you to tell me you understand."

He put his fist to his forehead, then brought it down, pointing with his index finger.

"Thank you," I said.

I was never sure how much was sinking in, but time after time he surprised me. "A sponge," Lidia had said the evening before. She'd handed him forks and told him to put one in front of each chair at the kitchen table, then marveled when he actually did it. While we ate, she'd watched him with his little fork, his slow bites and two-handed grip on his cup. "He takes it all in," she'd said, and I'd said, "Now if only he'd let it out."

From behind me, Charlie said, "Does he swim?"

"Yes."

"I'll take him while you work." Seeing my expression, he added, "Just in the shallows, right beside the dock. You'll be able to see us the whole time."

Swim! Frankie signed.

"We'll see," I said.

"Kiddo," said Charlie to Frankie, his tone conspiratorial. He smiled faintly, almost without moving his lips. There were pale lines of skin in the creases of his crow's-feet. "What your mom doesn't know is that I used to be a bona-fide sailor. Every week I swim miles around this house."

I love swimming, signed Frankie to Charlie, crossing his wrists, then moving his hands in a hasty breaststroke.

"All right," I said. "Enough with the hard sell."

Charlie grinned. So you have teeth, I thought.

He led us down the short hallway and through one of the doors. There was a standing desk and wooden stool under the north-facing window, and two headboards and mattresses were propped against the wall in one corner. The wood paneling was a dingy white, and half of the linoleum floor was covered by bankers boxes stacked two or three high. On the desk was a ceramic mug filled with black pencils with very fine points, a gray rubber eraser the size and shape of a matchbox, and something brass and ridged, the size and shape of a child's fist: a pencil sharpener.

I remembered the bit of business I needed to convey. That morning, I'd called Charlie's lawyer from Lidia's kitchen phone, and we'd made an appointment for me to stop by his office to sign papers. "I meant to mention," I said to Charlie, "Mr. Riggs says there's a gallery that wants to be in touch. The Abyss, it's called."

"Don't call him *Mr. Riggs*. Makes you sound like a kid." His voice softened. "I'll send a note."

Frankie looked back and forth between us. I stared at the piles of boxes.

"I've been told I need to get organized," said Charlie. "That's where you come in."

He went to a box and lifted the lid. I peered in. On top was a drawing similar to the ones I'd seen at the printer: a lead-lined octopus, tentacles waving wildly across a book page dense with type. Underneath this piece of paper, which Charlie handed to Frankie, was another octopus, tentacles in a different configuration, eyes fiercer. There were another dozen boxes in the room.

Frankie wandered away, staring at the octopus in his hands.

"Hey," I said to get his attention. I signed, rolling my hands over one another, *Be gentle*. To Charlie, I pointed to another stack of boxes. "May I?"

Charlie nodded and I pulled off a lid. The drawing on top was of a sea horse, its equine nostrils flaring.

"You drew all of these?" I said.

He nodded, frowning. "I'm supposed to *file* them. Squid in one box, barracuda in another, that kind of thing. There's a gallery in the Gables, they want a series of conflict scenes, dark stuff—they're calling the show 'Battles of the Deep.'" He rolled his eyes at the name. He was agitated, bouncing a little on the balls of his feet, as if the entire enterprise made him itch.

"I think I understand," I said.

"Every time I try to make heads or tails, I think I might drown."

"Sure," I said. And because it was the elephant in the stifling hot room, I stated the obvious. "You're prolific."

He cupped his face in one hand. It was the oddest gesture, one of compliant self-regard and introspection, almost feminine. Then his hand dropped and he looked away. "I've been doing it a long time," he said. "To tell the truth, I don't even remember how I started."

I said, "I read once that when people say that—*to tell the truth*, or *to be honest*—they're lying."

"I read that, too."

"You've been here ten years?"

"A little over ten, yes."

"What did you do before?"

He sighed and sat down on one of the file boxes, facing me. He tugged at the hems of his jeans, baring his ankles, then rested his hands on his knees. "I was an engineer."

"What kind of engineer?"

"Civil."

"What's that?"

"Buildings, bridges, roads. Structural integrity." He waited a beat. "What else?"

"What else what?"

"What else do you want to know?"

"What's my title?"

"What do you want it to be?"

"Errand girl? First mate?"

"Runner." He sighed again. "You're my runner."

"What happened to your last runner?"

"He quit a few months ago. He's sailing around the world."

"You're kidding."

"He's halfway across the Atlantic."

"And before him?"

"Another fellow, a college student."

"And before that?"

"Before that I had a boat."

"What happened to it?"

"Sank," he said.

"So much for structural integrity."

To my surprise, he chuckled. He stood and pushed a box toward me with his foot. "I'll get you a chair," he said, and left the room.

I opened another box and inside found another sea horse, then a clipper ship, then a detailed view of the Miami skyline from the perspective of the very room where I stood. All were drawn in fine, dark strokes, medical in precision, like something out of a textbook. You could study every vertebrae, every muscle, from one of these drawings.

He came back with a mug. "Coffee," he said. "A little creamer, no sugar."

"That's fine."

I held up the drawing of the skyline to the window. I could see the real-life buildings and their replicas in one glance: the county courthouse, One Biscayne Tower, the bridge to Virginia Key and the larger one to Key Biscayne. "This is amazing," I said. "They all are."

He cleared his throat. "Choose a dozen to take to Henry Gale. He'll add color."

"Choose a dozen based on what?"

He shrugged. "The word they used was *dangerous*, if I recall. I have some that should work. There's an octopus bringing down Freedom Tower. An electric eel lunging for a barracuda. A shark hunting. That sort of thing."

I raised my eyebrows at him. "You need a system."

His jaw tightened. "My system is hiring you."

"Right."

"Be ruthless. Put the shit with the shit, label it *shit*, put it away. Most of it's shit, to be honest." He looked at Frankie, who was staring up at him. "Sorry," he said.

Frankie smiled mischievously.

"*To be honest*," I said.

He started to move toward the door. "I'll be back in an hour. Then we could go swimming—it's okay?"

Frankie looked from Charlie to me and back again. *Swim*, he signed again. *Please*.

"You have to be very careful with him," I said to Charlie. "I don't know you."

"I told you," he said. "It's all uphill."

It was half an hour before I figured out a strategy. First I'd pulled out the contents of one box and started to sort into like piles, but after four similar octopi, each piece demanded a new pile: skyline, sea horse, nautilus, blowfish, brain coral, sea cucumber, sea urchin, needlefish, seashells, oysters, barracuda, whale shark, lobster, stone crab, and so on. Each creature was rendered so delicately, so fastidiously, that it seemed each must have taken weeks to complete, which could not have been the case. It was terrible, this wealth of detail, this avalanche of precision. I couldn't look away, on the one hand, but on the other hand they swam in front of me, each more intricate and evocative than the last.

There wasn't space to make so many piles, and I couldn't keep them all in my brain at once. I kept the ones of the skyline, the sea horses, and the octopi, put the rest back in their box, and moved it to the side. I opened another box, and the next four categories emerged: an octopus battling a clipper ship (this went into a pile for the gallery); a stingray, its fin swept up in motion; a scuba diver holding a brain coral in his gloved hand, a beam of sunlight breaking down through the water.

I gave Frankie a coloring book and a fistful of crayons from my tote, and he ambled to the corner and squatted in his usual, seemingly uncomfortable way, knees squaring into platforms for his arms. Whenever he sat like this, concentrating on some task, I was reminded of something I had no business forgetting in the first place: he lived in his own world. He could forget I existed, for seconds or even minutes at a time. This was astonishing.

By the time Charlie returned I'd made twelve good-size piles, and had sorted through about half of one box. Some pieces were dated, some titled, some signed, and some had no information at all. A handful were unfinished, as if deemed unworthy of further effort. These I put in their own pile. Every few minutes I came across a drawing I thought was hazier than the others, maybe done in dim light or with a less fine point on the pencil—but then I blinked and rubbed my eyes and second-guessed myself. Maybe, in fact, each was more precise than the last. I started to think about the tasks that would follow the current one, which in itself seemed endless. Every piece would need a signature and date and, if Charlie wanted, a title. And when finally the drawings were sorted by subject matter, each group would need to be sorted again by date. Or quality. Or something else I couldn't yet define. Also, there would need to be a central inventory of the entire collection, a glorified list. The project ballooned.

I found several pieces that might suit the gallery's needs. In one, a squid and an octopus brawled, tentacles locked, while a barracuda looked on wearily. This one was titled *Combat*, and the date was January 11, 1985. This man had lived in the middle of Biscayne Bay, drawing his pictures, since before Graham and I had moved into the cottage, since long before Frankie even existed.

I heard a door open and shut and Charlie appeared. By this point, Frankie had arranged items from my tote in a line on a clear patch of the floor—a lip gloss, a pair of sunglasses, a pen—and was jumping over each, then spacing them farther apart and starting again, a rudimentary hopscotch. He was restless.

Charlie had changed into green swim trunks and a white T-shirt. He carried a few business envelopes in one hand and held them out to me, watching Frankie as he hopped. "For Riggs," he said.

"I'll take them today." I put the envelopes in my tote.

Frankie went up to Charlie and signed a few times.

Charlie said, "Swim, swim, yes. Are you ready?"

Frankie nodded.

Charlie raised his eyebrows at me. "Are *you* ready?"

"Right downstairs?" I said, forcing him to maintain eye contact. "Where I can see you?"

"Right downstairs, yes."

The alternative to letting him go was not letting him go, which wasn't a great option, either. I saw nothing suspect or even heedless in Charlie, and I believed I could trust him.

I helped Frankie pull off his shirt. "Wear your shorts," I said. He'd left diapers behind early at his own insistence, but I'd brought spare clothes just in case. "*Be very safe*," I said to them both, hearing the anxious quiver in my own voice.

"We will," said Charlie, and Frankie followed him out of the room, sending a wave in my direction.

At the window I watched them make their way down the dock. The clouds had gone and the breeze had died. My son's shoulder blades cast slim shadows on the pale canvas of his back. Charlie said something and Frankie nodded eagerly. They lay down on their stomachs, heads bobbing over the dock's edge. Charlie splashed at the water and Frankie did the same. A silver swim ladder bucked gently on its hinges, and Charlie got up and stepped down a couple of rungs, then held out his arms. Frankie was hesitant, but then he leaned forward so Charlie could ease him into the water. The water reached Charlie's chest. At first, Frankie clung to him, but eventually he started to point his chin and scoop his hands and kick wildly, splashing and letting a little space grow between them. My heart buoyed. I watched for another minute or two, then went back to work.

AFTER AN HOUR—I CHECKED ON them regularly, wishing badly that I could abandon my task and just stand at the window spying, studying my son's joy like a scientist—they came upstairs wrapped in faded blue towels. Frankie trailed Charlie, eyelids heavy.

Sleep, he signed.

Every time he made the sign—and it wasn't rare for him to request sleep, even to beg for it—I'd had the same hopeful thought: maybe it skips a generation. I knew that many three-and-a-half-year-olds were sleeping less during the day or refusing naps entirely. For Frankie, this seemed far out of reach. Every day, no matter what was going on, he insisted on napping for a couple of hours or more.

"In here," said Charlie, opening a door.

In the room, there were two full beds and a wooden chest of drawers. Over the chest of drawers hung two oil paintings similar to the ones in the living room: wide poinciana canopy in one, palm trees and sandy beaches in the other. I'd seen enough of Charlie's work to know that he hadn't painted these himself. The beds were pressed against opposite walls, and the one that shared a wall with the room where I'd been working—the office, as I now thought of it—was the most carefully made, so I assumed the other was the bed where Charlie slept. Charlie pulled dry clothes from the dresser and left the room, tucking his chin to his chest as he went, as if he'd been intruding. After I helped Frankie wiggle into dry underwear, he climbed into the neatly made bed and pulled the sheets to his chest.

Read, he signed.

No book, I signed.

He pouted. *Sing*, he signed.

I was aware of Charlie beyond the doorway, within earshot. I sang the two lullabies I always sang, the two my mother always sang to me: "I See the Moon" and "Sleep, Baby, Sleep." When I was done, Frankie's blinks were long. I didn't see Charlie as I went back into the office, and for two hours I worked uninterrupted. The world was so quiet that the sound of the papers brushing together in my hands had the volume of another person in the room, speaking to me. I found myself humming as I sorted, and I stopped every so often to straighten my back and glance out the window. I made it through another box and opened a third. I'd begun to rethink my strategy of only sorting for a dozen subjects at a time, as it looked as if it could be days before I made a real dent that way, so I started ten new piles. I had to stop and straighten the increasingly messy stacks into a grid on the floor to allow for walkways. My back ached from bending. A boat passed, towing a skier. An airplane rushed overhead. Some of the piles grew to an inch thick, but some were still a single sheet by the time Frankie knocked on the wall between us.

Charlie appeared in the office doorway. "Is that the boy?" he said. "Ready for lunch?"

It had not occurred to me until that moment that he might have been lonely for companionship. Of course he was alone almost all of the time, but it seemed to me that a person who chooses a solitary life-style might be impervious to loneliness, or at least significantly more so than most of us. Maybe this isn't always the case. Maybe there are people who choose solitude for different reasons entirely.

Charlie prepared the same lunch, more or less, as the first time we'd come. Frankie, eyes swollen from swimming and sleep, wedged him-self into a corner of the sofa and sucked down a cup of water. Charlie brought the food to the table, then went back to the kitchen. When he returned again, he handed me a cold bottle of beer.

"It's like work and vacation at the same time," I said.

"It seems you'll never get through it, I know." He ate two cherry tomatoes at once. I watched his jawline as he chewed. "I've been put-ting it off for years."

"Why now?"

"Riggs has been nagging me. He says there needs to be an inven-tory, they need to be in storage."

"He's right."

"He's worried about a hurricane."

To mind came an image of his magnificent illustrations carpeting the ocean floor. Maybe an eel, flashing by, would catch a glimpse of its own frozen self.

He chewed on an olive, then pulled the pit from his mouth. "Get the pitted ones next time, for the kid."

"Okay." The heat drained me of energy, of appetite. I finished my beer. I said, "How long have you been showing your work?" The words sounded stiff and formal in my ears. It was hard to talk to an artist about his art without sounding like a dilettante or a rube.

"I met Henry Gale years ago," he said. "His father and my wife—anyway, they know each other. Henry put me in touch with a friend who had a gallery. We've done half a dozen shows, thereabout." He met my eyes and glanced away. "The money is pretty good. My wife—there are medical bills."

I'd forgotten that he was still married. He turned away a little, as if closing the door on that line of conversation.

"I've found a few options for the show," I said. I rose to fetch the pieces I'd culled. There were two of clipper ships being attacked—consumed, really—by giant octopi. In both, the modern Miami skyline fanned out behind the ship, giving the piece an apocalyptic quality, as if monstrous creatures and ghost ships might rise from the bay at any time. There was a menacing sea horse, dark lines along the scallops of its face, eyes slanted and cold, charging toward a smaller, milder sea horse. There was a whale shark stalking something off the page, zombie eyes cold as marbles. There was a sea snake flashing its fangs, its oily body suspended in midslither.

The last, which Charlie lingered over before setting it down with the others, was of a fish lying in a puddle of water on a dock, its mouth and eyes gaping. The scales of the fish—it was a bonefish, I think—were delicate and pretty, laid out in a pattern that reminded me of a nautical stencil. The scales were art in themselves.

"Drawn from life?" I said.

"From death." He pulled a stubby pencil from the table, turned over the drawings, and scribbled on the back of each. I gathered these were notes regarding color. "Take them to Henry Gale," he said.

I went into the office and found a file folder for them, then put it in my tote. When I returned, Frankie was pulling the last chunk of banana from a bowl. I bent to gather the dishes.

Charlie's eyes rested on my neck. "Can you stay awhile?" he said.

Please, signed Frankie to me.

"A little while," I said to them both, signing and speaking at the same time.

They went downstairs while I washed the dishes and wiped down the kitchen counter. The dish soap was running low, and I made a note to pick some up. When I came out onto the porch to check on Frankie, they were standing on the far square of the dock below. Frankie was watching as Charlie cast a fishing line and reeled it in. He handed it over and Frankie braced himself and took it, and together they reeled, Charlie's hand over Frankie's. Finally the lure, an iridescent plastic thing, burst out of the water. Charlie showed Frankie again how to cast the line, and when Frankie tried it by himself, the unwieldy pole got away from him and shot into the bay. In a flash, without removing his clothes, Charlie dove in after it, and when he emerged he had the pole over his head. He was grinning. He grabbed at the dock with his free hand and said something to Frankie—I didn't catch it—then hauled himself powerfully out of the water. He stood there dripping, breathing hard. He peeled off his wet shirt and dropped it to the dock, then started squeezing out the hems of his shorts. I felt the rare pleasure of watching an attractive man without being seen doing so, and I actually felt myself blush, standing there in the hot wind. I heard Charlie say, "That's quite an arm you've got, kiddo."

They went back to copiloting the fishing rod, Charlie in his soaked shorts and bare chest and Frankie in a mode of fierce concentration. I started to return to the piles and the boxes, and was facing away from them when the sound—that unfamiliar, bright beam of sound— reached me.

My son, laughing.

two

6

ON SUNDAYS, MY FATHER PLAYED a late afternoon show on the back patio at Tobacco Road, the oldest bar in Miami. The place was downtown on the river, locked inside a labyrinth of one-way streets and empty warehouses, and though I'd been there a dozen times, the band had already started playing by the time I was able to locate the entrance to the parking lot. It was full; I parked on the street. When finally we wound our way to the table Lidia had saved, we were disheveled and harried. I tried to brush Frankie's hair with my fingers but he pushed me away and scrambled onto Lidia's lap, reaching for her water glass. She pushed a sweaty margarita toward me.

"You made it!" she said.

"Barely," said Graham.

I shot him a look. He threw up his hands. I believed firmly that as long as he refused to drive, he had no voice in these matters.

I'd watched my father play music in fifty venues in my lifetime, everything from a soulless hotel bar to a gay dance club to a tiki bar in the Keys, where he'd played the ukulele. Now and again he'd played songs he'd written, though it had happened less over the years and I doubted he still wrote songs at all. This was a relief. His original songs had a folksy, bluesy sound, lots of tinny plucked guitar and melancholy piano, and they were, for the most part, love songs. The stories they conveyed, though, had nothing in common with my parents' story, which had started in college and continued through the one unplanned pregnancy and the marriage that followed. The disparity between the objects of affection in his songs and the tone and tenor of my parents' relationship had always confounded me. How is a person supposed to react when her father writes about the way a girl's shoulder slopes in the dawn light? He'd also written wry country songs about old Florida, alligators and airboats and frog legs and swamps, but these songs lacked the beating heart of his ballads. I'd understood early that my father's ambitions were somewhat confined, though I'd never gotten as clear a picture of his talent. Maybe every so often I perceived in his playing a certain tightness, a rehearsedness, that it seemed some musicians outgrew. In the next song it might be gone. I'd played piano as a kid, but my father had been an impatient teacher and I'd preferred to mimic his playing rather than read sheet music—a skill he was certain I needed to learn, though I never understood why—and eventually he gave up trying to teach me. Graham had always asserted that my father had a gift, but for whatever reason I could never wholly agree. I think my father sensed my skepticism, and it might have been one of the many reasons we were never closer. My mother had also played piano, but haltingly and effortfully, and she'd known only a few hymns by heart. As far as I knew, my father never had tried to teach her, though he did point it out when she was doing something wrong.

Though I was relieved that he no longer played original songs, I'd always enjoyed hearing my father's voice at the front of the band, out from under the muffled blanket of backup. He had a beautiful singing voice—throaty and understated and powerful. In life, my father was a poor conversationalist and a terrible listener. If you had something to say, you'd better get it out fast, before his eyes glazed over. One of the reasons I think he and Lidia were a good match was her tirelessness when it came to expressing herself. For Lidia, every day was filled with anecdotes, which she related energetically: the handsome young cashier at the Farm Store had winked when returning her change; stuck in traffic on I-95, she'd watched the man in the next car pick his nose for a full minute; her friend Damaris, in the hospital after minor elective surgery, had sworn the cafeteria served the best *ropa vieja* she'd ever eaten. The first time I met Lidia, she narrated for me her entire family history: she'd been born and raised in Puerto Rico, and her family had had money, though she conveyed that this meant that she'd lived in a nice house and had gone to private school, not that they'd enjoyed the kind of ostentatious wealth so common in South Florida, mansions and private yachts and full staff and so on. They'd moved to Miami in time for Lidia to start high school. Her mother had been Puerto Rican but her father had been Scottish, and from him she got the red in her hair and the pale freckles across her cheeks and arms.

My father, when he stood at the microphone, transformed from remote to robust and engaging. He enunciated and made eye contact. His voice sliced through the din. Every band he'd ever played with gave him a song or two per show. Once I heard him sing "Take Another Little Piece of My Heart" with a wedding band in Fort Lauderdale, and—I'm not exaggerating—ninety seconds into the song, every single person in the dance hall was focused on the stage. When over the years he'd introduced me to band mates, they'd always politely complimented his skills, but not until they mentioned his vocals did they betray a glint of real admiration. Why he never was a lead singer, I don't know for certain, but to be a lead singer you have to be a leader in general, which my father was not. I'd always liked about Graham that he strove, professionally. It seemed a sign of maturity, and there was a time when I'd believed it would mean good things for our family.

"I love to watch him," said Lidia, indicating my father on the small platform that substituted for a stage. "He's so comfortable up there."

Frankie moved to his own chair and rose onto his knees, trying to spot his grandfather through the crowd. Graham straightened his long legs between our table and the neighboring one, and every time someone walked by, he folded them up, then stretched out again.

"Do you want to trade seats?" I said to him.

"Why?" he said.

I shrugged. I motioned to Frankie and said, "Should we worry about the noise?"

He raised his eyebrows. "You're afraid of drowning him out?"

I sat back. This was the kind of joke he made every so often, and it cooled my blood. I had no idea whether other mothers were asked, subtly, to team up against their children—if I'd accused Graham of doing this, he would have said I was imagining things—but I had no instinct for how to respond. Here I was, worrying all the time about Frankie's speech, about whether I was being overly anxious or overly relaxed, and never could I count on Graham for reassurance. Mostly, he just seemed peeved about the problem, as if he'd been dealt into a game he'd never wanted to play.

We sat quietly through a couple of songs—or at least Frankie and Graham and I did, though Lidia leaned in every so often to make a comment in her stage whisper, about everything from the drummer's lewd T-shirt ("Inappropriate!") to the menu ("Order something! It's surprisingly good!") to the waitress's hair ("I think that cut is back in style, don't you?"). I did a lot of nodding. She made every occasion more festive. And if she caught a whiff of Graham's grouchiness or my hurt feelings, she did an admirable job of not showing it.

The last time I'd sat on that very patio, watching my father play, had been just after my mother's cancer had returned. I'd flown down to drive her to appointments and keep her company, and we'd decided on a whim to go out. It was the first time in years that she'd been to one of my father's gigs. Though I don't recall exactly, I think it must have been my idea. She'd mentioned that she and my father were "ships passing in the night," and maybe I thought seeing him play could help. At the show, she was restless and unsmiling, crossing and uncrossing her legs, taking careful sips of her drink and adjusting her blouse. Midshow, she leaned over to whisper that she needed to use the ladies' room. She hesitated before getting up. Then, instead of going inside, where maybe the line was long or the room smoky and crowded, she crossed the patio and parking lot and stepped onto a narrow strip of grass. There, within dim but full view of the band, she squatted between two parked cars, her long skirt pooling beneath her. When she returned, she polished off her margarita and ordered another, then started humming along, as if she'd unlocked a bit of happiness inside herself. I don't know if my father noticed, though I'm fairly certain that had been her goal: to be seen.

Frankie spilled his water and Lidia and I sopped it up with cocktail napkins. The waitress came by and flung down a stack of fresh ones. The band was Brazilian in flavor, loud for the small space. In the sweltering afternoon, with the parking lot and sluggish river just beyond the patio, the whole scene felt forced and artificial, as if we were all wishing we were either enjoying the show more or that we were somewhere else. I waited another song, then excused myself to use the restroom. Inside, it was dark and the red walls were cluttered with black-and-white photos of Old Miami. In one, dated 1911, a woman sat on a motorcycle wearing a long, heavy skirt, looking stubbornly at the camera, as if wondering what all the fuss was about.

When I got back to the table, I found Frankie had fished crayons from my bag and Lidia was talking to Graham, who kept his eyes on the band and grunted in acknowledgment. When I sat down, she leaned toward me, without breaking stride. "He just has this quality!" she said. "A twinkle in his eye when he plays. You know I don't like to stay up late—but your father! The energy he has! I swear, I'm younger but I feel older. Sometimes I drag myself out and I can't take my eyes off him. I mean, look at him! He's so handsome. This margarita is getting to me."

She possessed an emphatic, even-handed girlishness. In casual conversation, she mentioned people from her high school years with such regularity that you'd think she was in her twenties instead of her fifties. And at their wedding, she'd worn a tea-length peach taffeta dress that reminded me of an old-fashioned prom gown. She'd looked radiant.

"Do you sing?" I said over the music.

"Not a note. I know your mother had a good voice."

"She couldn't carry a tune," I said.

This was true. My mother had loved to sing, especially while playing the piano, but she'd had a painfully bad voice. It was something you got used to. Or, rather, it was something you were never not used to, if she was your mother.

"That's not what your father told me," said Lidia.

"Nevertheless," I said.

It irritated me that my father had told this particular lie. It was just like him, an unreservedly judgmental person, to refrain from speaking ill of the deceased, as if this could erase all prior unkindness and jigger history into a rosier light. I was defensive of my mother's inarguably bad voice. Who but me was willing to keep straight the facts of her life?

My father noticed us watching him and blew a kiss.

"Charmer!" said Lidia.

It's striking, the difference between one part of life and another. The man we watched perform was both my father and not my father. Lidia's husband, yes, but not my mother's. A second marriage was a different animal entirely from a first one. The mortgage, the raising of children, the deciding where to live and for how long—this was in the past. There should be another word for a second marriage like theirs, which was as distinct from the first as retirement from work.

Beside me, Graham was focusing intently on the band. Whatever I might have labeled his mood—grumpy at best, malicious at worst—there was nothing I could do to snap him out of it. So quickly, I knew, his work had started inspiring as much anxiety as energy and enthusiasm. There was a project in the late stages, a new way of studying extreme weather, and he'd been tossed into the thick of it. He'd been given a research fellowship, but his salary came out of two separate grants, including one from the U.S. Office of Naval Research, which named his position as associate scientist. He was making more than he'd ever made at Northwestern. Larry—this was Graham's old friend from McGill, who had gone out of his way to help Graham get the fellowship—had said that after the next round of grants came through at the end of the following summer, Graham had a good chance of being hired on the tenure track. This made me nervous—the carrot of tenure had been, for us, a dangerous one—but it excited Graham. He thought he'd earned it.

I leaned forward to kiss his cheek. He didn't move at first, but then his cheek nudged my lips, a gesture toward harmony.

Frankie tugged at my sleeve. *Milk, please*, he signed.

Milk was the object of a small, daily tug-of-war: he always wanted more, I always wanted him to have less, or else he wouldn't eat enough.

This time, before I could manage to reach into my bag, Graham turned, saying, "Wait." To Frankie, he said, "*Milk*. Can you say *milk*?"

Frankie rocked up onto his knees. Lidia and I looked between them. Frankie believed—I could see it in his face—that he was being asked to repeat himself more nicely, as I'd asked him to do no fewer than one thousand times. (I'd realized fast that there is a nice way to sign, and a not-nice way.) But this time, he'd asked nicely in the first place.

He faced his father and made the signs again: one hand opening and closing, thumb extended, then the same hand rubbing his chest in little circles, driving home the magic word. He wasn't typically defiant, my son—if anything, he was supplicant, sometimes desperately so. With Frankie, it was a matter of reading his body language and expression more than anything else. Maybe with another child, a verbal child, Graham wouldn't have gotten it so wrong. When you ask yourself if someone might have what my mother had called a *taste* for parenting, you might as well ask if that person has a taste for subtlety, that close cousin of compassion.

Frankie's little Thermos was in my bag. It would have taken a blink for Graham to pull it out, but instead he said again, "Can you *say* milk, Frankie?"

Frankie's hands dropped to his sides. He sat on his rump, his feet tucked beneath him. He picked up a crayon, drew a line, put it down again. The air grew thin.

I pulled the Thermos from my bag and set it in front of him, and Graham crossed his arms and turned back to watching the band. The waitress stumbled over his legs and shot him a glare, which he ignored.

The set was in full swing, the lead singer sweating over a cluster of dancers. I caught a whiff of cigarette smoke, which I took as a cue—an excuse, really—to leave. I leaned in to Graham, making my voice as lighthearted as possible. "Do you want to go when we go?"

"Let's finish the set." He brought his hand to his chest and rubbed in a circle. "*Please.*"

A wave of fury rose inside me. I blinked it back. It wasn't unlike Graham to push, with what I considered a certain brutishness, the issue of Frankie's talking. But it was unlike him to be snide. Frankie watched us, then stared down at his lap.

Graham grit his teeth a little and his eyes jumped from the band to the table and back. I glared at the back of his head. Finally, he turned to me, his mouth tight. "All right. I'm sorry, okay?"

I gathered our things. The set ended, and my father made his way over and lifted Frankie into his arms. "You're leaving?" he said. To Graham, he said, "You, too, *amigo*?"

"You look so handsome up there, *mi amor*," said Lidia.

"It's just a little smoky," I said to my father.

He shrugged. "It's not everyone's cup of tea."

I wanted to say: *There are things in the world that have nothing to do with you.* I bit my tongue.

"I've got an early morning," said Graham. This made no sense, knowing Graham, but he was making an effort.

By the time we'd made our way to the car, the band had started up again, and from the distance the music was clearer and more melodic, with breathing room between the instruments. We lingered before getting in the car—I was trying to decide on the best route home—and above us a streetlamp buzzed on, though there was only the slightest tinge of evening in the air. Graham sat on the trunk of the car and pulled Frankie up beside him. My eye caught the pale, tender swell of Graham's collarbone. The warm evening sunlight gave his hair a silver-gold sheen. Every time I hardened my heart to him, something softened it again. He'd said he was sorry, and I believed him.

To Frankie, he said, "I just wish you would talk to us, buddy."

Frankie leaned into his shoulder, scraping at a scar on his knee. Graham pulled him close.

"He will," I said to Graham. I'd said it so many times by that point, the words had lost all promise.

Graham swung himself to the ground and lifted Frankie, then settled him into his car seat. As he came back around to me—I was a few feet away, digging in my bag for keys—a sharp popping noise came from above. I ducked instinctively, then looked up. Along the trunk of my car were curved fragments of glass, and above us the bulb of the streetlamp was gone—why this happened, I have no idea—and in its casing remained only a single threatening shard. Graham stared down at his hand. Lightly embedded in his palm was a spear of moon-colored glass.

"My God," I said.

He pulled the glass from his flesh. There was a thin bloody thread left behind in his palm. He said, "Sometimes I don't know why you love me."

"Just be nice," I said. "That's all I want."

He shook his head absently, like this wasn't the right answer. He said, "Do you ever feel like nothing will be good again?"

• • •

THE LAST TIME GRAHAM AND I argued about whether to have a child had not been terribly different from the previous times, except that he'd finally allowed me to change his mind. I was just home from a baby shower I'd thrown with two friends from college. The head hostess, my old roommate Sara Brink, mother to ten-month-old twins, came up with the idea that we hostesses should fashion baby bumps from throw pillows, to wear under our clothes. As the only one from our group who had never been pregnant—the other hostess, Meg Pritchard, was expecting her first—I didn't want to do it. But I was wary of being the grown child, the one for whom the others must bend, so I went along. I put on the bump when I got to the restaurant and didn't look at myself in the mirror. I didn't know, then, what awaited me along the path to Frankie, but maybe I had a premonition, because it was impossible for me to foresee pregnancy as a happy time. At best I saw it as a rite of passage—unpleasant but satisfying. I intended to do it only once. This was something I'd said again and again to Graham, who didn't wholly believe me. He believed pregnancy and babies were some sort of addiction, and while he could vaguely stomach the idea of having one, more than one was unimaginable. The reasons he gave never varied: his age, his still-tenuous career, his sleep. This should have been a clue to me of his seriousness, even as my motley counterarguments scattered over us like buckshot.

I drove home from the shower without removing the pillow beneath my clothes. Graham was on the back deck. I stood in front of him until he noticed the bump.

"I'm pregnant," I said.

His eyebrows came together. "What's wrong?"

"I want a baby."

He frowned, but he didn't look irritated; he looked resigned.

I said, "No, that's not true. I don't care about having a baby. I want to be a mother."

It occurred to me, standing there in blotted makeup, that I should call my mother and share with her this morsel of gratitude, which was just occurring to me in that moment: that I wanted to have a baby because I'd so loved having her for a mother, that the two things were inextricable. It had been almost a year since her diagnosis and I'd visited six times. Air travel alone was eating at our savings, not to mention the time spent without paying clients. The possibility of making my mother a grandmother before she died—these were not the explicit terms of her illness yet, but the writing was on the wall—was so seductive, so galvanic, that the alternative seemed monstrous.

Graham closed his book. "I don't know if I can keep having this conversation."

"Please," I said. I kneeled. It had rained that morning and the wood of the deck was cool and smelled like a forest. "Please."

He sighed. "Sometimes I think it would be something. Me, a father?"

Could I picture it, even then? Could I imagine him having the patience or flexibility or focus? Did I realize these traits would be paramount? We seemed equally unlikely parents to me—this was my greatest miscalculation. Most people have children and part of them expands, another part contracts. We call this growth. We call it reordering priorities. I probably shouldn't admit it, but in my head I liken becoming a parent to cancer, maybe because one changed my life on the heels of the change brought by the other: it's this small thing inside you that swells as the baby grows, until it takes over. You can sort of remember what it was like before—maybe you vaguely recall a certain uncluttered pattern to your days and conversations and thoughts—but that ease of existence you once felt, that personal comfort, no longer matters.

I believed at the time that my inability to picture us as parents was a failure of imagination. We needed faith, I thought.

"I can see it," I lied.

He stood and put a palm squarely on my head. "I hate making you unhappy."

"Then don't."

His mouth was a thin line. "Damned if I do, damned if I don't." He took my hand, and pulled me inside to our bedroom.

7

SALLY LIVED IN A LARGE, shoddily built home with high ceilings and leaky windows, a formal foyer and a screened pool and a Jacuzzi tub as large as the *Lullaby*'s main berth. Between her house and the tightly wedged houses of her neighbors was an umbilical knot of roaring air conditioners. Frankie and I arrived for dinner two weeks after I started working at Stiltsville, and the moment we stepped into her chilly foyer, Sally handed me the number of her pediatrician. I'd asked for it on the phone earlier that week, but she'd been called away before digging it up. I'd never mentioned Frankie's speech problem to her, at least not in a way that was anything but offhand and unconcerned. I'd never wanted to have that conversation.

"She's sort of a ballbuster," Sally said as I slipped the paper into my bag. "Just ignore that part."

The walls of Sally's house had the chalky, overly smooth look of new construction covered in gray primer—they'd never been painted. At knee height, next to a hall tree heaped with clothes and books and beach towels, the wall was covered in concentric circles of lavender crayon.

She caught me glancing. "We're pretty shabby here," she said. "Forgive us."

I waved a hand. "I know a bit about shabby."

A shriek came from the living room. "Chaos," she said. She took the bottle of wine I'd brought and smoothed down her butter-colored sheath dress with one hand. She was the kind of mom who wore dresses, even if her only plans included hanging around the house with her kids, maybe hitting the grocery store.

Frankie peeked out from behind me, and Sally issued a squeal and pulled him into her arms, offering him juice, asking if he wanted a cup with a straw or a cup with dinosaurs on it. I followed them deeper into the house. It was a boisterous house, and not only because of the boys who dashed around the sunken living room, but also because of Sally's high-pitched outbursts, her generosity of spirit. I felt a pang of envy: I would never have a boisterous home. I'd been in other such homes, back in Illinois. There was crayon on the walls of those homes, too, and unfolded laundry heaped on sagging armchairs, and, out of sight, a maze of messy bedrooms and bathrooms. These houses wore me out. I wasn't fastidious, but I liked things to mostly be in their places, and with so many kids and so much space, these homes often reminded me of dollhouses that had been shaken like snow globes, leaving coloring books on the kitchen floor, exercise equipment in the entryway, a tricycle in the living room, a stack of mail on the coffee table. Big families made great neighbors, I'd noticed; strange kids stepped through the back door at all hours, then their parents came with a six-pack and requested help moving heavy furniture, or offered use of the pool or trampoline—and this, too, inspired in me that simultaneous discomfort and envy. I didn't like it about myself, but even as I wished I were the type of person who presided over this kind of casual, friendly, open home, I wanted people to call first. Whenever Lidia rang the cowbell at the *Lullaby*, I felt the hairs rise on the back of my neck, even if I wasn't at all unhappy to see her.

I was inflexible—this was the crux of it. And to have a big family, to have crayon marks on the never-painted walls, one needed to be flexible. It was something my mother had told me once, though I can no longer recall the context. "Georgia, if there were one thing I would want for you, it's that you'd just go with the flow," she'd said. This was before I'd had Frankie, but I'd filed away not only the comment itself, but also what went unspoken: we want more for our children than they manage to become. By the time I moved back to Miami, I'd gotten a taste of this wanting more, myself.

All three of Sally's boys were home. She'd said on the phone that the older two had been in camps in the morning, baseball for one and basketball for another, and the third had been in preschool. That afternoon they had clearly spent a while wreaking havoc in the house. Sally wouldn't be the type to structure the hours. She wouldn't guide them toward an activity or participate in one with them. She would grab a book and camp out in a comfortable chair where all the kids were in her sightline, and at four o'clock she would pour her first glass of wine.

The kids had made a fort from the cushions of the sectional sofa. One boy, red-haired and freckled like Sally, with her husband Stanley's puggish nose, sprang up from beneath a cushion. "Who are you?" he said loudly.

"*Manners,*" said Sally.

I gave the boy my name—I had only ever met the oldest, and that was when he was just a baby—and told him I was an old friend of his mom's. Before I could introduce Frankie, the boy ducked back into his fort. It rumbled. The youngest boy was at the dining table, which filled an open space off the living room, adjacent to the swinging door to the kitchen. The boy—also red-haired—was quietly coloring. Sheets of paper littered his end of the table. He didn't look up.

Sally handed me a glass of wine. "This is the part of the day when we do whatever we want," she said. She stooped beside Frankie and looked at him frankly. "What do you want to do?"

Frankie pointed at the dining table.

"Go on," she said, swatting his rump. "Carson! Share your colors!"

Carson watched Frankie climb onto a chair, then pushed a few sheets of paper and a plastic container of crayons his way. Frankie got to work.

"And what do you want to do?" said Sally to me.

"I love your home," I said.

She led me to a pair of loungers just beyond the living room's sliding glass doors. The air conditioner was on, but still she left the doors open and closed only the screens. The house gusted mouthfuls of cold air against my bare arms and moist cheeks.

"Stanley's picking up Chinese food," Sally said, tucking her legs beneath her. I could see Frankie through the screens, his dark head beside Carson's coppery one. The older boys whooped and one whined for his mother. She didn't seem to hear him. "Oh, I've got to tell you—you remember that cunt, Alice Ferguson?"

Alice Ferguson had been a year ahead of us in high school. Once, during a rare conversation, she'd told me that her boyfriend's penis was the size of a McDonald's French fry. I'd been horrified, less by the comparison than by the revelation itself.

"I don't remember her being *that*, exactly," I said.

"Anyway, she stops by my office this morning—she's starting a party-planning business—and get this: she's driving an Aston Martin convertible."

"Good lord," I said.

"I know."

"But who cares?"

"I know," she said. "No kids."

"What?"

"Alice—no kids."

"Don't be mean."

"I'm not. It's just, you know, the water heater broke last week, and the roof's leaking in Tuck's closet, and Maxwell needs his teeth fixed, and Stanley works every goddamned weekend."

We looked inside, where the two older kids were sparring with wrapping paper rolls. The oldest had his father's dark hair and wide cheekbones. His face was a little menacing until he smiled. As we watched, he trounced his brother and they started vying for head locks. I wondered if Sally would do something to break them up, but she just turned back to me.

"But then there's the love," she said.

"The love," I agreed.

She slapped my knee. "So you're headed to the Keys?"

This was a plan Graham had hatched just a few days earlier. There had been a vacation domino effect on his team at work: one of the lead investigators needed a day off, so his assistant took that day as well, and if they weren't working, then Graham's lead couldn't really work, so he took off, and so on. I'd gotten the feeling from the way Graham announced it—less like it was a vacation day than a lottery win—that days off, in this job, would be in short supply. I'd known that Graham's new position would involve an adjustment, though I'd underestimated the extent. In Illinois, he'd been home most afternoons, grading papers or preparing lectures in his study, the heavy double doors open to the rest of the house. Some days I'd set Frankie to play on the plush rug beneath Graham's desk and use that time to cook dinner or run an errand. Back when I still had appointments with clients, Graham had been available to watch Frankie, even if I had to drop him off at the college. It wasn't that Graham hadn't been working hard when he worked at home—he had been, relentlessly, which is one reason the tenure decision was so tough to take—but having his body in the house had lightened my load.

Without thinking about it, I'd assumed the position at Rosenstiel would be similar. Graham had warned me there would be hours at the lab in addition to the classroom, hours in committee meetings and writing grants and traveling, that research in his field was a team effort, and the team had to be present to work. But I'd been so desperate to leave Illinois that I'd heard only what I wanted to hear.

We were headed to the Dry Tortugas to kayak and camp for two nights. Frankie would stay with Lidia and my father, which worried me a little. They would heap on the love and attention, sure, but would they hold his hand when crossing the street? Would they remember to buckle his car seat? I'd heard somewhere that most accidents happen when the parents aren't around. I hadn't wanted to be the kind of mother who was never apart from her kid, not for his sake and not for my own. Somehow, this is exactly what I'd become.

"We leave Friday," I said.

"Before Carson was born, Stanley and I went to Sanibel for the weekend. All we did was talk about the boys and go to bed early, but it was nice."

"Three seems like a lot, I'll say."

"It's a lot." She lay back and closed her eyes. From inside came calls of victory from Tuck and whines from Maxwell. "This is my favorite part of the day," said Sally, which made me laugh lightly. "No, really. Stanley will be here soon and he's all rules and table manners, and I can't exactly blame him. In the morning it's dressing and brushing teeth and finding sneakers and getting out the door. At night it's cleaning up and baths and maybe, if we're lucky, Stan and I will stay up for a quickie." She sighed. "I remind myself every day to enjoy them, but then I forget again."

Carson had been tough to come by, same as Frankie. For both of us, there had been a regimen of pills and shots, disappointment month after month. Frankie was my fourth pregnancy in sixteen months. The first had made it to fifteen weeks, though the others had been briefer. After the third, Graham had lost the little heart he'd brought to the process. He'd begged me to stop trying. Then one night we found ourselves having regular, old-fashioned sex for no reason except boredom and friskiness. No one could have been more surprised than I to find myself without a period two weeks later. Just a week after that, Sally called with her news—she was halfway through by that point, but hadn't told anyone until she'd started to show. We didn't congratulate each other until each boy took breath.

When Frankie was a baby, I'd overheard a largely pregnant woman in the waiting room of my doctor's office, talking to another woman about anticipating her second. "They say the first one makes you a mother and the second one makes you a family," she'd said, glassy-eyed. I'd glared at her back as she'd waddled off after a nurse. Then what the fuck are we? I'd thought.

I'd been pregnant and I'd given birth, but I'd not gained admittance to that club of happy pregnant people planting and pruning their families like window boxes. To have considered another child would have been to consider another string of miscarriages. It wasn't a question of whether or not the eventual healthy child, if one were possible, might be worth it. It was a matter of sanity, survival. It was also a matter of trying to be a person who is sated by what she has, ending the cycle of wanting more, more, more. When I looked around, it always seemed I was alone in this way of thinking. Sally would never have asked if I was planning to have another. Everyone asked—even my father, who'd known about the miscarriages—but not Sally. Needless to say, Graham and I had never broached the subject; to have done so would have been, on my part, a violation of our tacit agreement.

At the dining table, a small negotiation was under way, an exchange of one color for another. Then both boys had their heads down again.

Sally saw me watching them. "Carson's my sensitive one. Late walker, late talker. They're making noise about holding him back from kindergarten."

"Really?"

She shifted toward me, gesturing with her elegant fingers. "There's this thing he does. He takes a black crayon or marker, and he makes these little loops all over a sheet of paper, like a sort of free-form spiderweb." She waited to see if I understood. "Then he meticulously—*meticulously*—shades each tiny section with a differ-ent color. He'll do it over and over, for more than an hour at a time. He's probably doing it right now. He needs the largest pack of crayons just to finish one, and even then he gets upset because he has to repeat a color once or twice. His teacher is alarmed. She called us in. She kept using the words *obsessive* and *compulsive*. Stanley was like, 'What's the problem? He's making nets to catch the light.' That's what Carson calls it, since he learned about the colors on the spectrum of light: *nets to catch the light*."

"It sounds beautiful," I said. I thought of the fan coral I'd seen just that morning, on a swim with Frankie and Charlie out at Stiltsville. Crooked jade hollows peeked between each ragged tooth of the coral, like rough sparkling gems.

"We have a few framed. Maybe we shouldn't encourage him, but he's going to be who he's going to be, I figure. Who gives a shit when he starts kindergarten?"

There was something drawn in her appearance, in the half-moons beneath her eyes and the way she pushed her hair away from her face. I took a swallow of my wine. I said, "When I asked about the pediatrician—there's some urgency. Frankie doesn't speak."

She searched my face. "Not at all?"

"Not at all."

"They checked his hearing?"

I nodded. "We've been waiting and seeing." I pressed my fingertips against the bridge of my nose. "Graham thinks I play it down. Maybe he's right."

She squeezed my knee. "It's probably nothing serious. Call Dr. Sonia. She won't freak out about it."

There came a commotion from inside. The bigger boys tore through the living room toward the front of the house. Then Stanley rounded the corner, wearing a tie and wingtips, one child in his arms and the other clinging to his leg, and a new sound cut through the melee: a deep, voluminous monster-roar coming from Stanley. As we watched, he tromped into the living room and crashed with the boys into the pillowy fort, bringing the whole thing down.

8

SINCE I'D BE LEAVING TOWN on a Friday, when I'd normally work, I told Charlie as soon as we arrived about my trip to the Dry Tortugas. He rubbed his chin and frowned, then said, "I guess that's fine."

He handed Frankie a small, rubbery orange octopus with catlike yellow eyes, and Frankie's face lighted up and he signed his thanks. Charlie had given Frankie one toy creature every day we'd visited. Early on, I'd asked him to please not give Frankie gifts behind my back, if he wouldn't mind. At this, he was unable to stifle a humoring smile. "Alrighty," he'd said.

Frankie had amassed a small gang of toy animals by this time, and he took them everywhere we went, all knocking around inside Graham's old canvas Dopp kit, which had a zipper with crooked teeth, so it took a long time to open and close. Upstairs at the stilt house, Frankie wrestled with the zipper, then lined up the toys on the linoleum floor, as if preparing them for battle. An orange octopus, a turquoise squid, a clown fish, a black manta ray, a gray shark, and the original yellow sea horse. Then he arranged them into a circle, as if having them reconcile. Then he put them in pairs.

In three weeks of coming to Stiltsville, I'd made it roughly a quarter of the way through Charlie's work. I no longer fought a swell of alarm each time Frankie stepped into the Zodiac or climbed the zigzagging stairs. I no longer checked repeatedly that his life vest was fastened, though he still wore it all the time at the house, except during his nap. Also, Charlie had convinced me that he shouldn't wear it swimming, that it would keep him from learning natural buoyancy. Each time we'd come, Charlie had fixed the same midday buffet, and once I'd teased him about his apparent aversion to cooking food, and he'd looked puzzled for a moment—I thought I might have crossed a line—then brought his fingers to his cheek. "You know," he said, "I can't remember the last time I so much as toasted bread." I brought Tupperware containers of tabbouleh and hummus, which he regarded skeptically at first; two days later, the containers were empty and he asked if I wouldn't mind bringing more. I told him about Lidia and her strict food schedule: Mondays were tuna casserole, Tuesdays lasagna, Fridays meat loaf. She ate fruit and deli chicken salad every day for lunch. The nights my father was at gigs, she either went out with her girlfriends or came down the lawn to eat with us. It was kind of her to cook for us three times a week, especially since preparing a meal in the *Lullaby*'s miniature galley was something I cared to do as rarely as possible. I found it fascinating and not a little admirable, the way she coped with her clear distaste for the culinary arts. Three meals, three nights, no substitutions.

"And this meat loaf," I said to Charlie, who for once listened with his gray eyes trained on mine. "It is really, really good."

Charlie had procured—I suspected Riggs visited regularly, but I didn't ask—a purple plastic fishing pole, child-size but still a little large for Frankie, which Charlie leaned against the generator room beside his own. When they went downstairs, Charlie carried his own pole and Frankie carried the smaller one, and they went together to the far end of the snaking dock, the rods propped against their shoulders. This was something that, like my father leading Frankie up the steps, reminded me of my mother. Or not of her, exactly, but of her absence. The empty vessel that consumed so much space, the thunderous void. I didn't believe in ghosts or spirits or even angels, though I'd always loved the idea of these things and wished I could believe—but how else to define the bellowing, chest-beating presence of absence?

Above the bunk in Frankie's shallow berth, I'd hung a photograph of Graham's mother, Julia, holding Frankie when he was five weeks old. Julia was a fragile person, less because of age than comportment and personality, and I remember worrying that she would drop into sleep and he would roll onto the polished marble floor of her sitting room. In the photo, her eyes are cast downward and you can't tell whether they are open, but there is a discernible tension in her arms, a mindfulness over the small life in her lap. I look at that photo, and I'm relieved that it exists and that I framed it, that it will not disappear down the sinkhole of photographs printed but never looked at again. But also, it gives me a pinch of regret. Naturally, there is no such photograph of Frankie with my mother. We started trying to get pregnant while she was still alive, but it took too long. As far as she knew, she had no grandchild.

Charlie wanted to drive the Zodiac. We'd fallen into the routine of taking a break after Frankie's nap for a swim around the house, but today he wanted to head out straightaway, before I got to work. He made the request while I was in the kitchen pouring water for Frankie. I had to ask him to repeat himself, he spoke so softly. He said, "I wondered if I might take us all on a ride in your boat."

"Where do you want to go?"

"For a swim. There's a good place, with shallows for the boy."

To Frankie, I said, "Let's lather up," and Frankie scrambled to get the suntan lotion from my bag.

I'd gotten into the habit of leaving the keys on the boat while it was docked. Frankie took up his usual spot next to the captain's seat, so I stood starboard of Charlie and gripped the metal rail that looped around the back of the bench. Charlie wore a canvas fishing hat with a strap tightened under his chin, and our hat brims collided when he turned to check the engine. "Excuse me," I said, leaning away. He didn't respond. His large hand pushed forward on the throttle, and he said, "Hang on," and then we were spitting smoothly into the channel. We turned to cut across the flats between Charlie's house and the house to the east—this was the stretch of shoal between houses, which in low tide was walkable and during very low tide broke the water's surface— and I gasped, fearing we'd run aground. But it was high tide. Charlie glanced at me. "We're fine," he said over the wind, then—this was the most unexpected gesture from him—he raised an arm and waved as we passed a red-painted house where a man, woman, and teenage girl sat on rocking chairs on the porch. All three waved back. It occurred to me, though there was no clear evidence of this, that Charlie might have been proud to drive by his neighbors with a woman and a child beside him.

I kept one eye on Frankie as we drove. I thought he might be wary of grabbing Charlie as he would me, if we bounced off a wave. I'd bought him little aviator sunglasses that slid down his fleshy nose and obscured much of his face, and he looked small but grown up, his gaze on the horizon.

We wound up at Soldier Key, a lump of uninhabited island south of Stiltsville. The world stilled when Charlie cut the engine, then filled with the noise of water slapping the hull and rushing up on the brief, seaweed-laced beach. A pair of gulls took off squawking from the island's thick mangroves. Charlie set the anchor while I helped Frankie into swim trunks patterned with cartoon turtles. He got Charlie's attention over my head.

Turtles, he signed, indicating his shorts.

"Maybe we'll see one for real," said Charlie.

Frankie saluted—this is something Charlie had taught him—and climbed onto the gunwale.

"You're in a good mood," I said to Charlie.

He frowned. "Am I?"

The week before, a miniature mask and snorkel had shown up at the stilt house, and after every swim since Frankie had signed excitedly about the sand dollars and urchins and starfish he'd seen underwater, using his hands to describe the creatures when he didn't know the words. Now Charlie fit the mask to Frankie's face, then lowered himself into the water and told Frankie to jump down, which he did. Sally and I had hired a teenager to give Carson and Frankie weekly swim lessons, though they hadn't yet started. I was wondering now if this was necessary. For Charlie, Frankie jumped through the air as if he'd never believed any harm could come to him by doing so, as if the act of falling into water posed no threat at all.

I'd taken to wearing my swimsuit, a modest black halter I'd bought on a whim, under my clothes, so I could pull off my shirt and get a little sun on my shoulders while we crossed the bay, and also to dispense with any awkward ducking into the bathroom before swimming. Now I felt nearly naked standing alone on the warm deck, blowing up an inner tube. I eased into the water holding the inner tube in front of me, then kicked toward the beach. The water was warm and soft, and the sandy seafloor was gluey underfoot. Frankie and Charlie stood with their masked faces in the water, hands moving back and forth at their sides.

Charlie took the inner tube from me and lifted Frankie into it, so he could hold on. They moved into deeper water, faces down and snorkels spiking into the air. I waded onto the beach and sat in the wet sand, shading my eyes. I could no longer hear Charlie's words, but every so often he tapped Frankie's shoulder, and Frankie's head popped up, the mask overwhelming his face like a parasite. Charlie pointed under the water, and Frankie adjusted and dipped again. When Frankie rocked forward to put his face in the water, the little turtles on his trunks crested the surface. It was too deep for him to stand, and every so often it looked like he might topple forward out of the inner tube. Each time, Charlie put out an arm for balance.

I had the thought that maybe Graham and Frankie and I could carve out some time to come to Soldier Key as a family, though my next thought was that this was unlikely. Graham didn't have a lot of free time. On the weekends, he'd taken long bike rides in the mornings, before Frankie and I were up, then made breakfast for us all, then worked at the banquette or on the deck through the afternoon. In addition to doing his own work, he was studying the work of his new team members, as if there might be a test. Knowing Graham, he was compensating for something he suspected had happened. Maybe there had been a conversation or meeting where he'd felt insufficiently prepared. Anytime I mentioned how many hours he was working, he looked wounded, as if I were betraying some common understanding about the importance of what he contributed to our family. Our situations, in his mind, were equitable: he worked and I took care of our son. His job wouldn't last forever, after all. If I wanted to stay in Miami, he would have to earn himself a more permanent place.

There was a certain logic, I had to admit. But still, there seemed to be some experience we were meant to be having as a family. I didn't know if other mothers felt this way, but I thought my own mother had, what with the way we'd paired up while my father orbited the universe on his own, colliding with us every so often, as if by chance. I grew up missing my father a little bit all of the time, looking around for him only to discover he'd left the house. The notion that Frankie was growing up the same way carved a rut in my heart.

There was something about the way Charlie stood in the ocean, his focus trained on my son, his muscular arms tensed in preparation to help Frankie stand or lift him out of the water. I remembered, watching them together, that my mother's old friend, Vivian, had had a daughter, which meant Charlie had a daughter. One could tell he was a father, looking at him. He wore fatherhood on his skin.

After Graham and I were married but before we'd decided—*I'd* decided—to try to have a baby, my mother had told me that she believed it wasn't a matter of being *meant* to be a parent. Rather, it was about inclination, like spicy food or heights. I think she meant to seem neutral on the subject, but I sensed an undercurrent of disapproval in her words, and I wondered if she believed that *I* did not possess this taste for parenthood, what with my moodiness and introspection, my only-child independence. It had always seemed that when my mother made a pronouncement about me, regardless of whether previously I'd believed the pronouncement was true, it *became* the truth. As if she not only had information that I didn't, but also had the power to mold my future self, which maybe she did. Once, I'd mentioned on the phone that I was in the process of reorganizing my kitchen cabinets, and she'd said, not rudely but with a thoughtlessness that asserted itself only after she started to get sick, that this seemed like a task for which I was ill-suited. "You've never had much of a head for that kind of thing," she said guilelessly. It wasn't only that my feelings were hurt by the comment, but also that I was perplexed by it. I'd assumed, until that conversation, that in fact I was perfectly capable of simple home organization. Suddenly, I believed the opposite.

If my mother had ever said that she thought I would be a good mother, maybe I could believe that I was.

Offshore, there came a shout—but it wasn't Charlie's, it was Frankie's, and then he was moving silently but frantically, scrabbling at Charlie's shoulders until Charlie was holding him and the inner tube was floating beside them. I stood up, but Charlie gave a reassuring wave.

"Stingray," he called.

Through the clear water I saw a gliding dark cloud of color, then the smooth flip of a fin. Frankie was grinning now, bouncing in Charlie's arms. Up came his hand beside Charlie's, and then, as the creature skated into deeper water, they both pointed emphatically to get my attention, signing for me to *Look, look, look.*

MAYBE IT WAS THE SEA air or the swimming or both, but at Stiltsville Frankie took marathon naps, stretching well into a third hour. I worked in the office while he slept, listening for his knocks against the wall, and every so often I trudged out to the kitchen for water or coffee and found Charlie napping on the sofa with his forearm over his eyes or sitting in the armchair under the heaping yarn, needles clicking.

After our swim at Soldier Key, Frankie's fingers and toes were pruned and his cheeks were the fruity pink of plums. I read him a book—I'd taken to leaving a few behind, along with spare clothes—and kissed his clammy hairline, and when I came out to get a glass of water, I found Charlie cutting limes at the kitchen counter. He dropped a slice into a bottle of beer and handed it over with a white paper napkin wrapped around the base. A salty, warm breeze swept in from the open doorway.

On the armchair was the bag of wool, and on top of the bag was a single knitted baby bootie made from cream-colored yarn. It was shaped less like a typical bootie than a prim little loafer, with a coconut button off to one side.

I said, "That's the cutest thing I've ever seen."

He grunted in acknowledgment.

"But you know that won't fit Frankie, right?" I said.

"You don't think?" he said.

I couldn't read him. "You're multitalented," I said.

"My wife taught me."

I spoke without thinking. "Why don't you bring the chair into the office? Keep me company?"

He shrugged and took a swallow of his beer, then handed it to me to hold. He hoisted the low chair into the office, set it down in the corner, and picked up his needles. For an hour or so we worked without speaking, me sorting and him knitting. I started an unopened box, having finished five or so completely, and when I pulled off the lid, expecting to see a starfish or octopus or clipper ship, I saw instead something new: a map. Along the top of the page was an intricate strip of hammocks along a peninsula, and at the tip of the peninsula was a stout lighthouse. The rest of the page was Biscayne Bay, including the finger-channels of Stiltsville, and at the bottom of the page, the land petered out, and there lay a necklace of squashed shapes: the Florida Keys. The map was drawn on a faded and yellowing page from a dictionary, headed with the words that bookended the content: *qualm* to *quick*. The weekend before, I'd stopped at an art supply store and bought a three-pack of fancy technical drawing pens and a battery-operated electric pencil sharpener. I used my own money for these and didn't submit the receipts to Riggs. Charlie thanked me politely when I handed over the packages, but as far as I could tell, none of it had been used.

The box revealed more maps on dictionary pages. One—the headers read *standard* to *stave*—offered more detail of the swampy hammocks and the textured stucco of the lighthouse, and in the center of the bay, near the mouth of the big channel, was a small bonefish. No Name Cove was detailed, with a tiny sailboat moored in its middle, and farther south was an inlet, water lines swirling. On one of the islands was a hexagonal structure: this was the fort on Garden Key in the Dry Tortugas, where Graham and I were headed in a few days. Another map showed Soldier Key with a smaller key beside it, titled *1905*.

Frankie was still asleep when I finished sorting the maps. Charlie looked up. In his lap lay the rounded tip of a second ivory loafer.

"Maps," I said to him, pointing to the box.

He put his finger to his lips, indicating the wall between the office and the main bedroom. "Yes, maps," he said.

"They're exquisite."

"They don't sell."

"I didn't know there used to be another island next to Soldier Key."

"Islands sink."

"Those little shoes," I said. "You're not making them for Frankie, are you?"

"No, I'm not." He bowed his head and continued to knit.

The afternoon sunlight filled the room like a substance, viscous and damp. I stood near the window and waited for a breeze to cool my face. To the east, a little fishing boat slowed as it approached the neighbors' house, its whine shifting into a low roar. The woman at the house— she was blond, a little older than I—went to greet the visitor, a thin dark-haired woman wearing a visor. The brunette was familiar, and I thought she might have been a woman named Marse Heiger, a friend of Lidia's who stopped by every few weeks. It was impossible to tell for certain. She and the blond woman embraced on the dock. I went back to my tasks.

Charlie fell asleep while I was working my way through another box. His head rested on the back of his chair, facing the wall. I'd never known an adult to nap as heavily, as unself-consciously, as he did. I envied him. After a while, I stood and stretched and watched the rise and fall of his chest under his T-shirt. His hands rested on the arms of the chair and his eyelids fluttered. I found myself touching his forearm.

He opened his eyes but didn't move. "What's going on?"

"Nothing. I just wondered something."

His mouth tightened a little. "What?"

I felt my face flush. "Can I ask," I said, "do you ever miss living on land?"

"Not a lot, no."

I was going to let it drop, but then he went on.

"I miss football, actually. Sometimes Riggs comes out and we watch on the set in his Bertram, but it's not the same."

"What else?"

"Gardening. My wife had the green thumb, but I held my own. We had an English garden around an old oak out back. I would spend hours on my knees, sweating into the roses." He rubbed his thighs. "Every so often I think I'd like to spend some time in my garden."

"I'd think you'd miss"—I searched for the word. "Freedom."

"I'm not sure we understand the term the same way."

"Freedom of movement, of space."

He motioned out the window. "You have more space on land?"

"Getting in a car and driving, that sort of freedom."

"Doesn't hold much appeal."

"Because of people?"

He nodded once. "Mostly."

"People don't hold appeal?"

"Not most, no."

"Is it hard to have me and Frankie around so much?"

"Not particularly. You can take that as a compliment."

"I do." I took a breath. "Why are you knitting those booties?"

We both looked down at the half-finished pair in his lap, the delicate coconut button.

"It's a little complicated," he said.

I sat down on the floor close to his chair. He wiped his forehead, then put his hands on his knees. He didn't look at me. "Maybe you know that I had a daughter," he said.

The past tense—*had a daughter*—landed in my gut. If I'd ever met his daughter, I didn't recall it.

"Sort of," I said.

"She died." He scratched at the stubble on his chin. "She was twenty-five. Married. Pregnant. This was ten years ago last December. Her husband, Sam, was an associate with my firm. I'd introduced them."

He said the last bit with a father's pride, but still my breath caught in my throat.

"No, no," he said, seeing my expression. "It was insulin shock. She was home alone. I came in the back with some ferns—sometimes on the weekends we did a little work in their yard—and I found her on the kitchen floor. There was orange juice spilled everywhere, but she hadn't gotten it to her mouth. Evidently." He checked to see if he should go on. "Her cat was making a lot of noise at her feet. I called the ambulance. I held her and tried to get her to swallow something. She was alive when I found her, but by the time they got there she was gone."

Age twenty-five. I'd been twenty-five when I met Graham. "Where was Sam?"

Charlie tensed. "He was at a job site. A pedestrian bridge at a college in Fort Lauderdale. His first big job. I'd made it happen."

"You liked him," I said.

"Very much. They had a good—" He searched for the word, then dropped it. "We thought they were too young when they got engaged, but we were wrong. Vivian was excited about the baby."

I tried to recall whether my mother had ever told me this story, but came up blank. I knew she'd kept things from me, truths of her life and of life in general, meaning to protect me. She would have believed telling me something like that would harm my spirit, I think—this was the kind of thing that had irritated me about her, once upon a time. Or maybe she did tell me of her friend's daughter's death, and I'd forgotten. I'd lived away from home at the time, after all, and had been in the process of falling in love. But the daughter and I must have been roughly the same age, and I didn't think I'd forget a story like that.

He looked at the little loafers in his lap. "It's Vivian's design," he said. "I mean, I'm sure other people have made baby shoes that look similar, but this was her pattern. She made them for years. She said they were her signature gift."

He was a thick-shouldered, square-jawed, sandpaper-faced older man, holding a soft woolen shoe smaller than his palm.

"They're a perfect gift," I said.

"She thought I needed something to occupy myself after Jenny died. Every time she made me sit down I felt like I couldn't stand it another minute." He glanced up at me. "I wasn't very nice about it."

"You learned."

He held up the shoe. "A little leather under here," he said, pointing at the sole, "and it's a slipper, for bigger kids."

"What else can you make?"

"Cardigans. Babies wear a lot of cardigans, even in the heat, have you noticed? And roomy little pants. Vivian called them *kicky* pants." On his face was a calmness I hadn't seen before. He noticed me staring and cleared his throat. "Once you've had a little practice, it's simple. Passes the time."

I knew I should return to work, but this was the most he'd ever spoken. "What happened to Sam?"

"He remarried. She's an attorney, a real go-getter. Her job moved them to Seattle. He writes letters."

"They have kids," I said.

"Two. Sam sends photos. A boy about Frankie's age named Simon. And a new one, a little girl named Jennifer." He touched the little shoe. "A nice gesture, naming the baby after her."

My hand came to my mouth. In my mind, this family assembled: Sam was a little stocky, a little unkempt, with a mop of dark hair and kind, weathered eyes. The wife had smooth, styled hair and wore tailored pants. She listened when Sam talked about his first wife. She let him cry. They went to breakfast on weekend mornings, and the kids were noisy and playful and the parents laughed at the baby's expressions and the boy's odd phrasings. The mother never had the feeling that something was missing, or if she did, it was fleeting and inconsequential. They mooned over the packages that came, every few months, from Florida. At least I hoped they mooned.

"There's no need to cry for me," said Charlie.

"I don't know how a person survives it," I said.

"Some people pick up, keep going. Some people drink, divorce."

I put my hand on the back of his hand. He frowned at it, but didn't move.

He said, "Some people go to sea, and they drown."

From the other room came the sound—at first soft, then more insistent—of Frankie's knuckles against the wall.

9

GRAHAM AND I PACKED SNORKELING gear, a tent and sleeping bags, groceries, and, because there was no freshwater where we
were headed, two dozen bottles of water. Lidia came down the lawn as
the sky was starting to lighten and settled on the *Lullaby*'s deck with a
newspaper. We'd said good-bye to Frankie the night before, explaining
again about our little vacation and how soon we'd be home. *Come back*,
he'd signed.

We stopped at a café in Tavernier for Cuban toast and coffee, then
kept driving. We passed through Islamorada, Duck Key, Marathon,
Big Pine. In the early hours, the sky was an unpleasant milky hue and
the air smelled thickly of swamp. But as the sun rose the sky deepened in color and the air cleared. In Key West, we rented kayaks and
strapped them to the roof of the car, then stopped at a bar in Old Town
that was known for its oysters. Graham had never eaten oysters, but he
was a good sport. I ordered a few of every kind and he grimaced at the
raw ones and scarfed down the Rockefellers. I told him that my mother
had always served oysters before Thanksgiving dinner. She'd placed a

sliver of lemon on each and added a dollop of cocktail sauce, turning each half-shell into a tiny plate. For the meal itself, she'd always invited a gamut of single, childless friends. My father tolerated the parade of strangers through the house because she always spent days preparing his favorite foods: moist turkey, corn bread stuffing, cranberry sauce, grilled asparagus with hollandaise, several kinds of pie. My mother had eaten sparingly, careful of her figure, but she'd watched with pride as my father dug in.

We found a room at a motel on the beach. Graham made me laugh by imitating the very serious desk clerk, who before handing over the room key had asked, as he shuffled ahead down the corridor, if we would be kind enough to move the bed away from the wall before engaging in "energetic coitus." Graham had a randy streak that I'd found crass when we met but over time had come to enjoy—it gave him an unpredictable quality. He climbed onto the bed after the clerk was gone, miming energetic coitus against the headboard, then bounced down on the satiny coverlet.

"Do you feel like a good hotel guest, wife?" he said, patting the bed. "Or a bad one?"

The next morning we were up early to catch the ferry, which made the two-hour passage to Garden Key, the largest of the Dry Tortugas, only once daily. The ferry was full, and after we pulled away from the dock, Graham took a map from his backpack and spread it across our laps. He'd circled snorkeling sites in red pen. We planned to camp two nights on the island, just outside the ramparts of Fort Jefferson, a Civil War–era marine fortress. There was also, said Graham, the option of paddling to Loggerhead, three miles across open water. The lady who'd rented us the kayaks had been skeptical when Graham mentioned this possibility—she'd asked about our experience, which was limited in my case to the lake behind our cottage and one trip to the Apostle Islands. Graham had just grinned gamely and assured her we'd be careful. When we docked, most of the passengers filed away to take a tour—they would return to Key West in a few hours—and Graham and I walked to the campground. It wasn't much more than a triangle of grass between the beach and Fort Jefferson itself, a hexagonal brick structure surrounded by a moat.

After unpacking, we walked the perimeter of the fort, weaving through the arched casements. Graham read from the guidebook. "It took sixteen million bricks to build this," he said. "Sixteen million bricks!"

Graham had a way of zeroing in on exactly what made history interesting. Being a tourist with him was like traveling with your best high school teacher, the one who put down the textbook and relayed some bit of trivia that brought an entire era to life. When I read a guidebook, the information lay flat on the page, details muddling. Not so for Graham. He read quickly through some parts of the guidebook's brief history—the fort was used as a prison and once housed five of the Lincoln assassination conspirators, including Dr. Samuel Mudd, who'd reset the bone in John Wilkes Booth's broken leg—then rested on the bricks. The fort had been erected entirely from a material that had to be hauled across miles of ocean, Graham emphasized; some ships capsized under the weight. And despite the inspired design, the place was never actually used as a fort. With the invention of cannon riflery, marine fortresses were rendered obsolete, and ships were sent instead.

One hundred and fifty years later, the mortar was deteriorating. Bricks littered the sandy moat floor. A wide plank stretched from a beached boat to the ramparts: they were rebuilding. A worker sat drinking from a water bottle under a royal palm, and Graham stopped to ask the man where he was staying. The man described apartments in the casements, where he and his coworkers were spending a ninety-day stint. There was a small bathroom and a table and a cot, said the man. He had a roommate, another mason. There were no telephones, no television. A boat came from Key West every week with water and pro-

visions, and the workers sent back mail and requests for alcohol, magazines, fishing supplies. Graham shook the man's hand when we said
good-bye, and we walked along the moat wall toward the campground.

I was distracted. Would Lidia remember Frankie's date to play with
Carson that afternoon? Would she sit with him while he ate, in case
he choked?

Graham said, "Can you imagine that job? I can't install a light fixture without making three trips to the hardware store."

"We'd be useless," I said.

"I wonder how different it is, being a bricklayer now versus back
then."

I hadn't been terribly interested in the fort when we'd first planned to
come. I'd considered the fort, the history, a toll we had to pay before we
could change into our suits and do a little snorkeling. As we'd meandered
through the rows of identical casements along the fort's perimeter, looking
through the old cannon windows housed in iron that, like the bricks, was
disintegrating, I'd been hungry and hot. How many times, in the decade
since Graham and I had met, had I had the experience of barely registering
something until he turned my head and forced me to look at it?

This curiosity, this connection with history—this was a quality that
I'd hoped he might impart to our son.

THAT AFTERNOON WE KAYAKED TO the closest island, Bush
Key. Onshore, we dried in the sun. From where we lay, we could see
tourists file out of the fort and back onto the ferry, and we watched the
boat shrink into the limitless blue. I was reminded of the distance we'd
put between ourselves and civilization, between ourselves and our son.
I commented that it would be something to see the islands from above,
the neat six-sided fort and the humpbacked shoals surrounding it. I was
thinking of Charlie's intricate maps.

Graham sat up and fished through his dry bag and pulled out a
brochure. On the cover was an aerial photograph of all of the Dry Tor-

tugas. "*Voilà*," he said, and lay back down again, dropping an arm over his eyes.

After an hour or so, we kayaked to Long Key, which was covered in scrub grasses and peppered with black-and-white frigates, their feathers shuddering in the breeze. The sun was starting to wane but the air was still hot. On the far side of the key, Graham stopped paddling and pointed: ahead, between the tiny island and the dark ocean, a round object bobbed. Graham started paddling toward it and I followed. The black shape surfaced and submerged again. When it came up a third time, we were just a boat's length away. I could see, from that distance, the glossy flat shell was not purely black but flecked with white. And it wasn't round, as it had seemed from a distance, but oval, with sharp creases down its length, as if it had been folded in several places and opened again. The turtle was at least five or six feet in diameter, almost as long as my kayak.

"It's not swimming," said Graham.

He was right. The creature appeared to rise and fall with the current, not moving forward at all. I was closest to its stubby rear flippers, which pushed ineptly against the water every few seconds, as if running out of power. When the meaty, oblong slab of its enormous head rose from the water, its eyes black and cold, I backed up a little. From directly across the wide carapace, which continued to dip and rise every thirty seconds, I could see the back flippers with their sluggish movements, and the thick spiked tail—but I could not see its front flippers.

Graham nudged the turtle with the blade of his paddle.

"Graham!" I said. The animal turned. The movement of its back flippers increased, as if in panic.

Graham stared into the water at something I couldn't see. "Holy hell," he said.

"What?"

"There's no front flipper. Just a stub and some blood."

My stomach turned. "What about the other one?"

Graham paddled around the head, then said, "It's here. It's caught."

"In what?"

"Some kind of line."

Movement in my peripheral vision snagged my attention: a dark shape on the surface of the water. When I turned to look, it was gone.

"We should get help," I said.

"I've got a knife."

He dug at his feet for his dry bag. As he moved, the kayak shifted beneath his weight and thumped against the turtle's massive domed back.

"Careful," I said. But the turtle didn't seem to notice. It dipped again and stayed down a while. Graham found the knife and waved me over. When our kayaks were side by side, facing opposite directions, he started to lift himself out.

"No," I said, thinking of the dark shape. "Something *took* that flipper."

"He's losing steam," said Graham.

The whole back-and-forth played out in my mind, the minutes of argument while the sun continued its descent and the waters darkened. There was no stopping him, I knew. Sometimes I thought that in becoming a parent, I'd morphed into an entirely different person, while he'd remained exactly the same person he'd always been. I found this bewildering. I steadied his boat with one hand and he lifted himself out, then swam slowly toward the turtle, holding his knife out of the water. The turtle surfaced again, but only barely.

Graham steadied himself on the creature's flank, then started hacking at the tangles of line, his face very close to the water. I couldn't see his work, but after a breathless minute his head rose, and, several yards beyond him, a dark fin broke the surface. I stared at the spot where it disappeared.

"Shark," I said to Graham.

"Where?"

I pointed with my paddle. "Five yards, maybe four."

I thought he might abandon the rescue altogether, or at least rush. Instead, he said, "Keep an eye out. They don't want me—they want our friend here."

"Graham, get back in the boat, please."

"Almost done."

A fin cut through the water off my port side. My God, I thought, they've surrounded us. Absurdly, I thought of jokes on the theme of circling sharks: lawyers, insurance salesmen, desperate older women.

"Hurry up," I said.

"Look." He pulled a knotted tangle from the water—ropey netting, maybe from a lobster trap—and ushered up a massive clawing flipper from beneath the turtle's body. Slowly, the flipper started to move. Graham kicked away as the turtle dived. "So long, friend," said Graham, then wrestled himself into his kayak.

When he was in, I let go of his boat and punched his upper arm. "Goddamn it," I said.

"Ow." He rubbed his arm, panting. "You never know what will happen, do you?"

This was something he'd said a dozen times. To be fair, it had always been more true with him than without him.

We looked in the direction the turtle had gone. After a moment, its carapace rose, milky spots reflecting the fading sunlight, then dived again. I didn't see another shark, but I stopped looking for them.

"I bet that thing weighed five hundred pounds," said Graham.

"You are reckless," I said.

"Don't say that."

I looked away from his lidded gaze, the heavy circles under his eyes. Begrudgingly, I said, "It's good you saved it."

"What choice did we have?"

I didn't answer, but I knew exactly what choice we'd had. Once, months before we'd moved, a friend had told me she'd recently ter-

minated a pregnancy at twenty-one weeks along, after an amnio revealed the baby had Down's. The reason she gave for the decision:
her living son, a healthy boy named Jeremy, who at that moment was
running naked through the sprinkler, trailed closely by Frankie. Their
penises bobbed and their coltish, miniature-man's legs kicked. Their
feet slapped the wet lawn. Of course she did it for him—for herself and
her husband, too, but mostly for Jeremy, whose standing at the center
of their universe would have inevitably slipped. I had no idea what I
would have done in her position, but I told my friend I understood her
decision, and it was true.

Where was that same instinct in my husband, to protect us at any
cost?

We paddled quietly until we reached the beach. I pulled my boat
ashore and sat in the sand. Graham stood above me, drinking from a
water bottle.

"I was scared," I said.

"You could try trusting me," he said, and walked away.

That night, Graham borrowed a nature guide from the young guys
at the campsite next to ours—they'd caught a bucket of lobster, and
cooked two for us—and thumbed through it until he came to a photograph of a massive black sea turtle. "Here's our friend," he said, handing me the book.

I squinted in the firelight. The leatherback sea turtle preferred deeper
waters beyond the continental shelf, but was occasionally sighted in the
Keys, en route from the Gulf to the Atlantic. "'Instead of scutes,'" I
read aloud, "'the leatherback has a thick, leathery skin covered in oils.'"

"Less revolting in person," said Graham.

The fort closed to visitors at dusk, but we sneaked in under a metal
chain. The starlight cast leaden shadows. I wanted to stick to the
perimeter—there were park rangers on the site, as well as a crew of
masons and engineers—but Graham walked straight into the open-air
courtyard and I followed him. There was the feeling, with Graham,

that no situation was too hairy to escape unscathed. There was the feeling that his largess—physical and psychological—sheltered me, as if my participation in any scheme was incidental. It was liberating.

The rampart walls rose around us, blocking all sight of the sea, though we could hear the push and pull of the tide. A black lighthouse squatted above us, catching the moonlight in its curves. There was the scattered noise of conversation coming from the barracks. From a powder magazine nearby came the low, otherworldly call of an owl, then a quick rustling in the sandy grass.

"Rats," said Graham.

"Let's go back," I said.

The owl made its noise again. "Look up," said Graham.

It was late and the sky was thick with stars. Was it possible I'd never seen such abundance in the night sky? I thought of Frankie. I wondered if Lidia had remembered not to give him milk before breakfast, if she'd helped him brush his teeth. I wondered if she was having trouble understanding him, if he was having trouble being understood.

"Magnificent," I said to Graham.

He pulled me in. My neck ached from looking up but I didn't stop.

Quietly, he said, "Just old light, that's all." I could hear the pleasure in his voice.

GRAHAM WANDERED THE ISLAND WHILE I slept. In the morning, we snorkeled and ate breakfast, then headed in the kayaks half a mile southeast to Bird Key, the site of the closest shipwreck. Graham lassoed our kayaks together and dropped anchor and hoisted a dive flag. We'd read that in the mid-1800s the Keys had been populated almost entirely by wreckers and pirates, and there were a thousand documented wrecks in the area, plus a rumored U-boat that had never been mapped. What was left behind after a wreck had been salvaged was either worthless or too cumbersome to float to shore, and so skeletons remained. Graham dived to the seafloor right away, but for a few moments I stayed at the surface, my face in the water, my body lifting and dropping with the surface current.

What lay beneath me in no way resembled a ship. I knew from the guidebook that there was such a thing as shipworms, termites of the sea, which ate away at wooden hulls, but I'd expected to see something—the slip of a keel or curve of a bowsprit, maybe—that recollected the vessel that had drowned there. Instead, there was coral of every color and shape, clumps of sea grass, fish darting here and there, and hundreds of bricks. The bricks were scattered along the seafloor as far as I could see, mustard yellow in color with etched lettering on the faces. Graham was a few yards from me, a plane of flesh along the water's rim. I dove toward a cluster of bricks and hovered there, trying to make out the etching: EVENS & HOWARD, ST. LOUIS. There was movement in the corner of my vision, and when I turned I caught the silver flank of a fleeing barracuda. I rose and cleaned my mask and heard Graham calling for me. I kicked toward him, taking in the colors and textures of the coral as I went, the scattered bricks, the bright darting fish. When I reached him, he put his hands on my shoulders and faced me away from the island.

"Look down," he said.

When I put my face in the water, I saw a massive iron propeller, each blade sheathed in toothy barnacles. There had been a ship here after all. I circled it. The act of snorkeling, to me, was like standing in a pitch-black room where you sense you are not alone, then lighting a match. It's a pleasure, certainly, to see up close what is shrouded from land, the busy citizenry of the sea—but it's also chilling. With the mask on, I had the feeling of wearing blinders, and each turn of my head could reveal something that had come forward from the deep, like this menacing piece of metalwork, its fat blades so stagnant that it seemed they might burst into motion if I continued to watch them. The rules of reality didn't seem to apply.

My heart was beating fast when I struggled into the kayak. The wind was up and the eastern sky was dark with storm. It would take half an hour to get back and haul up the boats, so it seemed unlikely that if rain was going to hit, we would get caught. But when I pulled up the anchor, Graham just sat catching his breath and looking west toward Loggerhead, a low ridge of foliage on the horizon. There was another lighthouse there, and a reef called Little Africa because of its shape. Graham wanted to go. The ferry captain had said that the island's caretaker invited visitors to sign a guest book. It was this— signing the guest book, leaving a mark—that drew Graham, specifi- cally. The crossing—I knew this from the woman at the kayak rental place—would be choppier than the waters between Garden Key and Long Key, with a crosscurrent that pulled straight out to sea. But not forging ahead would be, to Graham, like turning down the chance to send a memento into space.

I said, "I don't think we should go."

He arched his eyebrows and grinned at me. "Three miles, babe? We can do three miles in an hour."

I said, "We didn't tell anyone we were going."

"I feel good. Don't you feel good?"

I reached across the kayaks to touch Graham's shoulder. It was as close to him as I could get. "I feel pretty good," I said. "But it looks like rain."

"We'll beat it."

I looked behind us at Garden Key, so close and sheltering, then ahead at Loggerhead, which in truth didn't seem so far away. Graham took my hesitation as agreement. He started to head off and I followed, matching my strokes to his. After fifteen minutes or so, my arms started to tire. Even if I got there—without being pulled out to sea—I wasn't sure I would be able to turn around and head back. I didn't have a watch, but I figured it was around four o'clock. The sun wouldn't start to go down until eight; there was time. But still, as the distance increased between my kayak and the campsite, I found myself glancing over my shoulder and falling behind.

"Graham!" I shouted. I stopped paddling.

He waved me forward. I shook my head and he turned and came back. As he neared, waves lapped the prow of his boat, and my own boat rose and fell with the swells. If we stayed unmoving for long, we would be carried by the current.

"What's wrong?" he said.

"I want to go back."

He looked beyond me, gauging the distance. "It's as far back now as it is ahead. You can do it."

Could I? Strength, sapped momentarily by swimming and paddling, was already returning to my arms after the brief rest. Loggerhead drifted a little: we were moving, and quickly.

"The current," I said.

"We've got to keep moving."

"I'm not going," I said.

"Please come. I really want to go."

"Go. I'll head back."

"I can't go without you."

"Of course you can."

"Are you sure?"

"Yes. Be careful."

He cocked his head at me, then nodded. "You be careful," he said. He gave me a last look, then turned away.

Maybe a different man would not have left his wife. But I'd been sincere when I told him to go on without me; I had no illusions about Graham and the decision he would make. Graham didn't confuse love with overprotectiveness, as so many of us do. He'd always guarded his own independence, which as far as I was concerned left me free to guard mine. He'd always believed I could do pretty much anything that he could do, and to have stayed would have betrayed a lack of faith in me. His confidence in me gave me a fresh shot of courage.

I faced Garden Key and started paddling. After about five minutes, the wind picked up, jostling my kayak and pushing waves over the bow. The sky darkened. I was distracted by a thick limb of sunlight moving across the water's surface. I had to push harder with my right arm than my left, to fight the cross-pull of the current. A light rain started to fall, then grew heavier. When I looked behind me, I could see Graham making progress toward Loggerhead. Between us, off the stern of my boat, a flying fish whipped through the air. I kept going. My right arm ached, but I could see already that I would miss the beach if I didn't turn. I shifted my course so I was tacking toward the inlet, not perpendicular to the island but nearly so. The rain worsened. At one point, I lost sight of the lighthouse, though I could still see the beach. With spray hitting my face and waves splashing my boat, I kept going, and just before I reached the beach, I realized that I'd been speaking aloud into the rain. For several minutes, through gritted teeth, I'd been repeating the single word: *Frankie, Frankie, Frankie, Frankie, Frankie.*

GRAHAM'S FATHER DIED FROM AN aneurysm five years before Graham and I met. Once, after we were engaged, we sat together on the roof deck of my old apartment in Bucktown, and I asked about the years he'd spent in the minor leagues, and about how he'd first become interested in baseball. (A torn rotator cuff had forced him to quit, at which point he'd enrolled in graduate school.) He told me his father had been the one to nurture his talent, but his mouth had tightened as he said it, and I'd let it drop. Graham never spoke in a prolonged way about his father. All I knew about the man was that he'd met Graham's mother, Julia, in high school, and that while he'd served in Germany, she'd worked in a tire factory in their hometown of Ann Arbor, Michigan. I knew that he hadn't allowed Graham or his sister to attend church with their mother, which had reminded me of my own father. I knew that he'd spent the late portion of his career as a professor of biochemistry at the University of Chicago.

Years after that brief exchange on the roof deck, when Frankie was just over a year old, I found Graham standing at our kitchen sink in the middle of the night, staring out at the lake, which had recently started to thaw. The surface was marbled with dark, pooling patches of slush, like worn places on an old blanket. I could tell by Graham's bearing, the tension in his neck and shoulders, that he was awake.

It wasn't rare for us to bump into each other in the night, and usually we were quiet and respectful of each other, like ghosts with shared haunting grounds. But for no reason that I could discern, this night Graham started to talk. He said, "Did I ever tell you that as a kid I was afraid of being hit with the baseball?"

"That doesn't sound like you."

"Little League, when I was eleven. The coach told my parents I was fit for the outfield." He gave a wan smile. "So my father took me home and we threw the ball around a little, and every time it came near me—I remember it exactly—I cringed. I had a good arm, though. He could see that."

I had no idea where the story was going.

He continued. "He went inside and told me to wait, then came out with some twine from the garage. He stood me next to a tree and tied my wrists behind my back and told me to keep still. Then he walked away and picked up a baseball and pitched it at me."

I gasped. He glanced at me, then looked back at the lake.

"It wasn't so bad. After half a dozen hits or so, my mother came out and screamed at him. There were some ugly bruises on my chest and arms. The next week at practice, my coach didn't know what had come over me. He moved me to shortstop. You know the rest."

"That doesn't make it right," I said.

He shrugged. "Maybe not. I think about it a lot. Was he right, or wrong, or both?"

"He was wrong."

"Baseball put me through college. Baseball gave me confidence."

"There are other ways."

"But he didn't know any. Fathers are supposed to push their sons."

"He crossed the line."

"But how do you know where the line is," he said, "until after you've crossed it?"

A wave of frustration rose inside me. That I might be pitted as the indulgent mother because I didn't approve of a father pitching at his small, fearful son—in that moment, this seemed to encapsulate every disagreement we'd ever had about becoming parents, about whether people can become better versions of themselves for the sake of their children.

There was a sponge beside the sink. I threw it at him. "You are not your father."

He caught the sponge. "I know that," he said. "But what kind of father am I?"

THE RAIN HAD PASSED BY the time I got back to the tent. I changed into dry clothes and lay down for an hour, then walked back to stand on the moat wall and keep a lookout for Graham. Loggerhead was little more than a jagged horizontal line in the distance. I paced the wall. Finally, a yellow dot appeared in the choppy blue. The sun descended an inch, and after a while the little kayak grew in size and I could make out Graham in the boat, his strokes even and powerful, his hair faintly metallic in the dying sunlight. I waved until he stopped paddling to wave back. I dropped from the moat wall. When he came ashore, I helped him haul the boat onto the sand.

"Did you sign the guest book?" I said.

His smile was wholehearted. "Yes, I did."

"I'm glad."

I took a step toward the campsite, but he stopped me. "Let's wait for the sunset."

He pulled a bottle of water from his dry bag and took off his life jacket.

"I kind of wish I'd gone with you," I admitted.

"I wish you had, too." There was no reproach in his voice.

We pushed our toes into the sand. He said, "You used to trust me, Georgia."

This was true. For years, I'd trusted him nearly blindly. Life with Graham had always been filled with small excitements, like walking the frozen lake behind the cottage as the ice groaned and cracked under our feet. He'd taught me to use a kayak before dawn one night when neither of us could sleep. He'd made me practice maintaining the paddler's box so long that I grew frustrated, and only then did he reveal that he'd planned a kayaking trip through the Apostle Islands, where we would explore the sea caves and camp under the stars and—this part was scheduled specifically with me in mind, because it bored him to tears—tour as many Lake Superior lighthouses as possible.

"The stakes," I said. "They're higher now."

"I understand."

"Do you?" I said.

He didn't answer. He loved me too much to say what I believed he was thinking: *We used to have a different kind of marriage, and I liked that one better.*

He changed the subject. He was in a good mood, and wanted to stay that way. We got to talking about the research team he'd joined, which was studying how air and water interacted during hurricanes and typhoons. He didn't talk much about work normally, but I'd gleaned that despite the long hours, he liked his colleagues and the job itself. He'd spoken excitedly about a saltwater wave tank in the room next to his office, where a colleague spent twelve hours a day simulating hurricanes, and about how one of his office mates was working to determine the best paths for aircraft flying through storms.

Now, he explained, hands gesturing in the air between us, his team was about to deploy four new research buoys 250 miles off the coast of Jacksonville, in the thick of Hurricane Alley. The buoys would gather data about the force and temperature of the air and water during weather extremes, and about the sea spray that lubricates surging winds. A Scripps research ship would host the team offshore for weeks, maybe even months.

I was having difficulty following him—it seemed an odd time to launch into such a detailed explanation—but I liked how he talked about work to me as if we had the same basic foundation of knowledge.

He said, "The software that processes the data has a few glitches. I'm working them out. Larry's relieved to have a computer guy on the team. Everyone's headed up for the launch." He paused to drink from the water bottle. "The Scripps people need someone who knows the back end, just in case. It would be a mistake to count myself out." As he spoke, he wore grooves in the sand with his heels. "They're leaving next week."

Seeing my expression, he stopped talking. It was dawning on me what this conversation meant to convey. Graham knew I wanted him around more—of course he knew, though I prided myself on not repeating myself endlessly, the way my mother had. He was telling me that for the unforeseen future, my wish would not be granted. Not by a long shot.

I said, "I don't want you to go. But it doesn't sound like there's much choice."

"Are you saying I can go?"

"You're not asking my permission."

"But I'd like it."

"Go," I said, but my voice broke.

"It's a good opportunity," he said quietly.

We sat still for a moment. Maybe he assumed I'd been unpersuaded of the importance of the trip, that I didn't understand the relationship between his job—our bread and butter—and the work he'd be doing on this ship. But to me, all of that was beside the point. A year earlier, if Graham had announced that he was throwing himself more fully into work—well, I might have left him. Though I would not have admitted it, on some level I was grateful to Graham's work, to the fact that he'd immersed himself so fully. Otherwise, he might've wanted to go back to Round Lake.

Graham shifted forward to kneel in the sand. He pointed at the sun, which was falling fast toward the hazy horizon. "Here we go," he said. "Watch."

I watched. As the sun's midsection disappeared behind the horizon, a burst of iridescent green flashed at its apex, then was gone.

"Holy shit," I said.

The sun sank. The bruised sky closed in. Low waves lapped at our feet.

Graham said, "I know I disappoint you. I disappoint myself."

His hair luffed in the breeze, a nest of white feathers. I moved toward him but he shifted away. He stood and walked toward the campsite, then stopped to let me catch up. I knew he would spend that night, as he'd spent the night before, roaming the island. He hadn't packed the cuff because there was nowhere to fasten it. Anyway, he'd said, why bother?

In my mind, I closed a fist around the image of the green flash, that miracle of the natural world—summoned into existence, it seemed, by the man I married.

10

FOR OUR NINTH ANNIVERSARY—THIS was a year before we left Round Lake—we'd planned a weekend in Chicago, during which Frankie, who was almost three, would stay with Graham's mother and her husband in their apartment, and we would stay in a hotel. Graham was excited about a geology exhibit at the Field Museum, and I was excited to eat meals in loud restaurants crowded with adults. We were moderate in our ambitions, yes. It would have been the first time I'd left Frankie overnight.

The day before we'd planned to leave, I met a client and her family at their home in Skokie. An hour into our meeting, I received a call from the sitter, our next-door neighbor Kathy Lyman. Frankie had a fever of 104 degrees. I left my last remaining employee, a student named Tad Curry, in charge of packing up and collecting our fee, and headed home.

We left for the emergency room after Frankie's fever reached 106 and he had a febrile seizure in my arms. Harmless, as it turns out, but terrifying. Graham, of limited use in any emergency that required driving, held Frankie's hand in the backseat while I navigated the rain-wet streets to the hospital. I couldn't stop glancing at them in the rearview mirror, and at some point I had to veer roughly to avoid a deer standing in the middle of the road. I drove slowly after that, and by the time we reached the emergency room, my baby seemed more or less normal, if still warm to the touch.

Graham canceled our hotel reservations and called his mother. The next day, when Frankie's temperature was down, Graham lit on the idea of a last-minute overnight trip to a hotel water park on the edge of town. We argued about whether Frankie was healthy enough, and Graham said he'd take him down a few slides and that would be that. When had I abandoned all spontaneity? he asked. He had that way, when he got an idea in his head, of forcing that idea's inevitability—not only would we go, but we would enjoy ourselves. We checked into the hotel's last available room, a suite with a balcony overlooking a narrow strip of lawn, a parking lot, and an interstate. We were in a part of Round Lake that villagers didn't consider part of Round Lake at all. This was where they kept the chain grocery and restaurants, and next to the hotel there was a pool hall the size of an airport hangar. The hotel water park was something I'd been unfamiliar with before moving to the region. In Florida, water parks were built outdoors, but in the upper Midwest, where it might snow as late as May and early as October, they were built inside mammoth, chlorine-soaked structures with bad acoustics. Some had log cabin or wildlife themes, but many, like the one we visited that weekend, were simple: an intestine's worth of weaving fiberglass slides dumping out shrieking, brightly clad people.

It *was* fun. Frankie was agreeable and clingy. He roped his arms around Graham's neck each time they scooted together into the rushing water. They came out with openmouthed smiles, Frankie signing *Again! Again!* That night, we put Frankie down on the sofa bed, then sat a long time on the balcony, watching trucks rumble past on the interstate.

Earlier that month Graham had submitted his tenure materials; the committee was about to convene. He'd been warned by doctors about stress, but to me he seemed as relaxed as one could reasonably hope to be under the circumstances. He'd been warned, too, about changes in routine, but it didn't occur to either of us that one night in a comfortable hotel fifteen miles from home might pose a problem. I was especially sleepless, myself, those days, for no reason except the whim of my own insomnia. I was waiting it out. That night in the hotel, I fell gratefully asleep with Graham beside me, his body rigid and his eyes on the popcorn ceiling. Shortly, he would rise to read or take a walk, I assumed. I didn't worry about what might occupy him in the dark hours. Instead, I was thankful for that pleasant, underwater feeling of near-sleep. It's not overstating the case to say that I felt blessed by sleep when it came, as if it were tapping me with its wand.

Hours later, I woke to the sharp, unmistakable sound of shattering glass. Graham wasn't in bed. Frankie was wailing, but at first I didn't recognize the noise; he'd stopped using his voice months earlier. He was sitting up on the sofa bed, tears running down his face. He wasn't hurt. He pointed at the picture window, where vertical blinds swayed. Shards of glass covered the carpet. I went carefully to the window and looked out. Graham was lying on the strip of grass between the hotel and the parking lot, blood streaking his face and hands. He was crying out and holding his leg.

I did not decide, then and there, while my child wailed and my husband twisted on the ground, to leave Round Lake. I didn't realize that we would need to leave until long after the local paper had run its ungenerous article, which quoted our neighbors and their reports of odd goings-on at our home, none of which had ever been reported directly to me. In that article, which was accompanied by a piece about the Illinois Regional Center for the Study of Sleep, our neighbor Kathy Lyman, a garrulous woman who played in a bowling league several nights of the week, told a reporter that she'd "never felt safe" having us as neighbors. She said that if I wasn't aware of what was going on in my own house, I was "deaf, dumb, and blind." She told about the time she was woken in the night by Graham at the door in his pajamas, asking about the bat house in a "chilling voice." Another neighbor, someone I'd known only to wave hello, said that our house gave him "the willies," and cited the fact that Graham came and went and lights stayed on all night.

Even then, leaving didn't seem inevitable.

The night of our anniversary, in the moment that it took for the events to order themselves in my head, as I grabbed Frankie and headed for the phone, I did not think of moving away. But it did occur to me—not out of spite, but simply as a matter of course—that I would have no choice but to leave Graham.

Low hedges had partially broken his fall. He'd twisted an ankle and torn a ligament and cracked a kneecap, and he had a concussion. We spent the next twenty hours in the hospital, and when there wasn't a doctor or nurse in the room, there was often a pair of affable, baby-faced police officers, a woman and a man, who for a time acted inquisitive rather than interrogative. Their questions circled themselves, moved forward and backward in time. They took few notes. For a while I thought they were a little bumbling, that they were more curious about Graham's affliction than anything else, that they were just killing the hours and enjoying the snacks from the nurses' station. But after Graham's knee had been set and his head stitched, they returned to the room and read Graham his rights. It was then that I understood that all the chatting, the snacking, the pats on Frankie's shoulder—this was the light-handed, avuncular style of detectives who were good at their jobs. We hadn't been hoodwinked, exactly, but we'd—*I'd*—been naive.

Graham was charged with property damage and with recklessly endangering the welfare of a child. This last charge, we were told by the officers, who continued to treat us like pals, would probably be dropped. There was a lot of double-speak, a lot of explanations that didn't make much sense, but in the end I understood that they'd included the charge for two reasons. One was that we'd both admitted, in describing Graham's sleep problems over the years, that we'd known the extent of the situation and still let him remain in the care of our son. (I was not charged with reckless endangerment, and it didn't seem as if this had been under consideration.) The other reason was that without the charge, it was possible the right people wouldn't get the go-ahead to send the right kind of social worker to work with our family. The administrative shades of gray were lost on me. Something in me wanted to clarify in no uncertain terms that we did not need a social worker. But there was a smaller voice, too, that wondered why we wouldn't want some help. I called a lawyer from the phone at the nurses' station, realizing this was something I should have done hours before.

I couldn't help but wonder, at the time, how the same situation might have played out in Miami, which it seemed had a harsher but less passive-aggressive law enforcement culture. Maybe in Miami Graham would have been hauled off to jail, but there would have been no bones made about it, no soft-spoken cops repeatedly referring to my son by name, as if he were as much their responsibility as mine.

Graham's mother, Julia, came from Chicago. Reporters called. The lawyer haggled with the hotel and hashed out a figure for repairs. I drove over with a check and handed it to a jowly, silver-haired manager who lectured me about the difficulty of getting glass out of a deep-pile carpet. I reassured him that he would never see my family in his hotel again. The lawyer recommended that Graham check himself into Detention for a third, longer stint—this would look good to the court, he said—so we packed him up and drove him there right away. Kathy Lyman didn't show herself. A neighbor I barely knew, an elderly woman who'd known Julia in the old days, stopped by with a basket of muffins. How news spread even before the newspaper ran the story, I didn't know. "I'm so sorry for your troubles," said the neighbor as she handed me the basket.

She patted my hand. "Lord protect you." It was the first spot of sincere kindness in the ordeal. I could have wept in her frail arms.

Julia brought me the newspaper. There was no picture of Graham in his fugue state this time, but there was one of the broken window, taken from below, and one of Graham taken from outside his hospital room. In the photo, he scowled at an unseen person, an embittered expression on his face. I don't recall any anger in Graham that night, so I don't know how long the photographer must have waited to capture that look. When I think of Graham during those hours, the papery gown and the painkillers, his pliant answers to the unending questions, I recall only how dejected he was, how powerless and ashamed, when just the evening before he'd come whooshing out of a waterslide, his face as full of delight as I'd seen it. When I saw my husband's disgust with himself, any notion I'd had about my obligation to take Frankie away simply dissolved.

In the article, we were referred to as "eccentric neighbors," which I never understood. Surely, to be labeled as such, there must have been something other than Graham's parasomnia. Did it have to do with the fact that I hadn't grown up in the area? Was it Graham's prematurely white hair, his all-season bicycling and refusal to drive a car? Was there something about us I didn't recognize, some odd mannerism or behavior? It was more likely sloppy reporting than anything else, but still, I was humiliated.

The social worker visited me and Frankie at home every week. Her name was Claire David, and she was new to the work, perhaps a little out of her depth. There was Graham's parasomnia, yes, but that was overshadowed by Frankie's speech, which commanded the majority of her attention. She did not mention, not once, the possibility of a connection between the two. She sent a language pathologist to the house, and for two hours the pathologist watched Frankie and me play while scribbling in a notebook. A week later, I received a seventeen-page report in the mail, saying more or less what we already knew: there was no obvious learning defect. Frankie had great capabilities with sign language, and if signs counted as words, his vocabulary would have been par for his age.

There was no law on the books with regards to property damaged during the act of sleepwalking. There was something complicated about choosing an insanity defense versus a guilty defense, and for a while we tried to sort out the best course of action, but in the end the charges were dropped, and Graham paid a fine. Claire David's responsibilities toward us were dropped as well. Graham returned home after two months in Detention, his second leave of absence from the university, to find that he had not been granted tenure. Coupled with my business's decline, it seemed to me as if the ground had swelled beneath us like a tidal wave, lifting us from every mooring. Then Larry Birnbaum called with news of the Rosenstiel fellowship, and Graham applied, and we found harbor.

The night we decided to leave Round Lake, Graham lay down and I helped him fasten his cuff for the first time. Graham joked—our first joke, since!—that if I went to sleep angry he might never be allowed to leave the bed again. Then he lay very still, his eyes on the ceiling. His smile faded.

"I've never been afraid like this before," he said.

"Not even after waking up in the street?"

"I'm not afraid of hurting myself," he said, clenching his teeth.

I knew the answer, but still I asked. "What are you afraid of?"

He blinked at me. "Of hurting Frankie," he said, then turned his back. He trembled and I wanted to reach out to him, but something kept me still. It was weeks before I allowed myself to take a sleeping pill again. Nights, I wandered the house, alert for noise. When I was forced to lay down, I lay in Frankie's bed instead of my own, and held him until I was lulled to sleep by the tide of his warm breath.

IT RAINED ALL DAY AFTER we arrived home from the Dry Tortugas. I dozed on the sectional sofa in the *Lullaby*'s salon, then woke to find Graham and Frankie sitting at the banquette. Graham had one leg crossed over the other—he wore his shirt tucked into his belted pants, and shoes laced up, even inside. Frankie sat on his knees in robot underwear and a T-shirt, a pair of blunt kid scissors in one hand. He leaned far over the table, looking as if he might tumble into his father's lap. Graham was cutting even strips from cardstock, then folding each into a shape. Littering the table were pieces of Graham's work: little boxes with folding lids, cranes with pointed beaks, accordions of various sizes.

Frankie looked away from Graham long enough to squeeze one of the accordions between two fingers, then let it go. It soared over the table and landed on the floor.

I watched them without moving or making any sound. Each piece Graham finished, he handed to Frankie, who inspected it from every angle. Then Frankie placed the treasure among the others, and looked eagerly to Graham to make another. Whether Graham gleaned any pleasure from impressing his watchful, adoring son, I couldn't tell. After some time, Graham glanced toward the sofa, and his eyes found mine—I would have closed them and pretended to sleep, but I was too late—and I had a vision of us all sitting together, marveling over Graham's creations. I saw how it might have been, him showing off and the two of us egging him on.

Instead, Graham took my wakefulness as a cue to excuse himself. He stood, stretched, and walked into the main berth. Frankie sat back on his feet, opening and closing the lids of each little box, sending the accordions springing across the table. Maybe a different child, a child with speech, would have said, "Sit down? Play with me?" But not my son.

I'd seen Graham's origami skills before. On our fourth date, in an Italian restaurant in Wrigleyville, Graham made a tiny collared shirt from a dollar bill. I'm sure the look on my face as I'd watched his bony fingers work had been similar to Frankie's. Graham had blushed as he passed the object into my hands. But for reasons I never understood, Graham had made the treasure for me willingly, a token of affection, while for Frankie he did it out of duty and boredom.

Maybe it was unfair of me, but I felt a rush of anger when Graham rose from the table. My husband could have been a very good father—of this I am certain. He had it somewhere in him, the cells of parenting cancer. Instead, for reasons I will never understand, the cancer stopped growing midcourse, a kind of medical miracle.

I wondered if by filling Frankie's life, I'd eliminated any place for Graham. I wondered if Graham loved me in spite of himself, and he didn't have room to love anyone else. I wondered if Graham gave up a piece of himself to make me a mother, and was resigned from the start to losing me in the process. Sometimes this is what I choose to believe—that he gave me himself, and when it seemed he wasn't enough (might he have been?), he gave me more at his own expense.

So what did I do? I got off the sofa and poured Frankie a glass of milk. I brought a stack of puzzles to the table and let him choose one for us to work on together. That night, sitting at the table on the back deck after Frankie was in bed, I gave Graham the cold shoulder. When he asked what was wrong, I seethed a minute longer, gathering my thoughts, then said, "Why don't you like spending time with your son?" My voice was full of grit.

He didn't say anything. I turned toward him, primed to fight, but found him slumped in his chair, his forearm over his face, his long, angular body shaking as he silently sobbed. The advancing army inside me dispersed. I pulled his arm from his face and forced him to look at me.

"I don't know what's wrong with me," he said.

"Something is missing," I said.

"I know it," he said. "I do."

He never promised he'd try to change, never reassured me things would get better. He never lied to me—I did that for myself.

11

GRAHAM LEFT FOR JACKSONVILLE IN a van full of scientists at the end of that week. I got up early to drive him to Rosenstiel, and Frankie sat on my hip, waving sloppily at Graham while the van pulled away. We ate eggs at the dive bar at Dinner Key marina, watching the dayboaters maneuver from their slips, then headed out to Stiltsville. While I worked, Charlie and Frankie sat in rocking chairs on the porch. (When we'd first come, there had been only one rocker, but then two more showed up, which led me to think that Charlie must have had a house on land, where furniture remained as if in storage.) They were eating fruit Popsicles. I couldn't see them from the office window, but I could hear the slurping.

Every so often, Frankie's noise paused.

"What's that?" I heard Charlie say.

I had the urge to stop working and translate for them, but Charlie had been doing pretty well figuring out Frankie for himself.

A motor chugged by. "Them?" Charlie said. "Just looky-loos. Smile and wave and they'll go on their way."

Minutes later, a louder boat roared by, and Charlie said, "That's more power than the fellow's ever going to need, I guarantee you. And he's going to run aground in—yep, there he goes."

I called out the window. "What happened?"

"Guy ran aground," called Charlie. To Frankie, Charlie said, "Stuck! How do you like that?"

From across the water came a man's faint curses.

"That fellow is not happy, I'll tell you," said Charlie, chuckling. "No sir."

I thought I heard a soft giggle from Frankie, but I couldn't be sure. The slurping resumed.

That night, Sally came over after Stanley and the boys were in bed. We sat cross-legged on Lidia's back lawn, a bottle of wine between us, a stone's throw from the *Lullaby*, which was dark and still. Frankie was in bed. I told Sally about the Dry Tortugas—the fort, the sea turtle, the green flash.

"I've never seen it," she said about the flash. "But I hear it's quick."

Across the canal, I could see the parents of the family that lived there carrying a couple of their kids to bed in a lighted room. Off went the overhead light and on went a lamp.

I said, "Do you ever think about not being married anymore?"

"All the time."

"Really?"

"Sure. The other day I was loading the dishwasher—for like the fifth time in a twenty-four-hour period, right?—and Maxwell comes in because he's peed the bed. Stanley's asleep in front of the TV with his shoes on, so I go and change Max's pajamas and sheets and put him back to bed, and I put Tuck back to bed, because by this time he's up, too, and then I go back to the living room and Stanley's still there, still sleeping. So I go over and untie his shoes and slip them off, and I'm actually having this tender moment, thinking about how much I love all these slobs who live in my house. And I start to go back to the dishwasher, but out of the corner of my eye I see this white thing sticking out of the sofa cushion."

The swimming pool gurgled lightly. "Okay," I said.

"So this thing is right next to Stanley's ass, and I go to look closer, and it looks to me like a sock—probably Tuck's, because he likes to do this thing where he hides his socks—and when I pull it out of the cushion, ever-so-gently, I accidentally bump Stanley with my elbow, and he rears back like he's been attacked. He has this look on his face like he's going to kill me. Seriously. Then he realizes where he is or whatever, because he's like, 'Oh, it's you. I was *sleeping.*'"

I refilled my glass. The lamplight in the bedroom across the canal had gone out, and in another bedroom, a light went on. There were the parents again, with two more children.

Sally went on. "So I walk back to the kitchen with this sock in my hand, and suddenly all I can see, all around, is the mess. Like this sock is covered in crumbs from beneath the sofa cushion, and how do you keep on top of that, anyway? And the living room is full of toys and the bookshelves are all askew, and I start thinking about the kids' closets and what a fucking disaster they are. And I think, 'I cannot do this one more day.'"

"So what happened?"

"Nothing. I left the dishes. I went to bed. I don't really want to do it all—I just want to stop *feeling* like I should be doing it all. Stanley came in and woke me up with his stupid snoring."

"So all's well."

"No. I mean, yes, but there's more. The next day I have to meet this client in Kendall, and it takes like half an hour to get there, so I put on public radio—sometimes I put it on, when I'm in a mood—and there's this show on about a guy who, get this, was raped twenty years ago, when he was just eight, by a neighbor kid, who was sixteen at the time."

"I warn you," I said. "My skin has thinned."

"I know. It's the kid thing. But you've got to hear this."

"Go on."

"So the guy's describing what happened while they're at this older kid's house and their parents are upstairs having cocktails, and the older kid is supposed to be showing him his action figures or something, and instead he tells him to take off his clothes and holds a knife to him until he does it."

"Oh my God."

"I know, horrible. I mean, I know kids get raped, right? I know sick things happen? But there's something about this story, about the guy telling it so calmly on the radio, that makes me want to be right back there in that kid's bedroom and just—" She strangled the air. "I get *rattled*."

"Right."

"So I can't stand hearing it, but I can't turn it off. And the guy describes how afterward, the kid made him watch TV until his tears dried, then let him go back to his parents."

I took a deep breath.

"I know, I know. But wait. So I'm still driving, listening to this story, and I'm so upset that I feel physically ill. So I turn off the radio, and I just keep driving for a minute, but then I start crying so hard that I can't see the road—because, you know, that poor kid, and also Tuck and Carson and Maxwell—so I pull off at a gas station and call Stanley. And he freaks out because he thinks I've been in an accident or something, so I tell him I'm okay. I can hear the boys in the background, fighting over something, and I start to calm down."

She shook out her hair, then continued. "So I finally tell him that I just heard this story on the radio, and I'll never listen to public radio again, and he says—you know, he's a Republican, so he says that sounds like a good decision. And then I tell him about that little boy, and the knife, and the goddamned TV. And he's real quiet, and I can hear the kids hollering, and I tell him I don't ever want our boys—any of them—left alone with a teenage boy, period. And he says, 'Okay, okay,' like he just wants me to calm down. And I tell him I mean it, not even Salvatore or Bryan—those are his sister's kids. Never again."

Sally looked at me, gauging my reaction. She said, "So I think he's going to get all reasonable with me, like he's going to try to talk me down even though I still feel like I might be sick. He's going to *reason* with me, I think, and defend Salvatore and Bryan, because of course they're good kids. But at that moment, to me, there's no good teenage boy in the world. And bear in mind that I'm raising three boys, and one day they'll be teenagers, and the thought of one of them doing that—I cannot stand it.

"So I have this thought. I think that if Stanley does this, if he tries to reason with me, I'll kill him. No, I won't really kill him, but I'll divorce him. I'll take all his money. And the boys are whooping it up in the background and I know they're about to need some intervention, but Stanley doesn't hang up. He says, like it's no problem, 'All right. We won't leave them alone.' And I start crying all over again, from relief."

I exhaled. "Good for Stanley."

Sally's voice was low and steady. "So I tell him that if anyone ever hurts one of our boys I'll kill him with my bare hands, and Stanley says I'll have to beat him to it." She shook her head, as if willing the story from her memory. "Anyway, long story, I know, but after I hung up with him I had this thought: I don't love him like I did. But I love him in a new way, and we are in this thing together. We are going to raise these children or die trying." She finished her wine and pulled her knees to her chest. "Does that sound like I'm making excuses?"

"No," I said honestly.

"I swear, if he'd gone the other way—if he'd told me to be reasonable—I think a little bit of the marriage would have died then and there."

Marriages die in pieces, I thought. That's how it happens. I said, "Graham left on a trip for work. A month, he thinks. I'd bet a thousand dollars it will be longer."

She sighed. "Maybe it will be good. Absence and the heart and all that."

All the lights in the house across the canal were out except for the muted blue flashing of a television. Then a light went on in the kitchen, and the husband walked in and pulled down a bottle from a high cabinet, and at the same time the wife appeared at the back door and headed toward the canal. At first I thought she was approaching us, for some reason, but there was barely any light in Lidia's backyard, and I doubted she could even see us sitting there. She carried something—a towel. I thought maybe she was going to the boat—it was a forty-foot cruiser, surely stocked with a TV and full bar—but then she stepped to the edge of the dock, dropped the towel and her blouse, and dove into the canal.

"Good Lord," said Sally. "Aren't there alligators in there? What the hell is she doing?"

"I have no idea," I said.

There were alligators in the canal, yes. I knew this because my father was always talking about how over time the creatures were growing bolder, as if they'd been observing us and decided we weren't much of a threat. Two or three times a year, one came right up onto the bank and snatched a dog from its lead. My father had said that he fully expected to hear a knock at the door one of these days, and open it to find an alligator barging in, demanding a cold beer and a shower.

We watched as the neighbor woman slipped quickly through the dark water, pale limbs scissoring. Then she rounded the bend and her wake settled, and it was as if she'd never been there at all.

FRANKIE'S APPOINTMENT WITH SALLY'S PEDIATRICIAN came up a week after Graham left. I'm not sure exactly what I'd expected, but while we were in the waiting room, a woman in a white coat stopped to pick up a file from the reception area, and this woman had a doll's pinched blond curls and a double chin and smart eyeglasses—

this, I guess, is more or less what I'd thought our doctor would look like. Instead, after an intake in the exam room with a kind-eyed nurse wearing floral scrubs, there was a quick knock on the door, and in walked Dr. Sonia. She was no more than five feet in heels, with an arched, handsome nose and severe brows. She had dark skin—she was Filipina, I guessed—and under her open white coat she wore a plunging silk blouse and tight pencil skirt and black pumps. She introduced herself with a slight accent and did not smile.

When I'd made the appointment, the receptionist had asked about specific concerns, and I'd explained the one as calmly as possible. Dr. Sonia scanned Frankie's file—the nurse had skittered out of the room—and asked me to hold Frankie in my lap.

"Vaccinations?" she said as she listened to his chest.

I told her we'd been up to date until he was two, but we'd fallen behind since then. All of Frankie's records had been sent; I think the doctor just wanted me to acknowledge my own delinquency. When she asked Frankie to say "Ahh," he opened his mouth but didn't say anything. She checked his lymph nodes, his reflexes, his ears. When she was done, she inched back in her chair and regarded Frankie.

"He needs Hep B. The others can wait. Runny noses that don't seem to quit? Recurring fevers?"

"No," I said.

"So just the one thing," she said.

"Just the one thing." I smoothed the hair behind Frankie's ear. He looked back and forth between us, as if he knew what was coming next.

To Frankie, Dr. Sonia said, "You don't like to talk?"

He pushed out his lower lip and jutted his chin.

"Tell me," she said to me.

Frankie wriggled off my lap and beelined for a basket of books and toys in the corner. It was clear that Dr. Sonia was not a person who would suffer a mother unhinging in her office, so I steadied my voice. "It started when he was a year and a half. He'd been talking a little, a few words here and there, and then he stopped. It happened quickly, within a couple of months. Every so often he makes sounds, but not words." I thought of him crying in the hotel in Round Lake, laughing with Charlie at the stilt house. "They haven't found any kind of—" I moved my hands futilely, and all appropriate phrases left me. "They haven't found anything wrong with him. He listens, he communicates, he pays attention. He signs all day long, we both do. He's a great kid. He's *great*." My words felt very forceful leaving my mouth.

She regarded me, then turned to him. "Frankie," she said. "You don't want to talk?"

Frankie held up a toy bulldozer. I signed: *Speak?* He shook his head.

"Why not?" she said.

How long had it been since I'd even asked him? Had it been an entire year?

He came over and stood close, studying her face.

"We know you can hear," she said to him. She cupped his ears with her birdlike hands, then tugged on the lobes. "These are working, I think." He nodded. She rapped lightly on his skull. "Seems like this works, too."

He smiled.

She opened a drawer and pulled out a handful of flash cards showing pictures of animals: a cow, a dinosaur, a brown bear, a frog, a rabbit. "Frankie," she said, holding up the dinosaur card, "do you know what this guy says when he talks?"

Frankie nodded.

"Can you please tell me?"

He opened his mouth. He gave a very low roar. I took a breath.

She went on. "That's about right. But dinosaurs are very big and very scary, so they make a little more noise." She held up the cow card. "Can you tell me what this guy says?"

Frankie *moo*ed, then jumped a little in place and eyed the other cards in Dr. Sonia's lap. One by one, they went through each: the pig snorted, the bear growled, the frog croaked, all softly but clearly. When she got to the rabbit, she said, "Rabbits are quiet, but can you show me how they move?"

Frankie squatted, hands on the floor, and then he was off. He crossed the room, hop by hop, then returned the same way. A nurse came in and left a tray with a hypodermic needle and a vial, and Frankie stood up and eyed it suspiciously.

"Do you know what a shot is?" said Dr. Sonia.

Frankie nodded.

"And what sound does a boy make when he gets a shot?" said Dr. Sonia.

"Ow," said Frankie. Each sound was bracing, like a fall of cold water over my head.

"That's right," she said. She readied the needle. "Are you ready to say 'ow'?"

Frankie nodded. She leaned down and pulled up the hem of his shorts.

"Ow!" said Frankie. He rubbed his leg and glowered at her.

"You're like a voodoo doctor," I said to her.

"That only works once," she said. "Frankie, what's your favorite thing to do?"

He arced one arm, then the other.

"Swim?" she said, and he nodded. "What else do you like to do?"

He mimed casting a line.

"Fish," she said, nodding. "What else?"

He signed again: one hand flat and the other scrawling above it, pinkie finger out.

"Draw?" she said, and he nodded.

This was a recent development. He'd always enjoyed crayons and paper, but not until we'd started going out to Stiltsville had Frankie's interest deepened. Charlie had given him a box of colored pencils and a sketch pad, and was teaching him to draw human figures using a wooden manikin that moved at all the joints.

"Just as I suspected," said Dr. Sonia. "I like all of those things. And I like to be quiet, which I know you like. But sometimes I like to talk, too."

He knitted his brow. She got up and opened the door and called for the nurse, who appeared immediately. "Ten minutes," Dr. Sonia said, indicating Frankie. To Frankie, she said, "Get yourself a lollipop." He followed the nurse into the hall.

Dr. Sonia put a box of tissues in my lap. "All right," she said. "Here's what I see. He hears fine. Maybe there was some early hearing loss that wasn't caught, but I doubt it. There's a language and speech person I work with. Call her from the front desk, make an appointment. Tell her I said to make it speedy. Let's double-check what's already been checked, just in case."

"Okay," I said.

She picked up a pen. "How does he eat?"

"Fine."

"Any siblings?"

"No."

"How does he sleep?"

"Fine."

"What hours?"

"Down around seven, up around eight."

She frowned. "That's too much. Naps?"

"One, a couple of hours or so."

"Too much," she said again. "Stress in the family? Changes?"

"We just moved here. There's been some stress, yes."

"Divorce?"

"No."

"Do you want me to guess?"

I stammered. "There—there was an incident, back in Illinois.

Frankie's father has a—sleep disorder. He went through a window in the middle of the night. Frankie saw it happen."

She scribbled quickly. "Listen," she said, "when the speech therapist gets to your place, I want you to tell her what you just told me."

My mouth was so dry I couldn't lick my lips, couldn't swallow. "He stopped talking long before that."

"Just tell her."

"Okay."

She sighed. "There's something called *selective mutism*. I can't say for sure that's what's going on, but it's my best guess."

"I've never heard of that. Why haven't I heard of that?" I thought of the first, lengthy visit from the language pathologist back at the cottage, all those hours with the social worker.

"It's not easy to diagnose. And it's not something they'd just toss out."

I tried to speak evenly. "Maybe you think I'm an idiot. But I spend every day with my son. I spend every waking minute with him."

She tilted her head. "Why?"

"Why what?"

"Why do you spend every waking minute with him?"

I felt a surge of defensiveness. "I don't understand."

"Have you thought about preschool?"

"I thought maybe next year—"

"Put him in preschool. Two or three days a week, at least," she said. "Look, some kids don't need preschool, some do. It's not easy to let go—I know, I have four. I stayed home with the youngest until I'd forgotten how to dress myself."

This gave me pause over my own outfit, one of a few similar cotton skirts I wore almost every day, and a sleeveless blue T-shirt.

She continued. "We're not perfect teachers just because we're good mothers."

"You're saying—"

"I'm not saying it's your fault he doesn't speak." She placed one chilly hand on my shoulder, then took it away. "I don't know why he doesn't speak. Could be something, could be nothing. But most kids Frankie's age talk a great deal, and he doesn't. He needs to be around other kids. He can't talk like you talk, but my guess is that he can talk."

It was an enormous relief, this courage of conviction, this fortitude. But it made me feel spineless and ineffectual, which were two things I'd never thought of myself.

She saw my doubt. "I know," she said. "You wake up, you fix food, you clean up, you go to the store, you read him a book, fix more food. Then it's a new day."

"Yes," I said.

"And there's other stuff going on, sleepwalking husbands, what have you."

"Preschool?" I said.

"And the speech pathologist. Back here in a month, please."

She left the room, taking most of the oxygen with her, and the nurse returned with Frankie. We made an appointment at the front desk and walked to the car, each breath in my lungs deeper than the last.

On the way home, we were detoured by construction on LeJeune, and ended up on Ponce de Leon, a pretty street hedged by low coral walls and smooth pink sidewalks and ponytail palms. As I made my way around a neatly landscaped traffic circle, I noticed an unassuming storefront on the far side: the Abyss Gallery.

I parked and pulled Frankie out of his car seat. Just inside the gallery was a wall that ran parallel to the door, so not until we'd navigated the wall did we spot a cluster of frames filling one corner of the deep room. A man came from the back and I told him we were just looking. I made for the corner, where Charlie's name, CHARLES F. HICKS, was painted neatly across the wall in handsome letters. Above and beside his name were the prints I'd chosen—the drowning clipper ship, the menacing sea snake, the sparring sea horses. Since I'd last seen them,

Henry Gale had shaded them in jewel colors, which had given them depth and soul. And Henry had done something a little different with these: he'd burnished the shadows, lending the emerald and ruby and aquamarine a sinister appearance. Together, Henry's talent and Charlie's talent added up to something greater than their sum. Henry must have brought the portraits to the gallery himself, or sent a messenger. I hadn't been to the print shop in more than a week.

Beside me, Frankie stared. In his hand was a small brown walrus, the most recent addition to his collection. When he saw me watching him, his hand came up, pointing. And surely it was Dr. Sonia and her game, her commanding presence, but still nothing could have prepared me for what happened next. My son spoke one word, clear as sunlight: "Charlie!"

12

EVERY TIME I ARRIVED AT Stiltsville, I experienced a strong sense of inverted, irrational nostalgia. It was as if rather than being there in that moment, I was somewhere else, wishing I could be there. It wasn't unlike the feeling I had sometimes after putting Frankie to bed, even after a long day, even if I'd been relieved to say good night—sometimes I was seized by the desire to wake him just to be in his presence again, to reassure myself of him. The strange reverse-nostalgia itched at me every time I stepped from the boat to the stilt house dock, and it was several minutes before I could slough it off and relax. I think as much as anything else it was a weighty sense of gratitude, as well as the foreknowledge that whatever this was—this occupation, this friendship, this parallel life—it would not last forever.

In the forty-eight hours since Frankie had spoken Charlie's name, I had been unable to make contact with Graham. I'd known that once he was transferred to the research ship, which was called the *R. V. Roger Revelle*, getting him on the phone would be something of an ordeal, involving a message center on land that routed emergency calls and other messages, and a shared ship phone meant to be used sparingly. But until that time—and he wasn't scheduled to be transferred for a few more days—he was staying in a business hotel in Jacksonville with his colleagues and the team from Scripps, and I'd assumed getting in touch would be as easy as calling his room. This hadn't been the case. I'd left three messages at the front desk. Once, Lidia had taped a note to the screen door of the *Lullaby* saying he'd called me back on her line— there was no phone line leading out to Lidia's pier, which was a logistical complication that hadn't occurred to me when we'd bought the boat. The message, written in Lidia's sloppy script, had read: *Graham got your messages. Has been very, very busy. Love.*

Since I couldn't tell Graham, I told Lidia, who shrieked and squashed Frankie to her bosom, and Sally, who also shrieked. I planned to tell Charlie as soon as we saw him next. But when he came down the stilt house stairs to greet us, shirt unbuttoned and bare feet slapping the wood, talking about taking Frankie for a walk on the flats while the tide was still low—the impulse faded. I suppose I was sheepish about telling him because I hadn't yet told Graham, and because he figured so prominently in the story. Also, I wondered if he would appreciate the significance of what had happened, the magic of it. I'd already convinced myself not to make too much of Graham's response. Rather than being jubilant, as I'd been, it was likely he'd be impatient, as if I was excited over what amounted to very little. At the library, picking up books for Charlie, I'd read a little about selective mutism, and what I'd learned was not encouraging. In two days, Frankie's voice was already fading from my memory, but still each time I recalled it, I felt a shiver of glee.

Charlie handed Frankie a toy scuba diver, and Frankie rose to his toes, bouncing a little, and signed his thanks.

"We're off, then," said Charlie. "Okay, Mama?"

"Be good," I said to Frankie. I handed over the sunscreen and carried Charlie's cooler upstairs.

Some days, it was so hot and humid in the office, despite all the open windows, that the pages wilted in my hands. I wet my hair in the bathroom sink and wore a bandanna around my forehead to keep sweat from dripping onto the paper. Later that afternoon, while Frankie napped, Charlie sat in the low chair in the corner of the office, working on correspondence that he would send back with me to the mainland: letters to his wife and Henry Gale and Riggs, and usually at least one message for a curator interested in showing his work, which I would deliver. He silently steamed in the heat, breathing hard through his nose, his face flushed. He seemed to be making a point of not complaining, so I kept quiet until I couldn't take it anymore, at which point I simply said, "This heat is insufferable."

Charlie was out of his chair and heading into the hallway as soon as I spoke. I stayed where I was, kneeling in front of a pile of leatherback sea turtles—these had started to appear after I told Charlie what had happened in the Dry Tortugas—until he returned with a towel, which he tossed at me. "Let's go," he said.

Frankie had been asleep just under an hour. "I can't—"

"We'll be quick. Hurry up."

I found him on the porch, one leg over the railing. Balancing, he pulled off his shirt and dropped it to the deck, then swung over his other leg. I came up beside him and looked down at the jade water. The tide had risen—I could tell because it swallowed the barnacle line on the pilings—but beyond the patch of water, the dock doglegged. If I jumped too far from the house, I'd land on wood.

He saw the concern on my face. "Straight down," he said.

I was already wearing my suit, so I dropped my shorts and T-shirt to the deck and climbed over the rail. He put out his arm to steady me. Once we were seated side by side on the railing, we looked at each other. We were both grinning. His face took on a boyishness when he smiled; the lines around his mouth and eyes swapped their age for youth, his light eyes brightened. It was easy to forget, sometimes, that he was a quarter-century older than I was. He maneuvered until he was standing on the outside ledge, holding on behind his back. I did the same.

"Let's go at the same time," I said.

He put out his hand and we threaded fingers, which I hadn't expected.

He counted to three and we jumped. I lost his hand after we submerged. The water was warm and I let myself sink, landing softly on the seabed before coming up into the heat. We climbed onto the dock and wrapped ourselves in towels, then went back to work.

Half an hour later, I looked up. Charlie felt my attention on him and raised his eyes. I said, "We stopped by the Abyss Gallery on Monday."

He rested his cheek in his hand and waited.

"I don't want to make a big deal out of it," I said. "But when Frankie saw your art, he spoke."

"What did he say?"

I stared at the sea turtle in my hand, at the encyclopedia page beneath the artwork. The heading read: MINES AND MINING. "Just one word," I said. "Your name."

When I looked up, Charlie had one hand pressed to his lips, but I could tell he was smiling. "Isn't that something?" he said.

Later, after we'd made our way back to the *Lullaby*, I sent Frankie up the lawn with Lidia to take a bath, and set to cleaning out the tote I'd used since arriving in Miami. I threw out receipts and a half-eaten granola bar and a pair of dirty socks of Frankie's that I'd been carrying around for at least two weeks, and then I noticed something unfamiliar at the bottom of the bag. I pulled it out and held its dense weight in my palm, running a fingernail over the rough surface. It was a couple of inches tall, painted in antiqued powder blue. Hair in ropes, stomach tautly curved, fin flipped in motion: it was a small cast-iron mermaid, scalloped tail folded beneath her and one hand behind her head, expression a little wistful. I set her on the ledge above the sink while I washed dishes, but the feeling she gave me—hollow and exposed, as if I were being watched—rose up, and I took her to my berth and stashed her deep in the storage trundle. I returned to the salon, my heart beating fast.

But I needed to see her again. I retrieved her from the bunk and settled her on the windowsill above the kitchen sink, and that is where she stayed.

JELLYFISH SEASON CAME EARLY THAT year. I was in the office and Charlie and Frankie were sitting in the rocking chairs on the porch, taking turns with a pair of binoculars. Through the window, I heard Charlie say, "What is it?" When I looked out, I saw Frankie make the sign we'd learned, one hand against the other, pulling away and moving back again.

"What's that?" Charlie said.

I blurted, "Jellyfish!"

"They're early," said Charlie when I came out to the porch.

I couldn't see them at first, but a moment after they appeared the water was thick with them. They came in a wind sock pattern, a leviathan in aggregate, dense at the start before petering out. Charlie told us this was called a *bloom*, that it happened every summer, usually not until August. It was still only mid-July, but there had been a rash of small storms in the Atlantic, and they'd washed in prematurely.

We went down to the dock to watch them advance. These were moon jellies, the umbrellas cloudy along the rims and a bud of pink at the heart. Before the first one crossed in front of the dock, there was a flurry in my peripheral vision, and I turned to see Charlie drop his shirt and dive into the water. Frankie looked up at me and I gripped his shoulders. Charlie surfaced, facing the advancing battalion.

I called, "What are you doing?"

"Swimming!"

He dove again. When he came up, he was in the thick of the bloom, less than a foot from a jellyfish in every direction. He dove again and came up again in a different place. Each time he came up, he looked around to get his bearings, keeping his arms in close and staying buoyant using just his legs, and once—he was yards down the channel by this time, hemmed in on every side—he gingerly lifted one arm to wave. Frankie waved back. The look in Frankie's eyes as he watched Charlie was of pure amazement.

There was a feeling I'd had several times in my life, including when I realized I was in love with Graham: it was the smidgen of sadness that, at least for me, always accompanies happiness. The disquieting underbelly of loss that comes with getting something you badly want. The thing I'd always understood, even before my mother got sick, was that anything started will inevitably end, anything loved will be lost. I suppose it was possible that Frankie could see the dark underside of joy in my eyes when he looked up at me. Charlie was too distant to see it. He'd reached the far side of the bloom unharmed, and was treading back up the channel behind the jellies, like a shepherd. All he could see from that distance were my arms beckoning him back to us, my mouth open in laughter.

I SAID NOTHING TO CHARLIE about what I'd found in my bag. I didn't know how long it had been there, and as far as I knew—this is what I told myself—it had come from Frankie, lifted somewhere in a fit of love. It might even have come from Graham, though gifts from Graham had always tended to be practical in nature, sunglasses or a sweater or a new radio for my car. The following week, I was tasked with culling pieces for another show at the Abyss—Henry Gale had mentioned, in a giddy way that I found sweet, that the "Battles of the Deep" show had sold out—and I started with some of the recent sea turtles. I chose an eel and a couple of jellyfish, a squid and a nautilus, a starfish and seashell. The show would be called, simply, "Sea Creatures."

As I was moving boxes, reorganizing, a paper on Charlie's desk caught my eye. The desk was normally bare but for the pencils and eraser and sharpener—I'd seen him stand there only a few times—but today, beneath a glass saltshaker half-filled with rice, there was a drawing. It was rough and lined, not shaded like the others. The girl's hair was a little longer than mine, her arms and shoulders a touch more toned—and there was the matter of the scalloped tail and ridged dorsal fin. But there was no mistaking the rough curls and dark eyes and inky eyebrows, the plump cheeks, the beauty mark above the lip, the pointed chin, the spray of lines at the corner of each eye. She was seated on a dock with her tail curled beside her, her palm flat on the wood, and she smiled with her mouth open a little, as if she'd just come to the end of a sentence.

It was incredible, seeing myself rendered in Charlie's hand. It had been a long time since I'd considered—really considered—what I looked like.

When I was nineteen, home from my first year of college, my dying grandmother had lived in our guest room, occupying my mother's every bit of energy. They'd sat talking in bed in the mornings before I was up, a tray of coffee and toast between them, and once, after I'd woken early to meet Sally for windsurfing lessons, I'd overheard my mother and grandmother agreeing offhandedly that my "plain" face was mitigated, gratefully, by my "spectacular hair" and "lovely bosoms." I'd stopped short outside the room. They'd gone on to talk about, of all things, tea towels—how a few well-considered tea towels could freshen the look of an entire kitchen. The two conversations—my plain looks and the restorative powers of tea towels—have always been paired in my mind. As an adult, I came to realize that the notion about well-chosen tea towels was correct. I felt I had no choice but to agree that the assertion about my appearance was correct as well.

My mother never would have said such a thing to my face, even backhandedly. The most she'd ever said to me was that a little lipstick gives a girl some color. To hear her speak so unprotectively of my face was as jarring as it might have been to hear her having an orgasm. I left the house that morning red-faced, without saying good-bye.

My "lovely bosoms" had come early. I'd worn a training bra in third grade. Later, my friends would still be praying like zealots for the arrival of their own breasts while I'd taken to wearing oversize shirts to hide mine. My mother, also large-breasted, indulged my oversize-clothing phase and let me wear T-shirts over my swimsuits.

But it was my walk, not my face or premature breasts, that plagued my teenage years. I begged for lessons with a modeling coach to sort out my pigeon-toed gait. My father, after a particularly good tour season, relented, and the summer I was fifteen I spent Saturday mornings at the Fontainebleau hotel with an acting and modeling coach named Priscilla Teague. Again and again, I walked the length of a catwalk under Mrs. Teague's critical gaze, starting over each time my feet turned inward. I left every session close to tears. My mother begged me to quit. She told me I was perfect in her eyes, that this silly thing did not matter, that it was barely noticeable to anyone but me. I persevered, and the lessons did help to some extent, though still my natural walk comes through when I'm tired or self-conscious.

This mermaid version of me, filtered through Charlie's generous lens, came as a great relief. I wished my mother could have seen it.

Beside the mermaid on the dock were several small objects. It took a moment for me to sort out what they were, not because they weren't accurately portrayed but because I was having trouble focusing. My heart had quickened and my vision had blurred, as if I were underwater. Finally, I recognized them: a shark, a conch, and a scuba diver. Frankie's toys. I heard Charlie's steps in the hallway and looked up to see my discovery register on his face. From beyond him came the sounds of Frankie arranging bowls on a tray for lunch, his little feet shuffling.

I said, "Is this me?"

"Of course," Charlie said. He crossed his arms over his chest and cleared his throat.

"I love it."

"Good, because they want more. I'm working on a whole slew of Georgia mermaids."

"Really?"

"That one's just a sketch. Keep it. Call it a modeling fee."

He lingered a moment, then turned away. I found a plastic sleeve and slipped the drawing into my bag. I stood at the window and took in the sea air. Next door, Charlie's neighbors—husband and wife, no sign of the daughter—were poised to jump together off their porch the way we'd jumped off Charlie's. Their arms waved joyfully all the way down.

I SENT OFF A PACKAGE for baby Jennifer, kicky pants and matching cardigan and cream-colored loafers, and the following week when I checked Charlie's post office box, there was a letter with a Seattle postmark. In the car outside the post office, I held the envelope to the sunlight, and though I couldn't make out words, I could see that it was comprised of a few handwritten pages. When I handed the mail to Charlie, I saw him register the envelope, and though he didn't open it in my presence, it seemed to please him.

New mermaid drawings appeared. He didn't put them in boxes with the others. He left them on the standing desk—I pictured him there, one foot balanced on the other in that way he had, drawing me—and I sorted through them myself.

We didn't chitchat a great deal, Charlie and I. But once, while we were both in the office and Frankie was lying on his belly in the corner, working with his colored pencils, I found myself describing my failed business, all the way from how I'd started in the admissions office and worked my way up, to how my last client had told me, red fingernail stabbing the air in front of my face, that if her daughter didn't make it into her safety school, I would hear from their attorney. When I finished, Charlie was stifling a smile.

"What?" I said.

"Nothing."

"What?"

"I just—well, you don't strike me as particularly—how do I put it? Authoritative."

"I know," I said.

"Don't pout. I'd hire you. But I can just picture these nervous parents and their mopey kids. Everyone expecting you to perform a miracle."

"I didn't perform miracles. I wasn't trying to. I just wanted the kids to—concentrate, I guess. Show their best selves. I had this idea that if they would all just quit it with the oboe lessons and the volunteering on weekends, if they were sincere and knew what I knew about what colleges really want, even if they knew which colleges wouldn't want them in a million years—I thought I could help them get through it. I know it sounds naive."

"Maybe a little." He chuckled and shook his head. "I'm sorry. Desperate parents—you stood no chance."

I'd never thought of it this way, as doomed to fail from the start, like when a little shop opens up and the minute you see how the window is arranged, you know it'll be gone in a month. I'd been retracing my steps, trying to figure out where exactly I'd gone wrong. This other way of thinking about it was worse in a way, but in a way it was a relief.

"Don't dwell," he said, waving a hand.

This struck me as funny in itself. I laughed and he looked confused. I wiped my eyes. In front of me on the linoleum was a mess of sea animals, all seeming to swim together in the same brew. It struck me suddenly that it was possible, what Charlie had said—that it was no big deal that I'd wasted thousands of dollars and run a business into the ground. That I'd made foolish choices and had no one to blame but myself. Maybe all I'd needed after it happened was someone to tease me a bit, to take it all less seriously.

Once a week, we took the Zodiac to Soldier Key and roamed the beach. I forced Frankie into water wings—I'd bought them against the advice of his swim teacher—and both he and Charlie balked. "They reassure me," I said firmly, and they shut up about it. Frankie played a game where he tiptoed through the shallow water wearing his mask, then dipped quickly under, to spy on the fish as they went about their lives. He was undeterred by a lack of goings-on, and every so often, when he did manage to catch sight of a fish darting past, he squealed audibly. The sound thrilled me.

Charlie and I watched him from the shade of the hammocks at the water's frothy edge. I said, "My mother would have adored him. I mean, she really would have *adored* him." I felt the inadequacy of my own words.

Charlie cleared his throat. "I knew your mother a little."

I looked at him, his silver-stubbled jaw and lined eyes.

He kept his gaze on Frankie. He said, "Once, after Jenny died, I came home to this terrible racket in my house. Inside, there was your mother sitting at my piano, playing—"

"'A Mighty Fortress'?"

He nodded. "I must say—"

"She did not sing well."

"No, she did not. But she was belting it out, I'll tell you. And Viv and another lady were sitting there with their glasses raised, singing along. I said hello and went into the kitchen. Sometimes women can be a little intimidating, I find."

The image of Charlie shuffling in the doorway while my mother sang a rousing rendition of one of the three hymns she knew how to play, her fingers sliding around, missing every fifth or sixth note—it was easy to picture. "Probably best you got out of there," I said.

"I met your father once or twice. He was never one for the social stuff. I remember thinking we were probably two of a kind."

"Not really."

"As husbands go . . ." he said, but then he didn't finish his sentence. He said, "She was around a lot, in those days, usually when I wasn't home. Vivian said they laughed a lot. People get uncomfortable—it's not their fault—but not your mother."

"No, not her."

I'm not sure I ever saw my mother uncomfortable. I would have liked to ask her about this, to see if maybe there was some trick to it. How could we have been so alike in so many ways, and so unalike in this one?

The other hymns she knew by heart were "We Are Marching in the Light of God" and "I Love to Tell the Story." She could play a couple of others—"Amazing Grace" included—haltingly, with close peering at the sheet music. I had the urge to sit in that room, on the evening of Charlie's memory, and sing along. It was nothing I would have enjoyed while she was alive.

I said, "What happened after that?"

"What do you mean?"

"Did she stop coming over?"

He tossed a clump of seaweed into the shallows. "I doubt it. I don't know what happened next. I came here."

People get uncomfortable, I thought.

Frankie had gone from trying to catch the fish in his sights to trying to catch them with his hands. He ran to and fro, knees high, splashing and lunging, laughing in his soundless way each time he came up empty.

Charlie pointed to my boy. "She would have thought he hung the moon. She would have thought he was—" He took a breath. "Magical."

I sat quietly in the warm surf, letting this wash over me.

He said, "And you—she would've been damn proud."

ON THE WAY HOME FROM Soldier Key, Charlie throttled down, then killed the engine as we drifted over a shoal. Frankie and I looked at him for an explanation, and he said, "I have something to show you."

"What?" I said.

What? signed Frankie.

To Frankie, he said, "A while back I told your mom that I used to have a boat." He stepped to port and searched the water. "There," he said, pointing.

We peered into the clear, sunlit water. At first I didn't see much of anything, just sand spotted here and there with sea cucumber and ur- chins. But then we drifted, and into view came the white hull of a small boat, upended on the ocean floor.

"Your boat?" I said.

What happened? signed Frankie.

"Sank," said Charlie.

"How?" I said.

"My best guess? Hose clamp failed. It was late, getting dark."

The stilt house was half a mile away, maybe more. "What did you do? Did you swim?"

"Sure," he said. "But I hung around for a while first, to watch it go down."

"And you just left it here."

He shrugged. "Not much choice. All the maintenance, all the fuel—I was glad to be rid of it."

Frankie signed and I laughed.

"What?" said Charlie, looking between us.

"He said you littered," I said.

"Ha! Want to see more litter?"

Frankie nodded.

"You got it," said Charlie. He started the engine and turned away from the capsized boat, then puttered east, staring hard into the water. He cut the engine and told me to throw the anchor. "You'll need your mask," he said to me. "I'll take the boy down first."

It was an oft-ignored boating rule, I knew, to never leave a vessel unattended when anchored. Climbing into the Zodiac was a breeze— there was a level surface on the engine at exactly the right height—but still I appreciated his prudence. He helped Frankie adjust his mask, then jumped in and told Frankie to swim to him. He held him loosely on the surface as they peered into the green depths. They swam a few yards from the boat, then Frankie kicked excitedly and raised his face, waving with both hands and squirming in Charlie's arms.

I don't know the word! he signed.

"Let's surprise her," said Charlie to Frankie.

They peered down again, and after a few minutes returned to the boat, and it was my turn. I swam to where they'd been, my face in the water. What emerged from the depths did so abruptly, as if a curtain had been drawn. The plane of its lid was unnaturally black, the curve of its case instantly recognizable. I could see, scattered in the sand, a few ivory keys, and when I'd come to the far side of it, the keyboard itself was revealed, broken and dipping. A yellow fish darted into a crack. The whole thing had settled deeply into the seafloor, splintered and flattened like a crushed can. It must have been dropped from a good height.

"Crazy, right?" said Charlie when I climbed aboard.

What's the word? Frankie signed.

"Piano," I said. "We'll look it up."

"*Grand* piano," Charlie said.

To Charlie I said, "Do you know how it got here?"

He shrugged. "I figure someone was sick of practicing."

FRANKIE ASKED TO FISH EVERY time we arrived at Stiltsville, usually right after depositing whatever toy Charlie handed over into one of his little pockets. Unless the bay was too choppy, Charlie took him on the Zodiac for an hour or so while I worked. Sometimes I went along. Once, we drove out to the flats east of the radio tower, a stone's throw from the continental shelf, where the waves rose and the water darkened. Charlie handed me his rod so he could dig in my bag for snacks, and while I was holding it, there came a tug that nearly pulled the thing from my grip. I braced myself against the gunwale and struggled for some time, gaining ground and losing it. Charlie and Frankie whooped, Charlie with his voice and Frankie with his arms. For several long minutes, I was possessed—it is the only word—by the fight. My heart beat forcefully. When finally I was able to wrestle the struggling fish from the water, we saw that it was not a bonefish or sea trout or sea bass or tarpon, all of which we were used to catching and throwing back or frying up for lunch—it was a young bull shark, thirty or so pounds. The black eyes were mad with what looked to me like fear.

"Let him go!" I shouted to Charlie.

He got behind me and helped reel. The shark struggled. By the time we had him in the boat, we were both sweating and Frankie had moved to the prow, as far as he could get without going over, his eyes wide. Without thinking, I placed both hands on the shark's flank to keep him still—his skin was rough as a cat's tongue, the richest color of gray I'd ever seen—and Charlie lodged one foot in his mouth and reached in. Charlie pulled away the hook and I wrestled the shark over the side and dropped it, and we watched as he spent one stunned second hanging there, then flashed away.

"Mercy," said Charlie, breathing hard. To Frankie, he said, "Your mom's been holding out on us, kiddo."

That afternoon while Frankie slept, Charlie sat in his armchair, sifting through mail and peering down at it through his bifocals. I was supposed to take selections for the new Abyss show over to Henry Gale the next day, but I was having trouble choosing. I'd narrowed the field to twenty-one pieces, and I needed only fifteen. Charlie had made it clear that he wasn't interested in this part of the process. He had never so much as seen his work framed on a wall.

"Seriously," I said to him, facing the grid of drawings I'd laid out on the floor. "I can't decide. You have to help."

He didn't look up. "Close your eyes and point."

"I'm not going to do that."

"You're overthinking," he said. "As you tend to."

"Can I ask you a question?"

"Here we go," he said.

I waited.

"Yes," he said.

But I didn't know what I wanted to ask, exactly. I was keyed up from my battle with the bull shark, and I'd been thinking—this was near constant—about Frankie's speech and our appointment with Dr. Sonia and what I wasn't doing that I needed to be doing, what kind of mother I was and what kind I wasn't. One of the reasons I loved Stiltsville was the way it could blot out my anxieties, leaving only glimpses of the real world, like sunlight across a windshield. Today, though, I was agitated. Our appointment with the speech therapist was a few days off.

I said, "What should I be teaching Frankie? What's the most important thing for him to learn?"

Charlie pressed his hand to his cheek. "Kindness," he said.

This was reassuring. "I can handle that."

He started to go back to his work, but I stopped him.

"If you heard about me and Frankie," I said, "if you'd never met us and you just heard about us, about his not talking, and about us living on a boat and coming here and Graham being away. If you knew all that and nothing else—what would you think?"

He blinked at me, frowning. "I don't understand."

"Do you think—" I exhaled heavily. "Would you think we were strange? Would you be put off?"

"Put off? No."

"Would you pity us?"

"No."

I felt as if a strong wind had blown open a hatch inside me. My voice went high and breathless. "Would it sound like I was a bad mother?"

I put my hands on the warm linoleum and tried to focus on them, blinking back hot tears. Charlie came to my side and took up the same position, kneeling with both hands flat. His shoulder pressed against mine, his elbow against my elbow. For a while we stayed there, and then he said, "I would think none of those things."

I took a deep breath. "Sometimes I think that when I had Frankie, I became a little bit crazy. And a little bit invisible."

"Invisible to whom?" he said, ignoring the crazy part, which was diplomatic of him.

"I don't know."

And I really didn't know. Not to Graham—that wouldn't be fair. Graham still saw me, though I suspected he saw only the old me and turned away from what had mutated in me. Certainly I was invisible to Frankie, the way air and water were invisible, food and clothing and shelter; invisible to him as my own mother had been to me, as was his right.

"I'm being self-indulgent, I know," I said, shaking my head.

"Quiet," he said. In front of us, the drawings swam in their grid, becoming less and less distinct, as if they'd been left in the sunlight and had started to fade. I felt Charlie's eyes on me. He said, "You should have seen yourself today, reeling in that shark. You looked like you were fighting for your life."

He replaced his bifocals. His knees cracked as he rose. After he was seated again in his armchair, he spoke again. "We couldn't take our eyes off you."

LATER THAT WEEK, CHARLIE SAT down to start a pair of slippers for Simon. He'd used Frankie's feet as a guide, then sized up a little, and had taken my suggestion to line them with fleece instead of cotton. Casting on was the hard part, and he cursed a few times and unwound the yarn, then dropped his hands to his lap.

"You seem distracted," I said, and he grunted.

Intending to lighten the mood, I said, "You know, I think I'll finish by the end of month." I indicated the marked boxes that lined the wall. They were all filled with neatly labeled folders, and in each folder were portraits cased in individual plastic sleeves.

His voice was stone. "I would have thought you'd be finished by now."

I was stunned. He stared into his lap and made no move to continue with the slippers. He said, "I apologize."

I said nothing. He sighed and left the room, and after Frankie woke they went downstairs for a swim. We'd been staying later and later, almost to dinnertime, but that day I toweled off Frankie and packed us up before three o'clock. Charlie had arranged a big bowl of fruit for Frankie to practice drawing, and when I announced we were leaving early, Frankie signed histrionically in protest; I had to pick him up and carry him, kicking, down the stairs. Charlie dropped the lines into the Zodiac and I busied myself raising the engine and starting the motor. I knew I was being petulant, but I couldn't help myself. I hadn't realized how proud I'd been of the work, how protective of it.

"Check your bag," Charlie called out as I pulled away. When I got home, I took my tote into the main berth. In it I found a note written in that meticulous hand. It read: I'M A GRUMP. NOTHING TO DO WITH YOU. SO GRATEFUL. PLEASE FORGIVE. —C.

And the next time we saw each other, after I'd tied off and pushed the cooler onto the dock and climbed up, he touched my hair quickly—this was something he'd never done—and cleared his throat, then announced that he was very glad to see us.

three

13

GRAHAM AND I CONTINUED TO swap phone messages, including on the day of our tenth wedding anniversary, which otherwise passed without fanfare. Finally, I sat down to write him a letter. In it, I delivered three pieces of news. One was that Frankie had spoken. This was the most important item. Two, our tenants in Round Lake were moving out. I'd received the call that week. The wife was bored being so far from downtown, and she'd had it *up to here*—the husband's words—with the mice in the kitchen. They would lose two months' rent per the lease agreement, but we'd need to find a new tenant. We'd never considered selling the house. Not because we had plans to return (though I never could get a read on how open Graham was to the idea) but because it had been in his family so long, and to sell it would have been treason. I had some experience with familial treason, so I empathized. After my mother died, my father had sold or donated every piece of furniture, every table linen and dish, every tchotchke, and finally the house itself. My mother's clothes had arrived at the cottage in a pair of wardrobe boxes (the clothes were all too long on me or too small), and everything else was just gone. I still thought of things—the folding stepladder she kept beside the refrigerator, the Asian vases she'd made into table lamps, the library of psychology books she'd kept in the den—and wondered what had become of them. When I'd told my father, my voice straining to remain under control, that I would have liked to have kept a few things for myself, he was quiet for a moment, then said something about the expense of shipping. Men tend to be practical, I suppose. If he had known it would break my heart, he might have done things differently. As with so many things, there was no choice but to forgive.

The third thing I told Graham was that Frankie had had two hour-long appointments with a speech and language pathologist named Emily Barrett-Strout, and she'd more or less upheld Dr. Sonia's diagnosis of selective mutism. I told him we weren't sure yet what it would mean for Frankie. Typically, I explained, the disorder shows up in unusually anxious or shy children, and most of these children are able to speak in some circumstances if not in others. The diagnosis didn't quite fit, but it was the best we could do.

I gave no other details. I did not tell him that for the past week, since he'd first met with Emily, Frankie sometimes talked to me or Charlie, each word like found treasure offered with both hands. I did not tell him what Emily believed had caused Frankie's mutism, or what—this had been implied, never spoken—we might do to heal him for good.

I left out one more thing: the City of Coral Gables had left a notice taped to the *Lullaby*'s sliding door. The notice cited code ZC 4-408: *No houseboat, boat, watercraft or vessel may be used as an abode or place of dwelling while moored or tied up in any waterway or canal within the City.* The notice read WARNING at the top, and there was no fine. When the city would be back to follow up, I had no idea. I figured I probably had one more warning before I had to get serious about looking for a new place to live. When I first read the notice, I kept myself from panicking by remembering my mother's theory of juggling, to which she'd held tight: a person can keep only so many balls in the air at any given time. Something has to give.

When, during my junior year of college, my mother had been fired by Dr. Fuller for reasons I never knew, the juggling theory had substituted for reason, even for regret. "I dropped Fuller's balls," she'd said when I asked what had happened. "Men don't like that, honey." She was back working for Dr. Fuller by the following summer. Again I asked what had happened, and she told me only that he'd thought he could do without her, and he'd thought wrong. I found myself wondering about the words he'd chosen to win her back, whether he'd allowed his face to betray any measure of affection.

It felt odd keeping secrets from Graham. It felt like even more distance between us, which I suppose it was.

EMILY BARRETT-STROUT—*MISS EMILY*, as she introduced herself—arrived fifteen minutes late for our first appointment, looking more or less like what I'd originally expected of Dr. Sonia. She was older and plump, wearing nurselike clogs and oversize eyeglasses and a wraparound skirt. She had very pink cheeks and wore no makeup, and her face had a supple, youthful quality that didn't match the rest of her. When I let her in, she shook my hand and said something about leaving a file on the roof of her car. "It's scattered along I-95 by now," she said.

This seemed a bad start. "Are you talking about Frankie's records?"

"Goodness, no." She frowned. There was a pencil stuck behind her ear, caught in a web of flyaway silver hair, and she carried a multicolored woven bag that hit her hip when she walked. She dropped it heavily on the kitchen table.

Frankie eyed her and I introduced them. I poured a mug of coffee, but when I brought it to her, she said she preferred tea. I set a mug in the microwave, thinking this would be quicker than using the stove top, not to mention cooler in the humid morning. But I'd never used the microwave, which looked as old as the *Lullaby* herself. Sure enough, as soon as the water started to boil, the overhead lights blinked out and the hum of the microwave stopped.

"Oh, well," said Emily.

I went to the helm—a shallow, wood-paneled compartment in the corner of the salon—to fiddle with the breaker box. Emily sat cross-legged on the rug beside Frankie, sifting through a bag of toys she'd brought along. After the lights were back on, I finished making the tea and she took it. Otherwise, she pretended I was not there.

"Frankie," she said. "I like that name. Frankie, I bet you can tell me which of these toys is a fish and which is a bear."

She placed several toys in a line. He took the fish and pushed it toward her, then did the same with the bear.

"Sure, but which is which?" she said.

Frankie picked up the fish, then signed with his free hand: *Fish.*

"And?"

He picked up the bear and clawed the air. Whether this was actually the sign for *bear*, I didn't recall. Then, very quietly, he growled.

"That's what he says, but what's he called?"

Frankie stared at her.

"Frankie?" I said, and Miss Emily held up a hand to me.

He looked back and forth between us. "Bear," he said.

It was a small shock, every time.

Miss Emily picked up a pig. Frankie sighed, then said, "Pig."

She picked up a dog. "Dog," he said.

Weeks earlier, to convince me to start swim lessons with Frankie and Carson, Sally had relied heavily on one argument: that a child's parent is exactly the wrong person to teach that child to swim. I'd started the lessons not because I agreed with her, but because I thought it would be fun for Frankie and for me, and this had turned out to be true. Every weekend, Sally and I spent an hour drinking fresh orange juice in the shade while the older boys kicked around in the deep end and Frankie and Carson had their lesson in the shallow end. But I'd continued to hold fast to the belief that although Sally was right in general—parents shouldn't teach their kids to swim—she was wrong when it came to me and Frankie. I'd believed we were the exception.

What came to me, as I watched Frankie indulge Miss Emily in her game, was that every single parent in history had believed the same thing. We'd all been wrong.

"Okay," Emily said, cocking her head at him. "So you can talk. Why am I here?"

Frankie shrugged and looked longingly at the toys.

"Mom?" said Emily to me. "Take a walk?"

"I'd rather stay," I said.

"We'll be just a few minutes."

I closed the screen door behind me. When Emily saw me watching, she gave a look, so I stepped onto the dock and faced the canal. The house across the water was quiet—the kids were wherever they went on summer mornings, the father at work, the mother on errands or at the health club. A fishing boat trolled by. The captain was a middle-aged woman wearing a pink blouse. She waved as she passed. I sat down and let my legs hang over the water. I thought of the cast-iron mermaid sitting above the sink, which every so often Frankie climbed up to retrieve, so it might commune with his sea animals for a couple of hours.

Emily called for me through the screen door. Frankie was still on the rug, but Emily sat at the banquette. I sat across from her. Our knees bumped but she paid no attention.

"You already know what it isn't," she said. "It's not a hearing problem or a receptive disorder. This problem is expressive. I'm at a disadvantage, ironically, because—well, he spoke to me." She blinked her owlish eyes. "But I can tell you what I've seen before."

"How much?" I said.

"How much what?"

"How much did he talk?"

"Twenty or so words. No sentences, no pairs. We could have gone on and on, I think. He's in preschool?"

"Not yet." I'd enrolled him for the remainder of the summer session, but his first day was still a week off.

"His file says there's been some stress in the home," she said.

"I meant to mention it." I *had* meant to—really—but then she'd swept in and the power had blown, and it had gotten lost. I told her in bare terms the story of what had happened at the hotel in Round Lake. "He was not talking long before," I said.

She nodded. She took no notes. "You have trouble sleeping, too."

"I take pills. It's not too bad, nothing like Graham."

"Any changes lately?"

"Other than the move, not really."

"I like to meet both parents. Dad's at work?"

"Yes. I mean, he's working, but he's on a ship in Hurricane Alley. He left three weeks ago."

She raised her eyebrows. "That's a change, wouldn't you say?"

"Yes."

"Do you work?"

"Part-time. I'm sort of a personal assistant."

"Where is Frankie when you're working?"

"He's with me. It's casual."

Frankie lost interest in the toys and padded over to us. Emily winked at him without smiling. To me, she said, "You're an assistant to whom?"

I started to describe the situation, the kind of work I did and how we got ourselves out to Stiltsville, not knowing which facts were relevant and which were not.

Frankie interrupted. "Charlie," he said to Emily, then padded back to the rug.

"I swear he doesn't talk," I said.

"Gotcha," said Emily, then continued with her questions, as if nothing noteworthy had happened. Finally, she sat back and looked over at Frankie, regarding him as he played. She kept her voice low. "Here's what I'm thinking. You tell me that your husband has this problem, this sleepwalking. And you tell me that Frankie has witnessed at least one upsetting incident, that you know of. And you tell me that you sleep sporadically, usually on pills, and that your husband left town three weeks ago, and since then Frankie has spoken more than he has in two years."

We looked at each other. My legs started to tremble, then my arms. I felt a pulsing in my neck and something frenzied, something akin to rage, rising in my chest. Desperation, maybe. I said, as calmly as possible, "I don't think those things are related."

A look sparked across her features—sympathy, I think. She said, "Plenty of kids have expressive delay. That just might be what we're dealing with here, selective mutism *light*. He spends a few years taking it in before he lets it out."

Maybe she could tell I wasn't listening anymore, that the world had closed in and was thrumming in my ears, because she leaned forward, speaking slowly and holding my eyes with her own. "I will say that it concerns me," she said, "the matter of the timing."

Then I was up, crossing the room to Frankie, kneeling and squaring his shoulders. He looked at me, alarmed. I said, "Frankie, listen to me."

"Don't push him," said Emily.

"Frankie, do you feel—" I stopped. "Frankie, why don't you talk around Dad?" He shrugged. I struggled to control my voice. "Do you not feel safe around Dad?" I signed the word *safe* out of habit.

His mouth opened but he didn't say anything. He looked afraid. I was holding his shoulders too tightly. I felt Emily's arms circle my own, pulling me back.

"What are you saying to me?" I said.

I thought of Graham's story of his father and baseball, of Sally's horror story from the radio—but nothing stuck. I knew every inch of

Frankie's body. I spent almost every hour with him. Graham hardly spent any time alone with Frankie at all. He never had. But if it wasn't that, then what was it?

Then it came to me. Graham had never laid a hand on Frankie—I was certain of this. But then again, he hadn't needed to. A scene appeared in my mind: Graham waking in his underwear beside his friend Jackson's bed, Jackson's wife screaming, Graham seizing. Then my mind conjured another scene, and my blood ran cold. What if Frankie, as a baby or toddler, had woken in the night to find his own father standing in the room, unresponsive and unseeing? What if he'd said, in his early-language speech, "Daddy?" and the strange empty man had looked right through him. What if he'd repeated himself, babbling "Daddy? Daddy?" and the man simply turned and unhurriedly walked out without answering, without bending to pick him up or comfort him. What if this had happened time and again? It would have been like waking to find a monster in the room, all the more frightening for how the monster resembled his father.

The scene in my mind had the texture of real life, and I knew in my gut that this, or something very much like it, had happened to my boy.

I shook in Emily's arms. "I take pills," I said to her. "I have to, or I don't sleep. I don't know what happens in the night. I only wake to loud noise."

Frankie put a hand on my arm, then signed: *Okay, Mama? Okay?*

"Yes, baby," I said.

Emily sat back and crossed her legs. "Sometimes kids freeze up when there's something they don't understand. Sometimes they freeze so much they get used to being frozen."

I wiped my face.

She said, "I have to ask—when is your husband coming home?"

"A couple of weeks," I said.

She patted my hand. "We'll figure it out."

I rocked Frankie in my lap. I kissed his hair.

Before she got up from the rug, Emily said to Frankie, "How lucky you are to have such a good mother," and I had to take deep breaths before I could manage to get to my feet to see her out.

CARSON STARTED RUNNING IN DELIGHTED circles when Frankie entered the loud, colorful room at the preschool. They wouldn't have the same teacher, as I understood it, but their classes would share the same large space for most of the day, and they'd be on the playground together in the morning and afternoon. That morning, Frankie had refused to get dressed, then sat himself in his time-out corner as a protest. We were late. Frankie looked briefly pleased when Carson bounded over to greet him, but then he clambered into my arms and scowled at the room. I'd reminded him again and again that he was starting school, but until that morning it seemed he'd thought I was bluffing. When I'd pulled him from his car seat and he saw where we were, he looked at me as if I'd betrayed him.

His teacher's name was Carla. She was young—early twenties, if that—with two silver rings through her nose. But she had the straight spine and calm, confident bearing of someone who had been early to mature, which made me wonder about her background—not her training but her parentage, her home life. I set Frankie down next to her and he squirmed to get back to me. I stepped away, telling myself again that I was doing this *for* him, not *to* him.

When we'd toured, I'd spoken to the school's director about Frankie's speech. To Carla, I said, "You know he doesn't talk a lot, right? But he understands everything. He pays attention. So don't, you know, *not* talk to him."

"Don't worry." To Frankie, she said, "I hear you like fish."

He stared at her nose rings as she spoke, then nodded.

"Would you like to see our fish?"

On the far side of the room, a colorful aquarium spanned the length of a low table. He nodded again.

"Do you think you might help me feed them later?"

He nodded again. I blew him a kiss and walked out, feeling his eyes on my back.

EARLY THAT FRIDAY EVENING, AFTER Frankie and I'd spent most of the day cooped up on the *Lullaby*, me folding laundry and cleaning and him begging me to play with him, after two time-outs and one ugly episode wherein I yelled at him after he knocked over a pile of folded clothes, I decided we needed a change of scenery. I left the clothes strewn across the salon floor and went up to Lidia's house. I wrapped three slices from the pan of meat loaf resting on the stove top, grabbed a bottle of wine, and left a note of apology. I stuffed Frankie into his life vest and shuttled him onto the Zodiac. As I started the engine, something splashed across the canal. It took a moment before my brain sorted out the pale lines in the water, the steady forward movement: it was the mother from across the way. She turned to breathe, then her head was down again. She traveled straight up the center of the waterway. I sent something like a prayer of safety after her, then pulled away from the pier.

We'd never crossed to Stiltsville so late in the day. Ten minutes into the ride, as the melon sunset soaked into the violet horizon, I considered turning back. I forged on. The wind was blustery, lifting and dropping my hair, sending up spray over the gunwales.

Go away, wind! signed Frankie. I pulled him close and he buried his face in my torso.

Charlie came downstairs as I was tying up. Frankie stepped to the dock and peeled off his life jacket, as he'd taken to doing; I'd decided that he'd spent enough time at the stilt house to know to take care.

"How are you with surprises?" I said to Charlie.

"I can take them or leave them."

I handed him the meat loaf. "We brought dinner."

He held the package to his nose. "The famous meat loaf!"

After we ate—Charlie agreed the meat loaf was as good as I'd promised—Frankie and Charlie went from room to room, playing a version of hide-and-seek wherein Charlie always counted and Frankie always hid, each time in a different closet or corner. Though just that morning, he'd said "please" after I'd asked if he wanted orange juice with breakfast, he was still signing more than he spoke. After an hour or so, Frankie gave up hiding and climbed onto the sofa with his sea animals and asked for a blanket. I told him the grown-ups would be on the porch if he needed us.

Charlie and I sat in the rockers. He stretched his legs and steadied them on the porch railing. We drank wine from plastic cups and the wind swallowed our voices. I told him that I'd lost my cool with Frankie, that I'd yelled and he'd cried.

Inside, Frankie was moving his toys around on the coffee table. Another child might have been talking to them.

"It happens," Charlie said. "Mothers feel a lot of guilt about these things."

"Fathers don't?"

"They feel a little guilt. A limited amount."

"I hate it when he's sad."

"You can't protect him from suffering, you know."

"I can try."

There was the constant slapping of water against the pilings, a faint thread of voices and laughter from a house down the channel. The lights of the skyline blinked faintly. There was something in the way Charlie looked at the shore. Regret? I thought.

I said, "Do you ever think you'll go back?"

"I wondered how long."

"How long what?"

"Before you asked that."

"And what's the answer?"

He took a long drink of his wine. The cup covered his mouth and jaw, and all I could see were his sorrowful eyes, the way they folded at the corners. "I'll never go back."

"What makes you so sure?"

"Because I remember what it was like. I don't want to be like that again."

"Like what?"

"Angry, mostly. Scared." He stared at a point just beyond my knees. "I have a way of making other people miserable."

"I don't believe that."

He smiled. "Yes, you do."

"I'm not miserable."

"And I'm not on land."

There was no arguing. Over my shoulder, I could see Frankie moving around the coffee table, rearranging his animals, dragging his blanket along the floor and yawning.

I got to my feet reluctantly. "We'll be getting back," I said.

"Drive carefully, please."

The starlight threw soft shadows across his face. I thought of what he'd told me—it seemed long ago—about his daughter, and what happens to people after they lose a child.

"I'm glad you didn't drown," I said.

He looked confused, then his expression cleared. "Sweetheart," he said, "that's exactly what I did."

14

I'M EMBARRASSED TO ADMIT THAT I'd had barely any contact with Graham's mother, Julia, since we'd moved to Miami. Before we left, we'd talked about visiting at Christmas, but that was still a ways off. I'd sent a photo of Frankie and a brief update, with a crayon drawing I'd wheedled him into making for her, but it had been a month since then. I had not told her about the progress he'd made, though I think she would have been relieved to know of it.

The morning Graham called, I woke with her on my mind. This is the kind of thing for which my belief system has no vocabulary. I woke thinking of the leather driving gloves she always wore in the car. Why one would need such a thing, I never knew, but every time I watched her pull them on—they fit perfectly, as leather does only when it's very high quality and has been worn for years—I fell a little in love with the old-fashioned decadence of it.

She died in her sleep from complications from pneumonia. She was seventy-six years old. Graham had called Lidia's house every half an hour since dawn, but not until seven o'clock did Lidia answer, at which point she and my father came down the lawn and rang the cowbell. My father looked grave and Lidia's face was full of something like anxiety, though I guess it was sadness. She folded her hands in front of her stomach. I had the strange thought that I was about to be scolded, though for what, I didn't know. Leaving on lights in their house, maybe—this was one of my father's most tightly held pet peeves—or being too liberal with their groceries.

"Honey," Lidia said, then delivered the news in a motherly voice. We walked up the lawn so I could return Graham's call. Lidia carried Frankie in his pajamas. "Would I have liked her?" she said.

"She was a little cold," I said.

Immediately, I regretted saying it. It wasn't the most pertinent, not to mention flattering, fact I might have conveyed. But I'd been thinking that Lidia was warm, even at her most demanding, and that it's possible she would have found Julia remote, the way I had for many years.

"I didn't mean to say that," I said.

"It's forgotten." She took Frankie into the den to watch cartoons.

"Babe," said Graham when I was patched through. The line was full of white noise. His voice was weak. There was a high-pitched whistle in the background, and we waited it out. "I've been calling and calling."

"I'm so sorry. I wish we had a phone."

"Whose stupid idea was that boat, anyway?" He forced a breathy laugh.

"Are you okay?"

He cleared his throat. "I don't know. It hasn't hit me."

"Are you going today?"

"They'll shuttle me to shore today, but I can't get a flight until morning."

"I'll meet you there."

We stayed on the line for a moment, listening to static crackle between us. Then Graham said he loved me and would call with his flight information, and hung up.

I made hotel and flight reservations, then called Riggs and asked him to tell Charlie I wouldn't be back that week. The next morning, Lidia came down the lawn before Frankie woke, and I kissed him in his sleep and drove myself to the airport in the half-light, the streets mostly empty. When we landed in Chicago, the air had a funky green tinge—tornado weather. I rushed through O'Hare to meet Graham at his gate. Heaven knows why, but he tended to sleep heavily on planes, which meant he was usually late coming off, and this flight was no exception. The circles beneath his eyes were deeper than usual, and his clothes were loose and disheveled. He dropped his bags and buried his face in my hair.

"You're a sight," he said.

"Poor baby," I said.

He pressed his forehead against mine. I felt the pull of him—his familiar smell, the breadth of his shoulders, the pure white of his hair.

We rented a car and fought traffic in the Loop. Graham asked about Frankie's talking and I repeated what I'd told him in my letter. He tapped the window as we passed the little French restaurant where we'd had our first official date outside of Detention. We drove to his mother's apartment, where a group of women sat in the living room, a plate of coffee cake on the table. Julia's husband, Bob Winters, stood in the kitchen with a coffee mug in his hand. His eyes were rimmed and swollen, which moved me. Bob had paper-white hair, very thin at the crown, and liver-spotted hands. He was a big man, barrel-chested and hunched in the way of the very tall, and his clothes were starched, as if straight from the cleaners.

"Good of you to come," he said distractedly.

The apartment was spare and Scandinavian in style, the furniture low in profile and the walls adorned here and there with landscapes in dated wooden frames. The ladies cornered Graham, whispering sympathies, and I stepped onto the small balcony, where two robust ferns grew in clay pots. It was drizzling. The green hue was gone from the sky, replaced by honey-colored ribbons of evening sunlight streaking through the cloud cover. There was a loamy, agricultural odor in the air, a reminder of not-too-distant fields lined with hearty stalks of corn. A block away was the snaking green river, its color so different—so chemical and factory-fed—from that of the ocean. On a boat headed toward the wide disc of Lake Michigan, a group of tourists hunkered in ponchos.

Graham joined me. His eyebrows furrowed and he stared down at the tourist boat. After a minute, he said, "We never should have left Chicago."

I looked at him.

"We should have stayed here," he said. "We should have bought an apartment like this one. We never should have moved to the cottage."

"This apartment smells like old people," I said.

"You don't miss it?"

I shrugged. I had no desire to answer, to chase this line of thought to its unsettling conclusion. I did miss it, actually, but only a little. Chicago had always welcomed me—this was how I'd thought of it. It had been easy making a life there. But I'd been young. My concerns had been Laundromats and delis and bars. I had no experience being a grown-up, not to mention a mother, in Chicago. Besides, we'd moved to the cottage months before we were even married. Saying we shouldn't have moved was like saying we shouldn't have done everything else.

I went back inside but he stayed out, the mist falling on his hair. Inside, Bob's daughter, blond and largely pregnant, five or so years older than I, was straightening up in the kitchen. We greeted each other quietly. A couple of impeccably dressed women sat chatting in low voices at the breakfast table. Bob stood in front of a television set in the den, watching the Weather Channel. On the screen, a ferocious radar spiral moved haltingly across the southern Atlantic. The thing had yet to be declared a tropical depression, but it was intensifying just east of Bermuda, limping toward the Bahamas. I thought of Charlie and the stilt house, of wet winds lashing through the rooms, pulling the paintings off the walls and knocking the furniture around. I knew he followed weather events on the transistor radio in his kitchen. If this storm hit, would he go to shore?

The program switched to a commercial. "Nasty stuff," Bob said to me. I don't think he knew, in that moment, who I was. "Good of you to come," he said again.

I busied myself helping Bob's daughter in the kitchen. There was no ring on her finger, no sign of the baby's father. She said she was always surprised, when she saw me—three times now, including Julia's wedding—that I wasn't a Jew. "Because of your hair," she said in a sweet but spacey voice. I wondered if she was on something.

That night at the hotel, Graham shared a memory of being at the zoo with his mother and sister. He remembered the otters playing in their truncated river, pushing their furry bellies against the glass. They'd made his mother laugh out loud. He remembered his sister in a pink scarf and a brown derby coat. She'd held his hand while they rode the merry-go-round. His mother held him on her hip so he could better see the polar bears, who skulked in the dark reaches of their manufactured caves.

"My family is dead," he said.

"No, we're not," I said.

I held him and he kissed me. His mouth, his taste, was familiar but renewed, like finding something I'd thought I'd misplaced. "What if I lost you?" he said. His hands found the clasp on my skirt, and then the buttons of my shirt. His fingernails raked through my hair. We didn't make it to the bed. After, he held tight to me, tugging against my hand when I got up for water. I finally fell asleep under the heavy weight of his arm, and when I woke I lifted my head from the carpet to see him standing at the window without his clothes on, his palms pressed to the glass. I could tell from his breathing that he was awake. "Do not jump," I said loudly, and he turned around and laughed so hard he had to bend over to steady himself. He was dressed and ready to go by the time I woke again.

The funeral was in a Catholic church downtown. After the burial, we went back to Bob's apartment for a couple of hours, then we dropped off the car at the airport. At my gate, Graham fidgeted a little, avoiding my eyes, running a hand through his hair.

"You need a trim," I said.

He took a breath. "They moved me to my own bunk."

He tried to say it casually, like he was just making conversation, but he looked away after he spoke. I'm not proud of it, but in that instant, as I absorbed his words, I stepped away without moving a muscle. I told myself that if he'd wanted to talk about it, he would've mentioned it earlier. It's not that I didn't have the impulse to ask what had happened—but I fought it. Instead of pressing for information, I squeezed his hand, kissed him good-bye, and boarded my plane. He watched me go, the hurt plain on his face.

THE NEXT WEEK AT STILTSVILLE, I asked Charlie how he'd fared during the storm that had hit while I'd been out of town. He didn't answer right away. Frankie was on the sofa, facing the open window, watching a ship on the horizon, and for a moment we both watched him. He called out when anything interrupted the palette of sea and sky, combining the game of speaking with the game of spotting. "Air-peen! Moto-boat!"

To me, Charlie said, "I stayed here."

I wasn't surprised, but still I found myself suddenly, inexplicably frustrated with him.

He went on. "It wasn't much of anything. A little rain, a little wind."

"I can't believe Riggs let you stay," I said.

"He's not my father, Georgia."

I started to gather our things.

"Don't do that," he said.

Frankie turned to watch us. I said, "You can't stay here during a storm like that. It's not safe."

"If they don't evacuate on land, why evacuate out here?"

I stepped out to the porch. The wind was kicking up sea spray. Charlie came to stand next to me, his hands on the railing. "You don't know what you're talking about," he said. "This house has survived half a dozen hurricanes, for Christ's sake. It'll be here long after I'm gone."

"You have a home *there*." I gestured, and he glanced at the hazy skyline, as if the possibility of going to shore had never occurred to him.

"Not really," he said.

"I need you to promise you won't do that again."

This was a line I'd never crossed before, and he didn't like it. He refused to meet my eyes, and his mouth tightened. The words were hard on his tongue. "You were in *Chicago*," he said.

"So what? You could've gotten a ride. Don't blame—"

"I'm not saying—" He stopped. A step would have consumed the distance between us. "You were in Chicago," he said again, his voice softer. *"You were in Chicago."*

Maybe he'd thought that once I left, I wouldn't come back. I understood this concern because I'd been harboring the same one regarding Graham, even as I feared equally the day when he would return. But Charlie's voice broke a little as he spoke, and when he said it, the word *Chicago* brought Julia's funeral to mind, and the light rain and antiseptic apartment and too-green river. And Graham's haggard good-bye and our empty, cast-away cottage, and the feeling that something I'd loved deeply had moved on from me and no longer returned my love at all. It is possible to conjure an entire life from the ether, I thought, and lose it back to the ether again. It happens all the time. In Charlie's voice, the word *Chicago* took on new meaning. *Remote*, it said. *Lonely*.

"Next time, I won't be," I said.

From the living room came Frankie's pitchy voice. "Sailboat!"

Charlie kept his eyes on mine for another moment, then went to share my son's delight.

15

IT HAD BEEN FIVE WEEKS since Graham left, and Frankie was speaking more each day. First scattered, individual words—the reaches of his vocabulary stunned me—and then pairs and simple sentences. Once, when he was frustrated by the task of buckling the straps of his car seat, something he'd begun to insist on doing "by my own," I told him to take his time, and he sighed, exasperated. "I *have* my time!" he said, finally clicking the clasp.

The cotton-mouthiness of his speech remained, and his sentences lacked tense and flow; each word came out punctuated, as if read from individual cue cards. Emily Barrett-Strout wasn't concerned. She stopped by every Wednesday morning. I'd told Charlie we'd be late on those days, and when I told him why, his frown faded and he said, "Just hurry up."

One morning, I asked Frankie what he wanted for breakfast—we usually had either cereal or eggs—and he said, "Pancakes, please." We went up to Lidia's to raid the cabinets, and he learned quickly that talking would get him what he wanted: an extra book at bedtime, ice cream after dinner. Sometimes Frankie looked as surprised by his own voice as I was. One morning before dawn I woke to a warm hand on my arm. "Potty?" he said. Sometimes when it was dark he didn't want to go alone. After I brought him back, he looked up at me and said, "Sorry I wake you, Mama."

Did every mother feel, each time the word was formed, a small, soft hand petting her heart?

When I told Dr. Sonia what Emily had said—this was at a hasty follow-up appointment—she nodded and moved on, unimpressed. She was more interested in the fact that Frankie was sleeping less, going to bed later and waking earlier. She spent a long time recording this in his file. Frankie answered her questions in his mushy voice, his staccato diction, and she told him she expected to hear great things from him in the future.

Emily continued to ask when Graham would be home, but I had no answer for her. The storm season that year had been unusually calm, which, as far as I could tell from Graham's letters and the twice-weekly phone conversations we'd managed to schedule, meant more time offshore, adjusting and improving the equipment, but fewer chances to test it out. Emily might have sensed the quicksand that had become my immediate future, and she stepped delicately around it. Distantly, as if the entire notion were thickly swaddled, as if it were happening to someone else, I wondered if she might try to remove Frankie from my care if Graham did come home. This was as far ahead as I could see: when Graham came home, I would tell him about Emily's diagnosis, and he would pack up for Detention without my asking it of him. When he came home we'd try again to make a better life. This seemed the kind of plan made by the spouses of alcoholics or drug addicts—which is to say that it seemed a long shot, but worth a try.

I'd stopped taking my sleeping pills. Sometimes I slept anyway, with the hushed noise of the canal beneath the windows in my berth and the moonlight seeping across my sheets. If I couldn't sleep, I sat on the deck and watched the water make its way to the ocean. In these quiet, starlit moments, I felt a surge of affection for our watery retreat. Every few days, the neighbor woman came down her back terrace—did she really tiptoe out of her house, or did I just imagine it?—and dove into the water.

Sometimes I had a hard time staying awake through the day. Once at Stiltsville, during Frankie's nap, Charlie caught me yawning and told me to go rest in his bed. I would have refused, but I could not keep my eyes open. He closed the door behind me and I lay down, thinking it would not be possible for me to actually fall sleep there in the stifling room. I looked over at Frankie, sleeping uncovered with his mouth open and his cheeks flushed so deeply that they might have been painted, and fell asleep. I didn't wake until I felt Frankie tap my arm, then climb clumsily on top of me.

I COULD HAVE GONE OUT to Stiltsville while Frankie was in preschool, but I knew Charlie wouldn't like it—where his affection for Frankie stopped and his affection for me started, I could not have said—and for that matter, neither would Frankie. Instead, I went to Sally's place or helped Lidia in the yard or busied myself on the *Lullaby*, cleaning and cooking. Frankie cried a little whenever he had to get dressed to go to school, which broke my heart, and that weighed on me through the long hours. Then one day I dropped by Riggs's office to pick up my check, and on impulse asked him if he knew anyone who needed help two days a week.

"Sure," he said. "Me."

The following Tuesday, I sat compliantly as Riggs's regular secretary, Angela, taught me how he liked his phone to be answered, his messages recorded, his coffee made, and his dictation transcribed. Compared to figuring out how to work Riggs's office computer—there was a lost brief early on, which almost got me fired—learning to drive the Zodiac had been a breeze. Angela was going back to school to become a paralegal, and I'd fill in only for the rest of the summer semester; it was clear that Riggs didn't think I'd last much beyond that. But the pay was fine and the work absorbed the empty hours. Sometimes Riggs left his office door open—it was stuffy, even with a noisy window air-conditioning unit—and I could hear the murmurs and sniffles and sometimes the sobs of his clients, all women in the process of divorcing. I quickly formed the understanding that although Riggs was generally an unpleasant man, he reserved compassion for his clients. He was straight with them, never rushed them, and gave practical advice: how to shore up their personal credit, how to lay low with an affair and for how long, what to give up so that the custody fight might go more smoothly. (I noticed that he always told wives to give their husbands the family boat, and surmised that he'd had personal experience with this form of mollification.) He was done with appointments by 3:30 P.M., and by 4:00, when I was gathering my things to leave to pick up Frankie, he was halfway through a tumbler of bourbon.

A week or so after I started the job, Charlie asked how it was going. I said it was fine, which it was, except for the lost brief and also the fish in the saltwater tank in the waiting room, caught while Riggs was scuba diving in Aruba, which I'd overfed and killed. This had launched him into a red-faced tirade that ended with him wondering aloud why he had ever hired me and me leaving early. Two days later, when I'd stomped back in, he'd handed me two hundred dollars out of his wallet and called it a bonus.

"I wouldn't imagine it's easy, working for a man like him," said Charlie.

"It's really fine," I said.

"You must have some experience with difficult men. I guess I knew that." He smiled, and I understood that he was referring to himself. This was the kind of thing he said every so often—comments about putting up with him, about his bad habits—that surprised me. Compared to my father and Riggs and even Graham, though for different reasons entirely, Charlie was a puppy dog. But I understood from these offhand comments, and from the little I knew of his marriage, that he had not always been so.

So it wasn't entirely shocking when one evening I found myself sharing a bottle of wine with Lidia and her friend Marse, whom I'd met two or three times by that point, and Marse started to gossip about *the hermit* in a way that revealed she knew nothing of my relationship to him. (It was just like Lidia to express herself voluminously on the subject of her own business while remaining tight-lipped on the business of others.) Marse wore diamond stud earrings and a large cocktail ring and a smart tailored suit the color of hibiscus blossoms. She was older than I and younger than Lidia, and she'd lived in Miami all of her life. She was a partner in a law firm downtown. She dressed sexily, with plunging necklines and bare upper arms, but she had a hard edge about her that kept her from being pretty. One would be more apt to describe her as handsome. Her name was short for *Marilyn*, and rhymed with *arse*.

She said, "I hear he has a new whore. Small comfort that Viv is beyond caring, no?"

From what little I knew of her, I didn't think Marse was particularly insensitive. She spoke a little brazenly, but in the past I'd found it appealing; she had a lot of confidence. Normally, I could see why Lidia liked her.

I took a breath. "What did you say?" I said.

"I heard he has a new girl. This one has a kid, too."

Lidia sat back and crossed her legs. Her expression conveyed that she was going to let me handle this one, but she'd step in if I needed it.

"Who said that?"

"My friend Frances. She and her husband—I've known him forever—have the house next to his. Vivian didn't want her business known—you know how she was, or is, or whatever—so I've never talked to Frances about him." She looked at Lidia. "You've met her? They live down the waterway."

"Once or twice," said Lidia. "Pretty."

The last time I'd caught sight of Charlie's blond neighbor—
*France*s—she'd been in the rocking chair on her porch, wearing a wide-
brimmed canvas hat, her bare feet propped on the railing. Her husband
had sat down beside her and I'd thought they might have been holding
hands, but I couldn't tell for sure.

Maybe Marse sensed that the air had grown hostile, because she
said, "I really don't know anything about it. But Vivian's a friend, or
she used to be. Someone says something about the hermit, and my ears
perk up."

I stared at her.

"Do you know him?" she said.

"Sure," I said, reaching to pour myself more wine. "I'm the whore."

THE NEXT MORNING, I CALLED Riggs and claimed I was sick,
and as we were packing up for preschool, Frankie caught me throwing my sunhat into my tote. He told me to promise I would not go to
Stiltsville without him.

"Just this once," I said cautiously. "I have something very important
to talk to Charlie about."

At this, Frankie fell into hysterics. (There were times when it
seemed that all that vocalizing I'd yearned for was overrated.) He refused to put on his shoes. He signed so frantically that I couldn't understand him. We were running late, and I had no patience for the usual
round of one-two-threes and time-outs. Not seeing Charlie that day
was not an option.

I sat down at the banquette and pretended to read Graham's *El
Nuevo Herald*, which still arrived every morning. I didn't look up until
Frankie's wails quieted. "Are you ready?" I said.

"Don't go with no Frankie," he said, jutting his chin.

"Okay," I said. I crossed the fingers of my left hand. "I won't, but not
because you got mad."

I asked him to apologize, which he reluctantly did, and then he went to the screen door, where his little sneakers lay on their sides. He carried them in one hand and his backpack in the other, then looked over his shoulder at me, as if I was holding everything up.

The plan, which had formed over the past week, was that when the filing project was finished—it would take just one or two days more—we would get to work painting the stilt house, inside and out. As it was, all the walls were a smudged off-white. In the bathroom, the paint was peeling in long strips, and in the kitchen it was stained from cooking smoke and splatter. We would start with the office, then the main bedroom and living room and kitchen, then the bathroom. I was going to work on the interior and Charlie was going to use an extension ladder to paint the exterior. This had sounded risky when he'd first brought it up—alone in the middle of the bay, high on a ladder—but when I'd challenged him, Charlie just frowned at me and handed over a list of supplies. On the list, he'd written 4 GAL. INTERIOR PRIMER/PAINT and 4 GAL. EXTERIOR PRIMER/PAINT, but he hadn't specified a color. When I asked about this, he said dryly, "Surprise me."

So after dropping Frankie, I stopped and bought just one gallon of paint and one of primer, for the office. I chose a deep gray-blue called Marine. The man at the store who mixed the paint left a smear to dry on the can's lid, so the color would be visible from the outside. Charlie met me on the dock—he wasn't expecting me, but he knew the Zodiac's high-pitched buzz—and when he reached to take the paint, he frowned at the color.

"Blue? Really?"

"Yes." I dropped a bag of rollers and trays onto the dock, not looking at him.

"Where's the kiddo?"

"Preschool."

"Oh." He looked around, as if Frankie might have been hiding. He took the bag upstairs and I followed. I figured I'd ask him what I wanted to ask him and get back in the boat, but once we were in the office, he immediately opened the can with a screwdriver, then poured it into a pan.

"My, that is blue," he said.

"Forget it. I'll get white." I started to put the lid back on the paint, but he put a hand on my arm.

"What's wrong with you?"

"Nothing."

"I was married for forty years, Georgia."

"I met someone who knows you. A friend of Lidia's."

He sighed. "A friend of Vivian's, you mean."

"Yes."

"And?"

"And I guess there's been a little gossip about me. About us."

"Is this why you didn't bring the boy?"

"He's in preschool. No."

"So what you're asking—you're asking if—" He stopped. "Georgia, things used to be different for me."

"I gather that."

"It's been *years*."

I squatted over the paint, pressing the lid closed with my palms. My own heartbeat drummed in my ears.

"Jesus, you'd think they'd have forgotten all that by now," he said.

"They don't know you. Why would they forget what little they know?"

"You know me."

I stood up. "Do you want the paint or not?"

"What do you want me to say?"

The room was still and silent, dark for daytime because of thick, churning cloud cover. My palms were hot. "Your neighbors think I'm one of your whores."

His face went tight and he exhaled through his nose. He glanced out the window toward the red house, which was shuttered, no boat at the dock. "That's unfortunate. I don't know that I can fix that."

"So who are these women?"

He opened his palms. "I don't know what to tell you."

We stared at each other.

He said, "A while back I had a runner who brought girls when he came out. He liked to party. I guess I liked it, for a time."

I felt a little light-headed. "Why?"

"I'd left home. I was lonely."

"And?"

"Vivian started getting sick. I went back home for a while. This was about six years ago. We fought like idiots. *I* fought like an idiot. Then she got worse, and I put her in that place and came back here."

"And?"

"And that's that. You're acting like—"

"I don't like people thinking that way of me. Or of you."

"I don't either." His voice softened. "There were no more women, after I came back."

"Really?"

"Christ, Georgia." He gestured impatiently with both arms, as if to summon me toward him, but I stayed still.

Quietly, I said, "Maybe trust me on the paint color."

"Stay. We'll put up a coat."

He waited until I nodded, then brought me an old T-shirt and stepped out while I changed. We worked without talking. He took care of the edges with a paintbrush and I used a roller on the walls. He brought in his radio and played the jazz station and I found myself thinking of dancing with my mother in the kitchen, the way her broom skirt swayed, and the gold chains we both wore around our ankles, which we'd bought together in the Bahamas. At the thought of my mother, my eyes filled with hot tears. I had no idea when missing her might start to feel less like a physical wound, or if it ever would. When we'd finished priming the fourth wall, we moved the drop cloth back to the first wall, and Charlie stirred the blue paint with a clean brush.

We looked down into the can. "Okay, it might be too dark," I said.

"Here goes nothing," he said, and brought up the brush.

The color lightened as it dried. By the time we finished, my legs were covered in splatter and there was a streak across my cheek—I could feel it there, tightening on my skin as it dried. We sat down against the door and looked around, at the walls and the muddy sky through the windows. The room was reborn, even with the paint still drying and all the boxes crowded in a corner. I started to get up, but Charlie put a hand on my knee. "Wait," he said, then took away his hand.

"I don't want Frankie to be at school too long."

"Just a minute."

I sat back.

"I'm sorry about what we talked about. I don't want you to think—oh, I don't know."

"These friends of your wife's, they don't seem to think very highly of you."

"I suppose not."

What I said next came out fast. "Did you and your wife think about having more kids?"

He scratched his cheek. "We tried. We couldn't."

"I can't either. Frankie was an exception." I would never have said it aloud, but the word that came to mind was *miracle*. "Why does it seem like other people's lives are easier?"

He didn't say anything for a moment. My legs were crossed in front of me, my feet bare. He sat with his legs out straight, and I could feel the pressure of his upper arm against mine. His forearm lay across his thigh, the hair catching muted light from the window. He said, "Some are, but most aren't. Don't feel sorry for yourself." He waited. "I want to say—the thing about having one—if something happens, you're not a parent anymore. Just like that. I don't want to tell you what to do. But if we'd known, we might've tried harder."

I looked at him until he met my eyes. "Nothing is going to happen to Frankie," I said.

"No, of course not—"

"Nothing is going to happen to him."

"I didn't mean—"

"Don't say that again."

"I'm sorry. I shouldn't have said it."

I rubbed at a constellation of paint flecks on the front of the T-shirt he'd loaned me, which was now ruined. "I'm sorry you're not a father anymore."

He swallowed before speaking. "Riggs lost his son, you know. That's how we met. Grieving parents group, Vivian's idea. His boy would've been about your age." His eyes rested somewhere around my knees. "So would Jennifer."

For a moment, I watched the way his torso rose and fell. Then without thinking I pressed my chest against his shoulder and my nose against his jaw. He gave a little under my pressure, then steadied himself. My arm tightened around his waist and I felt his fingers against my shoulder, pulling me in. I was afraid of what might happen if I raised my face to his, so I burrowed against his warm skin, which smelled of salt and sunlight. When I felt I could, I pulled away from him, and went into the other room to change back into my own shirt.

WHAT I KNEW ABOUT VIVIAN Hicks, I learned mostly from Lidia and Charlie. She sewed and knitted, and also she collected antique cameras and used them to take photographs, which she developed herself in a backyard shed Charlie turned into a darkroom. She loved classical music, opera, and late-night variety shows, but had not witnessed a live performance of any kind, outside of plays at her daughter's school, until Charlie got tickets to a taping of *Ed Sullivan* at the

Deauville Hotel in Miami Beach. This was 1964. They went on their anniversary, and she was so excited beforehand that she couldn't eat. That night on the show, a band called the Beatles played for an American audience for only the second time. Charlie—this would embarrass him later—was unmoved by the music and aggravated by the hordes of screaming teenage girls in the audience. To him, it was all just a lot of lights and noise and crowds, then fighting traffic to get off the island. Vivian, on the other hand, was rapt.

She always had a dog, usually a corgi. One—Kismet was his name—buried its nose in a plastic bag he'd pulled from the trash, and, since his front legs were too short to pull it off, suffocated while they were out of the house. After that, Vivian went to the pound for her dogs, and once admitted to Charlie, with tears in her eyes, that although she loved her rescued dogs every bit as much as her corgis, she sometimes wished the rescues were just a little cuter.

She and Lidia used to meet before dawn in the Biltmore Hotel parking lot, to speed-walk the golf course before the golfers arrived. Once they were running late, and a golfer putted in their direction—meaning to move them along—and Vivian picked up the ball, put it in her pocket, and called the golfer a *motherfucker* to his face. Lidia laughed so hard she had trouble keeping up as Vivian hurried away.

Vivian wore a light pink bouclé suit to Jennifer's funeral because it had been Jennifer's favorite. After the funeral, she went to bed in the suit and didn't get out for two weeks. Lidia came over and changed her bedsheets and watered her plants and ran a washcloth over her face. She was at Vivian's house almost every day and didn't see Charlie more than once or twice. Charlie told me that he'd slept at Jennifer's house during some of this time, to be with Sam, though this seemed a strange choice to me. It was a year before he moved out to Stiltsville, and in that time Vivian left her bed and returned to church and knitting and walking the golf course, but she wasn't the same.

Vivian loved two men in her lifetime. The first was Charlie, whom she'd met in college. Then, after she went into the nursing home, she fell in love with Anthony Gale, Henry Gale's father, though that romance was something different entirely.

I wasn't sure how Charlie learned of Vivian's death, exactly. I assumed that Riggs got the news and hauled out to Stiltsville in his Bertram. I learned of it from Lidia, just as two weeks before I'd learned of Julia's death from her. She was in the living room after I'd dropped Frankie at preschool; I stopped in to use her phone. I called two marinas to ask about live-aboard slips—this was a task I'd been putting off too long—then noticed her sitting stock-still on the living room sofa, staring in the direction of the black television screen. Her eyes were bloodshot and she held a juice glass of whiskey. It was nine-thirty in the morning.

"Liver failure," she said, shrugging.

"I'm so sorry."

I asked if Charlie had been told.

"I suppose," she said. She narrowed her swollen eyes at me. "You know he left her. She was grieving and he left."

"He was grieving."

She waved a hand. I was too dense to bother trying to convince. "I heard you on the phone. You don't need to get a slip. Sell the boat, move in here. Stay as long as you want."

It was the obvious solution. But I was afraid of moving backward, of never gaining that footing I'd wanted so badly in moving to Miami. And besides, I'd grown fond of the *Lullaby*. I wasn't ready to let her go.

"Thank you," I said. I chose my words. "It's not that I wouldn't—"

"Forget it." She downed her drink.

"I hope you know I'm grateful. I want to give Frankie a home—"

"Understood." She stood up, wiping her hands on her slacks, but then it seemed she had nowhere to go, and she sat down again. She said, "I don't mean to be rough on you. I realize I'm not your mother."

It would have been indelicate to agree. If my mother had been alive and had made the same offer, I would have rolled my eyes, maybe even snapped at her. The most telling clue that Lidia and I were not related was how mannerly we were with each other, at least usually.

But I wanted to let her mother me just a little. "You know, I was thinking about something my mother said before I got pregnant with Frankie, about some people not being cut out to be parents. Do you think that's true?"

She blinked at me. "Your mother said some people aren't cut out to be parents?"

With no warning, as they tended to, my eyes filled. I nodded.

"And you think she meant you? Georgia, don't be stupid."

It took a minute, but I collected myself. "When is the funeral?"

"Sunday."

My father would be at the Tobacco Road gig. "I'll drive you. Frankie can go to Sally's."

"Why?"

"So you won't be alone."

She shrugged a little, as if it was of no consequence either way. I wasn't sure if the matter was decided, but I chose to think it was, and went into the kitchen to call Sally. When I came back, Lidia had refilled her drink. She looked up at me, and then her expression collapsed on itself, and she buried her face in her elbow and wept.

I'D ASSUMED IT WOULD BE just me and Lidia on the four-hour drive to Kissimmee, but Lidia directed me to Marse's Brickell Avenue condo before we left town, and there stood Marse on the sidewalk, wearing a red pantsuit and black sunglasses, hair blowing. Her condo was in a hulking, pyramid-shaped structure with blackened windows, and I could see whitecaps on the bay in the space between buildings. The royal palms that lined the street snapped in the wind. Marse leaned in to tell Lidia she tended to get carsick, and Lidia moved to the backseat.

"Hi," said Marse to me. "Still friends?"

"You bet," I said, and turned on the radio.

After we were on the expressway, Marse started shifting in her seat, pulling at her waistband. "This underwear rides up," she said. "I will be performing this maneuver from time to time."

"That's fine," I said.

Lidia cleared her throat.

"What?" said Marse. "Viv is dead, so I can't warn people about my panties?"

"Do we need to make a stop?" said Lidia.

"No, thank you," said Marse, sighing.

Lidia reached forward and turned off the radio. "Let's share pleasant memories of Vivian," she said.

The air conditioner hummed, pushing too-cold air against my cheeks. The low, cramped neighborhoods that lined the highway gave way to endless green groves. I'd always wished they'd erected Florida's turnpike along the water; the state's long neck offered some of the dullest driving in the country. In the Midwest, highways were nestled among rolling hills, white in winter and green in summer, among farmsteads with collapsing barns the color of dried blood. In the winter, horses wore heavy blankets and cows huddled together against fences, forming shifting tapestries.

Lidia said, "She hated church. You probably didn't know that, Marse. Once we were sitting together—Charlie wouldn't come, of course, and I wasn't married, not that any husband of mine would be caught dead—and the Father led us in prayer, and I bowed my head. I don't know what I was thinking about—my grocery list or something—but I was, you know, making good in the role of parishioner and all that. And then Viv leans over and pinches my arm and says, 'Wake up!'"

Marse's laugh was throaty and died fast. "I guess I understand her husband going nuts like that." She looked at me. "Sorry."

Lidia said, "He was grieving. People do it differently."

Marse said to Lidia, "I met Vivian the first time at your house, right after Jennifer decided not to go to college. Viv said Charlie was angry, and she'd told him to relax. She said all she'd learned in college was how to type a memo and meet a husband, and she could teach Jennifer that herself."

Lidia laughed lightly for a long time, and then we were quiet.

LIDIA DIRECTED ME THROUGH A maze of Kissimmee strip malls to the expansive Palms at Park Place Rest Home. I wasn't sure why we were stopping there, but she and Marse seemed to take the stop as a given, so I didn't ask. I trailed them as they checked in at the front desk. Vivian's room was located down a long hallway on the third floor. The carpet was bright green, and on the pale pink walls were watercolors of ducks on lakes and biplanes on runways. The door of the room was open, but Lidia knocked before entering. I was the last inside, so I was the last to see that Charlie was there, sitting in an armchair, his skin ashy and his eyes swollen. He moved as if to stand, but Lidia motioned for him not to bother. "Charlie," she said. "It's just terrible."

He noticed me standing in the doorway. He cocked his head.

"I'm so sorry," I said.

He looked awful in his stiff suit and shiny shoes and loosely knotted tie. Even the way he was sitting, spine straight against the back of the chair—he looked as if he wanted to leave but wasn't allowed. The room was small, with only a bed and chair and small dresser. Lidia and Marse sat on the floral bedspread. Charlie avoided looking at them.

"I thought we could pack her things," Lidia said.

"Yes, thank you. There might be something you ladies want. Her photographs are at the house. You should get some. I can give you a key."

"I have a key," said Lidia. "You don't want her photographs?"

"There are hundreds. Take some, leave the rest."

"Fine," said Lidia.

I wanted her to quit being so abrupt with him. But whatever was happening between them, it was years in the making.

It was Marse who stepped in. "I'd love to have one," she said. "She was so talented."

Lidia continued to look at Charlie without blinking. He stared at his lap and covered his mouth with one hand. Marse went to the closet and pulled down a suitcase and opened it on the bed. She brought down a stack of sweaters, then started to pull blouses and dresses off hangers and fold them neatly in the well of the suitcase. Lidia started to help but I didn't move.

"Is this okay?" Marse said to Charlie. He nodded, and they continued. Trip by trip, the closet emptied.

I felt a presence behind me and turned to find a man staring into the room. He had very light blue eyes, short dark hair with a graying cowlick, and a long, rectangular face with heavy jowls, though the rest of him was fit. He wore a short-sleeved plaid shirt tucked into tan pants, and black leather slippers.

"Good afternoon, Anthony," said Charlie impatiently.

The man nodded to Charlie. To Lidia and Marse, he said, "What are you doing?"

Lidia stopped. "We're packing Vivian's things, Anthony."

"I wish you wouldn't."

Lidia looked at Charlie, who shrugged. "Is there something in particular you'd like to have?" she said to Anthony.

He opened and closed his mouth. "Her pillow."

Lidia looked again at Charlie, who was staring out the window. She went to the head of the bed and took one of the pillows there. I moved out of the way, and ended up squeezed between the dresser and the wall.

Anthony hugged the pillow to his chest. To me, he said, "You're her daughter?"

"For Christ's sake," said Charlie.

I shook my head. "No, I'm not," I said to Anthony.

Anthony looked back at Lidia. "Perfume?" he said.

"No," said Charlie.

Anthony gave a soft whimper. "Her reading glasses, then. The purple ones. Please."

Lidia looked at Charlie, who said nothing. She went to the bedside table and brought back a pair of bifocals with a red beaded cord. Anthony took them carefully in one hand and continued to clutch the pillow with the other. No one spoke. Then Charlie stood up, saying, "Enough." He stepped to the dresser—we locked eyes as he went—and reached toward several squat bottles arranged on a mirrored tray. He hesitated. "Which one?" he said, speaking to Anthony but looking sideways at me.

"The pink one," said Anthony.

Charlie seemed to know which one Anthony would choose. It was the least full bottle. He sniffed it almost imperceptibly before handing it over. "Could you leave, please?"

"Thank you," mumbled Anthony.

Lidia patted his shoulder and he walked away. She went back to packing.

"I meant all of you," said Charlie.

Lidia dropped a sweater into the suitcase. "We'll come back after the service."

"I appreciate it," said Charlie. He held his hand up to his face, to shield it from sight. Marse and Lidia left the room, but I stayed behind.

"What are you doing here?" he said to me.

"I brought Lidia."

"I don't want you here."

"I'm sorry."

He glanced toward the open doorway, as if afraid of being caught, then reached for my hand. I was certain the ladies were just beyond the doorway, possibly listening. I kneeled beside the chair. His hand was cold in mine, the skin papery and dry. He took it away, touched his jaw with his fingers. "I wish you hadn't come," he said gently.

"Why?"

"It's odd, seeing you here."

"It's odd seeing you here, too."

This was true. I'd never seen him on solid land. It was as if he'd grown several sizes in his clothes and needed more air than the room could provide.

"Were you here when she died?" I said.

He nodded. "Riggs loaned me his car. After I got here it was only another hour or so. She didn't know who I was."

"Maybe she did."

"Don't be a child."

I blanched.

"Damn it," he said. "I apologize."

"Was it horrible?"

"Not particularly. Yes. It was quiet."

I thought of my mother's death, which had not been quiet. "That's better," I said.

"I held one hand, Anthony held the other. It's not like I didn't know it was coming. But I hadn't seen her in a year." He seemed to have trouble catching his breath. "So if I knew it was coming, how come I'm so—so—"

"I know." My mother's death, which had been inevitable for more than a year, was as shocking as a multicar pileup. I said, "You should let them pack up. It will help."

"That's fine."

"I can stay with you."

"No. Go." Up went his hand again, blocking his face. I touched it with my fingertips. I closed the door behind me as I went out. Lidia and Marse were in the hallway, looking abashed. We walked to the car without speaking. The service was still an hour off, so we went to a diner. Marse and Lidia each ordered a slice of pie, so I ordered one as well.

"He's a mess," said Marse.

To Lidia, I said, "Why do you hate him?"

"I guess I don't, really."

"Why did you send me to work for him?"

She took a small bite and chewed slowly. "I knew Vivian wanted someone who would be good to him."

"Vivian did?"

"She'd been so fond of your mom. And when you said you were moving back—well, it seemed like a good idea at the time."

"And now?"

She pursed her lips. "She worried about him, all those years. I never understood it."

Marse signaled the waitress for more coffee. "Poor Anthony," she said.

Lidia and I looked at her.

"What?" she said. "He sort of lost a wife, too."

"He has a wife," Lidia said. "She lives in Atlanta. Their son runs his business."

"Henry Gale," I said, making the connection for the first time. So this is how Charlie and Henry had met, linked by the inappropriate yet innocent coupling of their loved ones.

Lidia was smiling.

"What?" I said.

"I was just thinking about your father. Viv did not care for him. She thought I was crazy for marrying him, knowing how things had been with your mother. People can be wrong. And people can change, at least a little, which sometimes is enough. No one knows what goes on behind closed doors."

"I didn't think you were crazy," I said.

"I've always liked that about you."

THE SERVICE WAS IN A chapel not far from the rest home. Marse and Lidia and I sat in a row filled with women, some of whom I recognized from Lidia's backyard klatches. Lidia nodded to them or kissed cheeks. But then she went up to sit with Charlie, who until then had been the sole occupant of the front pew. Behind him sat Anthony Gale and a man with a helmet of thick black hair: Henry. I stared at his profile until he turned toward me. He gave a small, festive wave, then shrugged his shoulders and rolled his eyes a little, as if we were in cahoots. That someone was glad to see me was a great relief. When he turned away, he put his arm around his father's shoulders, which were shaking. I hadn't known, until putting two and two together that day, that Henry had a deteriorating parent. Sometimes I forgot that other people's parents can die. I wasn't even sure how Graham was handling his mother's death. The time I'd asked, during a brief phone chat, he'd seemed a little impatient with the question, as if he was tired of talking about it, or as if there was so much to say that there was no point even getting started.

Lidia and one other friend gave eulogies. Lidia told a story of driving to New Orleans with Vivian when they were nineteen, then talked about raising their kids together, then called Vivian one of the most resilient people she'd ever met. There was a photo of Vivian propped beside the lectern. In it, she wore a white blouse with a skewed collar, a rope of salt-and-pepper hair blowing across her neck. She shaded her eyes with one hand and smiled coyly. She looked like a European movie star. Normally, I found this kind of woman—beautiful, glamorous, graceful—off-putting, so I avoided looking at the photo, lest it spoil me on Vivian, who I now thought of protectively, as if I'd known her well.

My eyes drew to the back of Charlie's head, and I thought of the afternoon two weeks before when I'd trimmed his hair. He'd begged me, handing over the clippers. I had no experience, and had worked so slowly that he'd nodded off in the chair, his head jerking away from my hand.

Vivian's body would be taken back to Miami, so there was no trip to the cemetery, but the reception was back at the Palms at Park Place, in a hall that had likely seen hundreds of replicated gatherings. Coffee urns percolated noisily in the corner beside trays of crudités and squares of cheese and dry bricks of brownie. The wallpaper was gold-and-burgundy filigree, the furniture scuffed brass and worn maroon velvet.

Marse and I sat in the corner. "I need a nap and a glass of wine," she said, slipping off her heels. Then she straightened up and put her shoes back on. "I'll be right back."

Henry Gale found me. He sat and balanced a plate of food on his knee and offered to share it. We both ate from it until it was empty. I said, "I'm sorry about your father."

"It's going fast. But not fast enough for him to miss this." He waved a hand. "He's like a widower. And my mom's up in Georgia, playing bridge on Tuesdays and golf on Thursdays. She's kind of a widow, too." It seemed the notion had occurred to him for the first time. His cheeks above the dark beard were as pink and smooth as a child's. He stared at his own hands. They were large, fleshy hands, the palms faintly lined. I had the urge to take them in my own, but I kept still.

I said, "I loved the last batch of portraits. You're very talented."

He blushed. "Charlie's the artist. I'm just a technician." He cocked his head, regarding me. "I'll tell you a secret—I'm a little drunk. My father keeps a bottle of Scotch in his room, but he's forgotten it's there." His smile, engulfed by the abundant beard, was wry and sad. His shoulders slumped. "That's not nice of me, is it? Vivian was very nice."

"That's what I hear."

Marse came back with two paper cups and handed one to me. They were filled with sweet-smelling white wine. "Anniversary celebration next door," she said, scanning the room. "Vivian would've hated this. At least the old Vivian would have."

She looked Henry up and down, then introduced herself. She was older, but I could see them hitting it off, in an opposites-attract kind of way.

"I'll be around," she said to him, then crossed the room to a group of women, who parted to greet her. Nearby, Lidia was telling a woman in an apron that they needed to bring out more brownies and paper cups.

"Your friend," said Henry, motioning with his chin toward Marse. "Single?"

"Go for it," I said. I brushed crumbs from my lap and excused myself.

I checked first in Vivian's room. The door was open but the room was empty. I continued down the hall, then pushed open the heavy fire door to the stairwell, thinking I might find some back exit to a garden or lawn, but instead I found Charlie. He sat on a cement stair, slumped against the wall. He'd removed his jacket and tie and unbuttoned the top buttons of his shirt. His hair was a little askew, as if he'd run his hands through it without brushing it back into place. The lighting was dim and the air was cool. I was not at all surprised to find him there, in the least public place he could find. He looked as if he'd been returned to his own body.

"Nice service," I said.

He wiped his mouth. "I didn't speak."

"That doesn't matter."

I said it to myself as much as to him. I hadn't spoken, when it had been my turn. My father had left the podium expecting me to take his place—he'd choked up while speaking, which had surprised me— but I'd just sat still, feeling the cold wood of the church pew against the backs of my knees, thinking about driving to Key Biscayne in my mother's car, her hair electrified by wind, her expression resolute, hands at ten and two o'clock on the wheel. She'd hated to drive, especially in traffic, which in Miami was difficult to avoid. Usually I drove; why

I hadn't on the afternoon of this particular memory, I had no idea. Maybe Graham's aversion to driving hadn't turned me off, as surely it had many women before me, because it was familiar.

"She wasn't so perfect," said Charlie. "We build people up for this kind of thing."

"Of course she wasn't perfect," I said.

"When Jennifer died, she closed up. She blamed me."

"I doubt that's true," I said, thinking that Lidia seemed to believe the opposite. But how much could Lidia know about what went on in their marriage?

"She hated me." He looked up, a hint of cruelty in his eyes. "She said I'd dawdled on the way to Jenny's, that I'd lingered over coffee. She said I'd been putting off spending time with my child."

This hit me. It sounded like something I might have said to Graham, had I been in the habit of saying such things. But if something happened—something like what had happened to Jennifer— maybe I would say it.

"This is a dead end," I said.

He clenched his teeth. "Fuck her."

"Take a drink, please."

He took a long swallow from my cup, then handed it back. He slapped his palms on the step, and the sound echoed. "Get me out of here?" he said.

Then it was the two of us I pictured speeding away with the windows open. But when I moved toward him—I was going to give him a hand getting up—he pulled me down, so I was kneeling one step below where he sat. He tugged on the front of my blouse and I tipped toward him, and then his mouth was on mine. His whiskers were rough against my chin, his hands rough in my hair and on my neck. We tasted of the cheap wine. He cupped my breast with one hand and my waist with the other. Then I felt him lose heart. I tried to draw him back, but he pushed me away.

"Don't," I said.

"Stop. Stop, Georgia."

I pivoted away from him, breathing hard. I touched the places on my face where his stubble had scrubbed my skin. The weight of what I'd done started to press on me. I said, "I'm married."

"I'm not," he said.

His tone—mournful—reminded me that this wasn't about us at all. I stood up, smoothing my skirt, and before I knew it I was back in the carpeted hallway among the watercolors and elevator music. He did not follow or call out for me. I waited outside the reception hall until Lidia and Marse emerged, and together we went upstairs to gather the rest of Vivian's things. There was no sign of Charlie.

It was almost dark by the time we packed the car, and before we hit the interstate, Marse directed us to look up at the gossamer lavender clouds. She was one of a distinct sect of born-and-bred Floridians, people who couldn't imagine living anywhere else, like my father.

"I gave that Henry Gale my number," said Marse.

"Good for you," I said.

I glanced in the rearview mirror: Lidia's forehead was pressed against the window. Marse went on about Henry and I half-listened. After I dropped off Marse, Lidia didn't bother to move up next to me, and we didn't speak. Maybe my guilt was visible, a film on my skin. At Sally's house, I moved Frankie into his car seat without waking him, and Sally yawned and said she wanted to keep him for her own. When I hoisted him out of the car in Lidia's driveway, Lidia rubbed his back and looked at me with her sad eyes. "*Muchas gracias,*" she said finally, then turned away.

I guess he hadn't taken a key when he'd left, because Graham's body took shape in the darkness as I struggled down the lawn with Frankie in my arms. He was standing on the dock, looking out at the canal with his hands in his pockets. His hair reflected the moonlight. The sight of him made my heart race and my face heat up. He turned when he heard my footsteps, then reached to take Frankie from me. He kissed Frankie's hair, shushing quietly. I unlocked the sliding door and waited outside. I picked up a piece of paper from the table and strained to make it out in the low light coming through the glass. It was another citation from the City of Coral Gables. This time, they were giving us ten days to vacate, or they would confiscate the houseboat.

When Graham came back, he collapsed into a deck chair and pulled me onto his lap.

"You're back?" I said. I motioned to the citation. "And I guess we're out of here."

"Apparently," he said, letting his eyelids drop.

He rested his head on my chest. I brushed his hair with my fingers. "You're home?" I said again.

He nodded against me and sighed heavily. He didn't need to tell me that something other than love for his family had driven him off the ship. I knew this well enough.

That night, Graham slept, and I went to the roof deck and watched the surface of the canal shudder in the breeze. It was well after midnight. I figured that if the neighbor woman had taken a swim that night, she'd long since finished. But then I heard the whispering pull of her stroke, and I stood as she hauled herself out of the water.

"Hey," I hissed.

She spun around, pulling her towel tight. "Yes?"

"Did you call the police about us?"

She waited a second before answering. "It's against the law," she said.

"There are alligators in this water, you know."

"So I've heard," she said.

16

DID I BETRAY MY OWN son?

What happened next, I'll tell quickly, because it's difficult for me to do any other way.

Graham was back, loaded down and heavy-lidded with the weight of whatever had happened on the *R. V. Roger Revelle*. He didn't offer details, except to say he wasn't needed back at work for a while. I didn't press him. We kept Frankie home from preschool the next day and spent hours at the zoo. Frankie jumped and spun and made faces and pulled on Graham's hand and laughed aloud at his own silliness. His bliss was beautiful and difficult to watch. He and Graham spent a long time studying a gaggle of baby penguins in a glass incubator; they giggled each time one of the sleepy babies tripped or yawned. Graham tried to get Frankie to say what he wanted to do for his birthday, which was four days away. Did he want to learn to ride a bike? Did he want a cake in the shape of a sea animal? Frankie spoke but not a whole lot, and Graham looked a little spooked, but terribly proud, each time.

When I mentioned I'd been looking for a live-aboard slip at a marina close to Rosenstiel, Graham frowned. "Let's just sell the damn thing," he said. "We shouldn't have bought it in the first place."

"I don't know if we need to do that," I said, and he gave me a look. I let it drop.

We ate ice-cream cones that dripped aggressively in the heat, and Frankie ended up with a mess all over his face and hands and hair. Graham told him he looked like a chocolate monster, which Frankie found uproariously funny.

"Chaw-cot monster!" he shouted, splaying his fingers. *"Roar!"*

That night, Graham took his pills and I helped him fasten his cuff, then tiptoed out to check on Frankie, who had been in bed for three hours by that time. I was in the habit of checking on him almost every night, and typically I found him deeply asleep, face flushed and bedclothes bundled at his feet, pajama top bunched around his upper chest, showing the pooled flesh of his belly. I would whisper my love in his ear and tiptoe away.

This night, however, I found him not sleeping but fully awake, staring calmly but wide-eyed at the ceiling of his berth, bedclothes tucked neatly around his still body.

I knew then what had to happen. I shushed and sang to Frankie until his eyelids dropped. When Graham woke just after sunrise, he could tell from my demeanor that something was wrong. But he couldn't talk until he'd crawled from the cave of medicated sleep. I made pancakes and scrambled eggs. Frankie ate and drank and smiled but didn't speak. I fought the urge to shake the words out of him. For the first time I noticed something different—something I'd forgotten, maybe, or had never allowed myself to acknowledge—in his expression. It was a certain depth of consciousness, as if he'd shrunk a little inside his own skin, and now wore that skin like a costume. I could see my boy in there. I sat next to him at the table, powerless to stop myself from touching his hair, his shoulder, his warm back.

After breakfast, I took Frankie up to Lidia's, then came back to face

Graham. I told him the facts: what Emily Barrett-Strout had said the first time she'd met Frankie, the progress he'd made while Graham had been away, and what I'd seen the night before. I willed myself to be steely, but my voice trembled. "There is no choice," I said. "I love you. But you have to go."

"I'll go to Detention," Graham said, blinking back shocked tears. "I won't come back until things are better."

This was exactly what I'd once imagined happening. But I saw now that it had been a threadbare plan at best, and had unraveled somewhere along the line.

"You should go get better," I said. "But you can't come back to us." The act of saying the words took my breath away.

"I am so sorry," he said, his face in his hands.

I shook my head. He kept talking. He didn't know what was wrong with him, he said. He hated himself, but he loved me and Frankie. He said it time and again, that he loved our boy. His usual reticence, his moodiness, was gone, replaced by a slavish need that reminded me that he had recently lost his mother. My resolve shook but didn't crumble. I was surprised at the fervor with which he fought for us; I was touched by it. My urge to cower under Frankie, to push him forward as an excuse, was strong, so I quashed it, and by doing so was probably more tight-lipped than was fair. He offered to get his own apartment after coming back from Detention, until he could prove himself. He'd live apart from us for the rest of the marriage if it came to that, he said. These were desperate schemes, but he was completely serious, as if he believed our lives together made up a perfect puzzle with only one missing piece.

It was hours before he exhausted of protesting. His hands shook and his eyes were red-rimmed and swollen. I put on an air of finality. As my mother would have said, you have to fake it until you make it. "You'll be all right," I said. I fought the urge to tell him I would miss him, to take him in my arms.

"I can't imagine that's true," he said, biting down on the words.

I wanted to tell him I was sorry. Not for making him leave, but for the loss of all that we used to have together, which was now officially and irrevocably gone. I was sorry, too, that he'd lost his mother—this devastation had gotten buried under our own—and I was sorry because he was a loyal person, a person who held on even when things were not right. I understood that I had gone a long way toward ruining his life although he had not ruined mine. I wasn't willing to say it all—that I wanted more for Frankie than Graham was able to give, parasomnia aside. That I had made a mistake, not in having Frankie but in having him with Graham. I thought if I held back, it would be a kindness, that I might stop short of breaking his heart. But I knew, too, that by asking him to leave, I was revealing that I no longer had faith in him, which was the ugliest bit of it all.

He spent a long time dawdling over his bags. Meaning to help him, I went into the main berth and found him holding Charlie's early mermaid sketch, the one I'd brought home. It was still in its plastic sleeve. Graham must have found it in the back of the storage trundle.

In his expression there was anger, exhaustion, resignation. "Does this have anything to do with him?" he said.

"This is about our family."

I had no doubt that he could see the full truth—that my fidelity had been compromised—on my face. His haggard, beautiful features turned to stone.

He stopped at Lidia's to say good-bye and call a taxi. He said he'd return for his bikes and anything else he'd forgotten. This was a last-ditch effort to allow me to soften the lines of demarcation. I steadied myself and said that was fine, but to please call first. He looked as if he didn't recognize me. I stepped inside the house as he stepped out, and found Lidia standing in the kitchen with her hand on her hip, looking at me with what could only be described as pride.

Did I betray my own son?

I'd raised him, until that day, in a home I knew had the potential to be unsafe. I'd let him think each night when he went to bed that he might wake to some unimaginable chaos.

I did betray him, yes. And the fact that I did, along with everything that happened after, remains with me still.

four

17

THE DAY GRAHAM LEFT WAS a Friday. Frankie and I spent the rest of that day at Lidia's, treating her house like a recovery ward. She fussed over us, bringing cookies and milk on trays, asking hourly if we needed anything. Frankie requested animal crackers and she told him she'd run to get some. A minute later I heard her car start, and then she was back with two boxes and a bunch of fruit. I let Frankie watch cartoons until he crawled onto my lap and fell asleep. I moved him and covered him with a blanket, then went to the kitchen to call Dinner Key Marina. There was a slip for rent starting on the first of the month. The dockmaster required a deposit. I knew it would take more than I could muster to leave the house that day, so I promised to bring it the following morning, which he said would be fine. Then I called the Coral Gables Police Department and asked for the officer who had issued our most recent citation. I left a message promising to vacate the canal as soon as the slip was ready for us. I never heard back.

My father and Lidia came and went; my father, passing through, paused to rub my shoulder and kiss the top of my head. Every time someone entered the room, I spooked like a skittish animal. My voice was tinny and strained. In the late afternoon, bleached sunlight blazed through the living room windows. When Lidia noticed me shielding my eyes, she pulled the curtains, and I felt again like I could breathe. In lieu of anything resembling an evening meal, she brought out an enormous bowl of fresh, cold strawberries, and I ate one after another until they were gone. She brought a second bowl. I felt as if without those strawberries and their bold flavor in my mouth, their firm flesh under my teeth, I might have floated away, as untethered physically as I felt otherwise.

When I remember that day—oddly, the last day of relative peace for some time—I can vaguely recall the noise of the small television set Lidia kept in the kitchen, which my father watched while eating a meal. And I can recall a certain urgency in the voice of the meteorologist as he described what was happening eight hundred miles east of us, over the blue Atlantic. At some point, I fell asleep on the couch, the weather as distant as any other story writing itself outside the walls of that house.

When I blinked awake, it was almost dark. Frankie was eating a sandwich in front of the television. Lidia sat cross-legged beside him. She heard me stir. "There's a hurricane coming," she said.

"Really," I said.

Frankie twisted to face us. "For my birthday it coming?"

"Birthday hurricane," I said. "Exactly."

Like most South Floridians, I tended not to get worked up about weather events until they were nearly upon us. The system heading our way had been given a name forty-eight hours earlier, but I'd bet that most locals could not have said what that name was. I knew it, but only because Graham had brought it to my attention. He'd said that in a season full of dissolved weather events, this little storm might be the first thing with a bit of tooth to it.

After I put Frankie down in the guest room, Lidia and I watched the Weather Channel until I fell asleep on the sofa. I woke in the night to a blue flickering light, and found my father standing in front of the kitchen television, which was turned very low. I joined him. "What are you doing?" I said.

"Just thinking," he said. "Remember at the old house, all those high windows? What a chore. Your mother would make sandwiches before-hand. We'd live off pimento cheese for a week."

Half a dozen times during my childhood, he'd climbed a ladder to tape up the roofline windows of the family room. He'd stocked the garage with bottled water and batteries and ice. We'd all huddled around the television with my mother's sandwiches and homemade lemonade. Every hurricane in my lifetime had either dissolved or angled away before it could hit.

I found it jarring when my father showed nostalgia for our old life. "I remember," I said.

EARLY SATURDAY MORNING, FRANKIE AND I sat at the kitchen table with Lidia, eating cereal and talking about our trip to the zoo. Frankie was mostly quiet but spoke in spurts, and each time he spoke, he mentioned *Daddy*, which hurt my heart. I had no idea where Graham had gone the day before—probably to a hotel. I'd asked him to call when he was settled, but there had been no word. When the phone rang, Lidia answered, then handed me the receiver.

It was Riggs. "You're needed," he said.

Gusts of wind muffled the sound on his end. He was probably at the marina, dry-docking his boat.

"Where?" I said.

"Where do you think? Get out there."

The notion of seeing Charlie was daunting, but not because of the weather. The hurricane wouldn't make landfall until the following af-ternoon at the earliest, if it made landfall at all. The day was bright, blue, and cloudless.

I asked Lidia if she could watch Frankie while I helped Charlie, but at the mention of Stiltsville, Frankie protested. "Don't go without Frankie!" he said.

Lidia smoothed his hair. "Maybe today you want to be with Mama?" She looked pointedly at me.

"I'll pack us up," I said.

"Your father's gone for supplies. They're saying shelves are clearing out."

"I wouldn't worry," I said.

"Big storm coming!" said Frankie.

I went down to the *Lullaby* for my tote. This was the time of day when the boat's northern windows were shaded by the tangled hammocks that separated Lidia's dock from her neighbor's. The houseboat was quiet and warm, with no sign of the turmoil that had taken place, save for the way it turned my stomach to be there. Graham's cuff hung on its leash; his pills sat on the shelf above the bed. He had other bottles, I knew, but no other cuff. Maybe he didn't believe that alone in a hotel room there was any reason to use it, though naturally I would disagree. I left the sliding door unlocked in case Graham needed to get in, for the cuff or pills or anything else.

Months later, I would read an article—for a year, Andrew would be a household name—about a storm researcher named Frank Marks. (Marks was, incidentally, on faculty at Rosenstiel, and I would wonder if Graham had known him, if maybe Marks was the scientist in the office adjacent to Graham's, the one who spent his days studying waves in a simulator.) In the article, Marks told how that Saturday, when the storm was still two days from land, he and some colleagues boarded a jet plane in Puerto Rico and spent ten hours penetrating the eye, probing every wind and pressure change, buffeted by violent drafts and blinded by rain and hail. By the time Marks had landed, he knew better than anyone what we were in for.

On the ride to Stiltsville, Frankie, sitting beside me on the captain's bench, pretended to watch for whales. He pointed excitedly every so often, saying, "I spot one! Never mind, just a dolphin." And once, that's exactly what it was. I cut the engine. A group of pale bottlenose dolphins dipped and rose at our starboard side, then darted into the deep green distance.

Charlie met us on the dock. He lifted Frankie from the boat. "I didn't think you'd come," he said.

"Riggs called."

"I see."

"I would have come anyway."

"I choose to believe you."

"It's true." In that moment, I realized that it was.

He smiled, and something between us broke. We climbed the stairs. On the porch, file boxes—my boxes, as I thought of them—were stacked three-high.

"Now I know this is serious," I said.

"If I make for shore, the storm won't land. I guarantee it."

Frankie aimed for his usual spot beneath the picture window, but Charlie caught him by the shoulder, then pulled from his pocket a small black-and-white penguin.

"Penguin!" said Frankie, racing away.

"I appreciate you coming to the funeral," Charlie said, avoiding my eyes. "I'm sorry I was disagreeable."

I was quiet.

"And I'm sorry for—"

"Don't apologize."

"It was the timing, that's all," he said. "That awful place." He was staring at me now, his eyes intent. I felt myself leaning toward him, my side meeting his side. Behind the wall of our bodies, out of Frankie's sightline, our fingers touched.

"Graham came home," I said. "I asked him to move out."

He frowned and shook his head. "Poor fellow."

This irked me for some reason. Why wouldn't he be relieved, after all? Why wouldn't he reassure me that I'd done the right thing? But when I started to pull away, he tugged me back.

"I don't mean it that way," he said. "I just feel for the guy."

"I feel for him, too," I said.

"I know." He searched my eyes, his face inches from mine. I wanted to tell him he had nothing to do with me and Graham—was this purely true?—but then Frankie's voice came from the living room. "Ship!" he said excitedly, as if it was the first time he'd seen one from that very spot.

"We'd better get to it," said Charlie, and slapped me firmly on the behind.

FRANKIE AMUSED HIMSELF WITH A puzzle while Charlie and I made trip after trip to the Zodiac, filling the well of the little boat. By the time the space was full, it was so hot that Frankie was sweating through his shirt. We took a break to swim in the cloudy jade water off the dock. Frankie counted the sea urchins that littered the seabed, then the starfish. It seemed incredible that a storm might materialize from the empty sky. Charlie led us to the shallower water beneath the dock and pointed to a dark grouping in the shade, clumped around a piling.

"Lobsters," he said.

"What they doing?" said Frankie.

Charlie explained that they were molting. They did it at least once a year. "My house is their favorite place," he said. "The trappers don't know they come here."

"It's secret," said Frankie.

"They eat their own shells," said Charlie, wrinkling his nose.

"Yucky!" said Frankie.

I put Frankie down for a nap and Charlie and I listened to the radio for updates. The storm was still tracking toward South Florida—there was a possibility that the Bahamas would break its stride—but if it hit, it would do so late Sunday or early Monday, which meant it was still more than twenty-four hours away.

"It slowed down," I said to Charlie. "Isn't that good?"

"Sometimes a thing needs time to grow."

I had a thought. "Can we stay over tonight? We'll sleep in the office," I said. "I think Frankie would enjoy it, just this once." I didn't say: *In case the house is gone by Monday*. This seemed far-fetched. I had the feeling that all of it—the packing up and shipping out—was a bit of elaborate theater, and we had no choice but to play our parts.

His knee pressed against mine. "I'll sleep in the office. You two take my room."

And then—I don't know who started it—we were kissing softly, unhurriedly. This time, there was no reluctance. He was sure-handed and calm. I climbed onto his lap and his hands moved inside my shirt, his palms rough against my back. There was the feeling that life was speeding forward in an untenable way, that if I didn't do something to slow it down, it would spiral out of control. The feeling was not unwelcome.

Frankie called out for me when he woke. I pulled reluctantly away from Charlie, wiping my mouth. As I moved from the living room to the bedroom, I felt his gaze on my body.

We worked until late afternoon, at which point Charlie declared that the Zodiac would stand no more weight, and he would make a run to shore. He radioed Riggs to meet him at the marina, and I wrote a note asking Riggs to call Lidia and my father, to tell them we would be out for the night. Off Charlie went with the oil paintings from his walls—the fact that they were valuable was clear from the way he wrapped each carefully in cardboard and twine—and about half of the boxes of portraits. Charlie didn't want to bother with the furniture or his clothes or kitchen wares—whether this was because these items weren't worth much to him, or he was still skeptical the house would sustain damage, I wasn't sure—but I'd reminded him to at least pack a bag of essentials.

He would spend the following night, Sunday, at Riggs's condo, and I would spend it at Lidia's. I knew my father would have taped all the windows and stocked a cooler with sandwiches and soda. He would have hauled the patio furniture inside and secured the rosebushes beneath a tarp. I knew, too, he would have lengthened the mooring lines on the *Lullaby*, so it could rise and fall with the surging canal without snapping loose. All along the canal, backyards would have been bared of decoration, windows mummified with tape or shutters. When I thought of that next night, the night of the still-theoretical storm, I pictured me and Frankie and Lidia and my father huddled together in the living room, lights flickering and trees thrashing, and I felt a delighted shiver. Then came a pang of guilt: Graham would be alone.

Charlie headed off with a wave. While he was gone, Frankie and I drew pictures of stingrays and manatees at the kitchen counter, then sat on the porch, singing—this was Frankie's choice—Christmas carols. He asked questions about the hurricane: Is it here yet? Why did it get that name? Will it be wet or dry? Will it make it all the way to Mimi and Papi? Will we see it?

The sunlight thickened as evening approached. The breeze slowed, then died.

In the time I'd spent at the stilt house, I'd learned a good bit about its logistics. I knew that the generator came on only to cook meat or boil water, and for showers—Charlie didn't abide cold water—and I knew that Charlie always closed the bedroom and bathroom doors, to cut off the hottest part of the house. I knew that on particularly beastly days, Charlie draped dark sheets over the bedroom windows, keeping out as much heat as possible. I knew that sometimes this wasn't good enough, so he dragged one of the spare mattresses onto the eastern porch and slept there until his own bed was habitable again. I'd learned that there were mosquitoes at Stiltsville, but not many, and only on evenings with very little wind, and there were none of the no-see-ums that hounded us in the canal. There were a few cockroaches around, too, and once I'd asked Charlie where they came from—for a second I wondered if maybe they could swim—and he'd cocked his head at me. "They come with us," he said.

I turned on the generator to make dinner, and when I was finished and turned it off, the noise died abruptly and a hush descended. I went to the porch to scan the channel and was reminded, briefly and fondly, of how the midwestern sky gathered before a snowstorm, smelling faintly of tin and blotting out sound and light and all sense of distance.

It was distressing to be at the house without Charlie. Any fantasy I'd indulged of moving out there, even temporarily, revealed its foolishness for a number of reasons, not the least of which was—this was a surprise to me—I didn't much enjoy it. With no means of getting us home, I was jumpy and agitated. I followed Frankie every time he crossed the room or went to the bathroom, scooting close as we sat together. This was something that had been taken from me with motherhood— the ability to relax and enjoy something as idyllic as an evening on an island. After we ate, we worked on a jigsaw puzzle that was much too difficult for him. I offered heavy-handed assistance, my ear trained to the open doorway, listening for the Zodiac's high whine.

Finally, Charlie returned. The Zodiac's engine noise deepened in pitch and cut off. This is what it's like, I thought as I got up to greet him. It felt like waiting for rescue. I think for Charlie, the sound of a boat headed in his direction hastened his heartbeat the way the solitude hastened mine. I wondered what it felt like for him to head back knowing someone was waiting for him. Was this something he would even enjoy, if it happened regularly? Something told me it was not.

I watched from the porch as he stepped off the boat. He looked up pleasantly, his face youthful in the blue evening. "Do I smell food?" he said, then clapped a hand against his stomach.

We finished loading up the remaining boxes, then worked by candlelight over the puzzle. Charlie and I attended closely to Frankie,

bringing him bowl after bowl of cubed pineapple for dessert. I let him
stay up until his eyes took on their glassy look. He was excited to be
sleeping at the stilt house—he'd clapped and jumped around when I'd
told him—and I worried that he would be disappointed by the experience, which in reality would be not much different, for him, than a long
nap. I took my time tucking him in. I sang our usual songs and read
our usual books. The moonlight through the window blued his skin
and lips. He fought sleep. I sang again, read again, until he turned over,
pulling my hand alongside his body and burying it in his warm neck. A
few minutes later his grip loosened, and I moved away.

Charlie wasn't in the living room when I returned. The candles
were still burning, dripping clear wax onto the part of the puzzle we'd
completed. I blew them out. I stood in the dark until I was certain
Frankie was asleep. Once a week or so, he might rise in the night to
use the bathroom or drink water, and it occurred to me now to deliver
a glass to his bedside, just in case. But I didn't do it because I heard
footsteps on the porch, and Charlie appeared in the doorway.

"Coming?" he whispered. He put out a hand for me.

IT WAS TWO OR THREE in the morning—time blurs—when I
found myself standing on the far edge of the stilt house dock, having
negotiated its zigs and zags in near total darkness, my hand touching the flat top of each piling as I passed, feeling the cool cement on
my fingertips. Water slapped against the pilings. There was a smudge
of moonshine against the surface of the sky and on the planes of the
waves in the channel. Hot wind tugged at my hair. I doubted we were
the only ones out at Stiltsville, but it felt as if we were. The nerves I'd
felt the evening before were gone. It seemed to me, for a long moment,
that there was nothing to fear in the world. I imagined that Charlie and
Frankie and I had survived some kind of apocalypse. We would make
the most of our supplies. We would swim every day until our fingertips
pruned. Frankie and Charlie would fish, and we would cross the flats

at low tide and raid the red house for propane and canned goods and reading material. We would be happy.

My hair moved against my shoulders. The stars pushed down against the night, and the lights of downtown Miami swelled, as did the blinking red lights of the radio tower to the northeast, and the fat black stalk of the lighthouse, and the weathered wood beneath the soles of my feet. All of it heaved against me. I felt as if time had paused. The moments that followed would stretch into hours, days, weeks.

I'd left Charlie dozing on a bare, salty mattress we'd dragged from the office onto the side porch, beneath the window where Frankie slept. When I heard footsteps upstairs, I assumed he was coming to join me. But something was off—the steps were too flat-footed, too frantic. I turned, and in the darkness I made out the figure of my son, my baby, as he shuffled through the doorway and across the porch, then walked straight into the railing, as if it wasn't even there. I called his name. He reached for me before he slipped. Down he went into the wide space between rail and floor, and then he was falling through the dark. The sounds of the wind and my screams were joined by the thud of my son's head hitting the dock. His body slumped, suddenly boneless, half on the dock and half off of it. Then he tumbled over the edge, and disappeared into the dark water.

18

MY MEMORY OF THAT NIGHT is comprised of fragments, of flashes of dark and noise, of the sensation of Frankie's limp body in my arms.

Charlie came around the corner the instant Frankie stumbled. He shouted Frankie's name as I did. He crossed the porch and dived to the floor and reached through the railing. He would tell me later that, unbelievably, his fingertips brushed Frankie's ankle. I moved forward to try to catch my son's falling body, though I can't recall how quickly. Was there a second when I stood still, unable to command my own legs? Was this a crucial second?

He fell headfirst but also sideways, so his belly hit just after his head, followed by his legs, which missed the dock almost entirely.

Maybe Charlie felt Frankie's ankle against his fingers. Maybe he was that fast, but I was not. By the time I reached Frankie—could it have taken more than three long strides?—he'd been swallowed by the water.

Charlie launched over the porch rail. Frankie was in his arms before he surfaced. Then Frankie was in my arms, and in the darkness I could barely make out his eyes rolling in their sockets, the lids fluttering. Charlie was shouting at me to get in the boat, then we were moving fast across the bay. I sat on a box and hollered at Frankie to keep his eyes open, to stay awake, to talk to me. I told him we were going to get help, that he was going to be all right. I told him to squeeze my hand. If he did, I didn't feel it. He did open his eyes, though, and kept them on me, but it didn't seem as if he saw me. It seemed as if he was looking through me to the star-filled sky. I had the fleeting thought that it was just like him to space out when I was vying mightily for his attention.

The left side of his face swelled, forcing his eye shut. The skin turned blue. His right eye maintained its dazed assessment of the space of my face. There were no tears.

The Zodiac rode low under the weight of all that paper. I didn't notice, but then there was a sharp slapping sound and the engine stalled and we jerked to a stop. I slid forward and landed in the well of the boat, Frankie in my arms. From Charlie came shouting and cursing. I kept talking to Frankie, telling him it was going to be okay, and then Charlie was up at the bow, pitching a box over the gunwale. At first I thought he was doing this out of frustration, and I stumbled to my feet with Frankie, meaning to stop him. But when he bent again to hoist another box into his arms and pitched that one after the first, I understood. I wanted to help him but I couldn't manage to let go of Frankie. I turned away from Charlie's frantic heaving and rocked Frankie in my arms. There was a heavy splash as each box hit the water. The sound cut through the static of my desperation, a terrible reminder of how thoroughly the world had upended itself.

When the boxes were gone—all but the one beneath me—Charlie tried to start the boat, and after several attempts we were again on our way. The engine continued to make a choking noise and every few minutes gave off a high-pitched whine, as if losing a fight.

Mercy Hospital was on the bay, with a cement dock twenty yards from the emergency room entrance. The Zodiac bumped hard against the wall and Charlie jumped off with the spring line and pulled us in. He barked at me to hand him Frankie. By the time I'd made it off the boat, he was almost at the emergency room entrance, Frankie's legs flapping at his side as he ran.

Inside the bright ER, Charlie drew the attention of a doctor and two nurses in blue scrubs. They directed him to an open bed, where he lay Frankie on his back. The fall had been at least fifteen feet, he was telling them, maybe more. The team ignored me as they secured a brace around Frankie's neck and shined a penlight in his eyes and snapped fingers beside his face. The doctor asked if he'd lost consciousness, and seemed skeptical when I said that I didn't think he had, not completely. Charlie stood apart from the activity, hands clamped over his mouth in a way that I couldn't bear. Someone—it might have been me—told the doctors Frankie's name, and then they were saying it loudly and often. A nurse tickled his feet. The doctor was young, black-haired and dark-skinned, with a prominent Adam's apple and a smooth, calming Cuban accent. He told me there were no obvious signs of spinal injury—this, apparently, was the worst-case scenario—but they would take Frankie immediately for a CAT scan, to assess the swelling in his brain and check for broken bones. "You need to wait here," said the doctor firmly. Then Frankie's bed was being rolled away, and though I hadn't realized I'd been holding Frankie's hand, I felt his fingers slip out of my own.

They were gone twenty minutes. Someone led me to a hard plastic chair. Charlie had disappeared, but then he was back, saying they wouldn't let him in during the scan. His hands went to his mouth.

"Stop that," I said.

He dropped his hands. "I'm so sorry. I don't know what to say."

I didn't understand for a moment, but the look on his face, his rapid blinking and tight jaw, explained: he felt responsible. If he was going to insist on offering himself up for blame, I thought I might let him. "Shut up," I said.

He looked afraid of me. He took a step away. The doctor and nurses came back with Frankie on a gurney, and they headed into another room. One nurse explained that they'd seen a severe concussion and two skull fractures, one along Frankie's eye socket, just above the eye, and one below, along the jawline. They believed he'd broken at least two or three ribs, but were taking him for X-rays to make certain.

"We're giving him something to sleep," said the nurse.

"Why?" I said.

"We need him to be as still as possible for as long as possible," she said, then hurried off.

As she went, I heard myself call after her. "Did you tell him good night?" Then Charlie was holding me up, because I could no longer hold myself.

LATER, AFTER THE EVACUATION, I would have a hard time remembering that first night, the night before Andrew, without remembering shaking walls and roaring wind. But my mind plays tricks. The storm hadn't hit us yet. It hadn't even gotten close.

An unearthly orange finger of sunrise was visible through a window by the time a nurse came to move us to the Intensive Care Unit. Frankie was given a bed in the middle of a row of beds, with heavy blue curtains separating him from his neighbors. Charlie and I had decided not to call Lidia's house—this would be the first step in trying to get in touch with Graham—until the sun was up, so after he'd settled me in at Frankie's bedside, Charlie went off to find a phone. The doctor came by while he was gone. His name was Dr. Cristian Lomano. He explained again about the sedation: he was concerned about the swelling in Frankie's brain, which he called "extensive," and about permanent damage to the optic nerve.

"He's a pretty big kid," the doctor said, nodding in approval. "Big kids *bounce*." This was, apparently, a small bit of good fortune.

Half an hour later, Lidia and my father burst into the room. He was dressed in rumpled linen trousers and her face was unmade. The circles under her eyes had a satiny mauve tint. She paled at the sight of Frankie's battered face and touched my shoulder tentatively. She glanced at Charlie.

"Hello," she said quietly, bending down to Frankie.

"Don't bump him," said Charlie.

These were the instructions we'd received. The nurses had fitted snug bolsters along either side of Frankie's body, pinning him into place in a funereal way, and around his neck and head they'd assembled a brace made of white plastic. His body filled only a slice of the hospital bed. His bare chest was wrapped in gauze.

Lidia's hands recoiled. She cupped them at her collarbone. "*Mi' jo,*" she said in a whisper. Then she did something I'd never seen from her before. I'd never seen it from my mother, either. She pivoted into my father's arms and buried her face in his chest, saying, "*Harvey Harvey Harvey.*" He rubbed her arms and shushed gently. "He'll be okay," he said. Whether it occurred to my father that this might not be the case, I don't know. It wasn't in his character to imagine the worst. This was a defect, in my estimation. I've always believed that the worst hunts us, and to be caught unsuspecting is to be some kind of sucker.

From where I sat at Frankie's side, I was free to study the wasted landscape of his face. I'd seen the X-rays: above his left eye was a fracture the size and shape of a man's eyebrow, and beneath the same eye, along the upper jaw, was a second fracture the shape of a sickle, an inch long. Scans had confirmed three broken ribs. But these injuries were buried, like the cracks in the earth's crust that cause an ocean to swell, and what one could see plainly was this: his face had been flattened in parts and engorged in others. His brow line rose and sloped like the neck of a spoon. His cheekbone was a hard, purple knot reminiscent of a link of sausage, and it was so turgid that it blended into the bridge of his nose. The skin was eggplant-colored in places and bright red in places, and his right eyelid, which wasn't swollen at all, was the sweet coral pink of the inside of a shell.

I was repulsed by the sight of his face—not the gruesomeness but the evident pain. At the same time, I was unable to look away. Watching him, while around me Charlie and Lidia and my father whispered and shuffled, seemed a great responsibility, one I'd shirked and now embraced feverishly, like a convert. I'd been judged. This was clear. The verdict was on Frankie's face.

People speak of strength in times of crisis, as if strength were some great beast that swoops in to gird us, to repair our voices and limbs when it seems they might fail. But to this day, I don't know exactly what we mean when we speak of strength. Was it strength that I didn't sob? Was it strength that kept me from screaming myself hoarse at every nurse who pulled back the curtain around Frankie's bed, kept me from demanding to know if he would recover, and when? Every few minutes, I bit down hard on the urge to shake my boy until he opened his eyes. In my mind, this was the one thing he absolutely needed to do. My magical thinking settled on a specific fear: not that he would die or wake with severe brain damage—these possibilities were incomprehensible, though of course I felt a desperate, clawing fear of both—but that I might never again see his beautiful eyes open. The fact that this probably wouldn't happen for hours, possibly even a day, was inconceivable. It was as if I was being commanded to breathe deeply even as a hand tightened around my throat.

A nurse came by to urge Lidia and my father out to the waiting room. Before they left, Lidia handed Charlie a pair of brown leather loafers from her bag. They were my father's; Charlie put them on. I saw this happening in my peripheral vision, realizing for the first time that we had both come to the hospital without shoes. Charlie must have mentioned it when he called. Then Lidia crouched beside me, and I looked away from Frankie long enough to watch her pull a pair of pink suede slippers onto my feet, one at a time.

LATER, CHARLIE BROUGHT A CUP of coffee and pressed my hands around it. Lidia was in the waiting room and my father had left

to take the Zodiac home. The curtain around Frankie's bed slid noisily to one side, and there stood a thin black nurse in lilac scrubs. She
spoke in a heavy, overarticulated Haitian accent. "We have to evacuate," she said. "Your boy will go soon in the ambulance. You have a
ride?"

Charlie told her we did, but for a moment I didn't understand. Then
I remembered the hurricane, which—in my altered state, this seemed
horribly unjust—hadn't dissolved or even been delayed by Frankie's fall.
The nurse went on to explain that there was a bed at South Dade Memorial and Frankie would be transferred there with another patient;
there would be no room in the ambulance for me. I asked for reassurance that Frankie would not wake up while he was alone with strangers, and she gave it. She said that he would be among the first to leave.

There were 245 patients at Mercy that day. I would learn this later.
And, because three other hospitals were also evacuating, and because
the drop in barometric pressure and general anxiety would send many,
many women into premature labor, there was a citywide shortage of
ambulances and beds. This was the first time Mercy had ever evacuated, and in fact the chief of staff had lobbied against the hospital's
evacuation policy since it had been implemented years earlier. He'd
thought evacuation would waste resources and cause unnecessary risks
to patients. He was photographed, a day after the storm, standing in
several inches of water in Mercy's basement, a jagged hole at his back
where a window had been, a stingray dead at his feet. He admitted
readily, in the article I read, that he'd been wrong.

I kissed Frankie and Charlie pulled me away. We waited in Lidia's
car just outside the ambulance bay, me in the passenger seat and Charlie
in the backseat, and watched as Frankie was loaded in. We followed the
ambulance onto the road. Outside the window, my hometown looked
staged and unfamiliar, a replica of itself, as if someone had taken photographs and rebuilt the city to scale. About a mile from the hospital
we started to lag, and the ambulance pulled farther and farther ahead.

We came to a stop on the shoulder of the road, and then the ambulance was out of sight. "What's going on?" I said.

"We're being pulled over, sweetheart," said Lidia.

She rolled down her window and spoke to the police officer. I turned in my seat and found Charlie watching me. "We have to go," I said loudly.

He leaned forward. "We will. Hold on."

The police officer walked back to his patrol car and Lidia turned to me. She spoke like my own mother would have, with a possessive firmness, the way I would have spoken to Frankie. She said, "Georgia, I want you to count to one hundred. Do it slowly. Go."

By the time I was at eighty-seven, the officer was back. He gave Lidia a ticket for following too closely behind an ambulance. Then Lidia started the engine, and we got back on the road.

I LOCATED FRANKIE ON THE third floor of South Dade's east wing, where an ad hoc ward had been set up in a wide hallway outside the pediatric care unit. Frankie's bed was flush to the wall, and above it was a watercolor painting of a flock of flamingos standing along the rim of a green pond. At his feet was an empty bed, and in the bed at his head was a young girl, ten or so years old, sleeping with a thick wrap of gauze around her forehead. Charlie and Lidia had been stopped at the admitting desk and instructed to go home—whether they had, I didn't know, as I'd left them behind as soon as I was told where Frankie had been taken. I leaned close to Frankie's face. He smelled of sea salt. "You moved hospitals," I told him. "You'll be safe here." I pulled his blanket tighter. Then I was hit by a wave of exhaustion, and because there was no place else, I sat on the floor beside his bed.

The fact that I needed to let Graham know what had happened pecked at me. I wasn't sure, exactly, how to go about it. Now that I knew where Frankie was, I could go downstairs and find a telephone—

but who would I call? Finding a phone book and calling every hotel near Lidia's house would require more energy than I could muster.

A red-haired nurse with a hand tremor brought me a plastic chair. She said it had come from the cafeteria. "Guard it with your life," she said, and rushed away.

Charlie came up through a back staircase. He told me it was just after noon. There were no windows in that stretch of hallway, and time had become disordered and irrelevant, except that as the hours passed, it became more likely that Frankie would wake up. Charlie touched Frankie's foot. "I saw that young doctor," he said. "He'll be by soon."

I wiped my face.

"You should try to rest," he said.

"I keep hearing that sound."

He knew which one I meant. He closed his eyes, as if in prayer.

It seemed I'd never before understood the meaning of the word *regret*. Now it seemed regret was the desperate desire to reverse a specific amount of time. It was the need to purge from one's memory the sound of a boy's head hitting wood. It didn't seem to me that a tiny reversal of time was such a grand request to make of the universe. I would need only a few seconds changed, after all.

Frankie's expression remained empty and unfamiliar, and though I continued to feel physical pain when I looked at his broken face, I also started to feel a strange detachment from him, as if he were the sweet child of a neighbor or other acquaintance, and I was standing in until his real mother arrived. I'd felt the same curious detachment at my mother's bedside, before her death. I'd looked at her parched lips as she slept, thinking it was fortunate that I'd inherited my father's full ones instead of her thin, pale ones. Who thinks this in the hours before her own mother's death? Who feels any removal at all from the inert, battered body of her young son?

"Lie down," Charlie said.

The vinyl flooring smelled of cleanser. I forced myself to keep my eyes shut for what seemed like a long time, and when I opened them, a woman stood over me, casting a shadow in the fluorescence. She wore a blue silk blouse and a white coat and patent leather heels. It was Dr. Sonia.

I got to my feet. "Who called you?" I said.

"Dr. Lomano's nurse."

I vaguely recalled giving Dr. Sonia's name when asked about Frankie's pediatrician hours earlier. It was incredible to me that the staff at Mercy, still embroiled in evacuation, was organized enough not only to alert Dr. Sonia to Frankie's medical situation, but also to let her know that he'd been moved. This kind of efficiency would become less surprising in the days to come.

She stood at the head of Frankie's bed, reading through his chart. She pulled a penlight from her coat and thumbed open each of Frankie's pupils. "Are you the father?" she said, glancing doubtfully at Charlie.

"No," I said.

"Georgia." Her darkly lined eyes met mine. "What happened?"

She wrote in the file as I spoke. I started earlier than I needed to, with the phone call from Riggs, when I'd learned I was needed at Stiltsville. She didn't hurry me. I felt as if I were narrating a story from a book, except that as I closed in on the end, my voice started to fail. When I described standing on the dock alone and hearing a sound upstairs, I had to work to catch my breath.

"You heard him on the porch," she said, prompting me.

"I heard something. It was very dark. I assumed it was Charlie."

Dr. Sonia glanced over my shoulder at Charlie, her mouth a thin line. To her, I probably seemed like nothing more than your average cheating wife. I supposed that wasn't far from the truth.

"I spent an afternoon there once, at Stiltsville," she said. "I found it—how do I put it?—unsettling."

I said nothing.

"How long had Frankie been asleep?" she said.

"Hours. Five hours."

"Had he ever slept there before?"

"Yes, for naps."

"How far was the bedroom from the porch?"

"About twenty feet."

"Not far."

"No."

"Was the room locked?"

"Of course not."

"Was there a light on in the living room?"

"No."

"On the porch?"

"There was no light."

"Was the door to the porch closed?"

"No."

"How high was the porch?"

"Fifteen feet or so."

"Oh, Georgia," she said, touching the back of Frankie's hand. "How could you?"

I felt Charlie bracing me, his hands on my elbows. I heard him asking Dr. Sonia to leave, then insisting in a rising tone that she do so. She left. But it didn't much matter to me that she'd said what she did. It was simply as if she'd spoken my own thoughts. How could I? All those afternoons, all those naps, all those hours I'd spent with my young child in a house surrounded on all sides by water. I'd been the reckless one, I saw, not just the night before but every minute we'd spent at Stiltsville. My error in judgment had been enormous and unforgivable.

"Please find Graham," I said to Charlie. If I could do nothing else to help Frankie, I hoped at least I could deliver his father.

THE RED-HAIRED NURSE WITH THE tremor came down the hall at around 3:00 P.M., shooing all but a few visitors from around the beds. Charlie had yet to return. I sat stroking Frankie's hand for a long time, wishing I hadn't sent Charlie away—surely Lidia and my father were doing all anyone could to find Graham—but then I looked up to see a lean figure striding toward me, flopping white hair and jointed flamingo legs. He gripped my shoulder and studied Frankie's face. His own face was drawn.

"Where were you?" I said, my voice hoarse.

"Hotel," he said. "I called your father."

I gave him my chair. "How did you get here?"

"Lidia. She's in the waiting room—with your friend." His jaw clenched. "Hospital's trying to clear people out."

"They should go home. I'll tell them."

"I'm staying."

I nodded but made no move to leave.

"When will he wake up?" said Graham, his voice trickling to a whisper.

"Soon," I said.

"But he will wake up?"

On this point, I'd asked repeatedly for reassurance, and had received it. "Yes," I said. "He will."

Graham bit his lip. "I hate that you were out there with him."

Whether he meant Frankie or Charlie, I wasn't certain, and I didn't ask him to clarify.

I found Lidia and Charlie in one corner of the crowded waiting room. Nearby, a nurse was instructing a family to go home, and on a television screen above their heads a meteorologist explained that the hurricane was nearing Eleuthera, 180 miles southeast, bringing with it 150-mile-per-hour winds and twenty-foot surges. The meteorologist, Bryan Norcross, who would remain on air for two days straight, said the storm would reach South Florida in six hours, but the eye wouldn't hit until dawn.

Charlie made the slightest gesture in my direction, as if to embrace or at least touch me. I stepped back. "You should both go home," I said.

"I can't stand it," said Lidia.

"He'll be asleep for hours," I said.

Charlie's hands worked at his sides. "Can't I do something?"

"Please go," I said, backing away.

Somehow Graham had procured another chair while I was gone. He was such a resourceful person, I thought. He could solve any problem except the ones that really needed solving. I sat at Frankie's torso and Graham sat at his head. Graham's hands stroked the bedspread. It seemed to me that every decision we'd made, up to and including the move to Miami and the job running out to Stiltsville, had been undeniably wrong. We were unfit to lead our own lives.

"We should never have come here," I said, meaning Miami. "We should never have bought that fucking boat." I struggled to keep my voice under control. My hands flew about, and Graham raised his arms as if to protect himself. "You are a fool, buying that boat. You should go home."

I meant our other home, the cottage on Round Lake, which any day now would sit vacant. He might go back, I knew. Not because I was telling him to, but because there would not be enough to keep him here. I would be left behind in the town I'd fled years before, moored to my own bad choices.

Graham gripped me by the shoulders. I struggled a little, then went limp. "Take a breath," he said.

I started to cry. My voice barely made it out of my throat. "I don't want a divorce."

He exhaled. "Yes, you do."

Something in his tone grounded me, even as I recognized the sad and gentle anger in it, the enmity that had curdled between us. I wiped my face and took a deep breath. He let go of me and leaned forward to concentrate on the boy we'd made, who lay sleeping that unmuscular, invertebrate sleep.

What I'd feared most about leaving him was what I would be taking from Frankie. What I forgot, in those moments when I was undone by self-doubt, was all that Frankie would gain: sleep, speech, security.

Our red-haired nurse, whose name was Barb, stopped by every two hours. She checked Frankie's pupils and administered more sedative through his IV. "Lucky to get to sleep through this storm," she said in her hushed tone. I did my best to be polite, but what I was thinking was that it was not lucky at all, and I knew Frankie would agree with me. Later, when she was back again, Graham put a hand on her arm. "It's his birthday tomorrow," he said meaningfully. "He'll be four years old."

"Well, then," she said. "Let's make it a good one."

Another hour passed, and a different nurse came to confiscate our chairs. She was almost as tall as Graham and a little older, with silver-streaked hair and heavily inked tattoos showing beneath the sleeves of her scrubs. There were multiple holes in her ears, but she wore no jewelry and no makeup. The chairs were needed in the maternity ward, she told us. She crossed her arms and steadied her voice. "They're closing the streets. You have to leave."

"We're staying," I said.

"That won't be possible."

I realized that she'd been sent. Up and down the hall, the areas around patient beds had emptied of visitors. Graham and I were the problematic hangers-on, making difficult jobs more difficult.

Graham realized it, too. He wiped his face and sighed. "I'll go to your father's," he said to me. "I'll be back as soon as it's over."

"Your boy will sleep through it," said the nurse to him. "You should, too."

He touched Frankie's bruised cheek and leaned down to whisper into his ear and kiss his lips. As an afterthought, he kissed my forehead. Then he moved away slowly, as if fighting a tether.

"I'm staying," I said to the nurse after Graham was gone.

"I'll try to find a pillow," she said roughly.

Someone did bring a pillow and a blanket, but it wasn't that same intimidating nurse, and I never saw her again. Fifty percent of the hospital staff lost their homes that night; she might have been one of them. I would think of her many times, about her final words to Graham, and how none of us, least of all her, could have known what her advice would mean.

SOMEWHERE IN THE PEDIATRIC UNIT, there was a television tuned to the weather news. I heard snippets of storm-related talk from nurses who came and went, their voices agitated. I had no desire to learn more. Either the hurricane would hit furiously, possibly endangering us even within the hospital's walls, or it wouldn't. The only way that I might have become interested in the workings of the storm, its wind speed and direction and exact location at any given moment, was if Frankie woke and we could watch the news reports—or even the weather itself through a window—together.

I dozed on the floor as outside the winds rose and the rain started. The lights blinked out and then came back dimmer. I woke with a start to the sound of a metal tray rattling nearby; someone had dropped something in the pediatric unit, out of my sightline. It seemed that maybe Frankie reacted to the noise or my movement at his side with the slightest tremble of his head, but a moment later I decided it had been my imagination. The lights in the hallway cast shadows on his face. It seemed, if I wasn't fooling myself, that the swelling had gone down a touch. His nose seemed to assert itself a little more prominently from the rest of his face.

I pulled myself away, ostensibly to find coffee but really because I hoped to run into Nurse Barb and ask her to check on Frankie when she had a free moment. I clutched my precious blanket and pillow as I wandered down one hallway and another. The hospital, or at least that particular wing, was muffled in noise and movement. Even the workers who bustled past me seemed subdued and focused, as if they had no energy to spare. I found myself in a hallway that dead-ended. I kept going because at the very end was a large window. In late summer in Miami, the sun shone until eight-thirty or later, but that evening the sky was dark with cloud cover and thick with rain. Outside the window was the hospital's circular driveway, and the royal palms dotting the too-green lawn bowed in the wind. The four-lane street was empty of cars, and the traffic lights swayed on their lines. I turned away from the window and hurried back to Frankie's bed, intending to tell him, awake or not, what was happening outside. How the storm was rising. How he hadn't missed it yet.

It took me several seconds to locate him again, not because he had moved but because there was a man standing over his bed, which I hadn't expected. He had his hands in the pockets of his faded blue jeans. His salt-and-pepper hair was wet and disheveled.

"You're back?" I whispered.

He smiled his thin, frugal smile. "I was at Riggs's place but I couldn't stay. I sneaked in a side door. I found myself in the cafeteria. This is for you."

He handed me a large Styrofoam cup with a lid and straw. I thought maybe it was a soda—looking at it, I realized I was very thirsty and hungry—but when I took a sip, my mouth filled with the taste of cold, creamy chocolate ice cream.

"Oh my," I said. "Thank you."

"They turned off the freezers to save power. Free ice cream for everyone." He grimaced. "Is it okay that I'm here?"

I swallowed. "Yes."

"It's nasty out."

"How did you get here?"

"I sneaked the keys to Riggs's little sports car. It's been so long, I almost dropped the transmission."

"I wish he could see it," I said, meaning the storm, meaning Frankie.

"So do I," said Charlie.

I moved to my knees and pressed my chest against the side of bed. "Open your eyes, baby," I whispered to Frankie. Charlie knelt next to me and our shoulders pressed together. We hunched there for a long time. I finished my shake and wished I had another. My head started to drop and Charlie pulled me against him and I let him, but only as long as I had Frankie's hand firmly in grasp. Then, with my eyes closed against Charlie, I finally felt what I'd been waiting to feel for so many hours: my boy squeezed me back.

I WASN'T AT HER SIDE when my mother died. Neither was my father, who had a gig that night, as he'd had almost every night since she'd been diagnosed. (That year turned out to be the most productive of his career, a fact that we never discussed and my mother never openly acknowledged.) I was asleep in my old bedroom. The day before, I'd hired a night nurse despite my father's vehement opposition—the money, the waste, when here I was on loan from my other life, just as capable as anyone of lifting water to her lips or changing her sheets or turning her onto her side or reading her something unprovocative that neither of us would enjoy. Not until I was heavily pregnant, briefly on bed rest for high blood pressure, would I understand how physically uncomfortable and restless-making it is—worse, probably, for people with no experience with insomnia—to lie in one place for long stretches. This knowledge would have helped me in my nursing duties.

I think to some extent I believed, without having given it much thought, that a person should be able to do the work of dying quietly and restfully, like a battery draining of juice. My mother's death was cantankerous. She couldn't lie still, much less sleep, so neither could I. She moaned and called out nonsensically and once, twenty-four hours from death, sat up straight in bed and insisted that she wanted to go home. When I tried to calm her, she fought me off, limbs flailing, unknowingly flashing the room, catheter and all—giving Graham, who had just arrived from Chicago, a view he later joked was a good-bye to remember. I think when she so fervently insisted on going home, she meant the small, beachy home in Fort Lauderdale where she'd lived with her parents as a child. All I remembered of it, from my visits there before they died, were white walls and white carpeting, no adornment in the house except for a collection of ceramic angel figurines housed in an antique corner cabinet, which I was warned repeatedly by my soft-spoken grandparents not to touch. Through a picture window above the sofa, across the cement bulge of a causeway, was the ocean.

The drugs stopped helping eventually, despite ever-increasing dosages. If there was a way to make my mother comfortable, I never learned of it, and although making her more comfortable—so I, for any length of time, might be comfortable as well—was my primary objective every moment of the day, I never once sought assistance or even advice on the subject. I didn't so much as think to pick up a book on end-of-life care or ask for tips from the hospice doctor who stopped by every three or four days, and whose offerings were limited to prescribing painkillers and clucking his tongue each time I mentioned that she seemed persistently restless. A *fighter*, he called her repeatedly, as if bestowing a compliment. I cannot explain why I never thought to study up, so to speak, except that I was sleep-deprived, anguished, ill at ease. With so many things, it seems I am a person who isn't good at something until she's done it at least once. And I had only one chance to get this right.

I did not get it right. Despite my father's resistance, I found an overnight nurse in the phone book. My mother's health insurance, a plan partially subsidized by Dr. Fuller's practice, covered a few hours of hospice nursing each week but nothing overnight. I'm not sure why more wasn't covered, especially when she was already so close to the end, but I gleaned that the insurance establishment believes that people should take care of each other in this world, and not rely on professionals to do it for them.

The night nurse, whose name was Amelia, was in her fifties and wore her thick red hair in two high, ridiculous ponytails. It was immediately obvious that she was not a person with sufficient intelligence for the job, what with the medication schedule and need to adapt to unfamiliar situations. But I'd gone bargain hunting and found exactly that. She woke me twice, once before midnight and once a couple of hours later, to say that my mother was calling out. Not for me, *per se*— she hadn't looked straight at me or said my name in days, and I didn't think she missed me when I was out of the room—but in a sloppy and unintelligible way, half-phrases distorted by medication and pain. Amelia interpreted this to be the end. Both times she fetched me, I came to the living room, sat with my mother for half an hour, saw no behavior I hadn't seen before, and went back to bed.

I asked, after the second time, not to be woken again. I said this firmly, telling myself that I would need to do so, to get the point across.

The last time she summoned me was around 5:00 A.M. I was briefly annoyed, but soon enough knew this time was different. I came down the hall and into the room, and immediately, before even sitting at my mother's side or studying her hollowed-out features, paid Amelia and tried to send her home. She wouldn't leave; I gathered this was her protocol, to stay with the deceased for a certain amount of time. My father was still out—a late night, even for him. Amelia waited as I called the on-call hospice nurse, who told me I could have my mother sent directly to the funeral home I'd already chosen.

I asked Amelia what it had been like in the last seconds. I didn't expect much in the way of a fully drawn picture. She said my mother had taken a long breath, crossed her hands over her stomach—a gesture of resignation—and that was it. I think my mother died because she finally had some privacy from me, and I believe she would not have died that night if I had still been by her side; she would have continued to hang on. Whether I wish I had been there, I can't say.

Before they took my mother's body, I wrestled her wedding ring off her bloated finger—not pretty, and another thing I should have done earlier—and sat a moment at her side, holding her now-naked hand. I didn't cry. I didn't feel any kind of soulful presence in the room. She had been gone already, and now she was more gone. I felt relieved. My father came in as the room brightened; he'd seen the funeral home's van in the driveway. I looked at her face one last time—something in the set of her jaw seemed hard and unforgiving, which wasn't like her—and handed my father her ring, then went to bed.

Five years later, feeling the slight pressure of Frankie's hand in my own, I looked up into his face and saw that my boy, the love of my life, was awake and sluggishly blinking, his lips dry and parted as if poised to speak. In that moment, though it was nothing I'd ever thought possible, I felt the undeniable presence of my mother. I was careful with Frankie even as I embraced him, even as I called out for a nurse and my tears dropped onto his face, making him blink. All the time, my mother was with me, pulling me from where I'd been, a visitor at the bedside of a child who didn't seem quite my own and returning me to motherhood. As only she could do.

19

FRANKIE DID NOT, IN THE end, miss the storm. To this day he remembers some of that night, though much of the following nine weeks—recovery weeks, two steps forward and one step back, in the hospital and back at Lidia's—would be lost to him.

Nurse Barb was the first to respond. She bustled around Frankie, her voice low but animated, sending another nurse to get him water, checking his pupils and heart rate and blood pressure. She seemed if not as delighted as we were, then at least in the ballpark. Dr. Lomano showed up soon after, and he carefully removed the bolsters beside Frankie's torso, encouraging him to move his fingers and hands and arms if he could—and he could, thank heavens. Then he removed the neck and head braces and held Frankie's chin while encouraging him to move his head from side to side. This elicited several muffled cries and a brief burst of tears. The doctor put the neck part of the brace back on. This was a precaution, he told me, since it seemed the swelling had gone down and there was likely little danger now of spinal injury or hematoma. He inclined the bed so Frankie could look around.

Lost among the larger heartbreak was this small one, and I was the only one to witness it: Frankie wanted to speak but wasn't allowed. This was obvious from his repeated attempts to get out a sentence, but Dr. Lomano—he didn't mean to be insensitive, and his priority was on saving Frankie's strength and assessing damage—told him not to. So while the doctor conducted his tests—reflexes, pupils, range of motion of toes and feet and legs—Frankie bit his tongue, making every effort to be a good boy, as he'd so often been admonished to be. Finally, the doctor was finished. He asked Frankie if he was still thirsty, and instead of answering, Frankie took the cue that it was okay to speak. His voice was weak but deliberate. "The hurricane," he said. "Did it came?"

How I wished, in that moment, that I had not let Graham go home. How could I have, when there was any chance of this happening? How could he have let himself?

"It's here," said Charlie, and I said, "It came."

"Birthday hurricane," said Frankie, then closed his eyes. He was smiling.

THIS WAS NOT, IN THE moment, technically true. The outer tendrils of the storm had reached us, but the eyewall was still three hours away. The rains and winds had come first, slippery scouts, easing us into the real thing.

Dr. Lomano's nurse gave us instructions to wake Frankie every two hours to make sure his responses were still lucid, but otherwise to let him sleep. He was no longer under sedation, and without the drugs or the bolsters he slept in his usual way, with his mouth open and eyes slatted eerily and limbs spread. It was not difficult to wake him, and each time, he blinked and asked about the hurricane. Charlie and I had been taking turns checking the newscast and looking through the window down the hall, watching the palms bend calisthenically and electric-blue sparks flash in the distance, power lines snapping from their poles.

The eye reached Biscayne Bay at around 3:00 A.M. When Charlie told Frankie, Frankie licked his lips and studied Charlie's face. "The eye will look at your house," he said, as if in reassurance.

Charlie said, "That's what I'm afraid of, kiddo."

The hospital itself rumbled, and the lights, which for hours had been powered by generators, blinked off every so often. The ghostly noise of sweeping winds grew louder. Charlie grew restless. He could no longer sit beside me on the floor, giving me the warmth of his body and the hard pillow of his shoulder. He paced. Around 4:30 A.M., he said, "I have an idea."

He pulled me to my feet, then got on his hands and knees beneath the bed and fooled with the casters. He glanced down the hallway, then gestured for me to take hold of the foot of the bed. "Be gentle," he said, then started to pull Frankie's bed away from the wall.

I knew where he was headed. As we pushed Frankie's bed down one hallway and another, my heart raced, and I questioned whether what we were doing was wise or foolish, or enough of one to justify the other.

Nurse Barb spotted us. "Whoa, Nelly," she said, putting a hand on the mattress. "You're not supposed to move him."

I said, "It's just for a minute—"

"He's got to see the storm," Charlie said. "It's his birthday."

From where we stood, we could see through the window that the air outside was peppered with debris, palm fronds and sticks and leaves flying in every direction. I'd noticed tape on the windows of the pediatric unit, but this window was bare; it had been overlooked. It reminded me of a secret portal in a children's story. Frankie squirmed and we stared at him. "We'll be quick," I said.

Barb stepped back. "Support his neck if he sits up," she said. "And get back right away."

We positioned the head of the bed as close to the window as we could, and Charlie used the hand crank to raise the mattress. Frankie squirmed again and opened his eyes.

"Baby," I said. "Want to see the hurricane?"

"Hurricane *Andrew*," he said groggily.

"Smarty-pants," I said.

He rubbed his eyes. The chaotic dark was illuminated every few seconds by flashes of light. Charlie put up his arms to cut the reflection of the overhead light against the glass. I worried for a moment that something would strike the window with us crowded so close, but really there was no tooth in my fear. It was like watching a movie of a storm rather than the storm itself, and if it weren't for the rumbling walls and dimming lights and howling wind, I might have let go of my fear altogether.

Charlie and Frankie apparently felt no apprehension. Frankie inched down in the bed, wincing in discomfort, trying to get closer, and Charlie kneeled and propped him up so they were inches from the glass. Charlie cradled Frankie's head, brace and all, in the crook of his shoulder, and they would have looked so peaceful, sitting there together, except that as the minutes passed, they grew progressively more noisy. It started with Frankie, who despite our shushing couldn't keep himself from crying out, "Look there! Look there!" each time something appeared outside, lightning or flying debris or a palm tree in whiplash. Eventually, Charlie was giggling each time Frankie cried out, a giddy laugh I'd never heard from him before. Then Frankie was giggling, and even I succumbed.

Then Frankie quieted. "Look there," he said one last time, pointing down at a parking lot. The car closest to the street, a dark coupe, had started to move. Not in the controlled, deliberate way of a car being driven, but in a stuttering, sideways motion, in the direction of the empty street. The spaces next to the car were empty, so it was as if it had been stranded on its own vulnerable island. We watched it make its way into the street. Then there was a gust I could feel in the floor beneath my feet, and in one powerful motion the car tipped and rolled out of sight, end over end.

It was in those seconds, as we watched breathlessly, that the storm stopped being exciting. Charlie and Frankie shrank from the window.

"Time to get back," I said.

We lowered Frankie's mattress. He was asleep by the time we parked him in the hallway. Charlie and I sat on the floor, and I covered us both with the blanket and hugged the pillow to my chest. Charlie held my hand. I started to cry.

"Aren't you happy?" he said. "He's going to be okay."

How could I answer him? Of course I was relieved, even joyful. But I was also—and this is yet another thing I would be unable to explain—filled with the knowledge that we had lost something that night, though exactly what we'd lost had yet to be named. I cried because it seemed to me that something new was starting, and it would come with the force of this hurricane and last much, much longer.

LIDIA AND MY FATHER DIDN'T show up until late the next morning. A bed had come open in the pediatric unit and Frankie had been moved. The business of the hospital continued with a flow that amazed me. It was a wonder, I thought, that every member of the staff wasn't off in a corner, getting some shut-eye or having a drink.

I was lying beside Frankie in his bed, reading from a stack of books Nurse Barb had brought us, when they appeared. "Look who's awake!" I said brightly. But when I saw the anxiety on my father's face, my smile died.

"*Mi'jo*," said Lidia, coming to Frankie's side. From her bag she pulled a box of crayons and a sketch pad, and then leaned down to kiss him all over his face. My father shook Charlie's hand and said that he was sorry about Vivian. They exchanged a few words and then, with a glance in my direction, Charlie mumbled something about finding coffee, and slipped out of the room.

The phones were out, said my father, or else they would have called earlier. Lidia launched into a story about how their driveway had been blocked by one of Mr. Genovese's pruned trees, and how, to get out, my father had driven straight through his neighbor's hibiscus. In the rearview mirror, they'd seen Genovese gesture wildly at them from his semicircular front stoop.

"As if we'd caused all the mess!" she said to Frankie. "Hurricane Lidia!" She threw up her hands and he laughed.

"Georgia," said my father, and gestured for me to follow him into the hallway.

He stopped short once we were out of earshot, and I stepped aside to keep from bumping into him. "Is it the house?" I said. "Where's Graham?"

My father lifted his hands, palms upturned. "We don't know."

"What do you mean?"

"He came over last night. Lidia set him up in the guest room. This morning he wasn't there. The bed hadn't been slept in. His bikes are in the garage." He breathed hard through his nose. "We filed a police report." They'd knocked on every door in the neighborhood, he said, before they'd spotted a police cruiser cutting through a yard.

I pressed my palms to my eyes, trying to make sense of what he was saying. "Wait," I said. "Maybe he's at his office."

My father nodded. "Sure, maybe. But how would he have gotten there?"

"I don't know." What I was thinking was this: most likely, Graham had gotten up midsleep and gone out into the storm. Something had happened to him. Except—and this came as brief respite—if this had been the case, then the bed would have been slept in.

We returned to the room. My mind raced. My father bent down to kiss Frankie and tease him gruffly about his wounds, which in the daylight were both more gruesome, with their unearthly pinks and purples, and also less so, without the spectral shadows cast by overhead lighting.

I barely registered Frankie's giggling or Lidia's admonishments to my father to not make him laugh. In the back of my mind, an idea was forming. My father saw the alarm in my eyes, and then so did Lidia. She took my arm. "Don't worry—" she started, but I shook my head.

Quietly, I said, "Did you check the *Lullaby*?"

Horror registered on her features. But my father, who overheard, did not understand. He spoke in a low voice, so Frankie wouldn't catch it. "I'm sorry, sweetheart, I did the best I could with it, but the lines snapped."

"It sank?" I said.

He nodded. "All you can see of it is the propeller sticking out of the water. It's gone."

ANDREW WASN'T EXPECTED TO HIT Coral Gables dead-on. The storm's eye was predicted to hit farther south; these were the neighborhoods that evacuated. In Coral Gables, families went to sleep in their own beds that night assuming the storm would wake them when it came. Maybe they'd taped some windows and stocked their kitchens, as my father had, and those with boats on the canal had lengthened the mooring lines and doubled the knots. But they didn't expect to lose much more than a few shingles from their roofs, maybe a window or a shrub or two. Once the streets were cleared and the roofs fixed, Coral Gables would return to itself—less lush and certainly less neatly manicured, but wholly recognizable. South of the Gables, in the evacuation areas, including several developments like Sally's, the same could not be said. Sally would tell me later that out of the mounds of rubble scattered throughout her neighborhood she recognized her own house only because Stanley's candy-apple Porsche peeked out from beneath the collapsed garage, one headlight broken and one unbroken, as if winking.

This is the only half-plausible explanation—that the eye was not forecasted to hit the Gables—that I can find for the decision Graham made that night. There's also this: he loved weather, and he hated sleep.

In his experience, one was benevolent and the other malevolent; maybe he did not imagine the roles could reverse. Maybe he believed that the following days at Frankie's bedside would require as much strength as he could marshal, and he knew sleep would not visit him in Lidia's guest room. If the guest bed had been slept in, I might have convinced myself that he'd gone to the *Lullaby* and taken his pills and wrestled one-handed with his cuff all in the psychotic haze of half-sleep. Sometimes I managed to convince myself of this anyway. How much of a stretch would it be for a half-sleeping Graham to make his own bed after leaving it, after all?

But I don't really believe this is what happened. After he was found, still cuffed, at the bottom of the canal, every memory of the two of us together would fragment and reorder in my mind. Even the memory of that sea turtle in the Dry Tortugas, and his decision to leave me alone in my kayak while he went on to Loggerhead. Marrying a reckless man—and having a child with him—is a reckless act in itself. This was something I'd never admitted to myself.

Maybe if the story is told in a certain way, it would seem obvious to anyone that Graham had been untrustworthy all along. But I was there and I saw the way he cared for me, and so I have my doubts. It would be easier if I could believe it. It would remind me that no matter his intentions, he'd behaved carelessly not only with me and Frankie but also with himself. It would remind me that I'd been right to leave him.

But if I hadn't left him, hadn't succumbed to the pull I'd felt toward Charlie, then I might have tried to convince him to stay at Frankie's bedside with me, no matter what, for Frankie's sake. It had been selfish of me to let him go. It had been easier for me to be alone with Frankie, especially given the possibility that Charlie might return. If I'd coerced Graham to stay, I eventually would have ended up without a husband, but my son would still have a father.

20

FRANKIE'S ROOMMATE AT SOUTH DADE was a ten-year-old black boy named Antoine. Days before the storm, Antoine had been in a car accident with his parents, both of whom visited every morning and evening. Though I wondered how it could be that Antoine had been hurt so badly when they'd sustained only bruises and cuts, I never asked about it, and they were all so gentle and loving that I knew either parent would have cheerfully switched places with him. About once or twice a day, Antoine's pain medications stopped doing their job, and the nurses wouldn't give him more until it was time, so his parents held him while he softly cried. If his parents weren't there when it happened, I held him myself, wiping his nose and singing to him until Nurse Barb showed up.

The night of Frankie's birthday, as Hurricane Andrew skulked over Florida's western coast and limped into the Gulf, Lidia walked to a Publix close to the hospital. She told us when she returned that the store was being indiscriminately, almost lazily looted when she'd arrived, and she'd slipped a twenty-dollar bill under the locked manager's office door before walking out with a sheet cake, a half-deflated helium balloon, and a potted plant. Charlie disappeared for a few hours, then returned with construction paper, glue, string, and scissors, and sat in the corner working on a project, shooing me when I got close. I gathered paper plates and cups and soda from the cafeteria and made an IOU for a bike—the choice gave me pause, because Graham would have wanted to pick it out—then decorated the envelope using Frankie's crayons.

My father had been gone for hours, since he'd put two and two together and rushed off to find a working phone or a police officer. I hoped for Frankie's sake he would be gone until after our ramshackle party was finished.

Charlie worked for more than an hour. After he finished, he made a construction paper blindfold for Frankie and asked me and Lidia to step out. When he spoke to Lidia, he averted his eyes and lowered his voice, which reminded me of the way he'd been with me when we'd first met. Ten minutes later, he invited us back in, looking sheepish. He'd decorated the space above Frankie's bed with a variety of uncannily accurate cutouts of sea animals, each suspended on fishing line from its limbs or fins or tentacles, spinning and swaying in the air. A purple-and-pink octopus, a magenta-and-orange sea horse, a black shark with red teeth, a blue-and-green dolphin, a green-and-black turtle, a pink-and-white conch, and a red finger coral. Each was shaded and detailed in pencil. Altogether, the assembly looked like a snapshot of a particularly busy reef.

I thought of Graham's origami, then put the thought out of my head. Charlie removed Frankie's blindfold and Frankie squealed. "Sea creatures!"

"Happy birthday," said Charlie.

"I wish I had a camera," said Lidia.

More than anything else, I think it was those colorful mobiles, that act of love for her grandson, that gave Lidia the permission to forgive Charlie. I would never again hear so much as a skeptical word from her.

And it seemed, as we beamed at him and his cheeks reddened under the attention, that he knew it, and was proud. He was a man at least partially redeemed.

The hospital was not air-conditioned. They were conserving generator power for as long as possible, since no one knew how long the electricity would be out. The mayor had said it would be out for a week, but then experts in interviews had said that a week would be miraculous. So little did we all move around in Frankie's room that I barely registered the intensity of the heat and humidity, the ever-present skein of moisture on the backs of my neck and knees. Lidia had brought some of her own clothes for me, and for Frankie's party I wore a sleeveless linen sundress and a pair of underwear from the grocery store, where Lidia had gone again with a list and a wad of cash. This time, there had been an employee taking money, using a little plastic calculator to figure tax. Lidia said it was like the world outside was moving in slow motion. I thought to call Sally—we'd seen photographs of her neighborhood on the news—and went as far as picking up the phone beside Frankie's bed before remembering that the lines were dead.

Frankie started asking about his father an hour after the party wound down. I'd read him two books and turned off the light. Lidia had gone home; my father had not returned. I had very little hope that Graham would be found alive, though part of me tried to believe that maybe he simply didn't want to be found. Since the wheels of detective work were turning slowly—had my father yet been able to summon the police?—I lied. I told Frankie his father had to work, but was thinking of him every moment.

That night after Frankie and Charlie were asleep, I took a shower in the room's small bathroom, and wept under the tepid fall of the water.

The next morning, Lidia arrived without my father and explained in a whisper that he was still waiting for police divers to arrive. She set about unwrapping Cuban sandwiches and arranging them on plates, for Antoine's family as well as our own. Charlie, fidgety in Lidia's company, wandered off again. We'd spoken briefly the night before, in whispers, about Graham, and he'd been unconvinced by my theory. "Let's hope you're wrong," he'd said, squeezing my hand.

My father finally showed up—with Riggs, of all people—late that afternoon. Riggs brought a twine-tied pastry box and opened it at Frankie's side, wincing at the sight of Frankie's still-battered face. "That does not look good, kid," he said. "Have a *pastelito*."

I followed my father into the hallway. Lidia came up quickly behind us, and by the time she was at my side I had taken in the look on my father's face, and started to weaken on my own feet. I didn't cry, exactly, but in Lidia's strong arms I found myself shaking, thinking less of Graham than of Frankie, of his fatherless future. After my father told me everything that had happened since he'd left the hospital, he offered to take care of having the houseboat brought up and taken away, and of having Graham's body cremated, which is what he would have wanted. I found it touching that my father knew to make this offer. The work of death, therefore, was off my plate, and I could tend to the more imposing task of telling my son that his father was dead.

MY FATHER HAD DRIVEN STRAIGHT to the Coral Gables Police Department from the hospital, but the missing-person case he'd started was still in limbo, waiting to be active until forty-eight hours had passed. The officer who'd opened that case was out, so a different officer took notes as my father explained the situation. The officer interrupted to ask if my father was talking about the same ratty Sumerset houseboat he'd been ticketing for weeks, behind the three-thousand block of Granada Boulevard.

My father said that, yes, he was speaking of the same boat. Then he explained Graham's sleep disorder and described the night in Chicago when Graham had caused the accident, and the night in Round Lake when he'd gone through the hotel window. I'd never discussed the details of either incident with my father—he must have heard the stories from Graham himself.

"What did the officer say?" I asked my father.

"He said, 'I'll be damned.' He said he'd rustle up some divers to take a look."

For the rest of the day, my father waited in the backyard, clearing debris. No boats came down the canal, no divers showed. I asked about the family in the mansion behind Lidia's, and he told me they'd cleared out; the yacht was gone. There was a broken glass door off their back patio, which my father drove over to close up with a sheet of plywood. I wonder, still, about the mother of that family and her canal swimming, about what she gained from it, about the risks people are willing to take when they want something badly. My father slept uneasily that night, dreaming of shipwrecks. He emphasized this, as if sleeping uneasily were a detail that would particularly interest me.

The next morning, Lidia left for the hospital and my father resumed his work in the backyard. Next door, Felix Genovese hacked through the destroyed mangrove wall, and without bothering with banter asked my father about his fuel reserves. Lines at gas stations were a mile long, there was no reason to think marina fuel docks were open, and the Genoveses were itching to get out of town. The canal was slightly less impenetrable than the streets, and they planned to make their way to the bay in their sport fisher, then head up to Sarasota, where their daughter lived. But they needed a bit more fuel than they had on hand to make it as far as Fort Lauderdale, where they could buy more. He was willing to pay.

"Tell you what," said my father, and offered one car's worth of fuel if his neighbor would do him a favor. Genovese agreed without asking questions. My father stared hard at the propeller sticking out of the murky canal. "Wait here," he said. He went inside and changed into swim trunks, then got rope and a mask and snorkel from the garage.

He told Genovese to hold one end of the rope. "Felix," said my father, "can I trust you?"

Genovese shrugged. "Sure."

My father pointed to the canal. "I've got to go down there, and I want you to make sure I get back up."

"I don't swim," said Genovese, who had a pool in his backyard.

"Just hold on," said my father. "Don't let go. I'll be careful, but if you feel me tug hard a few times, I want you to pull me out."

Genovese looked nervous, but he puffed out his chest—these are my father's words—and called my father a lunatic.

I found it distressing how willing my father was to do this frankly terrifying thing. For Graham in death he was brave, when during his own wife's death he'd been such a phony. Not only had my father made no grand gestures toward the end of her life, but he hadn't even made the little gestures, dispensing medicine or talking to doctors, canceling a show or two to stay by her side. Maybe in Graham's case, my father's morbid curiosity got the better of him, but it seemed like more than that. It seemed like he wanted to see Graham for himself, to be the first person to face the end of Graham's life, instead of waiting for strangers in city-issued wet suits to confirm it. Or maybe my father was plainly uncomfortable with the in-between of life and death, the anticipation, and diving for Graham was, in its way, the same as disappearing during his wife's demise: he preferred to avoid the wait entirely.

My father tied the rope around his chest and eased off the pier into the water, dog-paddling through floating debris. He waved at Felix Genovese, who waved back, then he dived. He came to the screen doors of the *Lullaby* first, then made his way around the starboard side to the window over the banquette, which was broken enough to push through. He came up for air first, made it through the window and as far as Frankie's little bunk before retreating. He couldn't dive long enough to reach the main berth if he swam through the boat.

He breathed at the surface for a long time, buffering his nerve, then dived once more. But this time he went down at the bow, knowing he wouldn't be able to fit through the small windows there even if they'd shattered. Instead, he swam to the forward window on the starboard side, and held on to the trim so he could get a good look inside.

The mattress had come off the bed and fallen toward the door, barricading it. The trundle storage had come open and clothes floated midroom, as if worn by sea-ghosts. Graham's body hovered where the mattress had been, silver hair covering his eyes, bedsheets twisted around his torso and legs. His arm was tethered to the wall.

My father came up heaving, just in time to stop Genovese from jumping in after him.

It was not Genovese but Riggs who took my father back to the police station to report what he'd seen, then brought him to the hospital. My father had emptied his own car's fuel tank for Genovese, and Lidia had her car at the hospital, so it was dumb luck that while my father was contemplating using Graham's bicycle for transportation, he heard a knock on the door, and there stood Riggs. Behind Riggs was a gleaming black Mercedes-Benz. Riggs introduced himself and said something about Charlie having taken his car.

"Isn't *that* your car?" said my father, gesturing to the Mercedes.

"Charlie took my other car."

My father invited him in. Within minutes, he'd told Riggs the story of Graham's disappearance and discovery. They headed together to the police station.

"It's the damndest thing," said my father to me. "Can you please tell me why he did this?"

I shook my head. I could not, and cannot still.

RIGGS HAD COME TO THE hospital with sad news of his own to deliver. He'd brought Polaroids and handed them to Charlie, clapping him on the shoulder. "Sorry to bear bad tidings, friend," he said.

Charlie took the news stiffly, nodding and shrugging at each photograph of his fallen home, blinking rapidly. "Well," he kept saying. "Well."

Riggs seemed reluctant to leave even though there was no place for him to sit. Lidia went off and returned half an hour later with two patio chairs, tags hanging from the aluminum frames. She also brought jigsaw puzzles, and Charlie found a cafeteria tray and lay it on Frankie's lap. He and Riggs edged up close to the bed and with Frankie's eager assistance got to work. I sat beside them breathing deeply, trying not to arouse Frankie's suspicion.

Later, I dozed lightly in the corner on a floor pillow Lidia had brought from her den, and it was in my semiconscious state that I heard, as if through a fog, the sound of high heels clacking into the room. I opened my eyes to find Dr. Sonia standing at the foot of Frankie's bed, absorbing the stares of Riggs and Charlie, who were paused midpuzzle with pieces in their hands.

Frankie took it on himself to be the welcoming voice. "Hi! You came for me?" he said.

"I did," she said.

I got to my feet. "What are you doing here?"

"Checking in," she said, opening Frankie's file. "You look better," she said to Frankie.

"I'm an a-nem-o-ne," said Frankie.

This is something Charlie had told him, after Frankie had insisted we let him look at his face in a mirror. Because of all the colors.

"You don't need to be here," I said.

"I disagree," she said.

I came to her side and pulled the file from her hands. "You're no longer his doctor."

She blinked at me. "You want an apology? I'm sorry. I'm a mother. I know these things can happen."

I glanced at Frankie, but at Charlie's urging he'd gone back to working on the puzzle. I moved her into the hallway. "Thank you for coming," I said, blocking the door.

"Look," she said, speaking through her teeth; it was satisfying to see her lose control a little bit. "It's your choice, but I came because I wanted to see how Frankie's recovering. I'd think you'd appreciate a second opinion."

This was a good point. "He's doing well."

"Has he walked? He should be walking."

"Just once."

This was not strictly true. He'd gotten out of bed the day before with Nurse Barb's help, but had been unable to make it as far as the doorway before crying out, whether from weakness or rib pain, we didn't know. Dr. Lomano said his muscles were tired, and they'd try again when he had more energy.

"Get him out of bed," said Dr. Sonia. "Make him walk three times a day. You won't know how his recovery is going until he's moving around. The swelling is going down—that's good. I'd like to get a look at his pupils, test his reflexes."

"They're doing all of that."

"And I'm sure they're doing a good job. But many hands, lighter work."

I didn't think this was an apt aphorism but let it slide. I handed over Frankie's file and she sat on the edge of his bed and started in with question after question. How much was he eating? What did he remember of the evening before he fell? How old was he? Who were his friends at preschool? Every three or four questions, his mind would wander and she'd ask him firmly to pay attention. Eventually she seemed satisfied, and had him lie down and follow her penlight with his eyes and wiggle his toes and reach out to slap her hand with each of his. She repeated the last exercise several times. Each time, his right hand slapped hers dead-on, but his left landed off-center.

"Hmm," she said, closing the file. "Let's get you up."

"Right now?" I said.

"Right now." She pulled back Frankie's blanket. He edged off the bed and my breath caught, but then he was standing with a firm hold on Dr. Sonia's arm. They made it to the doorway. "Watch," she said to me as they passed.

It was not that he was having trouble walking, exactly, but that he was walking—I'm still not sure how to put it—*differently*. His right foot planted but his left foot dragged a little, toe-first, then pivoted and dragged a little along the heel. It took me several steps to even be able to tell what was strange, the difference was so minor.

Halfway down the hallway, Frankie collapsed. I rushed forward, but by the time I'd gotten there, he was in Dr. Sonia's arms, gripping her neck like a bride in the embrace of a tiny, immaculate groom. "His leg seized," she said.

"The left one," I said, and she nodded.

Frankie was crying and scared. I tucked him back in bed and Charlie comforted him while Dr. Sonia commanded me outside to talk.

"I'm not sure what it is," she said. "Some misfire in his brain. His memory is good, but his balance is off and this thing with the leg could be something. I'll talk to Lomano."

"Thank you," I said.

"It's my job," she said, and turned on a heel.

Riggs left an hour or so later. The lights on Antoine's side of the room went out and I watched his parents leave the room, raising a hand to them as they went. Charlie collapsed into the chair next to mine. I told Frankie it was time for bed and he said good night to each of his sea creatures individually. When he was done—he said good night to the shark twice—Charlie started reading him a book aloud. But it had been a long day and Frankie's eyes were heavy by the second page. Charlie didn't have the heart to finish with no audience. The overhead lights flickered and the sea animals swayed, as if settling in for the night.

"When will you tell him?" said Charlie once Frankie was asleep.

"Tomorrow," I said.

"Do you want me to be with you?"

"No. Thank you."

"We could find a counselor. Or maybe Lidia—"

"No." I shook my head.

"You don't have to do it alone."

"It's the only way I can do it."

His face was filled with shadows, long in the jawline and heavy under the eyes. It was impossible for me to think of sex, in those moments, or even of attraction. It was impossible to recollect the night we'd been together without feeling shame blunted by deeply suppressed joy. But the fact that he was there in that chair beside me was no small comfort. After a while, he moved to the floor cushion with a blanket and, confident that Frankie would sleep straight through, I grabbed a windbreaker Lidia had hung in the closet, slipped the stack of Polaroids Riggs had brought into my pocket, kissed sleeping Frankie, and left the room.

In the hospital cafeteria there was a fairly raucous poker tournament going on, spanning several tables and peopled with a mix of EMTs and nurses and aides. I stood watching the games for a while, then walked through the hectic ER and into the night.

I stood in the glow of a window and shuffled through the Polaroids. The first was of a sun-dappled blanket of green water, through which the outline of Charlie's old stove top was visible, its four black burners distorted by wavelets. The second was of a piling lying in shallows. The last was of blue sky over emerald water, and in the corner a slanted white piling—not Charlie's, but his neighbor's. The empty swath of water and sky was, I understood, where Charlie's house had stood. It hadn't been decimated or, as with the neighbor's house, plucked from its still-fixed pilings: it had been erased. There would come a time, years later, when I missed the stilt house, when I mourned its loss on

Charlie's behalf and even on Frankie's. But that night it was as if I'd confirmed the death of a sworn enemy, and I felt only relief.

I WOKE FRANKIE AT DAWN. I said his name quietly, so as not to disturb Charlie, and watched him wake without opening his eyes. He smiled a little in pretend sleep, and I continued to say his name in a singsong voice until he couldn't resist anymore, and his eyes popped open. He looked at me with the delight of a person revealing a happy secret. It was enough to start me weeping right then.

I'd begged for and received a wheelchair from the nurses' station, along with caution not to have him gone for long. I put two cups and a carton of orange juice in his lap and wheeled him down the hall, shushing gently each time he asked where we were going, to a service elevator, which at the ground level opened onto a loading dock. I'd made this same trip the night before, alone. We wheeled through the warehouse and out into the citrus light of new morning, then across the back acre of the hospital property. There had been a man-made pond there, but now there was only a marshy dip in the earth. I muscled through a thicket of bromeliads, red blooms spilling lewdly from their centers, doing my best to not jostle Frankie too much. We crossed the street and ducked between houses until we reached the elbow of the canal. We were at the far corner of someone's large backyard—there was a swing set, which Frankie eyed longingly—but I guessed that we were hidden from view by the mounds of fallen foliage.

At the water's edge, I helped Frankie from his chair and he sat down on the bank.

"Picnic," said Frankie. "The storm crashed the trees?"

"Yes. But they'll come back."

The sunlight was growing but still there was a slice of moon in the sky. There were bird sounds in the distance and water lapped the bank. "I have something important to tell you," I said.

"What?" he said.

I didn't speak right away. I was choosing the words, or rehearsing the ones I'd chosen.

He said, "Do we talk about Daddy?"

I kept myself from pulling him to me, from stroking his cheek and kissing his hair. It was important, I felt, that we have this conversation eye to eye. I said, "Yes, honey. Daddy had an accident."

Frankie shook his head. "*Frankie* had accident."

"Yes, you had an accident, but you're going to be okay. Dad had an accident, too, and his was very bad. He's not going to be okay."

Frankie finished his juice and set the cup down on the grass. It tipped and he righted it, and it tipped again and he righted it again. If I'd been delivering a different talk—about remembering to pick up toys after playing or saying *please* and *thank you*—I would have been frustrated by his inattention. But I knew that this was only the first of many times this news would be delivered. If Frankie had been a year or two older, he might have been able to start the long dive into grief right away. But at barely four, he would have to ingest the information in morsels.

"Daddy's gone," I said quietly. "He's not coming home anymore."

He stared, as if waiting for me to finish.

I said, "It's very, very sad."

"Why he gone?"

"Because in this bad accident, Daddy died. We're not going to see him anymore."

"Daddy's gone," he said, nodding. Then something in the canal caught his eye. I couldn't bear to look away from his face, which moved quickly from confusion to joy. When I did look, I saw that a white heron had taken flight from the brush and was heading away from us down the center of the canal. I watched it as long as I could make it out, but when I glanced at Frankie, he was looking straight up, at the brightening sky.

"Sun coming up," he said. He looked at me to share his delight. "Good morning!"

He did his best to scramble to his feet—he wanted to climb into my lap, I believe—but something failed when he tried to make his legs work beneath him, and he toppled face-first onto the dewy lawn.

I hunted down Nurse Barb before returning Frankie to his bed, and she promised to send Dr. Lomano as soon as he was free. This took close to an hour, during which I explained to Charlie what had happened. Frankie was restless, so Charlie distracted him by showing him the Polaroids, which Frankie found more fascinating than sad, it seemed. Charlie talked about how sometimes, in a bad storm, things sink, and this had happened not only to the stilt house but also to the *Lullaby*, which wouldn't be his home anymore.

I wondered how much bad news it was wise to dispense at one time. How do young children grieve? I didn't have the language of the angels and heaven and eternal life at my disposal. These would have been useful tools. They would have been useful for my own grief, even.

"But where the house *go*?" said Frankie.

"Lots of places," said Charlie. "Some of it probably ended up here on land. Maybe you'll be at the beach one day and a piece of my house will wash up at your feet."

"You're teasing," said Frankie.

"It's mostly underwater, kiddo," said Charlie. "On the ocean floor."

"House for fishes?" said Frankie.

"Exactly."

They continued down this road of logic: if the house was now underwater, then surely it would be occupied by any number of affable sea animals. Frankie asked about the likelihood of each creature using the house: Did Charlie think an octopus would sleep in his—Frankie's—bed? Would a jellyfish use the potty? Could a sea slug climb the swim ladder? I realized that Charlie understood as much about the toddler mind as anyone I'd known. He was helping Frankie not by creating a sea-themed fantasy, but by giving him exactly the information needed to transition from one reality—the stilt house, standing and true—to a new reality, wherein the house still existed (would it be possible, in Frankie's mind, for a house to no longer exist?) but had been put to use in an entirely different way. I could think of no charming fiction to ease his other, more devastating transition.

"Did the octopus need a new house, too?" said Frankie, discerning somehow that the hurricane had taken the octopus's old house and this is why Charlie had given over his own, as an act of charity.

"That's right," said Charlie.

Frankie continued to connect his own scattered dots, and Charlie agreed again and again, with all of it.

"Where my house going to be?" said Frankie.

"At your Mimi's house, at least for a while."

This notion—that we did not have a home—had not sunken in for me until this moment. I'd been feeling horrible for Sally's family and for others like them, but I'd forgotten, maybe because the *Lullaby* had been our home so briefly, or because what we'd lost in its demise was so much greater, that when we were released from the hospital, not only would Graham be gone but so would everything else—clothes, beds, books, toys. We were among the displaced. Lidia's house had, it seemed, played the role she'd always wanted it to play, the cushion to our fall. If not for the simple fact of its existence, I might have lost my mind.

Dr. Lomano was concerned about Frankie's legs. He'd spoken to Dr. Sonia the day before, had ordered tests. In bed, Frankie's legs worked fine. Even the left one, which had failed with Dr. Sonia and with me, responded to each of Dr. Lomano's commands without trouble. Before the doctor left the room, Frankie said to him, "My daddy had an accident tomorrow."

This was something Frankie did, confusing *yesterday* and *tomorrow*, using them interchangeably. Of course Dr. Lomano didn't know that. He smiled gamely. "Tomorrow he did?" he said.

"It's sad. He not coming home."

The doctor's smile faded. He looked at me.

"That's right, baby," I said, smoothing Frankie's hair. "That's exactly right. Daddy had an accident, and we're not going to see him anymore."

Frankie nodded. "See? Mommy talk about it, when the bird flied."

"I'm very sorry to hear that, Frankie," said the doctor.

"Me, too," Frankie said. He pointed above the bed. "See my octopus friend right there? See my sea horse friend right there?"

And the doctor, to his credit, stayed several minutes more, paying close attention as Frankie introduced each of his creatures. Frankie struggled to a kneeling position and Dr. Lomano helped him, and I watched Frankie's little fingertips as he touched the animals, sending them swaying.

21

RIGGS RETURNED THE FOLLOWING EVENING with pizza for everyone. Lidia brought her rarely used knitting supplies, and Charlie set to examining them while we all ate. Usually when Lidia or my father were in the room, Charlie slipped out to attend to some errand or another, but this time he sat down in one of the lawn chairs, and after the pizza was finished, he and Lidia started knitting.

I was reading to Frankie when Sally and Carson came in. The book blocked my view of the doorway, so it wasn't until Carson jumped on the bed and was chastised by Sally that I even realized they were there. I threw myself into her arms and helped Carson stand at Frankie's feet so he could see the floating animals up close. Sally took off her shoes and sat with Carson and Frankie on the bed, chatting and playing cat's cradle with some of Lidia's yarn. When I asked about rebuilding the house, she shrugged and said she figured they might as well. They didn't rise to leave until bedtime.

Sally pulled my hands to her chest before going out and asked quietly how Frankie was doing.

"Ask again in a few days," I said.

"My Lord," she said, her eyes dampening. "You've got quite a full plate, don't you?"

"I was thinking the same of you."

"Oh, I hated that house, anyway." She tilted her head. "Except sometimes. It's strange, all our stuff is gone, but I can't bring myself to care very much. Stanley cried about his Porsche."

"He'll get another."

"Maybe we'll live at the Hampton Suites for the rest of our lives. Free breakfast."

The next day, we woke to find phone service had been restored. I used a phone at the nurses' station to call Graham's mother's husband, Bob Winters, and tell him what had happened to Graham. I spent a long time listening to his labored breathing and confused questions. He mentioned that his daughter and her new baby were living with him, and as if to prove it a baby cried out in the background.

Next, I called Graham's colleague Larry Birnbaum, who had read about Graham's death in the newspaper. He'd been trying to get in touch with me to let me know I was welcome to pick up the few items left behind in Graham's office. There was an old photo of me and Frankie, he said, a stack of weather maps Graham had collected over the years, and a few books. I declined. Larry mentioned, offhandedly, that he'd boxed the items up after Graham's last day. After we hung up, the way he'd put it nagged at me, and I called back. After some misunderstanding, I finally wrangled from Larry this fact: Graham had been dismissed from his job with Rosenstiel at the same time that he'd left the *Revelle*. The details of his flight from the ship remained unclear, but Larry said something about keeping the whole thing private, out of respect for me and my son. He also mentioned pointedly, as if this were a detail prominent in my mind, that he knew Graham had bought supplementary insurance out of pocket, so although his work-subsidized plan was canceled when he was let go, the second plan would still pay out.

This was the first I'd thought of insurance. Larry transferred me to a woman in human resources who gave me the number of the company representative who worked with Graham's team, and from her I learned that Graham had bought a sizable plan just before he'd left for the *Revelle*. There were forms to fill out; she would send them.

When I reentered the room, I found a kind of party in full swing: my father with his ukulele propped on one knee, Riggs nodding along in conversation with Lidia, and Frankie sitting up in bed playing a bumbling—but apparently hilarious—game of handball with Antoine, wherein if Antoine couldn't swat back or catch the ball, Frankie ambled to get it while Antoine's mother shadowed him in case he needed help. Charlie was not in the room. For a moment, I stood watching the scene from the doorway, thinking that Graham should have been there, too. But then I remembered something. It was something I would need to continue to remember, throughout those months after Graham's death. I might have missed him, but Graham would not have wanted to be there, in the thick of any kind of domestic chaos. He would have been eyeing the door, as he'd done the evening we'd returned from the Dry Tortugas and he'd made origami for Frankie while I napped. And his own discomfort would have continued to hurt him as much as it hurt me.

Whether he meant to kill himself, I still don't know. He couldn't have been certain the *Lullaby* would sink, after all. The insurance company would request all his medical records from Detention, but in the end the policy would pay out. I assume Graham bought it because he could not ignore the perils of living in a place surrounded by water, and out of love and concern for his family. And it made a difference. That money would continue to provide the only kind of peace of mind he'd ever been able to give us.

OVER THE COURSE OF OUR three hospital-bound weeks, Frankie's walking continued to improve, with fewer incidents of the *seizing behavior*, as Dr. Lomano called it. There was one other thing, which the doctor said was unlikely to go away, but also unlikely to cause much trouble: when Frankie looked at you straight on, his left eye wandered slightly to the outside of his vision. This was due either to trauma to the retina or mixed messages from the brain left over from the swelling. Objects in Frankie's far peripheral vision might appear flattened or smaller than they really were, skewed almost undetectably. If Frankie noticed this, he didn't mention anything, and I didn't ask him about it. I would need to have his vision tested twice a year to make sure the problem, which the doctor called *strabismus*, didn't worsen.

When I asked Dr. Sonia about it, she shrugged. "I can barely even see it," she said. "What's the big problem?"

It continued to be reassuring and frustrating both, working with her.

Sally and her boys were at loose ends in the hotel suite, all their camps canceled for the remainder of the summer. And so more days than not, they came by with sandwiches and cookies and games, and the older boys horsed around in the lounge or took themselves on expeditions through the hospital while Carson and Frankie played with Legos or action figures and Sally and I chatted. Charlie made himself scarce when people visited and showed up again after they left; he never exchanged more than a few words with Sally, though he and my father and Lidia always made polite conversation before Charlie headed out. I teased Charlie that he was practically an imaginary friend.

Though he'd started out spending nights in Frankie's room, there was no truly comfortable place for visitors to sleep—I'd been squeezing into Frankie's small bed and Charlie had been taking the floor or the short lounge sofa—so eventually I convinced Charlie to spend nights at Riggs's. A day or two later, Nurse Barb was moved by my homelessness and new widowhood to bring a cot, which she squeezed between Frankie's bed and the wall. There, with only me and Frankie and Antoine in the room at night, I slept soundly for the first time in years. Despite everything, I have many contented memories of our time in the hospital, though none as precious as that of falling asleep beside my lightly snoring son, secure that his sleep would be a typical child's sleep, filled with dreams and not much else.

For Nurse Barb's birthday, Lidia brought a cake and candles and party hats, and Frankie made her a card. We took up a collection from the other families in the unit and celebrated in the lounge, and when she opened the card she cried and her mascara ran.

Riggs became a near-daily fixture in the room, stopping by with *pastelitos* and Cuban coffee in the late morning, handing off coloring books to Frankie and Antoine and paperwork to Charlie, who always turned up shortly after sunrise. The paperwork, I gathered, though Charlie was tight-lipped on the subject, had to do with repairs to Charlie's house in South Miami, which hadn't been occupied since Vivian had left for the rest home. With Riggs's help, Charlie hired roofers, painters, plumbers, and even an interior designer (someone Riggs was dating), who was in charge of choosing wall paint and wallpaper, some furniture, a few rugs. Every day brought some new hiccup. The neighbors' tree trimmer was blocking the driveway and the roofers couldn't get in. Then the painters found lead in the exterior trim paint and renegotiated their fee. Then the flooring people said the downstairs wood could be refinished but the upstairs might be better off with new carpeting, so extensive was the water damage.

I needled Charlie for information, but he continued to be evasive. "What's the problem with the floors?" I'd say, and he'd say, "I don't really know." I'd say, "What colors were you hoping for?" and he'd shrug. "Blues, yellows, maybe even some pink."

"You just want to be back at Stiltsville," I'd said, and he shrugged again, avoiding my eyes.

We had both reached the end of an era in our lives. When I looked forward, I couldn't see far, which made me distinctly uncomfortable. When I mentioned this to Lidia, she reassured me. "Make no decisions!" she said. "Come to my house, settle in, get Frankie back in preschool! Then figure out your plan."

This seemed at once very good advice and also impossible to follow. Wasn't a shaky plan better than no plan at all? Temporary housing in Lidia's guest room was comforting and familiar, but unfeasible long-term. When I explained this to Sally, she reminded me that her five-person family was living in a hotel suite next door to a Denny's, and that they would continue to live there for months, maybe even a year. She said she'd already gained five pounds. She guessed this was because there was so little cleaning to do.

"But you're rebuilding your house," I said. "I'm not rebuilding anything."

"So build one," she said. "There are plenty of empty lots these days."

There was the remote possibility of moving back to Round Lake, where the cottage now sat empty.

"Illinois?" said Sally. "No."

"Good schools," I said.

"You stay here," she said. "With us." She gestured around the room. Sally and I sat cross-legged on my cot, and on the far side of Frankie's bed he and Carson ate ice cream in the patio chairs and Lidia knitted. Riggs was propped at the foot of Antoine's bed, teaching him a card trick he'd been teaching Carson and Frankie a few minutes before. (Riggs's ease with kids reminded me that he'd lost his son, which reminded me again to be grateful for Frankie's recovery.) Even Henry Gale had stopped by a few times—he'd been giving out free printing to anyone whose pet had gone missing in the storm, for posting flyers—and Marse Heiger had called earlier that day to say she'd be coming by with dinner. She'd been working long hours in a volunteer phone bank in the lobby of her condo building. Was she allowed to bring wine to a hospital? she'd asked, and after I passed the question on to the room, Lidia and Sally clapped enthusiastically and told me to tell her to smuggle it in a Thermos.

More than once I let myself wonder if Charlie would invite Frankie and me to live with him in the house in South Miami, which I'd gathered had plenty of room. I'd told myself if and when the time came to decline. There had been no discussion of a shared future. We'd never so much as eaten a meal in a restaurant or watched a movie together. We'd never spoken on the phone or kissed in public. Imagining us together, in a traditional way, was like imagining life on another planet. It had shades of a reality that was familiar to me, but all the indistinct details kept muddling the picture.

Riggs went home, my father had a gig, and Stanley came by to pick up the kids but Sally stayed. Charlie hung around even though Sally and Lidia were still in the room, but it was quiet, relatively speaking, when Marse arrived.

"You've certainly settled in," said Marse to me, eyeing the mobiles. A few had torn from handling and Charlie had taped them. Whenever a door opened in the hallway, they fluttered. "You know," she said to Frankie, examining his fading wounds, "you're supposed to land in the *water*." He giggled.

The wine was poured and the sandwiches were distributed. Marse told a story about a homeless man who worked beside her at the phone bank, who kept asking her out on dates. Once, she'd actually consented— nothing had materialized with Henry Gale—and they'd ended up at the Barnacle, an historic home on the bay in Coconut Grove, listening to people play guitar and drinking dark liquor out of a brown-bagged bottle, her paramour in sweatpants and she in a suit. Lidia started hiccupping loudly during Marse's story, which made all of us laugh, including Frankie. Charlie was quiet in the storm of girl-talk but seemed content enough, sitting with his legs crossed and his fingertips against his cheek. Every few minutes I felt his eyes on me. I warmed under his gaze. In the time we'd spent at the hospital, we'd done little more than touch hands. When it was just us and Frankie, I kept some distance between us and he respected it. But now I felt the surfacing of a distinct urge.

Nurse Barb came by to ask us to quiet down, which Charlie took as a cue to leave. I followed him into the hall to say good-bye, and he pulled me into a supply closet. "This," he said, and kissed me hard on the mouth. "I have been waiting for this."

"I—" I said, but then his mouth was on mine again, his hands inside the waistband of my jeans.

"I love watching you," he said when we came up for air.

His brow pressed against mine. I liked the way our shoulders met almost evenly, as if we'd been carved in mirror image from one large substance. But as he pulled me in, more and more urgent, I felt myself receding. My lips numbed. Sorrow rose in my chest. I felt that it was possible—just possible—that our time had come and gone.

"Come back," he said.

I shook my head.

"It's okay," he said quietly.

What I was thinking was that in an hour or so I would change into my night clothes and slip into my cot beside Frankie, and we'd read as many books as we could before he drifted off. And despite the wine and the lightened mood, my focus was still consumed by my boy, on our upcoming release from the safe and predictable hospital routine, on our untamable future. The last time I'd let my focus stray, I'd almost lost him.

"This hospital—" I said.

"Don't worry." He kissed my brow and cleared his throat. "I have a favor to ask you."

I waited.

"I need to show you the house. Tomorrow, if you can get away."

"I'll try," I said.

I'd been leaving the hospital once a day with Lidia or alone, to walk to the store or around the block. But I'd never been gone long, and Charlie and I hadn't set foot out of doors together.

He stepped out of the closet and I followed him. He kissed me once and walked away with his hands in his pockets and his shoulders rounded. The noise level in our room had risen again, and I stood, listening to the happy sounds, the gabbing and teasing and giggling. If Charlie wanted me to visit his home, I believed, it could only mean one thing: he planned to throw us a life preserver. And though I hated to think of a time when Frankie and I would not see him daily, I felt more certain than ever that this was not the right future for us.

LIDIA AND MY FATHER AND Charlie showed up at roughly the same time the following morning. I took one of the bagels Lidia had brought, kissed Frankie, and left the hospital with Charlie in Riggs's little sports car. Around us, Miami was struggling to return to normal. On every corner loomed a pile of debris, and between the piles the neighborhoods looked sparse and trim, uncluttered by typical growth, like newly groomed eyebrows. Almost every house was missing roof tiles or was topped with men on their knees, hammering. I'd heard that laborers were streaming into the area from as far away as Virginia and the Carolinas, taking advantage of the glut of work. Insurance companies were fast-tracking claims and lengthening their lists of providers. Even pool boys were in high demand, and every store in South Florida had run out of lawn mowers and hedge trimmers. People who had never before so much as watered their own lawns now spent hours landscaping. In many neighborhoods, the electricity still had not returned. We could tell these neighborhoods because everyone was outside, sitting in loungers or talking to neighbors.

Charlie's home sat on property that took up an entire city block just a few streets off Sunset Drive, one of the area's main arteries. The house was surrounded by a hodgepodge of new, tightly packed two-story homes on small lots, and ranch homes with portacacheres. His was a white farmhouse with a detached garage set back from the road behind a low limestone wall and semicircular gravel driveway, shaded by an immense sea grape tree on one side and a live oak on the other.

The oak was rimmed at the base by a ring of bushy ferns—the English garden Charlie had mentioned had been overgrown. There was a truck in the driveway, and a few men worked on the roof. Charlie waved to them and they waved back. The stone wall continued around the perimeter, deteriorating in spots, sprouting air plants and moss from its crannies. There were no sidewalks in this neighborhood, and across the street to the east of Charlie's property was a tangled wooded area dotted here and there with what looked like headstones.

"Is that a cemetery?" I said.

Charlie grappled with the front door lock. "Vivian's parents are buried there."

"Is that legal?"

"Not anymore."

I stumbled on a crooked cement step, then followed Charlie inside. To the right was a formal dining room with sheets over the table and a crack in the picture window. On the wall were patches of fresh paint, each about a square foot in area: a light aquamarine, a dark coral, and a light coral.

"I'm supposed to make some decisions," said Charlie when he saw me eyeing the colors. "You'd be doing me a favor if you'd just choose for me."

"You got it," I said.

To the left of the front door was a living room with a fireplace, the mantel bare and the furniture covered, and through the living room was a small kitchen with a back door and a window over the sink, through which I could appreciate the depth of the property. The back of the house was shielded from neighbors by a thicket of gumbo limbo trees, several messy areca palms, and a towering and craggy banyan, its thickest vines burrowing into the ground.

"I'm surprised you haven't been vandalized," I said.

"Who says I haven't?"

He led me out back and around to the garage, which was locked with a padlock and chain. Behind the garage was a patio and covered barbecue pit. The area was littered with beer cans and soda bottles.

"Nothing too sinister," Charlie said. "Just neighborhood kids."

We picked up the cans and bottles and dropped them in a trash can at the back of the house. As we walked, he spoke slowly, as if to be certain I was listening. "Vivian's grandfather brought the family down to plant pineapple groves," he said. He indicated the back of the property and the acres beyond. "When that didn't work out, he planted palm trees instead. Her father sold off most of the land when she was a girl."

On the far side of the house was an empty swimming pool and a cabana. There were boards over the cabana's door and windows and a baby blue diving board lay on its side on the limestone patio. It was incredible to me that, given its current state, this had ever been a house where a family had thrived.

"The city made me take it out," he said, gesturing to the diving board. "Jenny and her friends loved that thing. They'd lie on it for hours, head to toe." He seemed to be picturing her there. "The pool is over nine feet deep. It feeds from a well, so it's very, very cold."

As we started to step back into the kitchen, we heard someone calling Charlie's name from the front yard. A man appeared at the side of the house wearing khaki shorts and a golf shirt, waving congenially.

"Barton," said Charlie. "How have you been?"

They shook hands. Charlie didn't smile, but he leaned toward his neighbor in a welcoming way, and the man seemed genuinely glad to see him.

"It's been ages," said Barton.

I introduced myself and we shook hands.

"So sorry about Vivian," said Barton to Charlie. "Moving back in?"

"Thinking about it," said Charlie.

"Glad to hear it." The men nodded at each other. "Well, I'll be seeing you," said Barton.

"My best to Sandy and the girls," said Charlie.

Inside, with Barton's receding back framed in a living room window, I said, "Goodness, you're neighborly. Who would have guessed?"

"He's a decent fellow. Always comes by with a big bucket of key limes when his trees start to drop."

"Will you be happy here?"

He sat down on the white-sheeted living room sofa. Above our heads came the sounds of multiple hammers. He looked around the room as if trying to picture himself there. "I really couldn't say."

I was very aware of the fact that we were alone, but also that there were people working unseen above our heads and bright sunlight streaming in through the windows. "Do you have a pencil? I'll help with those paint colors."

Charlie went to the kitchen and returned with a pencil, then sank back onto the couch. The air was hot and sour. I wore a tank top under my shirt, so I took off my shirt and tossed it into Charlie's lap.

The designer had painted a few squares of color on a wall in each room. In the living room, the options were stacked in a reading nook beside an antique hutch; there, I circled a buttery yellow. In the kitchen, I circled a deep marine blue that reminded me of the office at the stilt house, along with a swatch of brightly colored wax cloth from a few options taped over the sink, for curtains. In the dining room, I circled the darker of the two coral colors. Behind the dining room was a sunroom with a terra-cotta floor, bare of furniture; there, I circled a light aquamarine. Off the sunroom was a bathroom with only one swatch on the wall: the lighter of the corals from the dining room. I circled it in approval, then took myself upstairs. As I went, I glanced into the living room. Charlie lay with his head propped on one arm of the sofa, and as our eyes met, my heartbeat sped up.

Upstairs were three bedrooms—chalky gray-blue for the master bedroom and baby blue for the master bath, cream for the larger of the two other bedrooms and taupe for the third. In the hallway were strips of wallpaper in toile and floral prints, and I circled one covered in cheery hibiscus blooms. In the closet of the master bedroom was a large, open box, and when I peered inside I found hundreds of what I assumed were Vivian's photographs. I wanted to thumb through them but forced myself to close the closet door.

Off the master bedroom was a screened sleeping porch with a wide-plank wood floor that needed a good sweep. Through the screens I could see the patchy lawn stippled with acorns, the mossy rock wall, the cabana's pitched roof. Just beyond the perimeter of palms was the crystal blue of a neighbor's swimming pool. I could no more easily imagine Charlie lounging on the sleeping porch with a newspaper, swimming in the pool, or using the barbecue, than I could imagine him choosing wallpaper for the hallway. We were alike, it seemed. We both had a place to go, but that place wasn't the right one at all.

Before going downstairs, I stood on the sleeping porch and fanned my face, trying to cool off. I looked down at the disrepair of the pool and grounds, so lovely in their own way even in that state, and hardened my resolve: when he asked, I would decline, for his sake as much as my own.

His eyes were closed when I came back downstairs. There was a sheen of perspiration on his stubbled cheeks, and he'd pulled up the hems of his jeans, baring his ankles. I circled one ankle with my hand and his eyes opened. "I'm done," I said.

He touched his cheek. "Come on," he said, pulling me down by the wrist. His hands dug in my hair and his thigh spread my legs. My resolve weakened.

We were still at the house when the roofers took their lunch break. The terrible hammering stopped. I started to feel pulled back to the hospital, back to Frankie, and hurried to dress. But Charlie put on each of his shoes and buttoned his shirt so deliberately that it occurred to me that he was biding time. Before I could ask him what was going on, the doorbell rang and there stood a pert forty-something woman in a ponytail and linen pants suit. She was pretty in a calculated way, with a glossy, heart-shaped mouth.

"Victoria," said Charlie.

"Did you make any decisions?" she said brightly.

"We did!" he said, then introduced me. "This is the decorator," he said to me.

"Designer," corrected Victoria.

"I love those corals," I said.

"This house begs for old Florida tones. All the white—I shudder." She laughed loudly, then gestured for us to follow her into the kitchen. From a briefcase she pulled a file filled with pictures of cabinets and laid them out on the counter. Then she pulled out four squares of stone countertops in hues of white and gray. "The clock ticks," she said.

"We were headed out, actually," I said.

Charlie put a hand on my waist. "Just one more minute." He put the photos in my hand. "Please."

I understood then that this had been his plan all along. Not for me to just see the house, but for me to make these choices for him, even to meet Victoria; he'd been stalling until she arrived. And it was easy, picking out someone else's kitchen cabinets and countertops. It took me all of five minutes, after which Victoria led me through the house, pulling out photographs of ceiling fans with palm blades and upholstery options for the dining room chairs and living room sofa. When Graham and I had made some of these same choices at the cottage, it had taken weeks. What energy we are capable of wasting, when nothing more urgent is going on.

No, Frankie and I would not return to Round Lake. Whether I would sell the cottage or keep it, maybe for Frankie or as an investment, I wasn't sure, but there was no need to decide right away.

Finally we were done. We left Victoria behind in the house. The roofers had returned to their hammering. Sunlight dappled the driveway. As we drove away, I looked back at the house, which only an hour before had seemed so shabby and unloved, and saw it now as simply tarnished, in need of a spit and shine and not much else. I didn't think Charlie would be happy there, but I was happy for him.

"So what do you think?" he said when we were in the car. He didn't look at me. I studied his hard-set jaw, the lines of his handsome face.

"I think you have a beautiful home," I said. "The designer was a good idea."

"I'm getting the friend-of-the-boyfriend discount."

"She's getting divorced?"

"How did you know?"

"Just a hunch."

"Riggs is smitten. It's 'Victoria this, Victoria that . . .'" He trailed off.

We parked at the hospital and I started to get out of the car, then stopped. "Charlie—"

"I've got a couple errands to run," he said. "Henry Gale's shop, for one."

"We'll see you tonight?"

He hesitated. "Not tonight, no." He pressed his palms against his thighs. He didn't look at me. "I've got a few things to catch up on."

"I have something to tell you."

He raised his eyes. "All right."

"If you're thinking—I don't know if you are, but if you are—that we might live together . . ."

His smile was soft, apologetic. I saw that I'd been foolish. I saw, too, something I'd been ignoring, which had been right in front of me the whole time: he was much, much older than I. He had no intention of starting over, at least not in the way I might one day start over.

"I wasn't thinking that," he said.

"Of course not," I said. You're a *hermit*, I thought. And though I'd been certain, or nearly so, that living together would not have worked, I was crushed to realize it had never been under consideration.

He opened his mouth to say more, but I didn't want to hear it. I kissed him quickly on the cheek, but when he pulled me in for more, I broke away.

"Tell the boy," he said before I shut the door, "I miss him."

I waved good-bye over my shoulder. That evening, when I undressed for a shower, I could smell him on my clothes and in my hair. I sat on the toilet seat as the small hospital bathroom filled with steam, thinking that he had most certainly—I was almost sure of it—said, "Tell the boy I miss him," and not, as it had started to sound when repeated in my mind, "Tell the boy *I'll* miss him."

22

A WEEK LATER, FRANKIE WAS discharged from the hospital after having been there twenty days. Lidia and I stood on chairs and pulled the mobiles from the ceiling as Frankie called out, "Gently! Gently!" The swelling was all but gone, the bruising reduced to a mustard stain under his left eye.

He'd asked after Charlie every morning, and every morning I'd told him the same thing: "He's gone now, but he misses you." Eventually, I knew, he would stop asking. I found it very sad, the promise of his short memory, but also very comforting.

We took away with us a roster of exercises that Dr. Lomano believed would help keep the still-unexplained seizing behavior at bay. I made an appointment with an ophthalmologist to check on the strabismus, which continued to appear when Frankie was tired. We donated a large box of puzzles, toys, and books to the pediatric lounge.

Riggs had brought the mortgage papers to the hospital. He'd gone over them with me while I bit my thumb to keep from crying. A notary looked on as I signed where Riggs told me to sign. When I was done,

Charlie's house and its property, including the grounds across the street, belonged to me. I didn't ask where he had gone; I knew Riggs wouldn't tell me, but also I believed I already knew. Most likely, Charlie had been planning to go since long before meeting me and Frankie, had been waiting until after Vivian's death. For a long time I would wonder why we weren't enough to keep him around. I would wonder if there might have been something I could have said or done to make him stay. But there was the matter of our age difference, which would only have become more relevant as time passed, and there was the matter of his preference for solitude. Riggs was also sorry to see him go, I knew. He gave me back my job when Angela quit to go to school full-time, and though the two years I spent as his assistant weren't easy, he never again raised his voice to me, which is saying a lot.

We held a memorial service for Graham in Lidia's backyard, and there, for the first time, I met Larry Birnbaum in the flesh, along with a dozen of Graham's Rosenstiel colleagues. Larry had light green eyes and a deep tan and receding blond hair. He showed me wallet photographs of his four towheaded daughters. After we'd spread half of Graham's ashes in the canal and Lidia had served key lime pie, Larry and I sat together on the pier, and he told me in as much detail as he could what had happened on the *Revelle*. After, I was more certain that Graham had meant, or at least hoped, to take his own life. But I kept this to myself, for selfish reasons and also because that's what he had wanted.

IT WAS A MONTH BEFORE the farmhouse was ready for us. In the meantime, Frankie slept in the guest room at Lidia's and, unwilling to provoke the sleep gods, I slept beside him instead of in the den Lidia had cleared out for me. One afternoon, Marse Heiger picked up me and Lidia in her boat and ferried us out to Stiltsville to see for ourselves what had been lost. It took a while to find the watery land where Charlie's house had stood. We were able to, finally, only because a few of his neighbors' pilings remained. We puttered fifty yards west of the pilings and circled until we spotted Charlie's refrigerator and oven beneath the surface. Nearby was a barstool and a kitchen cabinet and nothing else.

"*Dios mio,*" said Lidia.

Marse shuddered visibly. "Can you imagine?"

I had been imagining it, in fact. The windows might have blown out first, followed by the eaves and the roof. How does a floor give way? How does a dock splinter? What does it sound like when a wall collapses? I focused on these images and tried to block out the one that kept coming: Frankie falling, and landing.

On the return, I asked Marse to keep our speed low and stick close to the shoals, so I could scan the water for Charlie's boxes. I wondered what the drawings would look like if I found them. Would they be unrecognizable, after all that time in the water, or would they be preserved, fish-nibbled but otherwise intact? I found no trace. Maybe Charlie went back for them himself, though with the storm and tides, it's more likely that they were carried out to sea. I like to think that they still exist somewhere, which leaves the possibility that they will be found.

For a long time I remained fixated on the accident. In particular, I circled around one question: What must it have been like for Charlie, during that swollen heartbeat of time while Frankie was falling? If I'd been faster, Frankie might have fallen into my arms; I might have broken his fall. But if Charlie had been faster, Frankie might not have fallen at all. I think this distinction instilled in Charlie an unbearable guilt, one that echoed the pain of having arrived too late to save his daughter. And I think this guilt helps explain why he left us the way he did, without saying good-bye. Without, even, any recognition of his love or ours.

I think Frankie missed him even more than I did. Whether he missed him as much as he missed his father, I couldn't say, but the fact that both men disappeared from his life within a week of each other was a blow from which he will never fully recover.

By the time we moved into the farmhouse—there was not much to move—the new paint smell had faded. Despite its face-lift, the house has echoing acoustics, leaky windows, noisy floorboards, and a persistent ant problem in the kitchen. I live with the choices I made so hastily that afternoon when I first visited, and for the most part they were good ones.

When we arrived, I found a new wooden manikin like Charlie's in the closet in Frankie's room. And in the closet of the master bedroom was the ruined T-shirt I'd worn the afternoon we'd painted the office; it still smelled of me. I wasn't sure if this was his way of acknowledging what we'd shared or of making sure I knew that what we'd shared was finished. Vivian's photographs were gone, but I pestered Riggs until one day at work he dropped an envelope on my desk. There had been at least a couple hundred in the box I'd seen, but in the envelope there were only five, all black-and white: the banyan behind the farmhouse; the house casting a sharp shadow across the lawn; the areca palms on a windy day; a hibiscus in bloom in the side yard. The fifth was of the pool, and in the water a female figure wearing a dark suit swam away from the camera. I framed the photographs and hung them in the upstairs hallway, where they remain to this day.

I spent a lot of time that first year trying to put Frankie's accident in the past. I tried not to dote on him, to give him space to get used to the changed circumstances of our lives, but he clung to me. At bedtime, he screamed unless I agreed to stay the night in his bed, and during the day he followed me from room to room. We were on rocky ground for a while, sanity-wise. I filled the swimming pool but he refused to go near it. Among all he lost, then, there was also swimming and water, games of Marco Polo and pool parties, the beach and the ocean and fishing. My father brought a child-size acoustic guitar and taught Frankie to play. Lidia brought craft projects and a small trampoline and picked him up every few days to go to the airport to see planes or the marina to see boats. One day, she brought him an easel and a set of watercolors and pencils, and from then on the house was littered with his master-pieces: fish of every shape and color, the farmhouse, the live oak, me.

My sleeplessness returned. I took up the habit of swimming laps before bed, which helps. Still, many mornings find me watching from the sleeping porch as sunlight spills into the grooves of the oak. We are surrounded by neighbors, but the rambling house and property feel to me like they exist in a separate time and place. I think of Vivian often. I wish I could thank her.

After we'd been in the farmhouse more than a year, I placed an ad in the Round Lake newspaper and found a new tenant for the cottage, another academic looking for a place to write his dissertation. I flew out and hired a local caretaker to put in the dock every spring and take it out in early winter, to set mousetraps and clear them, to winterize the pipes and have the chimney swept in the fall. I found myself glad that this place that once had been my home wouldn't be gone from me forever. I put away Graham's old posters, the gifts from his father, to save for Frankie. Before I returned to Florida, I spread the last part of Graham's ashes off the pier and spent the evening on the back deck, recalling the evening we'd made our lopsided decision to start a family.

And so I own two houses, neither of which feels like it truly belongs to me. Sometimes I daydream of a time after Frankie is out of the house when I might move into a soulless condo with no ghosts haunting the cupboards. Not because I'd rather live in such a place, but because I wonder what it's like to break with the past.

THERE IS ONLY ONE STORY I haven't yet told. It involves a young woman named Anna Fitzgerald, who, during the second semester of her graduate work at the Rosenstiel School of Atmospheric and Marine Science, was awarded a spot on the *R. V. Roger Revelle*. I've seen photographs: she was a very tall, pale person, with a prominent nose and poor posture, pretty in a way that she didn't seem to recognize. Graham's one-time roommate, a German-born Scripps student named Alfonso, did recognize it, and campaigned for her affections as soon as she was transferred to the ship. He and Anna had a habit of meeting at night on the stern deck, beneath the pilothouse, where they spent an hour or two talking and watching the shoreline lights. One night, a sleepwalking Graham happened on them, and for reasons no one but I can imagine, Graham charged at Anna with both arms extended, taking her completely by surprise and pushing her over the ship rail into the blue-black depths of the Atlantic.

I can imagine it, yes. Sometimes I even think I can explain it, though it's an explanation that falls short of pure logic, and therefore would be one that Graham would loathe on its face. Anna and I don't resemble each other, and Alfonso, who had rejected Graham's friendship after a tumultuous month of bunking together, doesn't resemble Graham, so the parallels are not perfect. But Graham was no dummy, and I think my pleasure at having escaped our shared life, however impermanently we believed that escape was at the time, was evident to him, even if it wasn't yet evident to me. He was in a state of heartbreak and loss, over me and Frankie as well as his mother, feeling no small measure of anger at me and at himself.

Anna lived. Alfonso punched Graham in the gut, sent up a flare from a nearby lifeboat, grabbed a life preserver, and jumped in after her. If they had been standing anywhere but the stern, where the ship rail was lower, it's unlikely Graham would have had the power, in his state, to force her over. And if the ship had not been anchored, she likely would have drowned. As it was, it's a wonder that she did not hit anything on the way down, not the gunwale or the anchor line or something in the dark water. It is a wonder that she was able to surface, and I'm grateful still.

Graham was transferred to shore and arrested by the Jacksonville police. He refused to hand over Lidia's phone number, so I was not contacted. By the time he returned to us, he was out on bail posted by Larry

Birnbaum and a psychiatric evaluation had been ordered. And although he would have returned to Detention willingly rather than lose me and Frankie, I know that being institutionalized without the freedom to leave would have seemed to him the end of anything workable in life.

Learning what Graham did to Anna Fitzgerald released me from some of my guilt, over leaving him and over Frankie's accident. I still wake in the night, my heart racing, with an agonizing image in mind: Graham on the deck of a ship, standing behind not Anna Fitzgerald but Frankie, arms up and ready to push. After I wake, I play it out. I save Frankie, again and again, but not by jumping in after him. I save him by knocking Graham to the floor before he can do his damage. In my edited version of imaginary events—as real to me in the dark hours as the clock ticking on the nightstand—Frankie turns to find his mother open-armed behind him, and his father, no kind of villain, alive and awake.

EARLY ON THE MORNING OF Frankie's first day of kindergarten, we walked across the street to wait for the school bus. Barton Callaway was standing at the corner with his daughter, a fifth grader. I snapped photos and asked Barton to take one of Frankie and me together. Barton's daughter helped Frankie take the first giant step onto the bus, and then Frankie sat alone at a window, clutching his backpack. After the bus turned the corner, I asked Barton to take a photo of me standing alone in the breaking light with the farmhouse in the background. He did. Then he gave me an encouraging shake of the shoulder and went inside. After the photos were processed, I dropped them at Riggs's office, knowing they would find their way.

It has been eight years since Charlie left, and I haven't seen or spoken to him since. Still, we haven't really lost touch. Every six months or so, Riggs drops by with a box: a handmade sweater or a book or art supplies for Frankie. If there is a note—usually there isn't one—it is brief. FOR THE BOY. —C.

Riggs passes on details about us. This was clear after I mentioned that I'd taken Frankie to his first baseball game, and there followed a new glove and season tickets. I mentioned Frankie's obsession with all things prehistoric, and three months later there was a new show at the Abyss: "Sea Monsters," featuring the extinct *megalodon*, a shark the size of a tanker. For Frankie's seventh birthday a book arrived, a biography of Mary Anning, the twelve-year-old girl in nineteenth-century England who discovered fossils of a monstrous prehistoric dolphin called *Ichthyosaurus*. We spent hours on our hands and knees in the backyard, excavating with spades and paintbrushes.

I grew careful about what I shared. I didn't tell Riggs about Frankie's broken arm after climbing the live oak when he was eight. I didn't mention when he was nine that he gave an older boy a bloody nose after the boy called him a *bastard*. I keep to myself the fact that he no longer swims.

Henry Gale and I closed in on each other over a span of years. As I remember it, one day I looked up and there he was, the dark beard and easy chuckle and ruddy cheeks, the two-handed handshake, the respectful affection for Frankie. He'd been waiting for me to notice him. He and Charlie were in contact for a time; they sent work back and forth. Then one day Henry received a note from Riggs—whether this had to do with our growing intimacy, I don't know—explaining that Charlie had found an illustrator closer to home and thanking him for the years of partnership. Henry's father still lives at the Palms at Park Place, though he's lost his eyesight and doesn't remember us when we visit. For the foreseeable future, Henry keeps his own house.

Frankie stopped sleeping through the night when he was ten years old. I put in a high, ugly pool fence with a locked gate and I keep the key hidden. I installed a house alarm. This will work until he's old enough to come and go on his own, which is coming soon; I'll need new strategies. He wanders the upstairs at all hours, reading books and playing, but I haven't seen any evidence—knock on wood—that he has his father's parasomnia rather than my run-of-the-mill insomnia. I pray that this continues to be the case.

For his eleventh birthday he asked for art lessons, and I enrolled him in drawing classes at the Lowe Art Museum on University of Miami's campus. After dropping him off the first day, I wandered through the rooms and came upon a collection of paintings I recognized: the Florida scenes from Charlie's stilt house, which he'd rescued on his trip to shore the night before Hurricane Andrew. A wall plaque noted that the works, all important pieces by artists known collectively as the Florida Highwaymen, had been donated in the name of Jennifer Elizabeth Hicks.

Today Frankie is tall for his age, talkative enough when he's not in a mood, broad-shouldered and energetic, with his father's stork legs and my woolly dark hair. When he isn't drawing or painting, he's playing baseball or guitar. He gets headaches from time to time, and every so often when you're facing him straight-on you might perceive that slight angling of his left eye, as if its attention has wandered. Sometimes, after practice or a long session playing guitar with his grandfather, I catch him limping or rubbing his arm, and I wonder if the horrors that brushed past us that night have returned to take what is theirs.

This past spring, one of Frankie's drawings was included in an art fair at his school. Henry and I went to see the piece framed on the wall, a blue ribbon hooked over one corner. The picture, which was done with a set of technical drawing pens sent by Charlie—the same brand I'd bought for Charlie so long before, which he'd never used—was of me sitting in the chaise lounge on the sleeping porch, a book open in my lap. I don't want to overstate my son's talent, but there is no question that he has an eye for proportions and light, and that he rendered me well, with my unruly hair and the way I cross my legs when I'm lost in thought. Studying it, I found myself distracted; not by what was on the page, exactly, but by the mood. It's disconcerting to think of him catching me off guard, steeped in melancholy. Maybe he'd seen me sitting just so on my private porch, orange light gathering beyond the screens. Or maybe he'd seen me in my own world a hundred times, and drew from a composite of memories.

When the art fair was over, I asked Henry to make a color print and mailed the print to Riggs. I included a photograph of me and Frankie standing in front of the picture, my face lit up with pride.

Charlie's work continues to hang in the Abyss and RZ galleries. One box of mermaids survived Andrew and these showed up shortly after he left. They sold quickly; I bought one of them myself. After the mermaids came the houseboats. Some were shabby like the *Lullaby*, some glass-walled or strung up with holiday lights, some shingled in cedar shake like the roof of the old stilt house. In a few, you could see the dark, still water where they rest, low hills in the background. I bought two, including one of a boat featured so frequently that I gleaned it was his own, though it just as well might be the one he sees most clearly from his desk.

Seven stilt houses survived Andrew. I've been on the bay with Marse and Lidia many times—Frankie refuses to go—but we haven't visited Stiltsville since the day we went looking for the remains of Charlie's house. In fact, it's been so long since I've allowed myself to think of the place, of the way it was before Frankie's accident, that when three months ago Riggs dropped off a box filled with drawings of the houses, I was shocked by the sight of them. There were dozens of each house, all drawn from the perspective of Charlie's porch, rendered in noon sunlight and late sunset and stormy weather. Sorting through them was like sifting through his memories.

Riggs asked me to organize the drawings and choose two dozen for a show at the Abyss; he gave no explanation for why after all this time the task fell back to me. I worked every night for a week, and Frankie and I saw the show the day it opened. I'd assumed the portraits would inspire Frankie to ask questions about Stiltsville and the summer we'd spent there, and I was right. I told him about fishing and swimming and the jellyfish bloom. I told him about the time we caught a bull shark, about the sunken boat and flattened piano, about the lobsters who came to shed their shells. I said nothing about his language delay or about the accident, which he barely remembers, and very little about Charlie. I know from experience that children understand more than we intend for them to.

I make an effort to mention Graham often, and Frankie claims to remember him well, considering. I've told him time and again how much his father would have enjoyed watching him play baseball. I've told him that Graham would have been proud to know that Frankie was never afraid of the ball, though I don't tell him why.

Graham is woven throughout our lives, yes, but so is Charlie. He is here in the house and yard and pool, in the English garden I've resurrected around the base of the live oak, and he is with Frankie every time Frankie picks up a pencil or paintbrush. He is even, somehow, in Frankie himself: every so often, when he is drawing or painting, Frankie stands with one foot balanced on top of the other, a stubborn and resolute expression on his face. I like to imagine that at that precise moment, three thousand miles across the country, Charlie is standing the same way, wearing the same expression.

In that last box of Stiltsville portraits, there was only one lonely drawing of Charlie's old house. It was at the very bottom of the box, so I came upon it last. In the drawing, the house is crowned by storm clouds and spotlighted by one wide ray of sunlight, surrounded by dark, choppy water. I didn't send this one to the Abyss; I wasn't meant to. I stowed it in the drawer where I keep my mermaids. I find that it doesn't hurt to look at this picture, the way it would have years ago. At least it doesn't hurt much. There's the zigzagging dock and crooked staircase and imposing Mansard roof, the wavelets catching the last dregs of sunlight in their slopes. And if you look closely, you can just barely make out a pair of tiny figures holding hands on the porch, poised to leap.

Acknowledgments

THIS BOOK WAS IMPROVED IMMENSELY by my generous early readers: John Stewart, Miriam Gershow, Joseph O'Malley, and Curtis Sittenfeld. For not only reading but providing in-person encouragement and expertise, I'm so grateful to Jesse Lee Kercheval, Michelle Wildgen, Judith Claire Mitchell, and Jean Reynolds Page. For cheering me on piece by piece and being a steadfast partner in all publishing hijinks, I thank my agent, Emily Forland. Also, I'm so grateful to work again with my smart and tireless editor, Jennifer Barth.

In researching parasomnia, I'm indebted in particular to the short film *Sleep Runners*, by Carlos H. Schenck, M.D., and to comedian Mike Birbiglia's hilarious monologue "Sleepwalk with Me," which originally inspired me to ask the question: what would it be like to live with a parasomniac? I also want to thank Dr. Jeremy Peacock for clarifying details related to parasomnia and selective mutism.

I am so grateful for the generosity of the PEN/American Center and the Bingham family.

For taking the time to share the painful memory of his son's terrible childhood accident, I thank my friend Rick Corey.

The inspiration for Charlie came from a hermit who lived alone at Stiltsville in the 1980s, whom I never met. I've always hoped that, like Charlie, he found a suitable alternative after his stilt house was destroyed in Hurricane Andrew.

For his unfailing support, bravery, and humor throughout our shared adventures, I thank John Stewart.

About the author

About the book

Read on

Insights,
Interviews
& More...

Powell's Q&A with Susanna Daniel

This interview originally appeared on Powells.com.

Describe your latest book.

My second novel, *Sea Creatures*, spans one summer in the lives of Georgia Quillian, her parasomniac husband, Graham (more on parasomnia later), and their three-year-old son, Frankie, who has recently stopped verbalizing. Like *Stiltsville*, my first novel, *Sea Creatures* is set partially in a house built on stilts in the middle of Biscayne Bay, where Georgia works as a personal assistant for a reclusive artist named Charlie Hicks. As Graham's new work and personal limitations pull him away from them, Georgia and Frankie come to depend on Charlie's steadfast attention and Stiltsville's remote beauty. Also, there's a really big hurricane.

Why do you write?

I've said before that I believe writers are, for the most part, hermits at heart. I live with two young children and another adult, my husband, and I adore all of them—but if I didn't hole up in my office and write for hours at a time, how would I justify spending so much time alone with my private obsessions and daydreams?

Name the best television series of all time, and explain why it's the best.

I've really loved *Rome, Friday Night Lights, The Americans.* But for me, great shows and most-loved shows are not always the same thing. The two shows I recall most fondly are both artistically uneven, and both were a little heavy on schmaltz—but both are full of smart, passionate writing and very relatable characters: *Sex and the City* and *Judging Amy.* The final episode of *SATC*, which demonstrates how each woman matured in her own particular way, slayed me. And as Judge Amy (as I call her), Amy Brenneman made working motherhood look harried and unsatisfying but also redeemed by small, precious wins.

Offer a favorite sentence or passage from another writer.

My earworms:
From Andre Dubus's pitch-perfect "A Father's Story," an imagined conversation between the Catholic narrator, who has done something for which he cannot forgive himself, and his god:

So, He says, you love her more than
    you love Me.
I love her more than I love truth.
Then you love in weakness,
    He says.
As You love me, I say, and I go with
    an apple or carrot out to the barn.

And the author's dedication from a terrific book for kids called *I'm the* ▶

Powell's Q&A with Susanna Daniel
(continued)

Biggest Thing in the Ocean! by Kevin Sherry, which gets me every time I read it: "For my parents, who were always the biggest thing in my ocean."

Describe the best breakfast of your life.

The ideal breakfast is an egg-and-cheese burrito with salsa and avocado and hot sauce, and the best version I've ever tasted was at a dive in the Castro, circa 1999.

In Sea Creatures, Georgia is an insomniac and her husband, Graham, is a parasomniac, and they meet at a sleep clinic. Why did you want to write about sleep disorders?

For two reasons. One is that my own insomnia has waxed and waned since I was twenty-one years old. I've learned a slew of coping strategies (as has my husband), and at this point my insomnia barely bleeds into my daytime life at all. But still I feel the sulking fear that my manageable insomnia might one day erupt into a full-blown sleep disorder, the way minor drug use can break out into a full-blown addiction, putting at risk my family, my work, and my sanity.

Second, I was inspired by a monologue I heard a few years ago on the *Moth Radio Hour* on NPR, by a comedian named Mike Birbiglia, who has since starred in a film adaptation of that monologue called *Sleepwalk with*

Me. The monologue is a comic take on a parasomniac's struggle—the night terrors and sleepwalking and even one dramatic event that inspired me to write a similar event into my book. It left me wondering: in all seriousness, what would it be like to be *married* to a parasomniac? *Sea Creatures* puts that situation under a microscope.

Share an interesting experience you've had with one of your readers.

About a year after my first novel came out, I was coming around to the fact that I wanted to write an entire novel about a character who was briefly introduced at the tail end of *Stiltsville*: a man known as the hermit, based on a real person who lived at Stiltsville full-time. At the Miami Book Fair in 2011, a woman who waited in line to have her book signed pulled three photographs out of her purse—all showed a younger version of herself in a bikini with a man on the porch of the real hermit's stilt house. As it turned out, she'd spent much of the 1980s visiting the freewheeling hippie, who left Florida after Hurricane Andrew and went to Brazil to live in another form of semisolitude. Those photos, and the effort she made to show them to me—this was a big nudge from the universe, and I went on to write *Sea Creatures*. ◠

The Story Behind
Sea Creatures

I KNEW BEFORE I STARTED that
I wanted to write a book about parental
ambivalence, about a marriage in which
one partner wants children and the other
doesn't. I started a book with a story
line involving a woman whose husband
declares years into their marriage that he
will not father her children, but I threw
away two hundred pages of this story—
let's call it a novel, to be generous—in
2010. Then in 2011, I wrote a slightly
different story and threw away another
hundred pages. This is when I hit on
a third story, one that whittled away
the plotlines and themes that weren't
working and left this heartbroken,
flawed woman and her impossible
choice.

I don't think I could have written
Sea Creatures if I hadn't already
stumbled through hundreds of pages
of chaotic mess, but this particular
story—the third and final—came out
in one coherent, dignified whole. It's the
kind of thing where you're not quite sure
how it happened, but you thank the
heavens that it did.

It took me ten years to write my first
novel, *Stiltsville*, which grew in fits and
starts from a story I wrote when I was
in graduate school—the story became
a chapter of the novel, and was later cut
entirely. If I had intended from the start
to write a novel, I think I would have
buckled under the pressure, considering
my lack of experience. So I tricked

myself into it by writing a second story about the characters, then a third, and so on. I didn't so much write *Stiltsville* as piece it together. The sixth chapter came first, then the third, then the fifth. I wrote the ending long before I wrote the second chapter, which gave me the most trouble. Then I cut that first-written chapter and another one, and rewrote the whole thing to make it cohesive.

Sea Creatures, in contrast, took a little less than a year, and though I didn't know how it would end when I started out, at least I knew from page one that I was writing a novel, and that it would have a conventional three- or four-part structure and take place over the course of one summer. I had a limited amount of confidence that I could pull off the trick of writing a second book, but it was enough.

Because *Stiltsville* was my first, it will always be special to me. It made me as much as I made it. As my teacher Chris Offutt said once, "You put your entire life up to that point into the first novel." How could I ever match that, in terms of my personal connection to the story?

That's one of the challenges of the second book. And I believe that by throwing away as much as I did, by keeping myself open only to the meatiest, most deeply felt story I wanted to tell, I was able to rise to that challenge.

Another challenge of the second book is to try to recover some of the wide-eyed naïveté of the first book. People asked me, about *Stiltsville*, how I had the courage to write an entire novel about ▶

a happy marriage. I answered that I'd never realized I wasn't supposed to.

With the second, you know what you're "supposed" to do or not do, whether you want that knowledge or not. I tried not to let myself be influenced, but there's no doubt that compared to the quiet simplicity of *Stiltsville*'s story, *Sea Creatures* contains more forward drive. And it is not the story of a happy marriage.

In *Stiltsville*, I tried to convey the complexities of domestic life, the compromises and joys and heartaches of marriage and parenthood. In *Sea Creatures*, I've concentrated more on the high stakes and instability of the same institutions.

Both of my books are narrated with a degree of intimacy that isn't typical of most domestic dramas, and with a sweep through time that gives the reader a sense not only of the past and present but also of how the characters' futures will unfurl. As a reader, I feel most gratified by characters who are so fully formed by the end of a novel that I mourn their exits from my life; I develop my characters with this goal in mind.

Graham, the husband and father in *Sea Creatures*, has a severe case of parasomnia, which is a category of sleep disorder that encompasses somnambulism (sleepwalking), sleep terrors, sleep violence, and other erratic behavior. He's been a parasomniac since age eleven, so some of my research focused on sleep disorders in children, when and how they emerge. I also researched coping mechanisms, safety issues, effects on spouses (parasomniacs have a high rate of divorce, suicide, and so-called "accidental suicide"), and long-term psychological effects.

I have insomnia, and I had been experiencing a particularly bad bout when I started writing this story. That bout lasted nine months, until after I'd finished a draft of the novel. I don't have parasomnia, but I've thought a lot about how sleep disorders affect not only the afflicted person but also his or her spouse, children, work. A severe sleep disorder is nearly unbearable, and to marry a person with such a disorder is to take on a great burden. To have a child with that person could be regarded as a reckless act in itself.

Mutism—specifically, selective mutism—is three-year-old Frankie's diagnosis in the novel (though this diagnosis isn't made until halfway through, when the reason behind the problem is uncovered). Selective mutism is related to anxiety, not intelligence or aptitude. My own now-articulate three-year-old didn't speak until he was two, which started me thinking about what it would've meant for our family if he had never started speaking at all. ∾

Author's Picks

Stories and essays, Andre Dubus

Until I was closely acquainted with Andre Dubus and his many beautiful stories and essays (*Selected Stories* is a good place to start), I had no idea how voice and narrative drive could transform a character's banal domestic situation into something chilling, exquisite, and profound. From Dubus I learned not to shy away from powerful emotion on the page, to not be coy about or dismissive of sentiment, and how to describe even a quiet scene in such vivid detail that the reader cannot look away. I frequently reread Dubus's powerful essay collection, *Meditations from a Movable Chair,* in which he writes at length about his Catholicism and the roadside accident that confined him to a wheelchair for the last thirteen years of his life. Every time I assigned a Dubus story or essay to a class, several students become instant fans—his work is all-consuming and addictive.

The Age of Grief, Jane Smiley

Perhaps my favorite novella of all time—a passionate, mournful recounting by a husband of the change that comes to his home life when his wife has an affair. At the end of the story, the narrator and his wife and their three children all come down with a terrible stomach flu, and the way this utterly domestic inconvenience interrupts the downward spiral of the marriage—a reminder, in the worst and best way, of the commitment the couple has made to each other—is astonishing.

Home, Marilynne Robinson

Of Robinson's great novels, this is the one that, for me, is most exciting in its fusion of language, detail, and character. The end is so powerfully satisfying that it brings the entire story to a new level of meaning. This is a story that unself-consciously answers the question (admittedly, this might concern the writer in me more than the reader): *What is a story?*

Light in August, William Faulkner

A rich, fluid novel of character and determinism—this is Faulkner's most accessible and also most instructive book, in my opinion. The inevitability of the story, how it rises organically from the characters, who are trapped but also invigorated by their limitations and circumstances—this is fiction at its most bold and honest.

Stories and novels, William Maxwell

I came late to William Maxwell, but once I read one novel—*They Came Like Swallows* was my first, and a great place to start—I wasted no time in devouring everything he's written, including his collected letters and even books written not by him but about him, like Alec Wilkinson's lovely *My Mentor,* which ▶

Author's Picks *(continued)*

makes me wish not only that I could
write like Maxwell, with an unparalleled
degree of tenderness and precision and
clarity, but also that I could know him
personally. ✑

Also by Susanna Daniel

One sunny morning in 1969, near the end of her first trip to Miami, twenty-six-year-old Frances Ellerby finds herself in a place called Stiltsville, a community of houses built on pilings in the middle of Biscayne Bay.

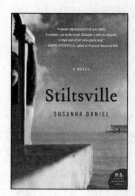

It's the first time the Atlanta native has been out on the open water, and she's captivated. On the dock of a stilt house, with the dazzling skyline in the distance and the unknowable ocean beneath her, she meets the house's owner, Dennis DuVal—and a new future reveals itself.

Turning away from her quiet, predictable life back home, Frances moves to Miami to be with Dennis. Over time, she earns the confidence of his wild-at-heart sister and wins the approval of his oldest friend. Frances and Dennis marry and have a child— but rather than growing complacent about their good fortune, they continue to face the challenges of intimacy and the complicated city they call home.

Stiltsville is the family's island oasis— until suddenly it's gone, and Frances is forced to figure out how to make her family work on dry land. Against a backdrop of lush tropical beauty, Frances and Dennis struggle with the mutability of love and Florida's weather, as well as temptation, chaos, and disappointment. But just when Frances thinks she's reached some semblance of higher ground, she must

Also by Susanna Daniel *(continued)*

confront an obstacle so great that even the lessons she's learned about navigating the uncharted waters of family life can't keep them afloat.

Susanna Daniel weaves "a sweet serenade to southern Florida, and a moving account of a woman's life" (*Huffington Post*) into a modern yet enduring story of a marriage's beginning, maturity, and heartbreaking demise.

Don't miss the next book by your favorite author. Sign up now for AuthorTracker by visiting www.AuthorTracker.com.